A New Heaven and a New Earth

St Cuthbert and the Conquest of the North

— Katharine Tiernan —

Sacristy
Press

Sacristy Press
PO Box 612, Durham, DH1 9HT

www.sacristy.co.uk

First published in 2020 by Sacristy Press, Durham

Sacristy Limited, registered in England & Wales, number 7565667

British Library Cataloguing-in-Publication Data
A catalogue record for the book is available from the British Library

Paperback ISBN 978-1-78959-125-5

I have persecuted the natives of England beyond all reason. Whether gentle or simple I have cruelly oppressed them. Many I unjustly disinherited and killed innumerable multitudes by famine or the sword. I was the barbarous murderer of many thousands both young and old of that fine race of people.

Deathbed confession of William the Conqueror;
Orderic Vitalis's "Ecclesiastical History"

Then I saw a new heaven and a new earth, for the first heaven and the first earth had passed away, and there was no longer any sea. I saw the Holy City, the new Jerusalem, coming down out of heaven from God, prepared as a bride beautifully dressed for her husband. And I heard a loud voice from the throne saying, "Look! God's dwelling-place is now among the people, and he will dwell with them. They will be his people, and God himself will be with them and be their God. He will wipe every tear from their eyes. There will be no more death or mourning or crying or pain, for the old order of things has passed away." He who was seated on the throne said, "I am making everything new!" Then he said, "Write this down, for these words are trustworthy and true."

The Revelation of St John the Divine, chapter 21, verses 1–5

Edinburgh

Lindisfarne

Melrose

R. Tweed

Tughall

•••••••••••••••
ROMAN ROADS

DERE STREET

Cheviot Hills

Bedlington

HADRIAN'S WALL

Corbridge

Monkchester
(Newcastle)

R. Tyne

Chester-le-Street

Durham

R. Wear

R. Eden

DERE STREET

R. Tees

York

THE LAND
BETWEEN
TYNE & WEAR
AN ARTIST'S IMPRESSION

NOT TO SCALE

● Bedlington

HADRIAN'S WALL

Tynemouth ●

Monkchester
(Newcastle) ●

● Jarrow

Gateshead ●

Corbridge ●

Whitburn ●

R. Tyne

Monkwearmouth ●

DERE STREET

Chester-le-Street ●

Durham ●

R. Wear

Contents

PART 1
THE SERVANTS OF ST CUTHBERT

AD 1068–1072

CHAPTER 1

THORGOT

Lincoln, 1068

One of these was Thorgot, deriving his descent from no ignoble race of the Angles, who was one amongst others who, after the conquest of England by the Normans, were kept as hostages for all Lindsey in the castle of Lincoln.

Simeon's "History of the Kings of England"

Yes, I am Thorgot. It has often been tut-tutted at for a pagan name, but I pay no heed. My mother was Norse, that's all, and that was nothing unusual in the Danelaw. There were more Danes and Norse in Lincoln than English. And if it seems a far cry from the Danelaw to Durham, why, that's the tale I'm here to tell.

I grew up speaking Norse, but my father wanted me to be a scholar, so English it was. By the time I left the Minster school, I could read and write in Latin and English, reckon out a row of figures, and order a melody into parts and harmonies. I was a ready scholar, but the monks were more interested in my voice than my studies. A voice like an angel, they said. I had to sing at every endless service when I would rather have been down at the harbour on the ships with my father. I hoped it would come to an end when my voice broke, but no. Better than before, they said. I knew the psalms by heart, hymns, liturgies, all of it. It was to be my salvation, though not in the way you might expect.

When Duke William and the Normans came along it was nothing to us. We'd had Danish kings, Saxon kings—now a Norman king. What difference would it make? Lincoln was a snug little port, far enough inland to be out of reach of pirates and raiders, and if you were wide awake, there was money to be made. My father was shrewd. He'd made enough from his ships to buy an estate for himself, and by the time I was twenty there was land for me as well.

In the spring of 1068, William arrived in Lincoln on his way back from the fighting in York. The aldermen turned out to greet him and brought out provisions to give him a feast. We were used to it. We lived on the crossroads of the kingdom. There was always some princeling passing through, and Lincoln merchants tried to keep on the right side of whoever looked like being in power. Duke William called himself king for now, but in a year's time it could be Sweyn Forkbeard for all we knew. We'd had Danish kings before. There weren't many who cared enough to take up arms for young Edgar the Atheling. He'd hardly had time to grow a beard when Harold fought at Hastings. We gave hospitality to William and showed him the town.

And that was our mistake. As soon as he set foot in the upper town, built where the Roman fort had stood, he had eyes for nothing but the view. It was a clear day, and from the top of the escarpment you can see for miles. He'd ridden down Ermine Street from York; now he could see the endless straight line of it stretching south with hardly a bend to London. And to the west the Fosse Way unrolled into the distance, just as the Romans had left it. Then and there, I do believe, William's mind started scheming.

Two months later he sent a detachment of soldiers into the town, and the word was that they would talk with the Witan. Now, my father sat on the Witan, not I, but he sent me in his place. I persuaded him. I thought he was too cautious. I was twenty years old and so full of myself I thought I could see off the Normans single-handed. I was to pay the price for my arrogance. If I'd not been so full of my own opinion, I might yet be an alderman myself and cantor of Lincoln's fine new cathedral.

It was a trick, of course. The Normans had no intention of talking to us, then or now. We walked into the Witan Hall like songbirds flying into nets. William's man, FitzRobert, sat at the high table with papers before him and clerks around him. We never doubted he was there for the council. For sure, the hall was full of armed men, but that was the Normans. Everyone knew they never took their helmets off. His clerks took down our names and our landholdings, and when that was done, we sat on the benches. When the last man's name was taken down, FitzRobert looked up and nodded to his soldiers.

It all happened in a second. Four soldiers grabbed me, roped me and pulled my arms tight against my body so I could scarcely draw breath. The hall was in chaos, men struggling, and the Normans shouting at each other in French. I was tied up with the other men, so we were forced to move in line. Then they pushed us out of the hall, down the street, through the town, shuffling along with armed men on either side of us cuffing our heads. Everyone came running to their doorsteps. The Normans let them stare. That's what they wanted, to make sure everyone knew what was happening. They took us down to their camp by the river, fastened off the ropes that held us together to a post and left us standing. My heart was hammering so hard that I could hear nothing else. As soon as I caught my breath I looked around. There were two men in front of me. I turned my head and saw three more tied on behind me. Six of us. There had been three times as many at the Witan. Why us? Why me? I wasn't even an alderman! I was standing in for my father! Outrage burned through me, so strong I felt I could burst my bonds like Samson in the temple. I strained and tugged with all my strength at the ropes that bound me. They hardly stretched. When I recovered my breath, I roared out,

"What are the bastards doing? Tell them to free us!"

The man in front of me twisted round. I saw it was Godwin, the leader of the Witan. He was an even-tempered man but that day his face was grim.

"Save your breath, Thorgot."

It was not meant unkindly, but I would have hit him if my arms had been free. I looked again and saw that the other five were aldermen. Respected older men. My father's friends. I was the only young man they had taken. The injustice of it sent me into another spasm of fury. But when I had recovered myself, I realized the other men were talking.

"If they'd wanted to kill us, they'd have done it already," Godwin was saying. "They'll hold us hostage."

The last word leaped out at me. Hostage. That word was to go round my head a thousand times in the days to come. All that I was, all that I planned to be, was reduced to this: I am a hostage.

We were shut up in a house that belonged to Morcar, a friend of my father's. I had often run in and out of Morcar's hall when I was a boy. There was no running in and out now. Not even to piss. Only buckets at the back of the hall, and the place stank before the first week was out. The soldiers must have found the stench as foul as we did, and they took to bringing in a couple of servants whose job it was to empty them. They had to make up the fire, clean out the mess the guards left behind them and bring in supplies. If the servant so much as glanced at us a soldier slapped his head.

At first, the old men talked as if they were still in the Witan, going over and over what was happening, what we could do, whether we could make terms. All they agreed on was that the Normans had taken our town and we were being held against resistance. If there was rebellion in the town, our throats would be cut. Feeble old dotards, I thought. I was furious with them for their cowardly talk. There was only one thing worth talking about in my opinion. Escape. But they ignored me, and after a few days we all fell silent. One of them, Bertred, often wept. It was a terrible sound in the silence, an old man weeping like a child.

In the mornings, the guards brought in a pile of bread, small ale, sometimes a round of cheese or an onion or two. Godwin would share it out, and we ate slowly, making the most of each mouthful. We had a table, but only a couple of small benches. I let the old men sit. I stood and chewed and tried to think of nothing but the food in my mouth. Once it was gone, the long day stretched ahead. The Normans kept the casements shut; there was no air, no glimpse of the sky. I paced up and down, up and down. I counted every roof truss, every knot in the wood of every plank. Outside it was springtime with the land breaking into loveliness and we were penned up in the shadow. I was in a torment of restlessness. My life had been stolen.

To make the time pass I started to watch the Norman soldiers who guarded us, started to listen to them, trying to make out their slippery language. I watched the guard change, waited for one of them to unbuckle his sword or lay his dagger on the table. I dreamed of seizing a sword and fighting my way to freedom. I was no swordsman, never had been, and any trained soldier would have cut me down in a moment, but my anger was so great I was certain I could overcome.

They were there, always. The Normans never let go of their weapons. If you woke at night and looked up, there would be half a dozen men sitting round the hearth fire, armed and in mail vests, drinking and dicing. They treated us like a pack of curs. If a hostage wandered too close to the hearth or happened to get in the way, they would strike the man hard across the head and drive him away with kicks and curses. We learned quickly enough to keep to our end of the hall. Only old Bertred couldn't remember. The shock had turned his wits and he was forever wandering around, trying to get out. One day a soldier grabbed a whip and started thrashing him, screaming abuse at him like a demon. We ran to pull him away and the blows came down on us instead. I was so maddened I went for the throat of the soldier closest to me. Next thing I knew I was on the floor with blood running down my face and Godwin beside me. He was shaking.

"Control yourself," he said. "Do you want to get us all killed?"

We awoke soon after dawn, to the sound of a sudden commotion outside. We heard men being marched past the house, on and on. There must have been hundreds of them. Then the uproar started. Norman voices shouting orders, yelling at people, horses neighing and pounding the ground, the sound of blows and screams.

Close by us was a deafening noise of battering and hammering, with sudden loud crashes that made the hall shake. Every crash brought new dread. It was Sibba the carpenter who first understood.

"They're pulling down the houses," he said. Why would they do that? But we listened, and when the next crash came, we knew he was right. Roof timbers were toppling to the ground. After an interval we could hear horses with loads dragging and scraping along the ground.

Further away was another, constant noise like the low roar of the sea; the rasp of scores of picks and shovels hacking through soil, hitting stones with a resounding clang before the endless rhythm continued. On and on it went, throughout the day, and the next day and the next, till it became part of the monotony of our life. Our prison was like the eye of a storm. Within it, nothing happened, nothing moved. We had nothing to see, nothing to do. We were helpless. Outside, all around us, was uproar and commotion, a storm that never ceased. It was like nothing any of us had known. What were they doing? What could they be digging? Were they digging a ditch, a moat to surround the whole of the upper town? It would be madness. What else could they be building that took so long, that needed scores of men working day after day?

We were to find out. It must have been three months or more after we had first been taken prisoner and summer was nearly past. One morning the hall suddenly filled with soldiers, a score or more. It was no different to the first time—soldiers grabbing hold of me as if I were being taken for a pig-sticking, screaming at me while they pulled ropes round my arms—but this time I felt insanely elated. I was going to get out, at last! I was going to breathe fresh air; I was going to see the sky! The feeling was so strong that it overwhelmed everything. I didn't care what they did to me. In spite of all that we had heard I had no inkling of what awaited us.

As we stepped outside my high spirits drained out of me in seconds. I couldn't believe what I was seeing. The world I had left behind had vanished. I turned to the man behind me, to see if he saw it too, that I was not dreaming, but it was Bertred. His jaw sagged and his eyes were staring like a madman's. I turned away.

Morcar's hall, where we had been imprisoned, was in Lincoln's upper town, built within the bounds of the old Roman fort. It was fine and spacious with a view to the countryside beyond. The houses of the lower town ran down the slopes of the hill towards the harbour, where merchants like my father lived, traders and craftsmen. Now, as I stepped back out into the light, I saw that the upper town had gone. Where there had been lanes, workshops, yards and houses, there was bare black earth. I couldn't make sense of it. A hundred houses, more, had stood here. How could they be gone? How could the yards and gardens, the smoke of hearth fires and the cries of children, have disappeared? Where were the people? There was nothing but acre upon acre of churned-up mud and broken wood and plaster.

There was no time to think about it. The rope jerked me forward, catching me unaware. I stumbled forward before looking up. Then I saw it. In the north-east corner of the fort, where the old walls of the Romans had been crumbling into decay, was an immense black mound of earth, thirty feet or more in height. It was as if a great hill had suddenly sprung out of the earth. I could see sections of lath and plaster taken from some house sticking out of the side. Understanding pierced my amazement. The digging. That was what they had been digging. Peering upwards, I saw that squatting on top of the mound was a rough wooden fort, square as a box. It looked to be two storeys high with a roof sloping low on all sides. The whole construction was encircled with a ditch, too deep for me to see the bottom. As we were pulled closer, I saw there were men still working in it, stripped to the waist. There were scores of them, but they were silent. None of the usual banter and whistling of working men. No songs or jokes. They worked with their heads down, without respite. They didn't give us so much as a glance.

We were led over a wooden bridge across the moat, then up rough steps cut into the side of the mound. After three months of inactivity I found myself panting. I could hear Bertred behind me groaning and gasping. I prayed to God to help him.

Finally our ragged line reached the top of the steps, and we came into the fort. It was a roughly built room where more soldiers lounged on benches with their ale, watching us. We were pushed over to a ladder in the corner and climbed up, swaying and lurching against each other, till we reached the top floor. Finally, we were in our new prison. The ropes were cut from us, the soldiers gave us a few cuffs to keep us in our place and then climbed back down, lifting the ladder away behind them. We fell back onto the floor. No-one spoke. It was beyond words.

I no longer held aloof from the others. I pestered Godwin with questions, trying to understand what was happening in this nightmare world. Trade had often taken Godwin to Frankia and Normandy, and I found a new respect for his experience.

"That's what they do over there. Build castles. Look, when William landed at Hastings, that was the first thing he did," Godwin said. "He had a castle built. And at Dover. Before he even raised his sword. And that's what he's doing here."

"But why here? We welcomed them to Lincoln. The Witan did homage to William as king."

Godwin lowered his voice, even though the soldiers spoke not a word of English.

"They don't care whether we're for or against them. They mean to take it all whatever we do. The town. The land. They'll make us their slaves. In case we rebel against them, they'll have us build a great castle for them to hide in."

He nodded towards the windows.

"This mound that the fort sits on, they call the motte. Down below, where the upper town was, will be castle land now. All of it. Their bailey. They'll put a wall round it and build their barracks and their stables and their workshops inside. Maybe they'll rebuild the church. It'll be a little Normandy."

Godwin was right. Once the motte was finished, the Normans set the

Lincoln men to labour on a timber palisade to enclose the land, while the harvest rotted in fields all around the town and workshops stood silent. The castle bailey took up the whole area of the old town, twenty acres or more, and every English house that stood within its bounds had been torn down. By Godwin's count it was a hundred and sixty-six houses. A hundred and sixty-six! It was unbelievable. All those families, those households, driven out to make way for William's soldiers. I despised and hated them with all my heart. Edward needed no castles to rule the kingdom, nor Cnut before him. These foreigners would never be part of England. In those first days shut up in the castle I swore an oath to myself I would never submit to them.

The routine changed in our new prison. The soldiers lived below us, but the loft where they kept us also served as their look out. It was a large single room with casements on all sides, overhung by the roof to keep the rain out. At night, the ladder was taken out, and we were left alone. But at first light the ladder would bang against the opening in the floor, and four soldiers would climb up to open the casements and start the watch. They made us keep to our benches in the centre of the loft, but it was easy enough to see out. And you could see for miles. You could see the Fosse Way and Ermine Street, you could see every horse, every pedlar coming and going. Closer to home, you could see the men working down below, you could watch for any man standing idle or trying to sneak away. The image of the silent men we saw, digging out the Normans' vile ditch, still stuck in my mind. One day an impulse struck me. I'll sing for them, I thought. Something to console them. I decided on the saga of Weland, a man who knew exile. With the casements stood open for the watch, I knew my voice would be strong enough to carry out across the fort.

I said nothing to the others, but when I started to sing their heads jerked up quick enough.

"If a man sits in despair, deprived of all pleasure, his mind moves upon sorrow; it seems to him that there is no end to his share of hardship. Then he should remember that the wise Lord often moves about this middle-earth . . ."

The soldiers turned from the casements, uncertain. I saw one of them shrug to the others and turn back to the watch. Excitement rose in me. My voice grew stronger, and I sang on. I'd learned the saga from my Norse uncle, and it was long enough to pass a winter's evening. By the time I was done the day was half gone. I looked at my companions. They were smiling, shaking their heads, coming over to clap my shoulder.

Next morning, I was no sooner roused from sleep than I found Godwin at my side, all eagerness.

"Sing again, Thorgot, but let it be Christian. We can hear the bells from the church. You could sing the office. They can't forbid the service of God."

After that, when I heard the church bells tolling for service I would start up and sing the office. Some of the men joined in behind me. Soon we were as holy as a cell of monks, singing our way from dawn to dusk. It annoyed the guards. But they were Christians after their own sort and couldn't tell us to stop divine service. Did all my anger turn to piety? No, but it gave a shape to the day and I found the familiar words of the psalms comforting. The torment of my thoughts lessened.

Sometimes at the end of the day I would sing a lament to give voice to my sorrows, some tale of heroes slain or women grieving. One evening, I was in the midst of such a song, when I noticed a guard half-turned from the casement, looking at me.

I knew that look.

I had discovered long ago that my voice could open hearts. Most of the time I didn't draw a second glance from women. I was strongly built and broad-chested, but I could have used a few more inches to make me handsome. My hair was fair to the point of whiteness with not a curl in it. If I wore it long it hung lank as string, so I kept it short and trimmed my beard close. I had fair skin, pale blue eyes and a nose better suited to a larger face. I was often joking and laughing before I was taken hostage, and the laughter had left lines around my eyes and mouth. So at least I had a cheerful look. But it was my voice that brought women to my side. When I sang a sad ballad at a feast, I could see that look on half a dozen women's faces. They would gaze at me entranced, as if the song had spoken to their souls. Long after I'd finished, they would still be sitting silently. Later they would come up to me, some too bashful to speak, others looking deep into my eyes. In spite of my voice, I was no angel. I made good use of my talent.

And now, here, in this prison I saw it on the face of a Norman soldier. The look. He was gazing at me as soulfully as a woman. I let my voice sink a little deeper. When I glanced at him again, I knew I had taken a captive of my own. I gave no sign, but in the following days I watched him.

At first the Normans had all seemed the same to me, with their dark bearded faces and the mail vests they never took off. But after a while I could see differences in them. They were all soldiers, for sure, hard men used to cruelty. But in all their cursing and bravado and in the fights that broke out between them, I caught a whiff of something else. Of fear. It was always there, in their quickness to grab a sword, to beat a servant without cause. Even fear of us, five harmless old men and a youth who couldn't control himself. They were foreigners in a land where every man, woman and child wanted them dead. In the face of that soldier I saw a longing for something else. Something to speak to his soul.

Over the next few days, whenever he was on duty, I sang for him alone. Sometimes he glanced at me and our eyes met. When it was time for him to leave, I managed to hang around near the ladder. He let the others climb down before him, then he turned to me. "Good," he said, in his strange Norman accent, and clapped my arm. Then he was gone.

Next time it happened I tried a request. My hair and beard had grown long over the months we'd been imprisoned. I knew I must look like a savage. As he turned to look at me, I pointed at my hair and grimaced. He smiled. A couple of days later he slipped a comb and a pair of scissors into my hand. My heart started beating furiously. A comb and a pair of scissors, and I was wild with joy! That night we opened one of the casements to let the moonlight in and our prison turned into a barber's shop. We hacked away at each other's hair and I cut my own beard short. Although I couldn't see what I looked like with my new trim beard and hair, I felt something of my old self return to me.

The next morning one or two of the guards looked at us curiously, but they were used to ignoring us. They wouldn't stoop to remark on our appearance. When my friend arrived, I slipped the comb and scissors back into his hand. I wanted him to know I wouldn't cheat on him.

Though he was always turned towards the casement, keeping watch, he was aware of me. At the end of his watch I would hang around by the ladder. I tried another request. More than anything, I longed for clean linen. I was still wearing the clothes I had put on the morning of the Witan and I stank. More pointing and smiling by the ladder. Next morning he put something down on the floor by the ladder hole. I gave no sign of noticing. I waited all day and all evening, till it was dark and my companions were snoring. Then I took it up. It was a fine linen shirt, soft as a woman's touch. I nearly wept. I took off the old shirt, filthy and sweat-soaked, and put the clean linen one on.

So it went on. He started to wait for me openly by the ladder, to try and talk to me. "Je m'appelle Ortaire," he said, pointing to himself. "Tu chante vraiment bien." I knew well enough what he was saying. "Ego Thorgot. Gratias estis genus," I said in Latin. Would he understand? He looked surprised, but he nodded. He could understand simple phrases in Latin, and I started to pick up a few words of French. It pleased him to teach me. What else had I got to do? Sometimes I felt I would sooner spit than have their language on my tongue, but I knew that one day it might help me.

He was the same age as me, I learned. He owed service to one of William's knights, but he was weary of war. He wanted to go back to Normandy. I saw the longing in his face and I felt a spring of hope. He wanted to escape from his life as much as I did from mine. Could I risk it? Would he betray me?

"Si tibi dant auxilium vobis erit pater," I said. "If you'll help me out, my father will pay you. All you want." I told him my father's name and where he lived. I could hardly get the words out. If I had misjudged Ortaire, my father's life would be at stake as well as mine. Ortaire looked at me intently, uncertain. He understood well enough what I meant. I made myself hold his gaze without faltering. At last he gave a little nod.

The others noticed, of course. They knew Ortaire had taken a fancy to me—the comb and scissors were evidence enough of that. But I didn't tell them what I was planning. Better that nobody should know. Days went past, and Ortaire gave no sign. I sang the offices as usual and a song for him. At last one evening he hung back above the ladder till his companions had all reached the bottom. Then he looked at me. "Ce soir," he said.

I didn't lie down to sleep that night. I sat up on the bench waiting, hour after hour. At last I heard the tap of the ladder against the board. He came halfway up and shoved a bundle up to me. I unwrapped it and found a helmet and cloak. I understood at once what he meant me to do. I put the helmet onto my head and pulled the cloak around me. Then I had to get myself down the ladder, my heart beating so fast I could hardly breathe, every creak making me start like a rabbit. At last I was in the guardroom and saw him waiting for me. The other soldiers were sound asleep. We moved over to the door, opened it with hardly a sound, and I was out! Ortaire turned to climb down the steps and motioned me behind him. My feet slipped and stumbled; he put his hand on my back to steady me. Then we were at the bridge. A guard was waiting at the far end and called out. Ortaire shouted back a password I couldn't understand. I kept walking behind him, waiting for the guard to call me back and demand I repeat it. Nothing.

We walked across the bailey with the moon shining down on us. I pulled back my shoulders and tried to imitate Ortaire's long soldierly stride. Then the last gate. The last guard. This time he and Ortaire talked and laughed for several minutes as I edged behind him. At last he got up and swung the gate open for us. He clapped me on the back; I had to hold myself tight to stop flinching away. As soon as we were well away from the gatehouse, Ortaire started to run and I set off after him. We ran downhill till we reached a little copse by the river. Four horses were waiting under the trees, and in front of them, my father and two servants. I ran down and embraced him, my heart exploding with joy. Then I turned and hugged Ortaire as well. He was my saviour, Norman or not. My father came forward and gave him a bag of gold. The servant brought up a horse for him. Ortaire stowed the gold into the saddle bag and turned back to me.

He spoke urgently, gripping my arm, trying to tug me towards the horse. I realized he wanted me to go with him. My father came and stood behind me, his hand on my shoulder. Something about his presence checked the Norman. He was silent for a few moments, staring at me, and I could feel his emotion. "God bless you, Ortaire," I said. "I'll never forget what you've done for me. May you have a good life." I spoke truthfully, and I believe he understood me in some way. At last he turned away, swung himself up into the saddle and with a last wave was gone, heading for the London road.

CHAPTER 2

UNEXPECTED COMPANY

The North Sea, 1068

He at great risk privily made his escape to the Norwegians, who
were then loading a merchant vessel at Grimsby for Norway. In this
vessel also certain ambassadors, whom King William was sending
to Norway, had procured a passage . . .

Simeon's "History of the Kings of England"

I turned back to my father. What joy there was in my heart! Joy at my
freedom, but also towards my beloved father, who had been able to
understand Ortaire's intention and hold him to the point, who had
thought of every detail. And who had not hesitated to hand over half his
wealth for my sake. I held him to me tight and close. At last he stood back.

"You must go. They'll be after you as soon as day breaks."

Until that moment, I had thought no further forward than breaking
free of my captivity, of being once again in my father's house. But in an
instant, I saw it was impossible. They would notice my absence as soon as
the first watch came up the ladder. They would be after me.

"We need to get you out of the country. I've talked to a shipmaster, and
he's agreed to take you. It's a Norse ship, heading for Nidaros. They sailed
out of Lincoln yesterday, but they'll pick you up at Grimsby. Ride hard,
and you'll be there by midday."

I was silent, trying to take in what he was telling me. Norway. My mother's country. It would be a new life altogether. Suddenly I was excited. Why not? My father was right. I couldn't stay here. I couldn't stay in Lincoln or anywhere close by. What was left for me here?

"But you, father? Won't they come after you?"

"The Normans speak to no-one. They don't know I'm your father. I'll be home and back in bed before they come beating on doors. Don't worry."

We were both silent for a moment, his arm around me. At last he clapped me on the back.

"Come on. Time you were off. One of the servants will go with you. There's food in the pack and enough gold for the ship and when you land. And this."

He gave me a roll of parchments.

"Letters. Recommending you to the church in Nidaros. Might be useful."

A last embrace. Then I was up on the horse, and we were off into the night. It was the last time I ever saw my father.

I was never much of a horseman, and after months of idleness my body was soft as a woman's. After a couple of hours of hard riding I started to ache. By the time we reached Grimsby the Normans would have been pleased to know I was in agony. What a relief it was to slide out of the saddle! It was a bright day with a fresh wind, and we could see the ship already docked; a smart-looking craft, her timbers still fresh, and sails reefed in against a good sturdy mast. The master jumped ashore when he saw us. I took the pack my father had prepared for me and staggered over towards him, stiff as a crone.

"Heill ok sæll!" he shouted out to me, and without a moment's thought I found myself answering back to him in Norse as if I'd never spoken another language. I cracked a joke about my horse-riding, and soon we were both laughing. I pulled out the money and counted out the coin for him and slipped in a couple of extra for the sake of fellowship. By the time they heaved me onto the ship, we were the best of friends. Which turned out to be just as well.

The rowing men sat amidships, with the hold and spare benches behind. I sat close to the landward side as they pulled out of harbour, staring at the coast of England slipping away. My home and my country. Who knew when I might see it again? I was melancholy for a moment, but it couldn't cloud my freedom. It wasn't only captivity that had worn me down. It was fear—fear that some hothead in the town would make an attack—and God knows I might have if I'd been free. The Normans would have slit our throats without a second thought. I sat back on the bench and drank in my freedom.

The very next moment I got a shock that nearly sent me over the side. When I'd got on board, I'd noticed I wasn't the only passenger. There were four or five men in the stern wrapped up in thick cloaks with a couple of chests stacked alongside. I was too busy with my own thoughts to pay heed. But then, as the ship rounded the headland and made for the open sea, I heard them talking. I knew the language they were speaking. Thanks to Ortaire, I even understood a few words. They were Normans! I was on a ship with Normans! The shock was like freezing water rushing through every vein in my body, turning me to ice. I pulled the hood of my cloak over my head and turned myself half over the side of the ship. Then I listened.

Their voices were raised. They were arguing. That was nothing new for Normans, but I felt uneasy. Then I saw the captain heading down the ship towards them. They had an interpreter with them, and then I heard one of them speaking in broken Norse to the captain.

"Who is the man?" he asked. "The new passenger. From Grimsby?"

The captain turned away from me, and I didn't hear his answer. Next thing I knew, he was beside me.

"Seems these men don't like your company," he said.

"What are they doing on the ship?"

"Duke William's men. Envoys to the court at Nidaros. William doesn't want to upset trade in the Danelaw."

"Tip the bastards overboard," I said.

The captain looked at me askance.

"Want to know what they're saying? They think you're an escaped hostage. One of them says he recognizes you. He wants me to take you back to Lincoln."

I was flabbergasted. What dreadful twist of fate was this? To have escaped, to get so far, and then to find myself alongside the very men I was trying to escape! I started cursing with every evil oath I knew in Norse, in English. The captain shook me.

"Turn round," he said.

For a moment I thought of resisting. Then I felt defiant. I had paid for my passage; I was a free man. They had no rights over me. I turned, and at once I found myself staring at the Normans, at their dark mean faces. One of them broke out into shouts and gestures, pointing at me and yelling at the captain. He must have seen me at the castle. Or heard me. They'd all heard me, would all know who the singer was. The interpreter tugged at the captain's arm.

"Yes," he said. "Is the man. You take him back to Lincoln."

When I heard that I was on my feet. I stood on the other side of the captain, arguing for my life.

"They're the criminals, not me. They're thieves and murderers. They destroyed our town."

The interpreter shouted back:

"Do what I say, Captain. We tell the king if you help him."

"They'll kill me. You know they will. Once they get me off the ship, they'll hang me."

The captain looked from one of us to the other.

"Wait."

He went amidships and hunched down on a rowing bench next to the lead oarsman. Then he beckoned the mate, and the three of them sat talking in low voices and looking up at the sky. At last the captain stood up, nodding. He came back to us.

"Well," he said to the interpreter. "We've talked it over. We'd be happy to help but there's dirty weather blowing up. Look." He pointed to the sky behind us, and sure enough, the clouds were darkening. My heart leapt. "I've talked to my men and they think the same. It's no time to be going about."

Such gratitude flooded into my heart I could have wept. The Norman kept on shouting and arguing.

"This man's paid his passage, same as you have," said the captain. "It's no business of mine where he comes from. Take him to King Olaf with you. Let him be the judge."

And that was it. We could all see his mind was made up. He took my arm.

"You better come forrard," he said. "We'll sit you in the bows."

He squashed me in with the ropes and tackle behind the prow. My bones were aching, and I was already feeling queasy as the tall green waves rushed towards me. But I cared nothing for my pains. I blessed the captain and his men from the bottom of my heart and swore to myself that one day I would repay him. If the Normans could have heaved me overboard for sure they would have done it, but there were eight sturdy oarsmen, the captain and his mates between me and them. I felt snug and safe as a babe in his cradle, and in my heart I mocked my enemies.

CHAPTER 3

Nidaros

Norway, 1068

*He attained also the acquaintance of King Olave, who, as he was
of a very religious turn, cultivated learning amidst the cares of his
kingdom. Hearing therefore that a clerk had come from England
(which at that time was reckoned an important event) he took him
as his master learning psalmody.*

Simeon's "History of the Kings of England"

The dark skies we'd seen brought a run of sou'westerlies that sent us
scudding up the English coast. While the Normans sulked in the stern, I
made friends among the crew—all Norsemen, and happy to hear tales of
my adventures to while away the long sea hours. Sometimes I took over
an oar from one of them and spent hours hauling to and fro, watching
nothing but the dip and rise of the blade, the spray and the dark swell
of the ocean. How good it was to stretch my body after the long months
penned in prison, to feel strength in my limbs again! My life was returning
to me, the life I'd lost as a hostage. I wanted to seize it, to live twice as hard
to make up for it. I was young and driven with desire. Yet, even then, when
my mind was emptied by the long horizons of the sea, a different impulse
stirred in me. I paid it no heed.

After we'd passed the furthest tip of Scotland, we reached the Orkney

Isles. We put in to one of them for supplies, and I heard nothing but Norse spoken there. England was slipping away from me. Then we turned east across the empty ocean.

We made landfall after three nights at sea, though it was hard to tell where the coast started. Rocks and mountains loomed out of the waves only to fall away again into the mist. For days we held a course that was neither land nor sea, between cliffs and towering pinnacles of rock, past fantastic skerries hung with mist and islands thick with forest. After the long months in prison the voyage seemed like a dream to me. My mother had died when I was ten years old, but her stories of sea-monsters and faery islands came back to me then and filled my head with fancies. It was easy to believe them here. Once we sailed between two great rocks so close the men had to ship their oars to make the passage. It would be a cunning raider who made his way to Nidaros.

At last the ship sailed up a long inlet and out into the calm waters of a great fjord. It was ringed with dark blue mountains that faded into further peaks which grew paler in the distance. The water of the fjord was clear as glass. One of the sailors pointed.

"Look," he said, "that's Nidaros."

I strained my eyes. Far away, on the far side of the fjord, I could make out a darker shadow on the shore. As we pulled closer, I saw a jetty, wooden houses, a long hall. For a moment my spirits sank. A king's capital, this huddle of huts? After such a journey I'd imagined a great city with fantastic spires and palaces. But this! Lincoln was twice the town. I pushed my disappointment away. It was to be my home, if the fates allowed.

Nidaros lay at the river estuary. Meeting a high cliff just short of the shore, the Nid looped back inland for a few miles before finally entering the sea, creating a near-island with the river behind and the sea in front. It was a fine spot for a port. There was a long jetty near the river mouth, and we tied up alongside a couple of trading ships laden with timber and barrels of fish. Close to the harbour I could see line upon line of split fish hung out to cure. At once I had on my tongue the taste of dried cod, of the fish stews my mother loved to make. For a moment I felt her close again.

The captain saw to the unloading of the Normans' chests and their bales of English cloth brought as trade gifts for the king. They fussed over every item, opening the chests as if they feared the crew had pilfered from their hoard. Finally they were off, but looking all the time behind them to make sure the captain was bringing me along.

We made our way through narrow streets between the warehouses and workshops. Though it was no great city, Nidaros thronged with life. I saw every kind of craftsman along the harbour lanes, from silversmiths to shield-makers. There were huts and houses crowded close together, hearth smoke rising into the air and a clamour of calls and clattering on every side. Errand boys shoved past us in the narrow lanes, housewives stood arguing over fish, a trader shouted at a line of slaves to move along. They were roped together, stumbling forward, careless whether they stood or fell. When I saw them, I felt again the bite of rope against my flesh and tasted their despair. I prayed I might never be a prisoner again.

We made for the upper part of the town, where the king's palace sat on a rise above the river, looking out over the sea. Like every other building in town save one it was built of wood, but it was tall and finely made, with carvings of fierce-eyed dragons on every corbel end. The Norse have a land of endless forest and none can match their skill with wood, from their ships to their homesteads. This palace would have graced any town in England, had it not been for the heathen look of it. But once we'd passed through the great doors into the king's hall, I forgot to take notice of anything but the banging of my heart. I was terrified I would find myself roped up like a slave again, sent back with the Normans to face their vengeance. I prayed to God at that moment to let me find favour with the king. I swore to him that I'd be his faithful servant for ever if he would save me.

Then I found myself standing before the king.

The throne stood on a dais at the far end of the hall, carved of stone and covered with furs. The king wore a broad circlet of gold on his head, chains of gold set with jewels around his neck and thick gold rings on his arms. Against the darkness of the furs he seemed to glow. The gold reflected light back onto his pale skin. He was dressed in silks and linen with a deep blue cloak around his shoulders. I was dazzled. Then I had a moment of surprise. I saw he was young: seventeen or eighteen, maybe. Younger than me. The awe I felt lessened. I looked again. He had a short beard, newly grown, and long fair hair. He was tall, for sure, taller than me and strong enough for a warrior. He sat on his throne in all his magnificence still and silent as a hare in its form, watching.

Behind him stood his bodyguard, eight or nine fierce warriors in mail vests that made their chests look immensely broad. They stood with legs apart, shining axes held threateningly before them. To one side there were clerks writing at desks or scuttling about, taking notes and whispering in the king's ear. On the other side stood two white-bearded men in long robes who I took to be monks of some order, with stiff headdresses like bishops' mitres.

The audience began. The envoys went forward to greet the king, there was bowing and gifts of cloth and silver, fulsome speeches from the interpreter, stilted pleasantries from the envoys and all the while the king was still and moved not a muscle. I had never seen such stillness. At last when the interpreter ran out of compliments Olaf leaned forward slightly. His voice was not loud but clear and unhesitating.

"You are welcome to Nidaros. King William has been generous in his gifts. We send him our thanks and look forward to bringing prosperity to both our countries. My councillors will meet with you tomorrow to talk further of our terms."

He nodded his dismissal, but one of the Normans pushed the captain forward, with me beside him. The king looked at me.

"Who is this man?" he asked.

The captain spoke before the Norman interpreter had found his tongue.

"He's an Englishman, Lord, though his mother was Norse. After we took him on board the envoys here said they recognized him as a hostage. They wanted me to put about and return him to Lincoln, but as he was on a Norse ship, I brought him here for your judgement." He bowed, pleased to have got the matter off his hands.

I stepped forward immediately. I only had one chance, and I wasn't going to waste it arguing with the Normans.

"Great king, I am honoured to stand before you. Alas, the envoys"—I bowed to them politely and received black looks in return—"have misunderstood the reason for my voyage here to Nidaros, to the famous court of Norway. My name is Thorgot, and I come with the blessing of the reverend priests of the church of Lincoln. They commend me to you in order that I may share their holy rites and practices with the Norse people. They have heard many tales of your saintly kinsman St Olaf, and how with God's blessing he brought the Norse people to the religion of Christ."

I'd not wasted my time on the ship. I'd learned from the men that this King Olaf was the nephew of another Olaf, a Christian king martyred in battle against his heathen subjects and now revered as a saint. I stopped speaking and broke into a hymn in honour of St Olaf. I admit it had been composed in honour of another king, St Eadmund, but it was easy to adapt it. As I sang the king's face changed. At first to surprise, then his eyes widened. The set of his mouth softened a little.

When I finished there was a moment of silence. I placed my hand on my heart, bowed low, then dropped to my knees before him.

"I am servant to you and the Church, Lord, if you will have me. These letters will tell you more of me."

I held out the letters of recommendation my father had given me. Olaf nodded to one of the monks to take them up.

"Read them," the king told him. As the monk turned the parchment round and stuttered out a word or two, I understood that either his Latin was wanting or his Norse. I glanced at King Olaf. We were both young men. I knew he had the same urge to laugh that I felt. I dropped my eyes. When I looked up again, he held the papers out to me.

"Here, Master Thorgot. You must read them yourself."

So I read aloud the words the good bishop had penned about me, and all those hours I'd worn away in chantry were repaid me a thousand times over. It seemed that I was possessed of every virtue and was the finest cantor in the land. The Normans' interpreter tried to break in, but the king waved him away.

When I finished there was silence. I saw the eyes of his bodyguard upon me, those huge men with dour faces, and I felt the Normans' fury that I seemed somehow to have outwitted them, though they couldn't understand how. I was terrified by my own audacity. The king's face was still once more.

"Do you know the singing of the psalms? The singing and the ordering of them?" he asked me. It wasn't the question I'd expected.

"Psalmody, Lord? I have practised it since I was a boy."

He nodded. "Master Thorgot, we give you leave to remain. We will talk further."

One of the clerks in attendance took me out to a side room where men were sitting around playing dice and talking. He explained to me what the king's words meant; that I was to remain at court till the king sent for me. I should be ready to attend on him at any time. Then he handed me over to the steward. He took a good look at me to fix my face in his head, then explained the household to me—where I should sleep, what I could eat and drink, when the household took food together, and where I should sit at the table. Then I was on my own, with plenty of leisure to observe the household and wait on the king's pleasure. I wished I might have said farewell to the captain and his crew and thanked them for their goodness. I promised myself if I should stay in Nidaros I would meet with them again.

King Olaf didn't keep me waiting long. I'd hardly got used to walking on dry land again before a servant came for me and took me to the king's private apartment. It was very different from the great hall. As I was to learn, Olaf loved comfort. The room was hung with silk tapestries from the East; there were furs on the chairs and a polished table with wine and goblets made of glass. The fire burned not in an open hearth but in a fireplace with a chimney. The room smelled of pine and sweet spices.

After so many months in a bare prison, and a week or more in an open longship, I was half-swooning. I was shown to a chair opposite the king and a servant offered me wine. I had to stop myself gulping it down like a churl. I was a man of the Church, I reminded myself. The king mustn't think me a drunkard.

I tried to gather my wits and looked up at the king. His face was as still and unsmiling as it had been during the audience, but his eyes were alive with interest.

"Tell me about Lincoln," he said.

He wanted to know everything, about the town, about the church, about the learning I had, the music I knew. The first task he had for me was the very thing he'd asked at the audience. Psalmody. A strange thing, you might think, but I soon discovered that the church in Norway had no liturgy, no cantors to lead the services. It was hard to grasp. England has been Christian for centuries; psalms are sung and liturgy recited in every church. But Norway was still new to Christianity. Olaf's father, Harald Hardrada, had forced his people to convert at the edge of the sword, but there was little love for the new religion. True, they held St Olaf in high regard; they understood kings who were killed in battle. But not Christ, hanging like a thief on a cross. Their hearts were still with Odin.

Olaf took me to see a service in the wooden church where the bones of his saintly kinsman lay, the first church built in Nidaros. It was simple enough: a rectangular hall, with a dais for the altar and a small side chapel for the saint's shrine. The Mass was a muddled affair, with German missionaries speaking the psalms in Latin, while the folk listened. None of the clergy ventured to preach. Did they speak Norse, I wondered? I watched Olaf as we stood through the service. His face showed nothing. He stood without fidgeting or giving any sign of impatience. He bowed politely to the priests. I became aware that he was watching me, too. When we walked together afterwards, the bodyguard hot on our heels, he said, "These monks haven't been here long. They're not skilled in our language yet."

I was bewildered. Hadn't the country been Christian for years?

"My father argued with the Pope and threw out the missionaries he sent. I have invited them to return. My father brought in priests from Rus who worship in their own church."

So we went next to the Russian church, dedicated to the Holy Mother of God. It was the only stone building in all the town, and it was a wonder. I had seen nothing like it: a basilica with a long high nave that sloped down to aisles on either side behind arched columns, slender and finely carved. Above them were rows of windows to light the interior. At the far end was a wide apse with a rounded dome and it too was filled with light. The whole building was whitewashed and painted in bright patterns of ochre, red and yellow. How had this Eastern church come to Nidaros?

In Harald Hardrada's youth, Olaf told me, he had been exiled. He became a mercenary, found his way to Byzantium and became commander of the Emperor's Varangian Guard. He amassed huge wealth. When at last he became king of Norway, he had sent to Byzantium for masons skilled in secret arts to build a church in the Eastern style. All my days in Nidaros I loved to worship there, to hear voices borne heavenwards into the pure and wondrous loveliness of that dome.

But at that time it was the preserve of Hardrada's Russian priests, the robed and mitred men I had seen at court. Their liturgy was so strange you might have thought it another religion altogether, with their processions and icons, their swinging censers full of incense, their strange droning chants.

After all our churchgoing we went back to the palace, to Olaf's private apartment, sent for wine and talked. And talked. After many glasses of wine, I gave up the struggle to appear a sober churchman and roistered with Olaf as if we'd known each other all our lives. At last he clapped his goblet down on the table, leaned back on the furs lining his chair and stared directly at me.

"What am I to do about the Church?"

"Which tradition do you favour?"

He shrugged. "I was brought up to be a warrior, not a priest. I can't make these decisions. I was trained to run an army, not a Church."

"It's the same," I told him. "It's like an army. Bishops, priests, deacons—everyone has their duties and takes orders from above. The Pope's the general. He makes the rules. But you'll have to get rid of the Russians. They don't answer to the Pope."

He stared at me, assessing what I said.

"I shall make you my chaplain," Olaf announced a few days later.

"Chaplain, Lord? I'm not even a priest."

"It'll give you authority. They'll have to do what you want."

I had plenty of ideas.

"Norsemen should lead the Church, not foreigners. There needs to be a school—young men, boys, who can learn to read and sing. They'll have to learn Latin."

He shrugged. "Whatever you want."

I became the king's chaplain, though we spent more time carousing than praying. Olaf loved drinking. When he was in his cups, the silence fell away from him, and he would talk as freely as any other drunkard. I did my share of drinking, but I learned to be wary. I needed to listen. I had so much to learn. So much to do.

Some folk have wondered at it, that I should have found favour so easily. But to me, now, it seems no wonder. I was a fugitive, utterly alone, without kin to support me. Olaf, though he was surrounded by his bodyguard, councillors and clerics, was alone too. Some men in the bodyguard were close to him in age but they kept their distance. The priests and monks sent to Norway were men with customs and languages different from his. They weren't friends. But he and I could be companions. I knew enough of the Church to help him, I spoke Norse and we could drink together too. I was his man, and my loyalty was to him alone.

The Norse had won their wealth through warfare, through plunder and pillage. Olaf wanted something different. He wanted to make alliances, for his country to prosper through trade. He wanted the Church. Not because he was a passionate lover of God; to tell the truth, I sometimes wondered how much he grasped of Christian doctrine. But he understood that the Church could unite his country, could bring culture and learning. Olaf was fifteen when he had seen his father, Harald Hardrada, slaughtered at Stamford Bridge alongside six thousand of his men, the cream of the country's manhood. There could be no more war for a generation. There were no fighting men left. Peace was the only way.

"Norway was never enough for him," Olaf told me, of his father. "He was like a hound with rabies, he couldn't stop fighting. Every year he went to war with Denmark, just for the sake of a campaign. If anyone angered him, his sword would be out of the scabbard in a breath. You might count yourself lucky if he only beat you with it."

"He beat you?"

"My mother taught me to keep my face steady and my tongue still when I was near him, just as she did. Anything could send him into a rage."

That stillness, that silence had stayed with him. In Council he spoke little, even when hot words flew to and fro. It served him well. He kept his own council and few men knew what he was thinking. They called him Olaf Kyrre—Olaf the peacemaker. What choice did he have? He made treaties of friendship with William of Normandy, his father's sworn enemy. He accepted the Pope's authority. He even took a bride for the sake of peace, the daughter of King Svend of Denmark. As soon as Ingerid was of age, Olaf would be wed.

"When I am wed, we will find you a beautiful Norse girl. You'll have a household and a family and forget about England."

"I'm not a marrying man, Lord."

"Not a marrying man? I've never seen a man who wanted women more!"

It was true. I loved to spend time with women. Olaf had a mistress, a slender woman with skin like alabaster and a smile like sunshine. She and her friends were full of teasing and laughter, and I tasted their lips as often as I wanted. But something held me back. Would I one day, I thought, be a priest in more than name? The thought swam as deep below my will as the fish in the fjord.

CHAPTER 4

EDITH

Durham, January 1069

In the third year of his reign King William sent Earl Robert, surnamed de Comines, to the Northumbrians. But they all united in one feeling not to submit to a foreign lord, and determined either that they would put him to death, or that they all would fall together by the edge of the sword. Aethelwin, bishop of Durham, met Earl Robert at his approach and forewarned him of the snares laid for him. But he, thinking that no-one would be so daring, despised the warning. Entering Durham with seven hundred men, he allowed his men to act everywhere in a hostile manner, even slaying some of the yeomen of the church.

Simeon's "History of the Kings of England"

I married Raedgar on 14 October 1061. When we heard the news of the Norman victory at Hastings, Raedgar asked, what day was the battle fought? The fourteenth day of October, they told him. I wished he hadn't asked the man. It was our day to rejoice in; why should we have to think of slaughter and bloodshed on some field in Sussex?

Even now, three years after Hastings, the war seemed distant to me. It was nothing to do with us. Nothing to do with Durham and the Community. Our town was different. It was set apart for God. That's what

I told myself whenever I had to listen to the rumours round the hearth, the tales of revolt against the Normans, of battles and burning towns. Our lives went on as they always had. In those days it was impossible to imagine them changing.

I was to learn what fear was and to know it as my constant bedfellow. But back then all I had on my mind was the ale I had to brew. It was towards the end of January, the dark days when it seems like winter is never going to end and everyone is low in spirits. When the malt was stewed and ready to ferment I thought: honey. There was hardly any left but what was the point of keeping it? Now is the time to use it, I thought. We'll have sweet ale and it will cheer us up. I fetched the big jar from the store and a long spoon and scraped away. It had turned hard and crystalline over the winter, so in the end I poured in some hot water to loosen it. When it was all emptied out into the mash, I put the spoon in my mouth and sucked every last bit of sweetness off it.

With the weather so cold the brew had needed days to work. That morning, before I had heard anything, I had taken a peep and decided it was ready. Gudrun, my neighbour, came to help me and kept the cloth stretched steady while I ladled the mash out of the cask and through the sieve. The ale was pale yellow, and the smell of honey was like a summer's day, like daisies in a hay meadow.

"Mmm ... what a smell!" said Gudrun. I closed my eyes and drank it in.

"It's snowing outside."

"I know. Imagine that, a green winter, and then snow like this at the end of January."

"The Saint has sent it. It will keep the Normans away. They'll never bring an army north in this."

The thought of the Normans distracted me. I let the ladle tilt sideways.

"Edith! You're spilling it!"

It had run halfway down my sleeve in a dark sticky line. I straightened the ladle and scooped up the mash again.

When we had finished the sieving and stowed away all the jars filled with ale we went back into the hall. At once I could sniff trouble in the air.

A stranger was standing at the hearth and all the men were crowded round him, heads close together. Hunred, my son, was there, hanging round their heels. When he saw me, he ran over and started pulling at my arm.

"The soldiers are coming! I want to see!"

I looked up at one of the servants, and he nodded. "Yes. This man saw them at first light. They're coming up the road to the east."

"Will they come into Durham?" It was a foolish question. There was scarcely an hour of daylight left, and it was snowing. What else were they going to do?

"Unless Earl Cospatric and the rebels attack them first."

Durham had been besieged once before, when I was a child. The Scots had come rampaging down, but they hadn't broken our defences. Were we going to let the Normans into the town without a whimper?

"All right," I told Hunred. "We'll go and have a look. Put your boots on."

I pulled on my calfskin boots that would keep the snow out and took a heavy cloak off the peg. We had to push hard to get the door open with the snow blowing up against it. Then we were out, into the sudden coldness of the air. The snow was falling without a sound in big heavy flakes. Everything was covered—houses, fences, lanes. Just whiteness and a dark heavy sky above. Hunred was full of excitement, kicking the snow and snatching up handfuls to stuff into his mouth. In spite of the dread in my belly I felt excited too. The first snowfall of the winter.

We walked over to the edge of the promontory. You can stand up there and look all the way down to the road that runs on the far side of the Wear. Hunred came running up behind me, shouting as he threw his snowballs, but I caught hold of his hand and put a finger to my lips.

"Hush. Look down there."

The soldiers were riding beside the river, in threes and fours. Their horses' hooves had worn through the snow so you could see the brown earth of the track. The line of soldiers stretched away into the distance; dark men and horses, backs and heads whitened with snow. It was a procession that never seemed to end. I couldn't stop watching. Then

Gudrun was beside me, grabbing my shoulder to keep her footing. Even when she was steady, she still held on tight to me.

"Why doesn't Earl Cospatric attack them?" she said. "Didn't he swear to drive the Normans out?"

She hadn't stood there long enough, or she would have known the answer. They were too many. I had counted four times, five times, to a hundred; they were passing already when we had arrived, and still they were coming. If only the snow would swallow them up, I thought, smother them with soft flakes, like sheep in a drift. Then a horrible imagining took hold of me, of finding them weeks later in the thaw, horses lying with swollen bellies and soldiers dead in their chainmail.

Gudrun tugged at me. "Let's go back. I'm scared. They'll be at the gates soon." I called to Hunred, but he was spellbound, staring at the soldiers.

"Who are they?" he asked.

"Normans. Come on! Look—your hands are frozen."

He pulled off a branch for a sword, and ran ahead, waving it round and shouting "Kill them! Kill them!"

When we got home, Raedgar was waiting for us.

"Where've you been? I have to go. The bishop and elders of the Community will receive them."

"Outside? In the snow?"

"The men are clearing the ground outside the church. We'll wait for them there. We have to receive them hospitably."

I was angry, unsettled, frightened, all together. He bent down and turned my face to his.

"Don't worry."

I pressed my head against his bony shoulder to try and blot out the image of the dark line of riders. For a moment, with his body hard against mine and the smell of his sweat in my nose, I felt safe.

"We may have them for a night, maybe two, but they're heading north, up to Tynemouth."

"There's so many of them. Where are they all going to go?"

"We'll have to lodge some here. It could be a dozen or more. Tell the servants to let them have whatever they want—ale, bread, meat; whatever there is. Let them have it."

I was outraged. Whatever they want? It was January. There were hungry months to live through before the spring. And the new ale! Why should I give my honey ale to the Normans? I opened my mouth to refuse. Then I remembered what I had seen, that long line of soldiers. Perhaps it was a price we had to pay. I held my tongue.

Raedgar lowered his voice.

"I want you and Hunred to sleep in the stable tonight. Make it a game for him—take some food, anything. But make sure you can't be seen and keep him quiet."

I took him up into the hayloft above the stables. I'd been mistress of Raedgar's hall for nearly eight years and had never been up there. Why would I? Only the stablemen used it. It was a snug space under the beams with dry hay piled all around, but I was too pinched with fear to marvel at it. Why did Raedgar want to hide us? What did he fear the Normans would do to us? I pulled Hunred up the ladder beside me and tried to make a game of it.

"Look at this! We can make a nest in the hay and lay the rugs on it."

My voice came out strained and high. He stared at me.

"Will we be safe here, Mother?"

I saw how pale he was. He knew well enough it was no game.

"Yes. We'll be safe. But you must be very quiet, quieter than a little mouse. Then no-one will guess that we're here. Not even the servants."

We burrowed through the hay to the furthest end of the loft. I made two hay beds, side by side, and laid the rugs on top. Hardly a gleam of light showed through the thatch above us. The horses shifted in the stables below, pulling at hay and chewing; I could hear shouts, but they were far away. Hunred lay against me, and I heard his breathing turn to sleep. I pulled the blanket I had brought over him.

Then I heard voices draw close and the sound of horses, their hooves muffled in the snow but saddles creaking and stirrups chinking. Men were calling to each other outside the stable. I heard the words distinctly but could make no sense of them. It must be Frankish. They were Normans. I turned and spat into the hay.

Hunred woke up. I could hear the servants' voices below us in the stable, and then Raedgar's, irritated, giving orders.

"Treat them like guests. Take the horses. If there's not room in the stables, let ours stand out. Yes, give them feed! What do you think?"

There was commotion in the stables, horses being led in and the stableman arguing.

"There's ten of them or more. What are we meant to do with them? We can't put ours out on a night like this."

Then Alun spoke, Alun the steward.

"Do you know what happened down in the village? Do you?"

He lowered his voice so I could barely hear him.

"A man down the street by the gate, it was a cobbler, you know him. Herebert. They put four men to his door, and he wasn't quick enough to let them in. One of the Normans drew his sword and put it straight through him."

There was a moment of dead silence below. There was no more argument, only the sound of horses being moved, the stableman speaking softly to them as they whinnied protest and kicked out at the strangers. Then the ladder was set against the loft floor and I heard footsteps on the rung. I felt the hay moving as bundles were pulled out for the new horses. I put my arm around Hunred, and we shrank back against the wall.

The men finished, and for a time there was only the sound of the horses squealing and stamping as they settled. Then I heard noises coming from our hall; men talking, bursts of laughter, shouts. Once or twice I heard a woman screaming. The noise grew to a roar. It was the roar of a feasting night, men getting louder as they grew drunker, drowning out the sound of the musicians and wild singing taking its place. I knew that roar and often I was part of it. But these were songs I'd never heard before. Norman songs. I hated them, hated the thought of them drunk on my honey ale.

It went on and on, deep into the night. Hunred had fallen asleep again. I would have too, if it had been an ordinary feasting night. But the noise of this feast made me too bitter for rest. At last, sometime after midnight, it started to die down. A few shouts and outbursts of drunken song broke the night silence for a time. Then there was stillness.

The air in the loft was bitterly cold. Every breath froze in my nostrils. I pulled more hay down till there was only a breathing space left and held Hunred close against me. His small body was so warm. So sweet. I loved him more than anything in the world. I will never let them harm him, I thought. Never. Never. Before I had finished the thought I was asleep.

Hours later I woke up. The horses were restless, shifting and stamping below us. Light was coming through the thatch above me, little darts of light dimmed by the snow lying on the roof. But it was not the pale light of a winter dawn. It was like the light of torches. Fire, I thought suddenly.

At once I was wide awake. I pushed the hay aside, slid away from Hunred and crawled back to the other side of the loft where there was a loading hatch let into the wall. I felt for the rope and tugged it open, the heavy door coming down on me so suddenly that I was knocked sideways. When I pulled myself up the loft was filled with light, a fiery orange light that sent shadows leaping on the walls. I stared out into the night. Flames and bright smoke rose up into the darkness, reflecting off the snow. I could see the dark outline of the church behind the flames. It must be the bishop's palace on fire, I realized. No other house stood so close to the church. I could hear men shouting war cries and the sound of swords clashing hard together. It was the Northumbrian rebels. It must be. They must have come into the town in the night and now they were fighting the Normans. I turned cold with terror. What if they fired other houses? All the houses? What if they fired the stables and Hunred and I were burned alive in the hay?

I crawled back and tugged Hunred awake.

"Put your cloak on. Quick. We're going to find Father."

I pushed him ahead of me back through the hay. His body was still sluggish with sleep and I had to half-lift him down the ladder and out of the stable. He stood blinking outside in the red glare of the flames. I took his hand and we slipped and skidded along the snowy path to the house. I pushed the door open. There was not a sound inside, not a candle still burning. Surely they couldn't be asleep? I stared around at the shadowy shapes in the darkness. I set both doors open to let the light in.

At first what I saw seemed indeed to be men sleeping. They were slumped over benches or lying prone on the floor. I had seen drunk men asleep on the floor often enough; that was nothing to wonder at. It was the smell that made me understand. The hall smelled bloody, like a flesher's yard. I looked again. The hall was full of bodies. Dead men, lying on the floor or on the benches where they had slept. Their heads lolled to one side, their throats cut. Their hair and tunics were matted with blood. At the far end of the table there were signs of a scuffle, of drinking cups and platters knocked onto the floor and a man lying face down, a knife still in his back.

I thought only one thing: Hunred. He must not see this.

He was still at the threshold, staring out at the flames. A wash of relief went through me. He must not see it. I would take him back to the stables. To the fire. Anywhere. I put my arms round him.

"Mistress Edith."

I turned and saw Alun the steward, his eyes glittering black in the firelight.

"Alun! What has happened?"

"The Earl's men came. They made them open the gates in the lower town. They have murdered the Normans where they slept. Hundreds of them. In all the houses. In the town too."

A kind of sobbing came up into my throat, a sobbing revulsion that I could not stop. Alun held my arm, urgent.

"The master told me to wait with you and the boy. De Comines and the other Normans lodged in the bishop's palace were awake by the time the rebels got there and they held out against them. The rebels set the place alight to drive them out. The fire is near the church and the master is gone to it."

"The church? What do you mean? Is it on fire?"

"I don't know. He told me to wait here for you."

Panic seized me. I was certain I must go to the church at once. I tried to shake off his arm.

"Take the boy. I'm going to the shrine."

But Alun held me still, shaking his head.

"There's still fighting, mistress."

I tried to pull away and Hunred started to cry in sympathy.

"I want to see the fire!" he wailed, again and again.

I bent down to him, suddenly sober.

"We'll go later. When the soldiers are gone."

Alun took us back to the stable, back up into the loft. He brought wine he'd kept from the Normans and bread and cheese for Hunred. The wine steadied me. I pulled Hunred close to me and sang to him while he ate bits of bread and cheese. In spite of the terrors of the night, he fell asleep in my arms.

With first light I saw Raedgar's face looking up at me from the ladder, soot-blackened and exhausted. Hunred leapt up, flinging his arms around him as he climbed up beside us. He took Hunred on one arm, me on the other, and the three of us lay tight together in the hay. Hunred was the first to cry out,

"I had bread and cheese up here in the hayloft!"

"Did you keep some for me?"

"I ate it all! I ate it all!"

I looked at Raedgar. His face was so streaked with smoke that I couldn't see his expression.

"The shrine?"

"Safe. Thank God. Our prayers were answered."

Hunred stared at him.

"Did you put the fire out Daddy?"

Raedgar hugged him.

"No, not me. Not any of us. The Saint came to our aid. He turned the wind to the east, so the flames couldn't reach the church."

He took my hand and pressed it tightly.

"It was a miracle, Edith. I saw it with my own eyes. It had started to burn. We could never have saved it."

We were silent for a while. At last he pulled himself upright.

"I must go back to the church now. Keep the boy here as long as possible."

Then the stables filled with men, talking and arguing. They were English voices now, not Norman, but none of them I knew. A man shouted an order,

"Three horses. Every man to have three horses! Strap on the bodies as they are, we'll strip them later."

The stables were soon in commotion, horses neighing and kicking out, men cursing as they saddled up and jostled the horses through the doorway. When they were all gone, Hunred pulled at me.

"I want to go back to the house."

"Wait. Wait a little while. There's so much mess to clear up. We'll keep out of the way."

"Now, Mother! I want to go now!"

At last I rolled up the blanket and pulled his cloak round him.

"Stay close beside me or the soldiers will catch you."

When we went outside, the whiteness of the snow dazzled me for a moment. I looked up at the sky. A pale sun was visible through the grey clouds, but there was no other light. There were no flames. The palace must have burned out. There was a strange stillness in the air, only the shouts of the Northumbrian men, the rebels, echoing in the air. A man rode past us, a cap on his head and mail over his tunic. He was young, fair-haired with a new beard. He looked like any other English youth you might see taking a sack of grain home from market. But this boy had different goods. He led a string of three horses behind him, reins tied together. Lying over the saddle of each horse was a man's body, face down. The legs and feet were on one side, arms reaching forward on the other, bunched together and tied under the horse's belly, the faces hidden against the horses' flanks. They were taking the bodies away, with their swords and axes, helmets, cloaks. Plunder that would pay the men for their pains. The youth caught sight of me watching him.

"They won't trouble you any further!" He shouted. "The Norman scum are gone! Done for! That's the end of them in Northumbria!"

More riders followed, each with a string of horses. I felt sick to my soul. Was he right? Would it be the last of the Normans? Or would they return for vengeance? Hunred tugged at my hand. He looked up at me, his mouth half-open with shock. "Are they dead, Mother?" I nodded. How could I hide it from him? Soon the bodies would be gone from the hall and I could take him home.

In spite of the cold, I made the servants set the doors and casements open. As the light came in, I stood and stared. I hardly recognized what I was seeing. It was not my hall. Everything was in disorder; benches shoved sideways, a table tipped over with a charger of greasy meat scattered below, broken drinking vessels and jugs on the floor, a tapestry pulled down from the wall and soiled with blood. The hearth fire was out. I felt the very life of the house had been extinguished. The servants stood aghast beside me. At that moment I wanted to run, run from the hall, back to my father and never return. But he was in his grave, I reminded myself, and I must show courage. I gathered myself. I had to. I would work till we were rid of every trace, every mark of the Normans. It would be as if it had never happened. All we had to do was work.

"Clear the floor," I ordered. "We'll clear the floor first. Clear it all out, the floor rushes, everything. Keep the broken shards separate, put them in baskets."

Once I had started, it was a relief. It stopped me thinking. We would do without rushes till the thaw. I would burn juniper, for cleansing. I could send the maidservant out with Hunred to cut some. It would keep him out of the way. I called to Alun for wood, to kindle up the fire and heat water. I went to my stillroom for lavender water and let it run out over my hands and wiped my face with it. I had to do this. I couldn't ask Raedgar for help. He was the dean; he had to be with the elders. And the bishop. Had he survived? Had the Northumbrians let him escape? In my mind's eye I saw the blazing house, the Normans running out with burning clothes, the waiting men with their swords and axes. Robert de Comines hacked to pieces. It was too horrible to think of. No more thinking. Work. I turned back to the hall.

It was dark before Raedgar returned. By then the tables and benches were set upright, pine and juniper burned in the hearth and filled the hall with a smell of resin. I couldn't smell the blood now, but when I left the hall for a time and returned, the stench still lingered beneath the smoke. I set candles on the table and brought bread for him.

"Have you eaten?"

He shook his head. In the candlelight his face was gaunt as an old man's.

"Where's the boy?"

"With the servant. She took him out into the woods while we cleaned the hall. He's tired out."

I leaned towards him like a conspirator.

"Are they gone?"

"Yes. They've gone." He sighed deeply. "May God forgive them for their evil deeds."

He turned to me.

"The bishop warned de Comines, warned him it might be a trap, but the Norman wouldn't heed him. God knows the bishop has shown his loyalty. He has served as an ambassador for William, but de Comines treated him like a vassal. After the Normans' feast and riot was done God moved the bishop to leave the palace and spend the night in prayer. He was at the shrine when they set the palace alight."

He paused. His fists tightened till the knuckles were white.

"The rebels were ruthless, Edith. Please God I never see such a sight again. It was burned to the ground and de Comines and his men with it."

CHAPTER 5

The Inheritors

Durham, 1069

Concerning the Ravages of the Danes circa 870 and about the Seven Bearers of Saint Cuthbert:

At this time the people, exhausted by the long continuance of the labour, gradually ceased attendance on the holy body. Indeed they all went away, with the exception of the bishop, the abbot and those seven who were privileged to bestow more close and constant attendance on the holy body. These persons had resolved that as long as they lived they would never abandon it. Four of them, named Hunred, Stitheard, Edmund and Franco were of greater repute than the other three, and it is the boast of many persons in the province, as well clerks as laymen, that they are descended from one of these families, for they pride themselves on the faithful service which their ancestors rendered to Saint Cuthbert.

Simeon's "History of the Church of Durham", Chapter XXVI

It was a week before the last of the snow melted. Although the ground was sodden, work started at once on clearing away the ruins of the palace, and I was glad of it. Every time I looked at the charred posts the evil images of the night returned to me. Once all traces of the building were gone the clerks and elders came in procession with censors swinging, sprinkling holy water to cleanse the ground. The bishop had given orders that the new palace should be built on the site of the old one, as if he wanted to cover up what had happened. Wanted to pretend nothing had changed. If I had been him, I would have found a new place for my palace. Indeed, if I could, I would have found a new home for myself. A new hall, free of the spirits of murdered men and ghostly cries at midnight.

But I couldn't, and I had to content myself with scrubbing and scouring till my hands were sore to get rid of the last traces of death from under the floor rushes. I burned pine and juniper every day on the hearth, and I brought holy water from the shrine to sprinkle through the house. Hunred had seen the fire, knew men had died, but he had seen nothing of what had happened in the hall. I wanted life to go on for him in the ordinary way, for him to go to school and learn his lessons, for everything to be as it was. But the night had left its mark. He woke with nightmares and was hard to settle. He and his friends played new games of houses set alight and dreadful deaths. None of us could forget.

At the same time, our house was turned upside down. The palace had served as chapter house, ecclesiastical court and estate office for the community. The clerks and servants were housed there. Now somewhere else must be found, and since Raedgar was dean of the community, our house was taken over. The hall was constantly full of men coming and going, sitting in council, needing benches and tables, needing food. The bishop's steward was always at my side, telling me of the next meal I would be expected to provide.

"Where's it all to come from?" I demanded of Raedgar. "We can't feed them all."

"I will speak to the steward," he would promise, and forget in the next breath, because a thousand worries had fallen on his shoulders. All the deeds of the community had burned in the fire, so that he was constantly with the reeves and the clerks in the scriptorium, trying to work out what was lost and what they must replace before the Normans tried to take our land from us. I knew it was pointless to complain to him, but when I was utterly weary and distraught from it all, who else could I cry out to?

At night when we lay together, Raedgar was so spent that he would fall asleep in the midst of my complaining and all the consolation I had was his sleeping body.

Sometimes in the early hours I could bear it no longer and shook him awake.

"Will they come back? Will they be revenged on us?"

Raedgar would struggle out of sleep and mumble comfort. Always the same words.

"The king trusts Bishop Aethelwin. He used him as his envoy to the Scots last year. He won't hold the bishop or the Community responsible. Why would the bishop have his own palace burned down? How could a Community like ours bear arms? Everyone knows it was Cospatric and the Northumbrians."

It half-reassured me—not the words, but his waking presence. He would stroke my head, clumsy with fatigue, as if I were a child. Like an elder brother. Always kind, always patient. Always tired.

One weary morning, when I saw Hunred pulling on his boots to walk to the schoolhouse, a sudden impulse seized me. I called out to him to wait.

"I'm coming with you."

But when we left the house another boy was running up the slope towards the schoolhouse, and in a moment Hunred forgot me and ran after his friend. As I stood looking after the boys, I realized I was alone. I was never alone at that time. There was always someone in the hall wanting something, needing orders, fetching supplies. But now, instead of going back to the house I turned up the lane towards the church. As I drew close, the din of the men working on the new palace next door grew louder. A man whistled as he swept his adze to and fro, sending curls of wood-shavings flying. I heard the swing and thump of axes, the foreman shouting orders, apprentices clattering buckets. They had nothing else to trouble them; only the task in front of them; the blade cutting through wood, the spade slicing through soil. I wish I were a man, I thought. I reached the entrance to the church and pushed open the heavy door.

Inside, suddenly, there was silence. The stone walls were too thick for the sounds outside to penetrate. Most of the women I knew, even in the Community, wouldn't enter the church on their own, unattended. But my father had taught me differently, and besides, my lineage gave me rights. I pulled my shawl over my head and walked down the aisle.

The Saint's shrine stood behind the altar, then as now. Tall candles burned beside the coffin, lighting the embroidered canopy of gold that covered it. Beside it on a stand was the Gospel book, set open at the reading of the day. Even in mid-winter, there were gifts from pilgrims set against the wall—a cloth-covered basket, a couple of boxes, a purse. Standing there, before the shrine, I felt peace enter me. The Saint was still here. The fire had not touched the church. Had not touched the Saint. As I stood before the shrine my soul began to ease. Angels attend on the saints of God, and that morning I felt their wings stir the air. As I prayed a thought came to me, of my father's words when I had last stood there with him. "Don't trouble the Saint with all your petty worries," he had said. "Just listen. Wait and listen." I wondered what he had meant. But I was too weary to puzzle it out. I let my lips form the words of the shrine prayers and repeated them over and over till I was ready to go back into the world. Everyone would be wondering where I was.

In the old days, Raedgar used to sit with Hunred before he had his supper, going over the day's lessons with him. But for weeks now, since the fire, he'd hardly seen his father. Raedgar was up early and not back till long after Hunred was asleep.

"Why can't Father help me?" he grumbled, day after day. At last I told him to bring his slate and primer and took him into Raedgar's work room.

"Is father coming?" he asked.

"No. He's too busy. He doesn't have time for your lessons. I'll help you for now."

He stared at me, puzzled.

"Tell me then, what did you learn today?"

No answer. Just stares.

"Write it then. Write it on your slate. Show me how good your writing is."

Still baffled, he bent over his slate and started to write laboriously: "Hodie . . . "

I leaned over and read it. "Today . . . " I started to translate.

"But . . . " He was agitated now, his face red.

"What's the matter?"

"You can't teach me! You can't! Women can't read and write!"

I laughed at him. I picked up Raedgar's *Collectar* and started to read the Latin to him. After a few sentences I handed the book over to him. It was too hard for him, and he could barely stumble through the first line.

"There," I said. "You shouldn't think that women can't read and write. You can see your mother can."

How confused he looked! Why could his mother read? No-one else had a mother who could read. I took pity on him, pulling him close to me along the bench. I bent down and kissed his head.

"Don't get upset. I'll tell you why I learned to read."

Still his body was stiffened against me. "It's a story. Do you want to hear?" Now he was curious. He softened beside me and took a quick glance at my face.

"Remember Grandfather? My father who died last year?" Hunred nodded. "He was descended from one of the Saint's bearers, the men who preserved the body of the Saint when the Community had to flee from the Danes."

"Like Father's father."

"Yes. Like Father's father. When I was seven years old, the same age as you are now, my brother died of marsh fever. That left only me. There were no other boys to carry on the line. My father said, Edith will continue the line. She will inherit. My mother thought him mad, but he was grief-stricken at the loss of my brother, so she let him have his way. Every day he sat with me like this, teaching me as if I were a boy."

I stopped for a moment, caught in memories. It had been hard, and my father pushed me without pity. But I loved it. I loved being on my own with him. Loved being special. I tried with all my might to please him, and I became a good scholar. He was proud of me and made me read aloud to visitors who scoffed at him.

"Yes," said Hunred, "and what then?"

"My mother thought it was a great folly. As I grew older, she argued with him night and day. How can the girl become an elder? How can she serve in the shrine with all the men? You're ruining her. All she knows is Latin! She can hardly spin a straight thread!"

Hunred looked up at me and started to laugh.

"In the end, Grandmother won. I could read and write by then, in Latin and English, but I went back to spinning and weaving and my household tasks."

I had started to become a woman. My breasts were growing, and men were starting to look at me. I wasn't tall, but I had a slender waist and a long neck. Swan-neck, my mother called me. She would give me her amber necklace to wear and hold up the burnished metal mirror before me. "That's what'll please a man. Not Latin and scribing."

I turned back to Hunred.

"Grandmother had a plan."

"What?"

"To marry me to Raedgar. To Father. Although he was so much older than me. Because his family were descended from the shrine-bearers, so that if we had a son, he would inherit both lines."

"Me!" shouted Hunred.

"Yes. And that's why you are called Hunred, after my line. It consoled Grandfather for the loss of his son. And you're extra lucky, because when your father isn't here, your mother can help you with your lessons."

"No!" he shouted, laughing now. "No, no, no!"

He grabbed his slate and jumped off the bench. It was no good. He wanted his father. Just as I had wanted mine, I reminded myself. But it annoyed me. When he looked eagerly for me to chase him, I shook my head. Let him go his own way. Perhaps one day, I thought, I would have a girl, a little girl all my own. And I would teach her everything I knew.

CHAPTER 6

THE HARRYING OF
THE NORTH

Durham, 1069

The King stopped at nothing to hunt his enemies. He cut down many people and destroyed homes and land. Nowhere else had he shown such cruelty. This made a real change.

To his shame, William made no effort to control his fury, punishing the innocent with the guilty. He ordered that crops and herds, tools and food be burned to ashes. More than 100,000 people perished of starvation.

I have often praised William in this book, but I can say nothing good about this brutal slaughter. God will punish him.

**Orderic Vitalis's "Ecclesiastical History
of England and Normandy"**

The topping out of the new palace took place at the start of April. By Ascension Day, it was ready for the bishop and his court to move into. There was a great feast, and no-one was gladder at the celebrations than me. No more clerks wandering round my hall, no more scribes setting up tables in every corner. No more wheedling steward wanting dinner for half a dozen guests newly come. No more. We had our house to ourselves again. I had leisure to play with my son—and to visit my neighbour.

Before the fire, Gudrun and I used to be in and out of each other's houses most days. The other women of the Community were older than me; I wouldn't have entered their houses without invitation. But at Gudrun's I would pull open the door as if it were mine and call out to find her. Gudrun didn't care. She had a slapdash, lazy way of doing things, and it was nothing to her if she were interrupted. She was the daughter of a lord and used to servants waiting on her.

"Did it grieve you?" I asked her once. "Having to marry into the Community?"

She arched her eyebrows and made a face at me. She had full wide lips that were always pouting or smiling.

"Grieve me? I wept for three days! I wouldn't eat. I howled all night. But nothing would change father's mind. He wanted our family to have the Saint's protection. Then I met Leofric, and after that I thought it mightn't be so bad. You know how he is."

I did. Leofric was tall and timid, always eager to please his wife. He never complained if his meal wasn't ready or if the floor was covered with cloth for Gudrun's latest gown. Her father was always sending new finery for her—a bolt of blue linen or a silver necklace, a piece of venison or a box of sweetmeats.

"Ooh, try this!" she would say, and take a sugared marzipan in her long fingers and put it in my mouth. To this day the taste of almonds makes me think of Gudrun. I was dazzled by her. "My little nun," she called me, because I dressed so plainly, but I didn't care. I loved to have her as my friend. In those early summer days of May and June when life seemed almost normal again, we would sit outside with our spinning, watching the comings and goings of the Community and telling tales.

But all the talk that summer was of the rebels. The place seethed with rumours, and Gudrun always had the latest news. She was bolder than I and often went down to the marketplace with a servant to listen to the talk among the stalls. When she came back, I'd be waiting for her, eager and fearful. She huddled so close that I was swooning with the smell of her musky rose perfume as she hissed the latest news in my ear. Wessex had risen against the Normans. William was a prisoner in Shrewsbury. The Atheling was fled to Scotland. I half-believed every tale till the next one came along.

But September brought news close to home that we couldn't doubt. The Atheling had joined forces with Earl Cospatric and a Danish force sent by Swein of Denmark. Their army had taken York. They had burned the Normans' castle to the ground and half the city with it. As I listened to the news, it wasn't York I thought of. It was Durham. Would we be next?

"The rebels won't attack Durham," Gudrun said, full of worldly wisdom. "Why would they? York's different. Whoever controls York controls the north, and now the rebels hold it. They'll soon drive William out of Northumbria altogether."

Gudrun always favoured the rebels. One of her brothers fought with them. I tried to believe her, but even then I cared for the rebels as little as the Normans. At night fear often woke me.

But by November, even Gudrun admitted that the rebels were in trouble. Swein had left the alliance; William had given the Danes raiding rights along the coast to be rid of him. We knew that was true, for the Community owned lands along the coast and we'd heard news of raids. Then rumours started that William was bringing a great army north to retake York. It seemed we were beset on every side. Would to God that King Edward had been given long life, I thought. What furies had his death unleashed upon us! All the women went to pray at the shrine every day at that time. There used to be arguments amongst us in former times—fallings out over the children or servants or unfairness when provisions were shared. No longer. Old feuds fell away, and we turned to the Saint.

December brought hard weather that year, with frost and early snow. A fortnight before Christmas, Earl Cospatric came galloping into Durham as if demons were after him. He had hardly a score of men with him and no word of more to follow. They were lodged overnight with the bishop and in the morning Raedgar was called to Council.

It was already dark by the time he came home. I was standing at the hearth spinning and listening to Hunred's riddles. Hunred loved to tell riddles at that time but often forgot half the lines or even the answer, so I had to tease it out of him. We were laughing when Raedgar came in and neither of us saw him. He must have stood and watched us, till Hunred looked up and shouted, "Father!" When he came over to us, his face was in shadow, so I guessed nothing of his news. But when he embraced me, I felt his heart beat strident in his chest.

"You are precious to me, you and Hunred," he said, lips close to my ear. "Whatever happens to us." Then he held me as if he wanted never to let me go.

I was astonished. Why was he speaking like this? Raedgar, who so seldom spoke of love—what had happened? I turned to Hunred.

"You must do your lessons. Go and do them now so Father can come and check them in a minute."

He went off. Raedgar and I stood by the hearth. His words came out breathless.

"The news is bad, Edith. The worst. If Cospatric is to be believed."

He tried to calm himself. Raedgar, who always made light of danger. I took his hand.

"Tell me, Raedgar."

He took a breath. "Last month King William brought an army north to retake York."

I nodded. I knew that already. I stared at the embers glowing under the cooking pot and waited.

"Cospatric knew William's army was too strong for him. So he decided to abandon York and send his men out into the countryside to lay up for the winter. As soon as William and his army were gone south, he planned to recall them and take York again."

"Why will they not surrender? The fighting will never end."

Raedgar shook his head.

"When the king learned of this, he fell into a rage. He gave orders that all the country about York should be put to the sword and not a village left standing that might support the rebels."

His voice fell low, almost to a whisper.

"He's sent his soldiers out through every hamlet. Every homestead. Innocent people who have no truck with the rebels. The soldiers kill everyone they find. They burn the houses and slaughter the stock. Cospatric says he has sworn to lay waste all the land between York and Durham. All of it."

I knew terror then. It was as if all the fears of the last months had finally taken possession of me. At last I managed to whisper,

"Durham too?"

"Yes. Cospatric has come to warn us."

The night of the massacre came back to me. I saw again the dead men's bodies on the floor and smelled their blood. This time it would be our blood—Raedgar's, mine, Hunred's. I cursed them, cursed these soldiers who murdered as they pleased. What did it matter whether they were Norman or Saxon or Dane? I begged God to burn them all in hell.

Raedgar was speaking again, his voice steadier.

"We'll take the Saint's shrine to safety, as our ancestors did before us."

"Where will we go?"

"We'll go to Lindisfarne." He paused a moment and moved closer to me, speaking very quietly. "We can't be sure of Cospatric. It may serve him to get us out of Durham. I don't trust him. But the threat is too great. We must go."

Yes, I thought. We must go. Before their swords find us.

CHAPTER 7

THE FLIGHT

Northumbria, December 1069

When they were retreating towards the island with the body of the holy father, there was a powerful individual on the other side of the Tyne, whose name was Gyllowe Michael. This man inflicted many injuries upon the fugitives; he hindered them in their journey; he persecuted them; he plundered them and did them all the mischief he could. Not, however, without its punishment . . .

. . . upon the fourth day they reached the crossing to the island, accompanied by all the people of the saint. But as they happened to arrive there at the hour at which it was full tide, the bishop and the elders and the women and the children mourned and lamented with each other at the danger which they should incur from the winter's cold, which was sharper than usual . . . whilst they were in the midst of these lamentations, the sea suddenly receding at that point (but at no other), afforded them the means of passing over, whilst at every other point the tide was at its fullest. And thus, singing praises to God and his holy confessor did they reach the island dryshod, along with the holy body of its patron.

Simeon's "History of the Church of Durham", Chapter L1

The story of our ancestors, the seven bearers who had protected the Saint through all the hardships that beset them, was known to every child in the Community. I had told the story to Hunred countless times. When I pictured the bearers, the seven of them were always carrying the coffin of the Saint on their shoulders, striding tirelessly over hill and dale, or lying breathless in hiding from the bloodthirsty pursuit of the Danes. They were strong and stalwart, unwavering in their devotion. They carried no possessions, no food, but depended on God alone for their sustenance, just as the Saint taught us. The bearers had fled from Lindisfarne when destruction threatened, and now we were fleeing back to it. The story was repeating itself, only backwards.

But our flight was nothing like the story.

It was delayed a whole day for packing. Cospatric came on Tuesday night; the elders held council all Wednesday—and then all of Thursday was taken up with packing. Three days! When William's soldiers could have been upon us at any minute! The bishop insisted that all the treasures of the shrine must be packed up, all the documents taken from the library, all his vestments folded and taken. He cared more about possessions than anything else. What good would they do us if we were still lagging when the soldiers came? Gudrun was as bad. She was in and out of the house with gowns and cloaks, holding them up for me to decide which she should take.

And there were so many of us. The bearers had no families, no servants, no blankets and ale and baskets of bread. Their bishop had no clerks and priests to attend on him. But we seemed to be moving half the town to Lindisfarne. At last Raedgar intervened. Lindisfarne was a small island, he reasoned with the bishop, just a few farms, a church, a guesthouse. How would they house us all? We couldn't take servants. It must be only the seven families of the elders. Only two attendants for the bishop. All the others, the clerks and cantor, the reeves, the servants, must make their own way north and find shelter on the Community's other estates.

The lifting of the coffin was even worse. The elders struggled to lift it at all. The seven men were of different heights and two of the older men were not strong enough to bear it. As they started to carry it down the aisle it looked as if it might topple at any moment. A couple of servants had to be fetched to take their place and ease the coffin down into the cart. It was to be borne on a cart, not on men's shoulders. It was slid in with no more ceremony than a sack of barley, wedged in alongside the chests full of the bishop's treasures. We are not worthy of our ancestors, I thought.

It was Friday morning before the procession set off, through the gates and down through the town. One cart carried the shrine and all the Community's treasures. The other was piled high with bags and baskets, blankets and clothes, and all that we couldn't bear to leave behind. The two youngest children travelled in it too, crammed in among the bags. Hunred was in a sulk.

"Can I ride?" he'd asked me.

"No. It's a long journey. You'll go in the cart."

He started to whine, "I don't want to go in the cart, I don't want . . . ."

I slapped him. "You'll do as you're told." He looked at me with a stricken face. I squatted down beside him and held his arm.

"William's soldiers are coming, Hunred. There's no time for 'I want this' and 'I want that'. Get your cloak and your boots, and get into the cart."

He wouldn't look at me now. No wonder the bearers took no children with them, I thought.

The streets echoed with the noise of the cartwheels and the horses' hooves, but there was no other sound. No-one ran to their doors to bid us farewell; the town was already deserted. Everyone had fled. It was hardly light; sunrise was an hour away, and it was bitter cold. We cared nothing for that. It would keep the Norman soldiers abed till we were well quit of the town and heading north. I rode close beside Raedgar, happy to be moving at last. I scarcely thought of what lay ahead. I felt only relief to be gone.

✠

Messengers had been sent on ahead to our stopping places to give them time to make ready for us. We would go first to the Community's estate at Jarrow, where a monastery had once stood in the days before the Vikings. That first day, when we were still fresh, passed soon enough, though it was a ride of twenty miles. Raedgar, Hunred and I were lodged with a farmer and though he had only a bench for us to sleep on, that night I slept more soundly than I had for weeks. The Normans would not find us here.

The next day we rode west along the Tyne to the crossing place and then north to the next estate at Bedlington. It was a long, long ride and oh, what a relief to slide from the saddle! But there were few smiles to greet us and little warmth in the welcome. Something was amiss, I knew it. I could feel it. People lowered their eyes before us.

The night passed peacefully enough but we were soon to find out who they feared. The next day we were to set down in a small demesne at Causey. But when we were a few miles from it a party of horsemen came down the road towards us at a canter, so that we were forced to pull up. There were six or seven of them, armed men with swords and spears. Raedgar brought his horse close to mine.

"Don't fear—they're Northumbrian men. They'll do us no harm."

Their leader rode ahead towards us and reined his horse in alongside the bishop and his attendants. He wore a leather cap with long sides that hid his hair, but a fair beard showed below it. He might have been twenty or twice that age; his face was so weather-tanned that any trace of softness was gone. He sat upright in the saddle as if he were well used to sitting there. His blue eyes were mocking as he looked us over.

"What have we here, fellows?" he shouted to his men. "Here's a pretty little party!"

The bishop sank so far down in his saddle that it seemed he might slip off it altogether. One of his attendants called out,

"God give you good-day, sirs! We are travelling north to Lindisfarne."

"To Lindisfarne? It's a long time since St Cuthbert paid a visit to Lindisfarne!"

"Indeed, sire." The attendant faltered, looking to the bishop for help. The bishop pulled himself up and stuttered,

"The Normans—the Normans are laying waste the land."

"Your Norman friends won't help you now, eh Bishop? Won't repay the favour?"

"They—the Normans are no friends of ours."

"No friends? Why, it's not a year since you sat down to dinner in your palace with Robert de Comines! You warned him of our plans! Wasn't it lucky he didn't believe you? No more do we believe you, Bishop."

Beside me I felt Raedgar urge his horse forward. He rode up between the bishop and his tormentor.

"Sir, we are protectors before God of his holy Saint, Cuthbert. Our duty is to him alone, and we seek only a place of safety for his shrine. As you look to know his favour on Judgement Day, let us go forward in peace."

He sat straight on his horse and spoke without a tremor. I saw Hunred staring at him, and I was proud he saw his father's courage.

"Traitors are traitors, priest."

"We look for peace as Christ has taught us."

The man shrugged. "There is only one way peace will come—when every Norman is driven out of this land." He turned and beckoned his men forward.

"We won't stop you now. We'll just lighten your load for you."

They moved round the two carts. The bishop suddenly came to life, urging his horse forward.

"No! No! You mustn't touch the treasures of the Saint! You'll suffer sure damnation! No, no . . . "

One of the soldiers turned and shoved him hard in the chest. The bishop toppled and fell from his horse like a sack. He lay still on the ground. The soldiers rode past him without a second glance. As they went by us one of them turned in his saddle to stare at me.

"Look Gyllowe!" he shouted. "Look at this! The priests take their women with them!"

He rode up behind me, leaned over and ripped the headdress from my head. My hair fell round my shoulders. He was beside me now and pulled me towards him. I called on my ancestors and on St Cuthbert to protect me. I could see his sharp white teeth and parted lips, could smell his garlic breath. I saw he meant to kiss me. I wrenched my head away from him. Then Raedgar was shouting at him and tugging his horse forward till he was forced to let go of me.

"Are you animals?" Raedgar yelled at Gyllowe.

Gyllowe laughed. "Yes, so we are and we can sniff out a bitch on heat from half a mile away. Best keep her close, priest." Then he clapped his man on the back. "Come, we've other business first."

Then they were round the carts, knives out, prising open the chests and boxes, tipping out the bishop's treasures. Hunred jumped screaming out of the cart. Raedgar dismounted, caught Hunred and lifted him up onto the horse. Then he bent down to pick up my headdress from the ground and put it into my hands.

"Put it on," he whispered to me. "Cover your head." My hair was lying long and loose around my neck. I felt as if I were naked before the men. I started to fumble with the cloth. Then Gudrun rode over. She took the cloth from me and wound it round my head tight and secure till all my hair was hid and my shoulders were properly covered. She leaned over from her horse and held me close without a word. I felt tears starting from my eyes.

Meanwhile Gyllowe and his men were grabbing and looting, stuffing silver chalices and altar goods into their saddlebags. Only the Saint's coffin was left untouched. When they could carry no more, they were back onto their horses, and at once I was panic-struck that the man would return for me. But they made off with the treasure, shouting insults as they went.

No-one moved. It was impossible to grasp what had happened. One of the children started to cry. The bishop's attendants went to their master, but they couldn't rally him.

"He's taken a blow to the head." They looked at Raedgar. He was dean and with the bishop senseless he must take command. He stepped away from me.

"Lift him into the cart," said Raedgar. "We'll get help for him at Causey."

He looked around at the wreckage of chests and boxes strewn across the road.

"Get the chests stowed back on the cart. As fast as you can. We'll check them later. We must get moving before they return."

There was to be no rest for us. No-one would help us at Causey for fear of the rebels. Raedgar gave the order to continue, onwards, to the last estate at Tughall. I knew nothing of it, only that it was far away. We had ridden a day's journey already, but no-one gainsaid him. On and on we went. As the road unrolled endlessly before us, the horses grew slow. I was so tired I would have risked an army of rebels to let my body lie down.

The cold of the December evening tightened its grip on us. Every breath was like a freezing burn in my nostrils and throat. My feet and legs were numb, my body stiff beneath the jacket and cloak. My body was frozen and so were my spirits. The humiliation I had suffered so overcame me I felt I would never feel joy again. The stars came out, with a gibbous moon that gave us light enough to follow the path. If there had been any spark of life in me, I'd have marvelled at it, at the frost on the track glittering in the moonlight, the stars shining so bright in the blackness of the night. But my heart was closed to any marvel. The only glimmer of joy I felt came hours later, when I smelled the sea and saw the huts at Tughall.

"Let me rest!"

"When we get to Lindisfarne. Only one more day. Then you can rest all you like."

"Just an hour. Another hour."

"The weather's turning. We must get there before nightfall."

When at last I struggled outside, I could hear Raedgar shouting and cajoling outside one hut after another till we were all on the road again. When I sat in the saddle, every bone and muscle in my body shrieked.

Sleet cut my face. And yet I was glad he forced us on, away from Gyllowe. We would be safe when we got to Lindisfarne.

It was twenty miles or more and all the time the weather worsened. The wind had gone round to the east and sent squalls of hail off the sea. The horses hung their heads, unwilling to move forwards, so we had constantly to urge them on. After hours we passed close to the palace at Bamburgh set high on its great rock, but we dared not ask shelter of the Earl. Who knows what treachery we might suffer there? We struggled on, skirting an endless bay till in the distance we saw the low outline of the island. We were almost there.

As we rode close by the shore, we saw the tide was high. We thought nothing of it. Although none of us had ever been to Lindisfarne, we all knew that you could ride across the sands to the island. But when we came down onto the shore there were no sands to be seen. There was only a grey expanse of ocean, with angry breakers whipped up by the wind scudding across it. We thought we had not found the spot and rode on till we could see round to the very tip of the island. It was surrounded by water. There was no way across. It seemed impossible that there ever would be. We sat close together on our horses, half-blinded by the wind and sleet, staring at the sea and the unreachable land beyond.

There wasn't a habitation in sight. Not a soul to help us. There was nothing but the dunes and sharp-tipped marram grass for mile upon mile, and already the light was fading. Would we spend the night starved and shelterless in this wilderness? One of the women slid down from her horse, threw herself down on the sand and started keening. Within minutes three or four more had joined her, and the children, and the keening grew to a wail. It was the sound of despair. I felt it welling up in my own throat. I clung to the pommel to keep myself from joining them; I could not, I must not, for Raedgar's sake. The bishop was slumped in the cart, every cloak and blanket he could find wrapped around him and his eyes tight shut. It was up to Raedgar to save us.

His horse looked as dejected and sorry as the rest of us, with its back turned to the sea and the wind blowing its tail across its hocks. When

Raedgar dismounted, it stood motionless. It must have thought like the rest of us, where was there to go? Raedgar went over to the cart where the Saint's coffin lay and called out to the women.

"We'll pray to the Saint. Each of you. In turn."

He and the elders started the shrine prayers. The keening died down and the women and children straggled over to the cart till we were all gathered. We stood close, shouting the prayers into the wind with all our strength. One by one we went to the coffin and kissed the cold wood. All our despair was in those prayers. Only the Saint could save us.

When we were done, we turned back to the sea. At once we saw the shore had lengthened. The waters had drawn back a foot, a yard, more, and even as we watched, we could see them retreating. What had seemed like a great sea was shallow now. The waters still stretched before us, but they no longer threatened to swallow us up. I felt a little spring of hope. Had the Saint given us a miracle? As we stared, a man came down the shore towards us. It was a fisherman with a creel on his back, strong boots on his feet and cloths bound around his head, making his way home from his fish-traps.

"Never fear," he told us. "It's the east wind blowing it on that makes the water seem fearsome, but it'll clear back soon enough. You'll get over before nightfall. Best leave the carts though. They'll never get through with the mud still soft from the tide. You can fetch 'em over tomorrow."

I thought of the Israelites and the parting of the Red Sea. They could not have felt more joy than we did at the man's words. He showed Raedgar and the elders where we were to cross, with every counsel we needed for a safe passage.

"I'd take you over myself," he said, "but there's others waiting on me and my catch, so I'll give you good night."

But when I went to Raedgar to ride with him, he shook his head.

"I'll stay with the Saint. You take Hunred over."

"The cold will kill you. What good will that do the Saint? Or me, or Hunred?"

"I'll stay."

In the end, we left him in the cart with the last scraps of food we had. I hadn't the strength to argue. The bishop was propped up on Raedgar's horse with a servant behind him. Hunred rode pillion with me. With his small body pressed against mine the mare slipped and slopped her way through the mud and the water and the darkness till we felt at last firm ground beneath us. We had reached the island.

So it was that the Community of St Cuthbert came home to Lindisfarne.

CHAPTER 8

A TIME APART

Lindisfarne, 1070

I woke next morning to the sound of raised voices in the hut next door.

"It'll do? What do you mean? It's worse than a hovel!"

I pulled my hood over my ears. But it was no use. Once Gudrun flew into a temper it could last all morning.

"I'll fetch some . . . ." Leofric's voice tailed away.

"What good will that do? I'll lose it, I know I will!" She was weeping now.

She's frightened, I thought. She was with child and full of fears she would miscarry as she had the first one. I would go to her later. But not now. Leofric would have to bear it on his own. Besides, if she was unhappy with her lodging, it would only make her crosser to see ours.

We'd been put in the guesthouse. One side of it was for the bishop and his attendants. The other side was for us, the dean's family. It was plain enough, with sleeping benches along the wall and a plank table, but there was a hearth and a pot to set on it. And it was ours. We didn't have to lodge with a family. Gudrun would be mortified.

Hunred was still sleeping. I slipped outside, down to the shore to look for Raedgar and the carts. There was nothing to see but dun-coloured mudflats stretching away into the distance. Where had the water gone? I couldn't so much as glimpse the sea. In time, I would get accustomed to the tides, but they were a mystery to me then. Far away in the distance I could see the carts, but they hardly seemed to be moving and the wind was too bitter to stand vigil. I was half-frozen by the time I got back to the guesthouse. There was a stack of wood set ready by the hearth and I made up a good fire ready for Raedgar's return.

He was half-dead with cold when he got in and all his clothes were soaked through. I pulled off his wet cloak and made him strip down beside the fire, so I could dry his body with warm cloths. He stood swaying there like a stick-legged heron, so I had to hold him with one hand and rub with the other. Then I sat him on the bench so I could pull a dry shirt over his head, tugging and fumbling his arms through the sleeves. When he lay down, he was asleep in seconds. I put more blankets on him and built up the fire. I feared he would take a fever after such a chilling and I stayed inside all afternoon and evening to watch over him. Hunred ran in and out, telling me of all his discoveries on the island, of the snow that had started to fall, of the village boys he had met. There was no sign of Gudrun.

Raedgar woke late in the evening. Hunred was in bed, and I was getting ready for sleep. I had unbound my hair and was kneeling on the floor beside Raedgar's bench-bed combing it out. I felt him stir. He lifted his hand up and touched my hair. I thought of that other man's hands, who had torn the headdress from my hair, and at once I felt unclean. But Raedgar stroked it and held it to his cheek as if nothing were dearer to him.

"Edith."

I leaned over and rested my head on his shoulder.

"Do you want another blanket?"

"No. Keep me warm with your hair."

I spread it out over his chest, and the firelight made it shine red and gold. The shame I had suffered left me. I kissed him, but already he slept again.

For months, for years, since the war came and brought all our troubles, Raedgar had scarcely looked at me. He worked night and day. If he remembered, he would try to comfort me and calm my fears, but as man and wife we were strangers to each other. Even before the war, I had always known that the Community and the Saint were more important than me, that our marriage had been for the sake of an heir. I was fourteen when we married, and he more than twice my age. I was a child to him.

But now, on Lindisfarne, he had leisure to look at me again. Had it taken Gyllowe and his men to open his eyes? All day I felt his gaze on me. I grew wanton and let my shift slip down so he could see my breasts, or I brushed against him when I passed. He would put his arm around my waist, pulling me close to him. If we were unobserved, he would bend down and kiss my neck. I smiled back at him with parted lips. For the first time, I found pleasure in our love, and I could think of nothing but the nights. I felt no shame for it. Married love is no sin. Solomon's words sang round in my head:

> "How fair is thy love, my sister, my bride; How much better is thy love than wine! Thy lips, O my bride, drop as the honeycomb, Honey and milk are under thy tongue, And the smell of thy garments is like the smell of Lebanon."

Yet even then Raedgar was troubled by his desire. He couldn't stop himself questioning and worrying. Mass was the first thing.

"I cannot take the sacrament if I have lain with you," he said.

Where did such an idea come from?

"I heard nothing of that in our marriage vows," I would retort, and put my shift off to torment him.

"Stop!" he would cry and cover his eyes. I pulled his hands away and kissed his mouth.

Once, after a night of sweetness, he rose early and went out. Curious, I followed him. He went down to the little beach beneath the ridge, stripped off his clothes and plunged directly into the water. It was January. The water was so cold that your feet turned numb if you paddled for five minutes. He stood in it up to his neck, just as the Saint did in Father Bede's story. I ran home and snuggled back down under the warm covers, peeping between my eyelids as he came in. The fire was not yet made, but he stripped off his clothes next to the hearth and did his best to dry himself. His body was whey-coloured with cold. I wanted to laugh, to tease him, but I shut my eyes and pulled up the blanket. Did he think he was sinning, lying with his wife? Or did he have a sudden call to prayer? What a strange man my husband was. His heart was in love, but his head was full of doctrine, and the two warred together within him.

There was little for him or the other elders to do on the island. There were the daily offices at the church and the shrine prayers beside the Saint, and the elders still held council every day. But the council dealt with petty things—an argument between a family and their hosts, whether more provisions were required from Goswick. The war seemed far away. After all our troubles it was a time of blessed peace. Not for Gudrun. Although Leofric had managed to lodge her in the best hall in the village, she was restless and yearned for her own home. But I wanted our life on Lindisfarne never to end.

Hunred was happier even than I, having his father close. Raedgar found stones for him with holes right through and taught him to play jacks with them. They searched the shore for Cuddy's beads, hollow rings of stone which, according to the legend, had fallen from the Saint's rosary when he prayed in the sea. Hunred was always hungry and seemed to be growing taller by the day. There was no shortage of food. The island had fields ploughed out for barley and vegetables, and when the Community arrived the islanders brought in extra stores from the estates at Fenham and Goswick. There was fish and seal meat, wild goose and duck. We never went hungry.

Sometimes we went exploring round the island, all three of us together. On a winter's day Lindisfarne can be as dour as a Lenten penance, with hawthorn bushes bent against the blast, dull skies, driving rain and waves snapping at the stony shores. But when a fair day comes and the wind drops away, there is nowhere lovelier. The sea stretches away to the farthest horizon on every side, turning blue and indigo and glass-green in turn, shimmering and sparkling. Flocks of geese fly V-shaped across the skies, honking and calling. Hunred loved to climb the high rock at the seaward end of the island and look out for raiders' ships on the waves. On a fine day we could see the dark outline of Inner Farne where the Saint had had his retreat. It was scarcely a hide in width set in the midst of the sea, like a stepping-stone between heaven and earth.

Below, in the shelter of the rock on the shore-side, was a curved bay where the fishermen kept their boats pulled up on shingle. There were few visitors in those winter days, but once a trader pulled in to shelter from a storm and let us look at his bales of silk and linen, his finely wrought silver and platters bound for the king of Norway. He had perfumes too, of rose and spices. Raedgar found a coin for the man and bought a tiny blue glass phial for me. The scent of it was like a glowing breath of faraway Byzantium.

Though there was little left of the monastery save two half-ruined churches, to St Peter and to the Virgin Mary, the turf still carried the outlines of the cells where the first monks had lived and prayed. Cuthbert might have lived in one of them, I thought. I wandered between them, dreaming of his life then. We had laid the Saint's coffin inside the church of St Peter by the altar, in the very place it had stood until the heathen drove the monks away. Or so I fancied it, though Raedgar claimed the church had fallen into ruin after the Danes and what I saw was repaired or new built. What difference did it make? The Saint was back on Lindisfarne, and I felt certain it rejoiced him. It was simple and quiet. He would not miss all the gold and silver that surrounded him at Durham.

Not so Bishop Aethelwin. It was hard to say whether his broken skull or the loss of the treasure hurt him more. As soon as he could stand, he had his men go through every chest and make out a list of all that had been stolen. Though Raedgar told me it was a sin I couldn't hold the bishop in respect. He didn't belong to the Community. He had been forced on us by Canterbury because he was a monk and celibate. Edmund, our previous bishop, was married like all the other elders, but now it seemed bishops must be celibate. Aethelwin had been one of Edmund's advisers, and he seized his chance when Edmund died. He was appointed bishop from Canterbury without the Community's consent. That was nothing to him. He brought in his own advisers and talked only of estates and treasure, deeds and possession.

We stayed on the island for the Christmas feast and through the remainder of December, all of January and into February. By then it seemed that everyone was impatient to be gone, to get back to Durham. Gudrun would come to see me, holding up a gown.

"Look at this! The salt air has eaten the cloth half away and stained it too! I look like a churl!"

"You never would, Gudrun. You'll always be a beauty."

"No! My skin is worn to leather in this place. I might as well start planting parsnips."

As the Saint did, I felt like reminding her, but kept my mouth shut. After all, Gudrun had been brought up a lady. I no longer cared what gown I wore or what servants' work I had to do. None of that mattered to me. I was content. When I look back now, I think that God gave me those months to sustain me for what was to follow. I was in love with Raedgar, close to my son, close to the shrine of the Saint. I cared nothing for salt winds or simple lodgings. I shut out all thought of the war, of the death and destruction that was happening. I wanted to think only of love and of the light on the ocean.

It ended, of course. Messengers went to and fro till word came that it was safe for us to return to Durham. Everyone was ready to believe it but me. The reeves came from Durham to organize it all. Word was sent out through the district to the rest of the Community to make their return. Provisions were brought in to take back with us, for we heard there had been looting in Durham. We left with four carts this time, two of them packed full of sacks of grain, cheese, and barrels of salted fish. The horses were brought out and our journey started all over again. Hunred wept to leave, and I felt like weeping with him. The island was a place set apart. With every step we took across the sands returning to the mainland fears and troubles crept back into my heart. With every mile that separated us from Lindisfarne Raedgar grew more distant as his duties took him over. At least we saw no more of Gyllowe. When we reached Bedlington, all the talk was of his death. It seemed that after the Christmas feast he had taken a sudden fever and was dead within a day. I thought of his mocking eyes and the way he sat on his horse as if they were one. I couldn't imagine Gyllowe dead. An old man had seen him in a dream, wherein he had been taken by St Cuthbert to see Gyllowe screaming in the flames of hell. The bishop declared that the Saint had been revenged upon him for the evil he had done the Community.

"Do you think it's true?" I asked Raedgar. "About the Saint's revenge?" He looked at me. In his face I saw head and heart war together. In his heart he knew the Saint as love alone, but in the shallows of his mind such stories held him in thrall. He sighed.

"No," he said.

We had no joyous homecoming to Durham. There had been looting at Jarrow, and the soldiers had destroyed part of the old church there, out of spite when they found no treasure. As we neared Durham, we saw destruction everywhere. We rode past silent farms and hamlets where every hut and shed had been burned out and half-rotted carcasses lay on the ground. We saw not a soul. The countryside was empty. In the woods and banks, the first green shoots of spring were showing, but the fields lay barren all around. We grew more and more fearful of what awaited us at home.

We found the town stripped bare. It had been sacked, whether by William's men or Cospatric's we could not tell. In the church, the great crucifix above the altar had been torn down and pillaged of the gold and silver that had covered it. All the treasures that had adorned the walls had been stolen, and the church was as filthy as a stable. Our houses had been ransacked and anything they could carry off was gone—stores, clothes, hangings.

It was far worse outside, in the countryside beyond the town. The folk who had managed to escape with their lives had nothing. No home, no food and in the dead of winter. Durham was full of starving fugitives. They had fled to the shrine of the Saint for safety, only to find it empty; we had abandoned them.

There was no time to rest from the journey. The first task was to clean out the church, so the shrine could be reconsecrated. Anyone who had strength enough worked with us, till it was ready for the bishop and elders to fill with incense and carry the Saint's coffin back to his shrine. People filled the church from wall to wall to witness it. Here at least the world could be put back to order. But beyond the church's walls it was a different story. What were we to do with all who needed help? How were we to feed and house them? They could return to their villages and rebuild their huts, but how would they live? The Normans had not only stolen corn and cattle, but destroyed their tools, their ploughs and axes. They meant to drive them off the land for ever, to make it a desert where no rebel could find shelter.

Within days of our return Lindisfarne seemed like a dream, a moment in Paradise that was hardly imaginable in the suffering all around us. We did what we could. The guesthouse was overflowing, so we took people into our houses. We fed them, let them warm themselves beside the fire, listened to the terrible tales they had to tell.

It was so hard to find food for them all, now, at the worst time of year, when seed-corn needed to be set aside for sowing if we were not to have famine next year too. Each day, Alun, our steward, brought what he could find, and I would set a great pan over the hearth to cook a soup for everyone. I ate little in those days. I was still plump from the good food of Lindisfarne and felt ashamed when I saw women and children with shrunken bodies and staring eyes. Their clothes were hardly more than rags. I gave away all our blankets, all our spare clothes. I had never seen people so desperate.

Hunred hated it. He hated to see his clothes given away, hated to share his home constantly with strangers. All he could talk of was going back to Lindisfarne. Raedgar and I had little time to spend with him, and his school friends were scattered. He barricaded himself into Raedgar's room for hours on end, refusing anyone entry till his father came home. Then he would fling himself on the floor in tantrums like a toddler. At last I said to Raedgar,

"Take him with you. Let him sit with you in Council, go with you to visit the sick, whatever."

"He'll get bored."

"He's worse than bored here. He wants to be with you."

So he did. Hunred hung at Raedgar's side like a shadow. He had seen too much of war, more than a child should see, and it had made him fearful. He wanted everything to be the same, for life to return to its ordinary ways. So did we all.

When we were still in the thick of these troubles, news came that Malcolm of Scotland had taken an army down into Cumbria and was making his way along the Tyne, plundering as he went. I no longer asked or wondered why. In this new world of war, I had learned there was neither friend nor foe. Rather, there were two sorts of people: warriors whose great causes were a pretext for theft and slaughter; and us, the helpless, the innocent, who must suffer their violence. It bred an anger in me—no sudden rage but a settled contempt for the men who did these things. It cured me of my fear. I despised them and turned with all my heart to God and St Cuthbert. Only a fool would put his trust in princes.

It was at this time Raedgar came home one evening with a grim face. I thought the Scots would be upon us in the morning, but he had different tidings.

"The bishop has spoken with us this morning."

That was hardly news, so I waited.

"He says that the kingdom is in turmoil, that we are beset on every side by opposing forces. He fears the lordship of King William will be severe. He cannot reconcile himself to live under people whose language and customs are strange to him."

Indeed. It was thus for all of us, so why was it so special to Master Aethelwin? Then came the blow.

"He means to resign the bishopric and leave this land altogether."

I was shocked now. I stood and stared at Raedgar trying to grasp what he had told me.

"Resign the bishopric?"

"Yes. He plans to travel to Cologne and take refuge in a monastery there."

The coward! The miserable slighting coward, to sneak away at such a time of need! What a self-serving faint-heart he was!

I looked up and saw that Raedgar was watching me.

"There's more." He waited for me to listen.

"He has told us that he will take the bishop's portion to support him in his travels."

The bishop's portion. The share of the Community's treasure that was meant to be passed from one bishop to the next. He was a thief as well as a coward.

"God forbid! You must prevent him!"

I had more rants ready till I looked at Raedgar. He knew my opinion of the bishop and now he was teasing me with a half-smile on his face. My rancour blew out of me in a gasp.

"He's not worth your anger, Edith."

Suddenly we were laughing. Raedgar was right. He was better gone. But when the laughter was over my heart was heavy. More work than ever would fall on Raedgar's shoulders.

"Who will be bishop, when Aethelwin is gone?"

"Who can say? We'll have to wait for Canterbury to decide. Archbishop Lanfranc is William's man."

"Will it be a Norman?"

"If William holds the throne, he'll hold the Church too, and with no gentle hand. That's why Aethelwin is leaving. He fears William will be revenged on him for Robert de Comines' death."

A Norman bishop. A foreigner set over us, who would know nothing of the Community. Nothing of the Saint. Raedgar put his arm round me.

"Don't be downhearted. The Saint watches over his people. Whatever happens."

I had more news for Raedgar, but he was called for. It could wait. Amidst all the suffering and loss of our return, I had a secret consolation. As the weeks had passed and spring came forward, I found myself quickening too. I knew I was with child.

CHAPTER 9

Aldwin

Winchcombe, 1072

At this period there was a man named Aldwin, who was a presbyter of the province of the Mercians and prior of the monastery at Winchcombe. He had understood from Bede's History of the Angles that the province of the Northumbrians had formerly been peopled with numerous bands of monks and many troops of saints who while in the flesh lived not after the flesh but rejoiced in devoting themselves even while upon earth to a heavenly conversation. These places, that is, these monasteries, he earnestly desired to visit, even though he well knew that the monasteries themselves were reduced to ruins; and he wished, in imitation of such persons, to lead a life of poverty. So he came to the monastery of Evesham and explained his wishes to the brethren, two of whom forthwith associated themselves with him in carrying out the object he had in view. Elfwy, one of these, was a deacon; the other, who could not read, was named Reinfrid.

Simeon's "History of the Church of Durham", Chapter LVL

Have you known a time where words become suddenly alight with meaning and set a fire burning in you that consumes everything familiar? A fire that burns away the small cares and duties you once believed to be service enough, and leaves you with a single light, a single longing in your heart that will not leave you night or day? That others call a madness but that you know in every sinew and bone in your body to be truth itself?

So it was for me at that time. If you have not known it, then I cannot explain it to you, nor could I explain it to my brothers.

"For God's sake, Aldwin!" Brother Edwin cried. "Can't you see what's in front of you? Our land is being stolen from under our noses and you are talking to us about legends of long ago. Have you lost your wits?"

We were in Chapter. I could have said, my brother, see how anger is taking hold of you. But I knew he was tired, like all of us. Fear made him angry. That's how it was in the monastery in those years. Winchcombe was a great monastery with lands throughout Mercia. We wanted for nothing. Our vows of poverty had never been put to the test. But now, six years after the Conquest, our guesthouse was overflowing with men, women and children thrown off their land, starving and sick. We fed them, tried to comfort them, buried the dead. Edwin and the others worried all the time that we would be overwhelmed, that we would be unable to find food for them or ourselves and worse, that the monastery might lose its lands. The Normans were building their castles all about us, looking for land and careless whether it came from man or God. I was prior at that time. I sat through countless Chapter meetings, listening to all the fears, all the complaints, all the schemes to win the Normans over. It was endlessly wearisome. Fear closes the heart, and I saw how the brothers in my care struggled to live in charity with each other. Nevertheless, we continued to abide in the Rule and to find consolation in the guidance St Benedict had left for us.

When I was able, I spent time in study as the Rule advises. One winter afternoon I was taking down a commentary of St Augustine of Hippo from the shelf when another book tumbled to the floor. I stooped down to pick it up. I turned it over in surprise, looking for the title. I had thought I was familiar with every work in our library, but I had never seen this thin brown book, the leather binding worn and stained. How had I managed to overlook it in all the years I had passed at the monastery? And who knows

what made me find it then? I took it with me to my cell. What Brother
Edwin said was true—it was a history of our land from centuries ago. Yet
to me it was alive as nothing around me was. Written by the Venerable
Bede, himself a saintly man, it described the days when the Word of God
first came to the English, when men and women gave themselves up to
God without reserve and worked miracles in his name. The land of the
Northumbrians was filled with monasteries and convents governed by
saints. I read of the most holy father, Cuthbert, who renounced all worldly
comforts to live alone, and of others too numerous to mention.

The Venerable Father's history became a measure against which I set
my life. I saw how lukewarm my devotion had become. My mind was
filled with possession and belonging. When I sang the psalms, my mind
was full of cares. I had entered the monastery for the love of God, but love
had been all but extinguished in me. Now every reading of the Gospels
seemed like an exhortation to me.

There was no single moment when the revelation came to me. It formed
almost unnoticed till it had become a force in me so strong that I felt it
with every breath. At last I knew I must obey it. I went to see the abbot.

"Well," said the abbot. "Bede's *History of the Angles*. A very worthy
work, though it can speak little to our present time, I would have thought."

"Are not all times as one in Christ?" I asked him. "Does he not say, 'I
am the lord of the living not of the dead?'"

The abbot sighed. "Tell me what you are planning."

I took a moment before I spoke, to beg that the light in my heart be
known through my tongue.

"Christ has put it into my heart to travel to the land of the Northumbrians,
where his Word was first brought to our people. To seek out the places
where his holy saints spent their lives with God. I believe he wishes his
light to be rekindled in the kingdom he first sanctified."

The abbot stared at me for several moments.

"My dear prior, this is a wild vision. Things aren't as they were when
Father Bede was alive, you know. The Vikings laid waste to Northumbria
centuries ago. There's hardly a church left standing up there."

"Father, you speak truly. But it is not buildings that I seek."

"But stability, prior. You have taken an oath of stability. You can't just run off and leave the monastery."

"Nor do I wish it, Father. But I am certain that I am called to do this."

Our talks went on, week after week. I couldn't convince him. The abbot was a good man. A kind man. He was fair and just and never shirked his duties. He saw God like an earl, with himself as a trustworthy reeve who would always manage his lord's estates to the best advantage. He was not by nature a contemplative. He had no idea what would possess me to abandon comfort and possession.

At last, he told me that I might travel to the monastery at Evesham and speak to the brothers there. I think he hoped a change of scene might help me to return to my old self.

I spoke in Chapter at Evesham as truthfully as I was able. On the faces of my brothers there I saw the same look of bewilderment and pity I had seen back in Winchcombe. Truly, if I had been any less certain of my calling, I would have abandoned it there and then. But how can we know what effect our words have? All we can do is speak the truth as we know it. Although I thought their ears were closed, it turned out differently.

No-one spoke then. After a long silence the abbot thanked me, and the discussion moved to other matters. But afterwards, when I walked in the cloister, Reinfrid came and found me.

Reinfrid was a Norman. Was that not strange, that the first man to hear me was not a Saxon, but a Norman? I greeted him in Latin, and he nodded a response. He was head and shoulders taller than me, a fierce dark-featured man with black eyes looking down at me under heavy lids. It is no shame to say I felt afraid of him. I had seen too much of our people's sufferings for false courage.

He had brought a French-speaking man with him, Brother Cedd, for Reinfrid spoke little English at that time. Cedd told me Reinfrid's story while the Norman listened, watching him unsmiling. Reinfrid, I learned, was a knight. He had come over to England with King William and had fought for him, first at Hastings, then later against the rebels of the north. After the sacking of York, he had been one of those who had led his men through the hamlets and villages of Northumbria, firing houses and killing every man he saw. They had sacked Bede's former church at Jarrow. Finally, they had come to Whitby. As he stood amid the ruins of the ancient abbey, horror at his wickedness finally overcame him. He fell to his knees before his men and swore to give up his life to God. He left William's service and came to the south of England to find a monastery. He had asked to be admitted to Evesham.

So much his brother knew.

"Has your abbot accepted him into the monastery?" I asked Brother Cedd.

"Yes. The abbot believes he truly repents."

"Why here? There are monasteries enough in Normandy."

Cedd hesitated. He spoke to Reinfrid and they talked together in French. The brother turned back to me.

"He wants to—what's the word? Expiate. Atone. Here, in England. He wants to go with you, back to the north, to the place of his sins, to atone for what he did there."

I looked up at Reinfrid. He was frowning as he tried to understand Cedd's words. It made him look more menacing than ever. I felt a slight shudder go through me. Then, suddenly, he dropped to his knees in front of me, big man that he was. He bowed his head before me and tried to chew out a few words in English.

"Take me. For penitence."

For penitence. I took a deep breath. How could I deny him his repentance? It was for God to judge his sins, not me. I rallied. Commending myself and Reinfrid to Christ, I put my hand on his head and blessed him. It seemed that I had found my first companion.

He was not the only man from Evesham to join me. While I was still standing with Reinfrid, uncertain what to say, a young novice hurried through the cloister towards me.

"Father Aldwin, I heard your words, it was so … I want, I would like, I would like very much, very much, I . . . ."

"Will you join us?" I asked him, to get him to the end of his stuttering.

He looked at me with his eyes wide open, as if astonished with himself. He had a fresh, simple face. He would have been no more than a boy when the Normans came.

"I'm only a deacon, but . . . "

I took his hand. We smiled at each other. I could see his heart was not yet blunted with custom and care. He was full of eagerness, ready to throw himself into any adventure. At last he burst out with what he wanted to say.

"I want to come with you, Father. I want to see the places of the saints that you spoke of and follow in their footsteps!"

I was happy to hear him, yet a misgiving entered my mind. Hearing him speak, with all his youthfulness and innocence, for the first time I wondered at myself, wondered that I should lead others into hardship and danger. I had no worry on my own account, for I was certain that I was called to do it. But a youth like this? I spoke more gravely.

"You must be certain. There will be many dangers and hardships. There will be days when we hunger and thirst, when men may turn against us. You must be certain that God is calling you to do this."

"I am certain, Father. I am so, so … I mean I am very much, I am absolutely . . . ."

"Very well. But remember, you are not bound by any oath to me or any promise. If you find you can't continue, there is no shame in turning back. No shame at all."

"I won't, Father. I won't."

"What's your name?"

"Aelfwy."

A sprite. A warring sprite. Perhaps he would turn out to be our protector.

CHAPTER 10

ON THE WAY

England, 1072

It is a walk of some ten miles between the two abbeys of Evesham and Winchcombe and the lane between the two has been worn by generations of monks coming and going. On a May morning nowhere could be lovelier. The hawthorn and wild cherry were in blossom. A froth of cow-parsley was breaking out along the field edges and the air was loud with cuckoos. My heart lifted as I walked with my new companions. On such a morning God's grace seemed all about us.

Then I heard shouts in the distance and turned to see horsemen riding down the lane behind us. It was unexpected. Monks were accustomed to travel on foot. It could, I reasoned, be a visiting bishop or church officials. But I knew it was more likely to be Norman soldiers heading for Gloucester. As they drew close, I saw I was right. Half a dozen armed men, in their leather tunics and mail vests, swords hanging off their belts as if they feared attack, their horses' hooves churning up the lane. As they rode closer, instead of drawing to one side to pass us, they continued riding three abreast, so they filled the lane from side to side. I saw they intended to force us off the road. The Normans liked to make it clear that for them, we English people did not exist. They treated us like cattle. There was no time to brood on the matter. There was a thicket to our near side, with dense undergrowth right up to the side of the lane. They were coming at a trot, and I was about to jump headlong into the nettles and brambles when I saw Reinfrid step in front of the horse nearest us. He took hold of the bridle, pulled it to a stop and nodded to us to pass by. The rider went to draw his sword, but before it was fully out of the scabbard Reinfrid had reached up and grabbed hold of his sword arm. Seconds later the man was sprawling on his back on the ground. Reinfrid picked up his sword and stood over him, shouting in French at the other men. There was some argument but after a few minutes they moved the horses to form lines of two. The man on the ground got up and re-mounted with a groan of pain. Reinfrid gave him back his sword and some more words of advice in French. The whole party moved on without a backward look at us.

Aelfwy and I stood astonished at his strength. At his authority. "Thank you," I said at last. Reinfrid shook his head and shrugged.

"Bad men."

Yes, I thought. They were bad men, and Reinfrid had been able to call them to order. It was a moment of illumination. I had doubted Reinfrid. I had been reluctant to accept him. Now I saw that his presence was a mercy.

As the abbot had reminded me, we Benedictines take a vow of stability, intended to cure monks of discontent. It is no use thinking, I would do better in another monastery; I am not understood here; I need more intelligent company. You must stay, like it or not. I had spent the whole of my vocation at Winchcombe and had expected to die there. Was it discontent that made me want to leave? I had asked myself this question again and again, searching my conscience for hidden traces of self-will. I could only say it did not seem so. It came from another force entirely, stronger than my own will. Of course, discontent was how it appeared to the abbot, a mad whim that he was duty bound to check. But I was, after all, the prior, second only in seniority to him, and in the end, he felt he could no longer oppose me. He insisted only that Reinfrid and Aelfwy should be placed under my authority in the Rule and that I take charge of their souls. There was a solemn service before all the brethren where they took their vows and the abbot committed us to God. Afterwards I embraced each of my brothers in turn, asking for their forgiveness for any wrong I might have done them. We left the following morning after Lauds as simply and silently as if we were taking a day's visit.

As we walked out of the gates of the monastery, I felt the tightness in my chest give way. I was at peace with myself at last. We walked in silence, the three of us, out into a dull drizzle that soon covered our habits in a sheen of moisture. Aelfwy led the pack donkey, fussing and tugging at the panniers to distract himself from his bewilderment at what he had agreed to do. Reinfrid had a look of especial grimness about him as his staff hit the ground. That look came on him, I would learn, when he imposed some irksome penance upon himself. The penance now, for him, was walking. In his old life, he had ridden the length and breadth of England, ridden the strong Norman horses that left destruction in their wake. Now he had to walk like a peasant, and it was hard for his pride.

We had no horses. Only the donkey. She had wonderfully soft, long ears and patient eyes and her name was Freya. She won over even Reinfrid. I saw him when we were making camp for the night spend fully half an hour feeding her morsels of his supper and brushing down her coat. She was equally at home in French and English and listened to stories, grumbles or memories without judgement. When our feet were blistered and our legs aching, she plodded onwards without complaint. I felt we had a small saint in our midst.

We needed one. The early weeks were the hardest. None of us were used to walking constantly, hour after hour, day after day. The abbot had ordered us to continue the practice of the offices throughout our journey, but after the first week I took the decision to stop the night offices. Neither Aelfwy or Reinfrid were accustomed to the rhythm of night rising, and all of us were exhausted. We said Prime on waking, Sext at noon, then Vespers and Compline at night. It was enough to keep us recollected. It wasn't only the walking. Each day we had to find a hamlet or farm where folk would give us food; sometimes we were turned away and had to start the search again. If it was wet, we needed shelter. I had started the journey with a single intention—to endure all hardship and to trust in God's mercy to provide for us, as the saints of old had done. It was soon put to the test, though not as I had expected.

One day it rained unceasingly, steady heavy rain that soaked through every stitch of clothing and through the thick leather of our boots. We were walking a trackway which ran through high open country in an endless line. Water ran down our heads, our shoulders, our backs and chests. A bitter wind set our clothes flapping against our legs. On and on we went. At last on the horizon we saw a shepherd's hut with a good roof of thatched straw. My heart rose and at once I reproved myself. It was still only early afternoon, and we had hours left of the day to walk. Had I not sworn to suffer any hardship? What a faint-heart I was.

Reinfrid was leading Freya, and as we drew close to the hut, he led her towards the shelter. Her pace quickened behind him.

"No," I said. "It's not time to stop." I pointed to the road ahead so that he would understand my meaning.

He threw his hands out in that way the Normans have and lifted his eyes to heaven as if calling on God himself. He spoke in French, but I knew he was protesting. His voice got louder, and he turned to Aelfwy for support. Aelfwy nodded his head up and down.

"Truly, Father—I mean, I think Reinfrid means, it would be better, if there's no other shelter, maybe none at all . . . "

"No," I repeated. "It's not time to stop." I went over to Reinfrid, took Freya's reins from him and pulled her after me as I continued onwards along the road.

"Fool!" shouted Reinfrid. "You are fool!"

A novice should not shout at his master, but I had no wish to start imposing penances, so I decided not to hear him. I tugged hard at Freya to follow me, but she was as reluctant as my companions. Fortunately, I had some bread in my pocket, and I coaxed her along with that.

The rain grew stronger and stronger as we continued till it felt as if we were walking into a wall of water. It was impossible to tell what time of day it was or where we were. I was dazed by the battering of the wind and rain till I could scarcely put one foot in front of another. I lost all sense of time. At last I felt Reinfrid take me by the arm. He took Freya from me and led us both off the road. Somehow he had found a craggy hollow with an overhanging rock and a couple of trees that kept the worst of the rain off. When he let go of my arm, I felt myself sag down to the ground. Sodden and chilled though I was I fell at once into a deep sleep. I dreamed I was at the bottom of the sea swimming upwards and upwards through pale blue waters but never reaching the surface. When at last I burst above the waves, I was gasping for air. I sat up, panting. My body was strangely hot, and I could feel sweat running down my face and arms. It was dark all around me and I had no idea where I was. I stood up, tottered and fell back to the ground.

When I next came to consciousness, I found myself lying in a hut. It was quite still. I was warm and comfortable, and the rain had stopped. I could hear voices outside.

"Water," said the voice. There was a splashing. "Water. You try."

"Watter," said the second voice.

"Woman."

"Woehman."

It was Aelfwy and Reinfrid, I realized. An English lesson. I lay quite still. I didn't want to call out. I wanted to lie there and listen to them.

Aelfwy's method was alphabetical. Words first, then Reinfrid had to make a sentence. Somehow they had reached W already.

"Woehman," said Reinfrid. "I am 'appy wiz ze woehman."

"No," said Aelfwy. "No, no, not monks. You know, I mean, no, not, not monks. Not with women. No. Let's try another one. Wise. That's hard. Look . . . wise . . . " He must have made a face or a show, because Reinfrid laughed.

"Wise," he said. "I am wise in ze watter." Now they were both laughing, and I smiled too as I lay on my sickbed.

Although I smiled, the words struck my heart. The whole incident came back to me in a flash, and I saw I had not been wise. Reinfrid was right. I was a fool. God had given us what we needed, shelter from the storm, but I was so full of my own ideas that I could not see what was in front of me. Now I was sick, and the journey was delayed. My companions had brought me to shelter, had cared for me without reproach. I opened my heart to ask forgiveness for my folly, for my stubborn will.

In that early part of our journey, we kept close to the Fosse Way, heading first towards Leicester, then in the direction of Lincoln, though we kept out of both towns. For the most part the weather was mild in those early months of summer and the roads dry. Barley and wheat stood tall in the fields, and the sweet smell of haymaking was often in our nostrils. The air was dense with swallows swooping and diving. Yet the growth and greenness was deceptive. Early summer is always a hungry time of year when the crops are still months from harvesting and last year's stores are running low. But in the villages and farms we passed through there was worse than hunger. We found people close to starvation. The new Norman lords cared nothing for them or for the prosperity of the land. They were soldiers and they thought like soldiers; they wanted plunder. They pressed the villagers constantly with new tithes and taxes and thought nothing of taking sheep, pigs, cattle from them. For a family to lose their milking cow is a dreadful blow. To lose their winter grain means starvation. Yet still, when we monks came to their door, they would let us in, would find something for us. They were more desperate for comfort even than food. They needed to know that God had not deserted them. We listened to their troubles and gave them what consolation we could.

Some churchmen believe that the Normans came to harry England as a punishment for our sins. I look at it in a different way. Did not Christ himself suffer at the hands of the Romans? Had the Romans not conquered his people just as the Normans have ours? What Christ has taught us is to hold fast to the kingdom of heaven, whatever the injustice and suffering visited upon us in this world. He is with you in your pain, I told them. He suffers with you. What other consolation could I offer?

It was hard for Reinfrid at these times. He saw and tasted, day after day, the suffering his people had visited on England. He kept quiet, but often our hosts would realize that he was Norman and shrink from him, just as I had done. God had set Reinfrid a course of repentance harder than any monastery could have devised.

We saw other travellers—merchants with closely guarded packhorses, Norman knights with their entourage, messengers cantering past on sweating nags. Once or twice we were stopped by armed men—soldiers, robbers, what was the difference? They found nothing in our panniers that they wanted—a plain chalice and patten, vestments, a few books, bread and water for our noon meal. Reinfrid spoke to them in French, explaining that we were pilgrims. When they heard their own language, they left us alone.

Although Reinfrid was still a novice, we all wore the same travelling habits while we were on the road. But there all likeness ended. Reinfrid was a foot taller than Aelfwy and me, strongly built with a sword arm as thick as a house beam. He would have drawn attention in any company. He was not yet tonsured and wore his dark hair cut straight above the shoulders, but he had no trace of a beard. He liked to be clean-shaven and somehow managed to shave himself every morning, sharpening the knife-blade on his whetstone. For myself, I had decided not to trouble with such things. I was letting a beard grow and it was coming through in an uncomfortable stubble of white and grey that had me rubbing my face a dozen times a day. I tried to keep the tonsure, but I could feel hair brushing around my ears. Aelfwy was the same. A ring of golden curls was growing around his head that made him look like an angel. He was as slight as a girl beside Reinfrid. Both of us struggled to keep pace with the Norman's long stride; I made him lead the donkey to slow him down. What a strange sight we must have been to any onlooker!

Tutored by Aelfwy, Reinfrid's English was improving. In return, he taught us words and phrases of French. Sometimes our conversations along the way were so strange a mixture of languages, so full of misunderstanding and mistakes that miles would pass unnoticed in our laughter, strangely assorted though we were. Even in those early days we were good companions.

Although Reinfrid was a knight and of good birth in his own country, he was unlettered. From the beginning I had worried over this, as to whether a man could fulfil a monastic vocation if he were unable to read and write. Christianity is a revelation of the Word, from Moses to the Gospels. Monks spend much of their lives reading the Word of God, copying it, contemplating it, writing commentaries on it. How could an unlettered man come close to God? In those days of journeying I found my answer. All that mattered, I saw, was that Reinfrid had given himself to God in repentance. He had opened his heart. Aelfwy was the same. He was, as he had told me, only a deacon and was not deeply versed in the scriptures. Yet I could see that he knew more of Christ's love than many of the scholars we had in the abbey. Out on the road we were free; free of the troubles and concerns of running a monastery with all its land and possessions, its busy kitchen and larders, its storerooms and tithes. Here at last was true poverty for the sake of Christ. The three of us were wholehearted in our intention and it drew us together. We were brothers on the Way, though we were to be tested in ways we couldn't have imagined.

CHAPTER 11

POSSESSED

Northumbria, 1072

. . . it suddenly came to Cuthbert that she was in the grip of no ordinary illness; she was possessed. He consoled her husband: "Do not weep. It is not only the wicked who are stricken down in this way. God, in his inscrutable designs, sometimes lets the innocent in this world be blighted by the devil, in mind as well as in body."

As they approached the house, the evil spirit, unable to bear the coming of the Holy Spirit with whom Cuthbert was filled, suddenly departed. The woman, loosed from the chains of the devil, jumped up as though woken from a deep sleep . . .

Bede's "Life of Cuthbert", Chapter 17

As we made our way towards Nottingham, the land became thickly forested on all sides. The road north cut directly through the forest, but we took smaller trackways that were less frequented. We were constantly losing our way in the endless stands of oak and birch and glades of bracken, each one no different from the last. One evening, lost and hungry, we came upon a village deep in the forest. It was a remote place where the people had seen little of the Normans; they saw few strangers and were happy to welcome us. We were lodged together in a freeman's house, and he gave us cured ham and beans and barley bread for our supper. The man's wife and daughter served us at table; the girl took a fancy to Reinfrid and teased him for his poor English. It was pleasant to see him welcomed, to see him smile and join the laughter at the table. Aelfwy was persuaded to sing for them, and his stuttering disappeared miraculously as he sang. We all felt our spirits lifted, and even Freya was reluctant to leave next morning. I was to remember that evening as a glimpse of an older England; England before the Normans came.

But as our journey brought us closer to York, there were few such pleasant evenings. We heard many warnings from other travellers about what lay in store for us in the empty land. That's how they spoke of it, the empty land. The land that William's soldiers had laid waste. Three years had passed since then, but the destruction had been so great that it was still abandoned. Not entirely. They warned us that some of the dispossessed had turned outlaw and preyed on travellers to make a living.

"Make sure you fill up your bags," they told us in the last hamlet we stayed in. "You'll find nothing there."

One of the men looked at Freya and shook his head. "She'll not last. A donkey is a week's meat for an outlaw."

Thank God, fear did not afflict me. I was certain that our journey was God's will, whatever might befall us. But I should have looked beyond myself. It was then, I believe, that fear took hold of Aelfwy's spirits. He was not himself. He became quieter and his usual willingness turned into reluctance. I took little notice. I was more aware of Reinfrid's dark moods. His fear was different. Last time he had travelled the road he was one of William's soldiers, and he had given his sword to slaughter. Now he had to seek God's mercy for his evil deeds.

Though Dere Street runs directly north from York, Reinfrid counselled us that it was too much used by mounted Norman troops and companies. He led us instead on a quieter road to the east that kept us well clear of the city, out into open country. There were few other travellers on the road, and they grew fewer the further we travelled. At first, nothing seemed different. The countryside was green about us, with meadows and woodland on either side of the road. But soon we started to see fields that lay overgrown with nettles and docken. Others were almost bare, the earth covered with a white sheen of salt. There were no animals. No sheep or cows grazing the fields. We came to a village and could see at once it was deserted. Long grass grew up the side of the roofless houses and saplings sprouted through the walls. The pigsties and fences were broken down; coppiced hazel and hedgerows were halfway to full grown trees. Tracks through the grass showed where foxes and rabbits had their runs, and a buzzard circled overhead, its mewing cry the only sound in the air.

We were to see many more deserted settlements, large and small. Sometimes there were only grassy mounds to show where homes had once stood. A silence hung over these places that was different to the ordinary peace of the countryside. A silence filled with emptiness. With absence. So many homes, so many families, people and their geese, their cows and pigs. All gone. It was hard to comprehend such slaughter, how it could have been, village after village, farm after farm. The silence weighed down upon us.

The weather was unsettled, with days of overcast skies and sudden downpours that sent us running, but we shrank from taking shelter in the ruins. On our first night, Reinfrid had gone into a house that was still partly roofed but came out shaking his head.

"No."

I looked at him askance.

"There is bones."

We slept rough that night under trees, and the next. We rose early and walked longer, till exhaustion made us halt. There was only one thought in all our minds, to be quit of the empty land. We had brought bread enough to last four days, time enough, we hoped, to pass through, but we were still hungry. We scavenged the hedgerows for herbs and leaves to chew.

It was on the third day that we saw Aelfwy's trouble start. As we drew close to a deserted farmstead, he clapped his hands over his ears and started to run. When we caught up with him, he was pale, with sweat running down his face. When Reinfrid took his arm, Aelfwy stared at

him with so wild and strange a look that Reinfrid let go. I put Freya's lead
rope into Aelfwy's hands.

"Look, she wants you. You must look after her."

Freya might comfort him, I thought. So long as she had grass and
water and a handful of bread nothing troubled Freya. Aelfwy took the
rope and let the donkey walk him forward till evening. We found a hut,
a shepherd's bothy that had been left undamaged; it was scarcely large
enough for the three of us, but it gave us a roof against the rain. I thought
Aelfwy was simply exhausted, that sleep would restore him. But he woke
all through the night.

The hard ground in the hut and an empty belly kept me from sleeping
too, but they were not the cause of Aelfwy's trouble. Dreams plagued
him, and he talked in his sleep, strange confused words and sudden cries.
After hours of tossing to and fro, at last he leapt up and woke bewildered.
Reinfrid calmed him, persuaded him back to sleep, but he was soon awake
again, sitting bolt upright beside me and talking, on and on.

"No," he said. "No. I was wrong, I was wrong to, to come, at all. I see
it now. It was f . . . folly. A dream, that I would change, would, would be,
different. I can't, Father, can't, can't, can't . . . go on."

It was very early in the morning. I peered at him in the grey light. Ever
since leaving Winchcombe, Aelfwy's company had been a solace to me.
If ever I was troubled in my soul, I only had to look at his open face, his
ready smile, to feel my spirits lift. Not now. A frown had settled on his
forehead and made a deep groove between his eyes. His body was taut
with the trouble within him, and he fidgeted constantly with his hands,
picking at his fingers.

"In the night, Father," his voice dropped away almost to nothing. "I am
po . . . po . . . possessed, Father. An evil sp . . . spirit. Inside me."

I took his hand, but he pulled it away. "No, no! It will . . . it will enter
you." He flung himself away from me and started to weep. I felt tears come
to my own eyes, to see him so afflicted.

There was no hope of him sleeping now. I must sit with him, I thought,
trying to shake my own fatigue from me. I wanted nothing more than to

sleep for hours yet, but I pulled out my beads and started to pray aloud to try and calm his spirit.

When had this started? Days before, I decided. I should have been more aware. But what could I have done? He seemed beyond our help. Was he indeed possessed? I half-believed it. Who knew what spirits lingered in this unhappy land? I scoured my memory for the prayers of purification. It was so long since I had used them or even heard them.

As I sat there, the beads running through my fingers and thoughts coming and going in my mind, I fell into a state halfway between sleep and waking. My lips still moved, the words of the prayers continued, but my thoughts drifted till I was half-dreaming. One of Father Bede's stories of St Cuthbert came into my mind. It was as vivid to me as if spoken by the venerable father himself, and in my dreaming state I understood the story as a direction to me. I saw what he meant me to do. When I came to myself, I found the resolve already formed in my mind.

When Reinfrid woke, I asked him to take counsel with me. We left Aelfwy still huddled in the corner of the bothy and stood outside to talk in the drear light of another wet day.

"How far are we from Durham?"

"A day."

"I want to take Aelfwy to the shrine of St Cuthbert."

Reinfrid stared at me, at first surprised. Then he fell silent. I knew he was thinking it over and I was relieved. I needed his help.

"The Saint will help him?"

"Yes. Aelfwy believes he is possessed. It may be so. The place is full of spirits."

Reinfrid nodded. "You want to . . . " He searched for the word.

"Exorcise. Bring out the bad spirit."

Reinfrid started to walk up and down, staring at the ground. I waited.

"Durham—do you know what is there?"

"The shrine?"

"Yes, but King William builds there a castle. Since two, three years. Against the Scots people. And North people."

I grasped what Reinfrid was telling me. Somehow, so far from the Norman kingdom of the south, I expected to find Durham still a Saxon town. But I was living in the past. William meant to hold his kingdom in the north, and clearly he had chosen Durham as a stronghold. I knew Reinfrid was cautioning me. Our presence might cause questions that he preferred to leave unanswered. I too had no wish to encounter men of the church. I had learned at Winchcombe that what I had been called to do seemed a folly in the eyes of others. I would not have chosen to visit the town now, and I could see Reinfrid felt the same. But since Father Bede's voice was clear within me, I persisted.

"If we were to visit, how should we do it?"

Reinfrid didn't oppose me. There was goodness in him; I knew he was doing it for Aelfwy's sake. Once again, I wondered at the man. His soul was stained with the foulest crimes and yet he was capable of great kindness. I would never understand what soldiers do.

We talked together, trying out different plans. Should only Aelfwy and I enter the town, and leave Reinfrid outside to wait for us? What if we were prevented from finding each other? Should Reinfrid come with us and maintain a vow of silence? There was no point, I thought. Even in a monk's habit, he stood out at once as Norman—in his bearing, in his dark looks, in his speech. In the end we decided we would enter the town at night and seek lodgings at the guesthouse. We might leave Freya with a household outside the town. We would go early to the shrine, as soon as we might, and then be gone.

If we had had any doubts about the plan, Aelfwy's state convinced us. He still lay in the corner of the hut and would not speak with us. If we went near him, he flinched away from us and cried out, "L . . . leave me, leave me here. I ca . . . can't, can't go on," again and again.

We tried to persuade him to eat some bread to give him strength for the day's walk, but he wouldn't eat so much as a crust. At last we made ready to leave, with Freya standing outside the hut. Reinfrid lifted Aelfwy bodily; he cried out at first, then went limp in Reinfrid's arms. Dear God, I thought, blessed St Cuthbert, holy Father Bede, help us get him to Durham. Reinfrid managed to lift Aelfwy onto Freya's back and nodded to me to stand the other side. Together we held him upright and took some of his weight. Freya looked at us in protest. I bribed her with Aelfwy's bread and at last we were moving.

The day seemed endless. We had no bread left. Whenever we passed a stream, we filled our bellies with water to stave off the pangs of hunger, but it gave us no strength. I was tired out from the long marches of the previous days, and it was a constant struggle to keep Aelfwy from slumping sideways off Freya's back. At last, towards evening, we came alongside the river that encircles Durham. We saw first the stone towers of the church where the Saint's body lies, rising above the wooded cliffs of the riverside. Then as the road curved around, another building came into view. In spite of Reinfrid's warning, it shocked me. The Normans' castle was built on the steepest point of the cliffs, a black fortress on a great mound of earth and stone. It seemed to be leering down at us as we crawled along beneath it. The trees had been felled all about it and the land still lay bare as if violated. It was an evil thing to set beside the house of God.

The road led us to a wooden bridge that would take us into the town. Soldiers stood guard at either end. Reinfrid straightened himself up, shouted out a greeting and clapped their hands as if they were old friends and we passed over into the town. Although it was evening the place was still busy. Men were coming and going along the streets wheeling carts piled high with sacks and boxes. Children ran screaming through the alleyways. A couple of soldiers on horseback forced their way through and one of the horses left a dark pile of manure behind. The fresh strong smell choked my nostrils. We had been four days in the silence of the empty lands; we were exhausted and half-starved and the tumult all around felt like a dream. I had no idea where I was or where to go. I looked up at Aelfwy, swaying on Freya's back, his face ashen. Somehow Reinfrid kept us both going, up one narrow street after another, till we found ourselves in front of the gatehouse that gave access to the sanctuary. Once again Reinfrid spoke to the guards, their faces changed from surliness to respect, and we passed through. I thanked God for Reinfrid's strength. He had brought us all to safety.

Beyond the gates was the solace of the sanctuary. I sensed the quieter air and open ground, but I had no strength left to look about me. I wanted only to reach the guesthouse, to bring Aelfwy to safety and to rest my aching legs.

They brought us bowls of hot, steaming soup and I thought I had never eaten anything so good in all my life. Aelfwy sat staring at his bowl till Reinfrid took a spoon, put it in his hand and helped him get a spoonful into his mouth. He seemed to wake up then and started spooning away as readily as we were. I was even happier to see him eat than to taste the food in my own mouth. I blessed the charity of the brothers. Freya had been taken care of too, a stable found and a bucket of feed. When our meal was done, we were shown where we could sleep. There was straw on the pallets and blankets. I fell at once into so deep a sleep I would not have heard Aelfwy if he had been shrieking in my ears.

In the morning, I saw him lying quiet enough but staring at me.

"F..f . . . father. Wh..wh..where am I?"

"In a guesthouse. The house of St Cuthbert."

He stared at me, bewildered.

"The Saint will help you, Aelfwy. We have come to ask his help."

He understood now, and once again tears started to run down his face.

"I ca..ca..can't, I can't. I am not wor..worthy to stand bef..f..ore him."

"In Christ's eyes we are all worthy, Aelfwy. All worthy."

"No, no . . . ", and he wept some more. I took his hand and held it close. How frail and thin he was. He was not a strong man, either in body or mind. It was no fault of his. He was as God had created him. He had tried to overcome his weakness by throwing himself into the journey, but instead it had overwhelmed him. I remembered now my first misgivings and I blamed myself for not paying them more attention. I tried to comfort him.

"Our own weakness is of no account before God. If we were not weak, how could he help us? And look, did we not set out on our journey to find the saints of God? We are here now, close to blessed St Cuthbert."

He seemed to listen and no longer pulled his hand away so fearfully. But I knew our visit would be longer than we had planned. Unless Cuthbert granted us a miracle, it would be days before we could think of moving him.

Reinfrid slept on. My body was stiff and aching; I needed to move myself. I stepped outside. It was a bright, windy day with high cloud blowing across the sky, mid-morning at least. I looked about me. We had climbed through the town last night to the highest part of the half-island formed by the river, but here, where I stood, the ground was level. I could see the gatehouse in the bailey wall where we had entered last night and not far from it the huge motte of the new castle. I had seen its like in Gloucester, so it was not new to me, but here, where it stood within hallowed ground, it seemed a kind of sacrilege. The earth of the mound was still raw, and on top of it squatted the fortress with its beetle-browed roof and dark window slits. It bespoke nothing but malice. The drawbridge was lowered, and I could see that the men who came and went were not servants of God but men of war, armed with swords and spears. I prayed to God to forgive the men who had built it.

I turned my back on it and looked to the other end of the close, where the church and monastery stood. I would go and visit the shrine, I decided.

As I drew close, I saw the usual monastic buildings—a scriptorium, chapter house, school rooms. But there were other buildings too—large houses set on their own land with stabling and gardens behind—the kind of houses a prosperous merchant might live in. I was confused. Why were they here, in a monastic precinct? Who lived in them? As I passed one of the houses, the door opened, and a woman came out with a little girl. The woman was leaning down towards the child to wipe her mouth. When she was done, she swung the little girl up into her arms, laughing, and held her up in the air, squealing and squirming in her arms. I stood still, transfixed. The woman was young, and her laughing face was loveliness itself, she and the fair-haired child she held before her. It was a vision of innocence and happiness. And yet, at the same time, such was the affront to see them there, in that place, that a knife seemed to turn in my chest. This place was a monastery. A place where only men should be, set aside for men who had renounced the company of women for the sake of Christ.

She caught sight of me, smiled and called out a good day. I mumbled something in return and moved on towards the church, my heart beating hard. As I grew nearer, I could see men coming and going, in clerical dress as one would expect—but not tonsured. My bewilderment deepened. The door of the schoolhouse opened, and several boys tumbled out together. A tall youth ran past me without a glance. I turned to look after him and saw that the young woman was now standing at her gate, waiting for him. Suddenly I understood. He must be a priest's son. They were married men. Hereditary priests. Of course. I remembered hearing this, that the Community of St Cuthbert still went on in the old style, as a hereditary order with priests who held land. How extraordinary. A kind of relief filled me. Who was I to judge? We had tasted nothing but kindness from these people. We owed them nothing but gratitude. But I turned round and went back to the guesthouse.

I found a physician had come to see to Aelfwy. Like the men I had seen earlier he appeared to be a cleric but was untonsured. Kindly though he was, his attentions troubled Aelfwy, and the physician withdrew to speak with me alone.

"His mind is troubled," I told him. "He believes he was possessed by an evil spirit when we passed through the empty lands." The physician nodded.

"There are many who are afflicted in this way. I'll give you herbs for him. Can you read?"

"Yes."

"The tinctures should be taken with repetitions of the prayers I will give you. When you have them by heart, soak them and let him swallow them. He should go every day to the Saint, as often as he is able. It is beneficial to touch the coffin." He paused. "He is very weak. He needs food and rest. When the body is stronger the mind will grow stronger too." He looked at me. "Perhaps you too, father, are in need of rest. Have you travelled far?"

What should I tell him? It was pointless to try and conceal our purpose. We had been guided here. So I told him of our journey and the reason for it. As I spoke, I saw expressions pass across his face—surprise, deepening into astonishment and incredulity—that were unpleasantly familiar. Weariness overcame me. No doubt our story would soon be known by everyone.

It was difficult to explain the Durham Community to Reinfrid. The seven senior priests were all married men, with families, while the other clergy— deacons and lay clerics—might do as they pleased.

"Not celibate in Durham," Reinfrid remarked. He was happy to provoke me.

"It is a hereditary order. There were similar orders in the south of England before the reforms of the last century. True monastic life, as the first saints lived it, was lost in the north after the invasions of the Danes. God willing, it may be restored."

The Community still used the ancient liturgy from Lindisfarne. It must have been passed down for decades. They observed the day offices only, and they were seldom all present save for the tall ascetic man who was their dean. The church served as both monastic and parish church; at Sext and Vespers, the church was often filled with both men and women.

We took Aelfwy to all the offices and after each one we knelt before the shrine. It was covered in gold cloth and the walls hung with precious ornaments so that the very air seemed to glow. There was great peace in the presence of the Saint. Sometimes I felt that I was glimpsing the other world, beyond the veil of our earthly cares, as if the Saint from his great charity took us to his presence close to God. We were seldom alone. Men and women alike came to the shrine, many sick or troubled. It was truly a place of healing.

For Aelfwy, there was no sudden casting out of his demons, as I had imagined. Instead his fears fell away bit by bit. He found joy in staying close to the Saint and we saw him gradually returning to himself. When Sunday came, a solemn Mass was held, the clergy entered in procession and for the first time we saw the bishop. He wore all the vestments of his office yet despite them I could see at once he was not a native. He was olive-skinned and though his Latin was fluent, he spoke it with the intonation of the Franks. He must have been appointed by the king.

The very next day I was to find myself in his presence. After Mass, the dean had come to speak to me.

"You are welcome to our Community here at Durham, brother. Bishop Walcher has asked me what your purpose is here."

I tried to avoid the question. "Our brother Aelfwy has been unwell, and we give you thanks in God for your hospitality."

"Is he mending?"

"I believe so."

The dean looked at me. Although, like all the priests there, he was married, I could see he was in his heart a man of God. I decided to tell him what had been revealed to me and the true purpose of our journey. As I spoke, I saw not censure or disbelief in his face, but interest. Interest and understanding. I felt my heart open and I spoke freely. When I was done, he clasped my hand.

"It is a true vocation, to follow in the footsteps of the saints who were our forefathers. May God grant you success."

He was some years older than me. I saw in him the weariness I had known as prior at Winchcombe; the weariness of office, of the tasks and pettiness that fill the mind and leave little space for God. He understood what I was seeking.

"Come and join us," I said. He smiled and shook his head.

"My duty is here, to the shrine. It is the service God has called me to." He was abstracted for a moment before he recalled himself.

"I wish you well with all my heart. The bishop, too, is interested. He asks you to wait on him."

And so I found myself there, in the bishop's palace beside the castle. The audience hall was full of clerks and petitioners, but an attendant took me to a private chamber beyond it. It was spacious, with a fine Frankish tapestry hanging on the wall. It depicted what seemed to be a pagan scene, of women adorned with flowers and naked save for their long hair, dancing in a spring garden. I moved my gaze away and looked instead at the long table on the other side of the room, next to the hearth. There were silver cups on it and a platter of small cakes. Behind were shelves full of books and parchments. Bishop Walcher sat on a high-backed chair at one end of the table with a scribe at his side. For all the summer weather he wore thick long robes, splendid and stiff with embroidery. The attendant gave me a little push, and I went onto my knees before him. The bishop put out his hand for me to kiss his episcopal ring in the Roman fashion. A musky smell seemed to emanate from him, like calamus or myrrh. The light from the casement behind him obscured his face so I could see only the outline of his head with its embroidered cap.

"Take a seat." He waved me to the bench alongside the table and spoke to the attendant. "Give him wine." The man poured wine into a silver cup and placed it in front of me. I could see the bishop's face now. I was surprised to find an older man, in his fifties. The skin hung slackly around his jaw and nose like a mastiff. Only his eyes were bright and dark in his jowly face.

"Welcome, brother. Welcome indeed. We see too few brethren here in Durham. You've come from Winchcombe? A great house, I have heard."

He spoke in Latin, very fluently, but with a Frankish intonation that I found hard to follow. Nevertheless, I soon understood that he wanted to hear about Winchcombe, its history and its properties. Then he leaned forward towards me.

"I come from Liege, you know. A great house and well-endowed. But King William sent for me! What could I say! Of course, I was honoured to receive such a bishopric." He sighed.

"I'm not a monastic myself, and of course I've nothing against the Community here. But these married men, you know … I miss the company of the brothers back in Liege. Such refined and learned men! But one has to start somewhere. I plan to build a monastery here in Durham, you know. You don't need to look elsewhere."

"I thank you, Lord. But we are looking for retreat, not company."

"Very laudable but, you know, this country is a wilderness. Hardly safe. Even here, as you can see, one has to have protection. The dean says you are planning to venture up to Monkchester."

"Yes, Lord. In the footsteps of the saints."

"That's Waltheof's territory, you know. Earl Waltheof. William has appointed him Earl of Northumbria. An unwise appointment. A very changeable man. Not to be trusted."

"We won't trouble him for anything."

"But it's his *land*, don't you see? Monkchester is his land. He won't want you there. Not monks. Not from Durham."

I felt frustration, anger rising in me. I didn't want Walcher's interference or his advice. But I had not thought of this, that these places of the saints are someone's land. What concern would we be to them? I protested inwardly. These places were ruinous and uncared for.

"Lord, are these places not still the property of the Church?"

"Not there. Not Monkchester. The Earls have long since stolen that away."

I felt the bishop's eyes upon me. At that moment I wished with all my heart that we had never come to Durham. He was going to try and force me to stay there, I was certain. But his next words surprised me.

"I have another plan for you. There is another estate, south of the Tyne, that is still the property of the Community. It is the very site of Father

Bede's monastery of St Paul. It was cruelly used in the last wars but there is shelter there. The remains of the church and other buildings. And land, many hides. I will give you my blessing to make your hermitage at Jarrow. You will be under my protection and I will require your obedience."

It was, I knew, more than a blessing. It was an order. He was bargaining with me. He could give us what we needed but we must accept his authority. I had to struggle with myself. All my life, obedience has been the hardest vow of the Rule. Even though I know it to be an infallible way to God, there is something in me that refuses to submit. Now, before this venal bishop, this Frankish clerk, this usurper, I felt my whole being rise up in protest. How to contain myself? On an impulse I reached out, took the silver cup the attendant had put before me and gulped down some wine. The alcohol sent a different fire through my veins. The bishop pushed the cakes towards me.

"Try one. They're delicious."

Still hot with anger, I took a cake and put it in my mouth. It tasted of hazelnuts and honey and butter, sweet and melting. I let it linger round my mouth while I took hold of myself. Even in my turmoil, I tasted the sweetness beneath the bitter medicine of obedience. Jarrow. Father Bede's monastery. Had he not guided us here, and was he not now bringing us to our place of shelter? I made my decision. I got to my feet, a little unsteady from the wine, and went over to kneel before the bishop. I bent my head, kissed his ring, and promised my obedience.

We stayed on in Durham a few days more to give Aelfwy time to recover his strength. I found a great love in myself for the Saxon church where the Saint's shrine lay. Built when the Community first moved the body of the Saint to Durham more than seventy years ago, it had a wonderful strength and simplicity about it. The stone had been quarried from the cliffs on the riverbanks and was cleanly dressed in massive even blocks. There was a tower at the west entrance, and a second crossing tower at the centre. Within was a long aisled nave, lit by high arched windows. The walls were painted with images of Christ and of the Saint. For all the sorrows that afflicted the country round about, in the church there was a different order. A glimpse of eternity. I could see that Aelfwy had found repose here, and I felt reluctant to force him onward. But I knew within myself that we should leave.

"It's time to move on, Aelfwy." I put a hand on his shoulder. "For Reinfrid and I. Perhaps not for you. It may be that your place is here. Or that you should stay for a while and join us later. I'm certain these good people will find a place for you."

He looked confused. "I, ah, I must co . . . come with you."

"You don't have to. You can serve God in different ways. There's no shame in it."

"D . . . do you think I am too w . . . w...weak?"

It was hard to answer. I did fear that he would fall prey once again to the troubles that had beset him.

"It's in God's hands. Only he knows what strength you may be given."

"I w . . . w..want to come. I . . . I...I really, I mean, if you, if you, you and Reinfrid, w . . . w...will take me."

He looked up at me with that innocence of his, the openness that was the true state of his soul, and I thought, he is restored to himself. I felt so much love for him. I took him in my arms and embraced him till we were both laughing and smiling.

"Of course. Of course. We will all go together. Freya will take care of us."

The next day we left for Jarrow.

PART 2

THE NOVICE

1074–1075

CHAPTER 12

The King's Chaplain

Nidaros, 1074

In this way Thorgot had enough and to spare of good things flowing
in upon him by the bounty of king and noblemen. But as religious
impulses often change when they are distracted, his soul by degrees
declined from its former state, attracted in the course of events by
the pleasures of the world. But although unwilling of his own accord,
he was in time compelled to enter the home of his heavenly Father.
Simeon's "History of the Kings of England"

It was dawn one morning in early June. I was standing on a rock above Kyvannet, toes curled round damp lichen, staring down at the dark water of the lake. The sunrise had tinged it pink and silver and it was veiled with a steam of mist. Three of Olaf's men were already swimming, their bodies pale beneath the water. Although I had stripped off like the others, I was waiting for a moment to slip away. I hadn't enough Norse blood in me to share their passion for icy water. Olaf loved it, of course. He'd spent his childhood out here. When the light days came, he spent days swimming and hunting, forgetting all about running a kingdom.

"I'll stay back in Nidaros," I'd said to him before we left. I had a pile of plans and petitions on my desk crying for my attention. "I'll take care of everything. You can stay away as long as you want."

He slapped my shoulder.

"How long is it going to take you to become a Norseman? Come!" And he shouted to the servants to bring up a horse for me.

So I stood there, staring down into the water and shivering. Then Olaf was behind me. "Skraeling!" he shouted and gave me a shove between the shoulder blades. I toppled off the rock and into the water. The shock of it took every other thought and sensation from me. I gasped for breath. I flailed my arms and legs around till the sensation started to recede and my body reached the temperature of the water. Then, miraculously, I was no longer cold. I started to swim, ducking my head underwater where the kelp swayed to and fro, and little fish fled from me. I could see a body coming up behind me. I was sure it was Olaf. I whipped my fish-body around to burst out of the water in front of him and take my revenge, grabbing his shoulder to try and push him under. We wrestled and splashed for a few moments till we were both breathless with laughter.

"I am your chaplain!" I yelled, "Atone for your sin!" and with a last shove I pushed him under. "Repent!" I shouted as his head popped up, and we were laughing again.

The servants built a fire where we warmed ourselves afterwards, dripping and teeth-rattling, and then we ate. Bowls of skyr made from reindeer milk with honeycomb on top, soft barley bread and cured herring, blueberries picked from the forest. Sometimes now on fasting days I dream of those morning feasts and wish myself under a Norse sky once more.

"Have you seen the tracks?" said Olaf when we'd eaten. "Come hunting with us. It'll be a good day."

"I can't. The mason's waiting for me."

It was our great project at that time. Olaf wanted a cathedral in Nidaros that would rival the churches of Italy and Frankia. It was to be the shrine of his martyred uncle Olaf. We'd spent the winter months working with the masons on the plans; they were near complete, and the foundation stone would be laid when Olaf returned. It was going to be a miracle in stone. We used the mason Hardrada had brought to Nidaros for the

Holy Mother of God church, a silent man from the East who knew the secrets of Byzantium. It was laid out to the same dimensions as St Peter's in Rome—on a smaller scale, but still a building that would dwarf anything seen in Norway. It was to have columns like the Temple of Solomon. The mason knew his texts. It was all there in the Bible. According to the chronicler, Solomon's temple had pillars of thirty and five cubits high. Solomon had made chains, according to the text, and put them on the heads of the pillars.

"What are these chains?" Olaf asked the mason.

"Spirals, Lord. Carved into the stone," he told him. "Spirals going roundabout from base to top."

I was fascinated by the mason and his art. I learned about load and span, about the groins and ribs that would be needed for the vault above the choir where the sound of music and chanting would circle and echo as it did in the Holy Mother of God church. In another life I would have been a mason, I decided. But now my task was to take charge of the organisation. Scores of men were needed for the build. They would have to be housed and fed. New quarries would have to be dug and stone carted in. New taxes had to be introduced to pay for it all. And Olaf? The plans and arrangements bored him. His face would go still, and the blue eyes shadowed over. He disappeared into that faraway place in himself where no-one could reach him. I knew better than to pester him. We would meet for business in the evening, I would give him whatever documents needed his signature, and then we would drink.

It was evening by the time I got back to Nidaros. I'd been six years in Norway, and I had my own house by then, close to the palace. It was more like an office than a home; for all Olaf's efforts I wouldn't take a wife. So I lived alone, though there were always half a dozen clerks in the hall working away on documents and accounts, men waiting on the benches at the side to talk to me. That evening I was tired out from the long ride, and I sent them all away. Except for one. I could see he was a seaman and I asked him what his business was.

"The captain says to tell you *Sea-Dragon* is come into harbour this morning, Lord."

I gave him a coin.

"I'll come down after I've eaten."

In spite of all my duties, I found time to run a couple of ships. Between a morning in the choir and an afternoon working over plans I would go down to the harbour to drink ale with one of my captains and check over his cargo. The church was in my blood sure enough, but so was trade. My ships were the rope that bound me to my father. The finest timber and furs, the best of the fresh-run salmon and cod, the purest amber, always went to Lincoln, and his ships returned with fine cloth and silver, books and linen for me. They would always have papers for me. Letters from my father.

Although we were parted by so many miles of ocean I felt as close to him as if he lived in the next street. How proud he was of me! How he rejoiced in my success! I do believe it drove me onwards. The greatest joy I took in any success was to set it down in a letter to him. If the king gave me a rare jewel to reward me for my services, I would have it done up in a casket and sent to my father. I never forgot what he had done for me, how he had given all his gold and risked his life to free me.

He never urged me to return, though as the years went by it was often in my mind. But what would I find there? I knew from his letters that Lincoln was no longer the town of my boyhood. Like all the other merchants, my father had to learn to speak French and pay taxes to the Norman bailiffs. The aldermen no longer governed the town; the Normans did. Even the Saxon church was despised. They were building a new cathedral—not in the town, but safe inside the castle's bailey walls. It was a town within a town, my father said, and everyone knew who was master and who was servant. Even if it were safe for me to return, I had no wish to return to a life of servitude. Norway might be a lesser kingdom, but I mattered there. There was so much for me to do. What was there to return to?

My heart lifted that night at the thought of news and merchandise from England. As soon as I had changed my travelling clothes and eaten a good supper, I went down to the harbour. I shouted out my greetings to the captain. As he called back, I knew at once from his face that there was bad news. He had no papers to give me, no letters. He came ashore and stood before me.

"You've a face as long as Lent, man. What are your tidings?"

The man looked at his boots, reluctant to speak. I waited.

"Nothing wrong with the cargo, Lord, nor the voyage. But we have some ill news. From Lincoln."

"Tell it."

"It's your father, Lord. After the Easter feast he took a fever. The physicians did what they could, but he worsened . . ." He paused, swallowed.

"How is he now?"

"He is dead."

"My father? My father dead?"

"Two months since."

How could he have been dead two months and I not known of it? Not felt his spirit leave my heart? How could it be? I was seized with such a storm of anguish that I took hold of the man and shook him.

"No! No!"

His teeth rattled together, but he uttered no reproach. He was a good man, and he pitied me. At last I released him and turned away. Then the tears flooded my eyes, and I wept like a woman.

I was astonished at the force of my grief. I knew that I loved my father, loved and respected him. But I could not have foretold how his death would change me.

I couldn't hide my low spirits from Olaf when he returned.

"You're fortunate," he said, when I told him. "When my father died, I felt no grief at all. Only surprise. He had fought in so many battles I thought it was impossible to kill him."

"You've lost comrades though. Brothers in battle."

"Yes." He turned away. He was a warrior. They didn't speak of such things.

I tried to drown my grief in the long drinking sessions the king loved. It did no good. I hadn't the heart for it, but no matter how drunk Olaf was, he always noticed if I left early.

"What's wrong with you, man?"

"I'm sick."

It was true. I was heartsick. With my father's death a light in me went out. I lost interest in my life in Nidaros. The cathedral's foundation stone was laid; there was a great feast, and Olaf sat over it all in triumph. Building started in earnest on the choir and a camp sprang up beside the river to house all the workmen. The stone yard, where the masons in their aprons cut the formless stone into smooth blocks and columns, was a constant source of wonder to everyone. But my passion for it had gone. I wanted only to return to England and stand at my father's graveside. I knew Olaf wouldn't let me go. In spite of all the luxury and favour that surrounded me I started to feel like a prisoner. At last I could stand it no longer.

"My Lord King, I have to go home. I have to."

"Home? This is your home."

"You've made it home for me. You've been so generous. But … this grief. It gives me no peace. I have to go back to England. Back to my own people."

"The knife has cut deep, Thorgot. But wounds heal. They can heal here as well as in England."

He made me pause. Perhaps he was right. Perhaps I would feel this way wherever I was. I tried again to throw myself into my work, but it made no difference. Gradually, I began to understand myself better. With my father's death, I had become the head of the family. I had a sister, nine years my senior, who was married with a brood of children; she had no need of me, and my father had not remarried after my mother's death. But it was about more than family affairs. It was about my inheritance. My father had been his own man. He was a freeman, and his father and grandfather before him. It was that freedom I was heir to. But here, in Norway, I was a servant. Surrounded by wealth and honour, for sure. But in everything I thought or did I was ruled by the king. There was a bond between us. Love even. But we were not brothers. He was the king and I the servant. I was governed by his will. I had learned to read his moods, his wishes, in order to bring about what was needed. I held more influence over him than any of his councillors, but I was not a freeman. I wanted to honour my father. I wanted to live as he had done. Free.

I started to argue with Olaf, day after day. He was certain it was a passing thing, that I would recover. He made me promise to wait till autumn. I used the time to make arrangements for different men to take over from me. Bit by bit, I shed all my duties.

"You don't need me any longer," I told him. "The plans for the cathedral are done, the masons can take it forward. You have priests who speak Norse, you have your own cantor."

"Don't need you?" His face didn't change but his eyes were full of bitterness. I knew he felt I was betraying him.

But when autumn came and I was firm in my resolve, he showered me with gifts, as if all his love for me could be changed into gold.

"Go back to England," he said. "Take care of your sister and spend a winter or two talking English. Then you can come back to where you belong. We will be waiting for you."

His generosity cut me to the quick. Part of me was ready to throw my arms round him and swear never to leave. But in my deepest heart I knew I had to go.

I sailed in late September, when the birch trees around the fjord were turning to gold and the first cold winds were blowing down from the north, in a fine ship the king had given me. It was heavy with treasure, with chests of fine clothes and linen, with plate and glass. I would be able to live like a lord when I got home. But when I tried to think of my new life in England, I couldn't picture it. I was accustomed to planning and organizing, yet when it came to what I would do, where I would live, there was emptiness. How could I want to return so much and yet have no idea of how to do it? I refused to think about it. I would know when I got there, I told myself. The ship pushed off from the quayside, the rowers dipped their oars and found their rhythm and the green water of the fjord rushed past me. I shouted my last farewells. We passed the tiny island that stands outside the harbour and swung southwards out towards the sea. Nidaros disappeared from my view for ever.

We slipped down the coast, down the strange sea road I had first threaded six years earlier, between the looming rocks and skerries, small islands and their remote, clinging settlements. When we broke out into the open ocean there was a strong swell running and a south-easterly that sent us flying over the waves to Orkney. For the first time I saw whales, sending great spouts of spray high into the air, their mighty backs heaving clear of the water. They made a majestic procession through the ocean, a great company moving who knows where, calves clinging close to their dams. They paid no heed to us. I thought of Jonah, shipwrecked and swallowed by the whale, and a little shiver of dread ran through me. Could they really swallow a man? It was holy scripture, I reminded myself. Jonah was a prophet of God. Not a liar. The ship ran on before the wind, we made landfall and were into Kirkwall harbour as neatly as any sailor could wish. We would have a night ashore, take on provisions and head down the Scottish coast in the morning.

Next day the wind still blew more southerly than easterly, slowing our passage down the coast. Then, after a few days sailing, the weather turned stormy. The wind went round sharp to the east, bringing hail showers and sudden gusts that jerked the sail sideways and tossed the ship aloft. The air was loud with curses as the captain struggled to keep us on a steady course. I was soaked through to the skin with the sudden rise and fall of the ship, but I knew he could bring us through it. He had seen out storms far worse than this. The bad weather went on all day and we suffered what felt like endless hours of lurching and heaving. Towards the end of the afternoon, as he did whenever we passed a river mouth, the sailor on watch yelled out from the bows, "Tynemouth!" to help the captain set his course.

But the captain had little time to heed him. Soon after the shout from the watch the storm struck us with full force. What we had endured till now seemed slight discomfort. The wind became a howling gale, driving the waves higher and higher. Huge seas rushed upon us. The ship was flung about like driftwood, and I clung for dear life to the gunwale. Somehow the men managed to wrestle down the sail and then the captain let her drift close to shore in the hope of shelter. Blinding showers of hail tore through the air, so I could scarcely see from one end of the ship to the other. I prayed that all my goods had been stowed tight enough to keep them safe. At last came a respite, a lull when the wind seemed to drop and the rain slackened. I glanced up. For a single heart-stopping moment, before the fury of the storm returned and blinded me again, I glimpsed a cliff so close to the ship I could almost have stretched out and touched it. It seemed only yards away. Dear God, I thought, the captain has brought us in too close! I turned to shout a warning across the ship, but the next moment a shattering, cracking, splintering sound burst out from beneath me, so violent it seemed to jar my very bones. At once water started to surge upwards into the ship. My mind worked for just long enough to tell me: we have struck a rock. Then it was utter chaos. I could hear the captain bellowing orders and men shouting, while the water rose around us faster than I could have thought possible. The ship lurched sideways, and my body was suddenly thrown forward into the bilges. At once I was swallowed up in icy water, so cold that I was too shocked to know what was happening. An image flashed into my mind of falling from the rock at Kyvannet; I heard Olaf laughing in my ear. Then the solid ship was gone altogether, and my feet and legs were flailing in the water. In seconds, a wave rolled right over me. I fought my way back to the surface, gasping and choking with saltwater in my throat and nostrils. There was a short stillness between the waves, and in it I saw an oar that had floated up from the ship. With the last of my strength I reached out and grasped it. I pulled it close to my body and clung to it. Even when I lost consciousness, I must have clung to it still, for when they found me on the sands it was beside me.

I remember nothing of that shore or the good folk who found me and brought me to shelter. I lay half-dead and feverish for days, believing that I was in the belly of a whale from which I would not come forth alive. But, like Jonah, I was spat forth at last, back into the world. Only four of the sailors had survived beside me. We had been taken to a village named Whitburn, by a sheltered cove south of the cliffs where we were wrecked. It was no more than a line of fishermen's huts with nets drying outside and a few fields of barley; a poor enough place but the folk there had taken us in and cared for us. I gave them all the thanks I could, but I had nothing to reward them with.

"Was there nothing washed ashore?" I asked, again and again. "No chests? No bales or boxes?"

Always they told me, no master, nothing. As soon as I was strong enough, I staggered down to the cove and searched up and down. I could not believe that all my treasure, all my goods, had been swallowed up in the sea. The fishermen would come down at high tide to pull in their long-nets, and I would stare as the nets came in, hoping to find some remnant of my treasure among the fish. Nothing. It was folly. How would heavy chests and trunks be washed ashore? But I could not bring myself to believe it: I was a penniless beggar. I made crazy plans to get the fishermen to dredge the sea, to dive into the deeps—anything that would restore my wealth to me.

I should have been spending my time on my knees thanking God for my deliverance and the great mercy he had shown me. I am ashamed, now, of what I was then. But like Jonah I had been born a second time into the world. I was like an infant wailing for the moon.

At last I had to accept that I would never see my treasure again. God had stripped me of everything—my goods, my reputation, my prospects. I felt utter despair. If Olaf could only see me now! If he could know what had befallen me! I knew he would help me. But how could I send word to him? Who would believe me? I was dressed now in the clothes that had been found for me, rough woollen hose and tunic. I looked like the lowliest churl. "I am the Norse king's chaplain; please ask him to send me gold." Surely they would think my brains had been turned in the shipwreck.

Of the four men who had been rescued with me, three had survived. They planned to make their way to Tynemouth, find a ship to work their passage home and go back to their families. Should I go with them? Even then, even in my extremity, I didn't want to return. It would be humiliating, for sure, to crawl back and beg for a second chance. But it was more than that. In my despair one thing only seemed certain to me, that the hand of God was upon me. I could not escape Him. He had taken everything from me and flung me to the ground. I must submit myself utterly to Him.

When I was well and knew that I should no longer be a burden to my hosts, I thanked them with all my heart.

"I want to become a monk," I told them. "I want to join a monastery. Is there a monastery near here?"

I was ignorant. I had no idea that there were no monasteries in the North. I expected to be taken to some long-established house where I would enter as a novice. Nor did the village folk enlighten me. There was talk up and down the huts for a day or two till it was decided. They would take me to Durham.

CHAPTER 13

THE RULE

Northumbria, 1074

The morning I was to leave Whitburn I stooped under the doorway of the cramped hut, straightened up and let a sharp breath out to get the stench of fish out of my nostrils. I looked round for the horses. None. They hadn't brought them up yet, I thought. Then I saw the two men who were to be my guides waiting for me. They had staffs in their hands and packs on their shoulders. I was shocked. Walking, for me? I was used to riding everywhere. Even as I felt the shock, though, I knew what a fool I was. Why would these people have horses? I was a churl now. I had better get used to it. I mumbled a greeting to the men, and we set off.

The two of them loped along effortlessly, but my legs were unused to walking such distances. My feet were soon blistered in the borrowed shoes. I was still weak from the fevers I had suffered after the shipwreck, and I could hardly keep up with them. After a while, they took pity on me, lending me a staff and stuffing the shoes with moss. I was humiliated. I summoned my will. I resolved I would keep going, keep up, whatever it cost me.

We came to a river, the Wear—the same river, they told me, on which Durham stood. I prayed that we would soon be there. But the track wound on and on till it was close to noon. Then we came upon a different road, one of the old roads of the Romans. In a few miles, it led straight to an old fortress set on a rise above the river. I felt a moment of recognition. Though smaller, it was like the Roman fort at Lincoln. The same long walls, the same gatehouse. It felt like coming home.

"We'll rest here," my guides announced. They took me through a side gate into the fort. There were remains of the stone buildings the Romans had left behind but alongside them a village of sorts had grown up. A stone church stood against the walls. The men walked over to it and sat themselves comfortably against the walls in the sunshine. What a relief it was to sit and rest my aching feet! My two companions grinned as I gobbled down the bread and cheese they gave me. All thought was driven from my mind by hunger and fatigue. While we ate, they told me about the church we were resting our backs on. The monks from an abbey called Lindisfarne had brought their saint here, they told me, when they fled the Danes many years ago.

"They wandered the land for seven years. Then Guthred the Dane, king of York, had a vision that showed him the great power of the Saint. He gave St Cuthbert's people the fort here at Chester-le-Street and much land with it. For a hundred years, the shrine of St Cuthbert was in this very church."

"Not anymore?"

"No. The Saint lies at Durham now."

I felt awkward. I knew that there had been many saints in Northumbria in former times, but to tell the truth, that was all I knew.

"Why is the Saint—Cuthbert, is it? Why's he so honoured?"

They stared at me as if I were mad.

"I came from Lincoln," I said hastily. "We have few saints there."

Then the stories started. They told me of his life, of his miracles, of his love for creatures, of his healing powers. The longer they spoke, the drowsier I became. I gave thanks to this saint for granting me a rest.

"He is the protector of our people," concluded one of the guides. "It is great merit to visit his shrine."

I understood then. It wasn't simply an act of kindness, taking me to Durham. It was an opportunity to visit their saint and gain his blessing. They stood up, and I had to try and follow suit. They caught my arms to steady me till I could walk again. Then we went inside the church, built on the foundation of some Roman building. The light inside was dim, but on the wall beside the altar I could make out a painted figure. Candles burned before it.

"Is that . . . ?" I whispered.

"Yes."

They went and knelt before the image. I knelt beside them. It was that day, exhausted and bereft, that I said my first prayers to St Cuthbert.

We reached Durham at nightfall. I remember nothing of that first night except falling onto a straw pallet and sleeping. By the time I woke, my companions had already made their visit to the shrine and were standing outside, ready to set off for home, as fit and fresh as when we left. I embraced them and swore that if I ever had the means I would repay them for their kindness. Then I limped back into the guesthouse and went back to sleep. I was exhausted.

By the end of the day, I was confused as well. Was the place a monastery? It was like no monastery I had ever seen. For sure, there was a church, but there were houses all about where families were living, with children running around. There were no monks that I could see. The men who took care of the guesthouse were servants with a couple of priests visiting from time to time. I saw more soldiers than men of God. The Normans had flung up a great castle on the high ground above the river and hemmed in the sanctuary ground with a bailey wall. Every time I looked at the fortress I thought of the dark days of my imprisonment at Lincoln. Did God want me to live here, in the shadow of the Normans?

The story of the Community is well known now, but to me then it was a mystery. How strange a time it was! I was twenty-six years old, and for the last six years my pride and arrogance had grown apace. I had a high opinion of my own abilities and gave no thanks to God for what I accomplished. Between us, Olaf and I had reinvented his country. I thought I could do anything. I thought that I knew everything. Suddenly I was ignorant and helpless. All I could find in myself was weakness. That night I turned my face to the wall and wept.

When my desire to become a monk was made known, the dean came to see me. He explained the nature of the Community to me and why I could not enter on a monastic vocation there.

"However," he told me, "there is a small community newly founded at Jarrow. The conditions there are ascetic, but it is full of the light of Christ. If you are willing to undertake a novitiate there, the bishop will surely give you permission to join them."

Did I want to do that? Enter a new community? An ascetic one? Even as I asked myself the questions, I knew the answer. I had made the decision to become a monk. I couldn't set conditions on it. I had lost everything. What difference did it make, new or old, ascetic or luxurious? I said yes.

So next it was to the bishop, where the wealth and comfort of his hall reminded me so strongly of Olaf's palace I had to clench my teeth together to keep from howling with despair. I stood in my churl's clothes before the Frankish bishop. Walcher was his name. He stared in amazement when I spoke to him in Latin. For a wild moment I thought, I will tell him my story. I will tell him that I am chaplain to Olaf, king of the Norse. He will understand what I am, and he will give me employment here. But in the next instant I remembered the guard room at Lincoln Castle and the Normans who sailed with me to Nidaros and I knew. Never. Never would I take meat with the usurpers. I would rather have bread and water in the meanest cell in Jarrow. So I told him nothing, told him only it was my vocation to become a monk, and to seek his signature on the document to take with me. I lowered my eyes and backed out of his presence. I had no inkling, then, of what would pass between us.

Before I left Durham, I went to visit the shrine, where the coffin and altar were richly dressed in gold cloth and ornaments. With all the other pilgrims, I knelt before the body of the Saint. I thought of the church at Nidaros and of the fine cathedral that would one day house St Olaf's shrine. I had reverenced his shrine for the king's sake, but I had felt nothing in its presence. St Olaf was a warrior. I never heard anyone discuss his other virtues. But there, in the church in Durham, the stories the men from the village had told me came back to my mind. This was a saint who had given up everything for God. He spent years in solitude on a tiny island, without possession or comfort. He was a true follower of Christ. For the first time in all my misery I opened my heart and begged him to help me.

I walked alone to Jarrow, another long day's walk, with only bread in my pack for the journey. By the end of it I was longing to rest my eyes on the monastery walls. The dean at Durham had told me only that it had been a monastery in former times and had suffered attack from the Vikings. But as I walked through the dreary October countryside my imagination built a guesthouse with a roaring hearth fire, a cloister and chapter house, dormitories and refectory. So strong were the images in my head that when I reached Jarrow I was convinced at first that I had taken a wrong turn. What I saw was a narrow stone church, half broken down at the west end. Beside it were old stone buildings, some roofless with saplings and briars growing through them. Here and there a building had been cleared and a makeshift roof of thatch set over it. In between there were several circular huts of the poorest kind. A monastery, this? But as I stood in disbelief a young man in a monk's habit came out of one of the buildings. Seeing my bewilderment he came towards me.

"I am looking for the monastery of Jarrow," I said.

"Then you are welcome. You have found us. Where have you come from?"

It was too hard to explain. "Lincoln," I said.

"I am from the south too, from Evesham, a monastery near Gloucester. I came from there with Father Aldwin. He is our abbot." He smiled at me, such a sweet smile I might have taken comfort, but I was too distraught at my surroundings to notice.

"Have you come to see him? I'll take you."

He took me to one of the roofed-over buildings and called out for permission to enter. A voice responded. The monk pushed the door open and I found myself in a plain room. The walls had been roughly plastered and a wooden casement set in the window. As well as a table and bench, there was a pallet on the floor. Clearly it served as both cell and study for the abbot.

In the light from the open door I was able to see the abbot clearly. I thought at once of Cuthbert. Aldwin looked just as I had imagined such a saint. He had a full silver-grey beard that covered his cheeks and mouth, and more silver hair curling away from his tonsure down to his shoulders. A wooden cross hung around his neck. As he stood up from his desk and came to greet me, I saw that he was about the same height as me, but so thin that his habit hung loosely from his shoulders. His face, too, was thin with prominent cheekbones and nose, but I only noticed that later. What struck me first were his eyes, the light they held, as if his whole spirit were concentrated in them. He smiled at me with such kindness that I was suddenly undone. All my grief and loss, my exhaustion and confusion, welled up uncontrollably. I sank down onto the bench before him and sobbed. He put a hand on my shoulder and waited.

"My father is dead! I have lost my father!" More sobs. "The ship is wrecked, my treasure, everything, lost!" I looked up at him, tears running down my face. "Why has God done this to me?"

Aldwin didn't answer at once. He stood looking at me in his calm, kindly way. Then he said,

"In his mercy and wisdom God has brought you to this place."

I pulled my shoulder away from his hand. Brought me to this place? I wanted to shout at him. Brought me to this miserable ruin? To these hovels only fit for pigs? I was about to give way to another storm of weeping, this time mixed with rage at his failure to comfort me. Then a different thought struck me. Maybe he was right. I swallowed my sobs. Suddenly I felt foolish slumped on the bench and stumbled to my feet. I stood before him and bowed my head.

"What do I have to do?"

"Jarrow was home to Father Bede and to many saints and holy men. That's why we are here. Their grace is over it. You must pray to them constantly for their help and guidance."

He blessed me and turned away.

"We'll talk more later. First Brother Aelfwy will find you something to eat and drink. You're worn out."

The sweet-faced monk beside me tugged at my sleeve. I understood I was being dismissed.

"It's his time for prayer," he whispered in my ear. "Let's find some food. Have you walked far?"

So my life at Jarrow started. A hut was found for me and a rough woollen habit. I was always cold. Always uncomfortable. The food was rough and meagre. And I was the lowliest member of the community. I tried to bargain with Aldwin to let me become a monk straightaway. I was a churchman already, I pointed out, and I had held high office. I had been the royal chaplain. It wouldn't be necessary for me to undertake the novitiate.

Why was I in such a hurry? Because it seemed humiliating to me, versed as I was in all the practices and learning of the Church, to become a novice. There were only two other novices at that time. One of them, Morcar, was well-born, a son of the Earl of Northumbria, but he seemed to have spent more time learning swordcraft than book skills. He hardly knew a word of Latin. The other was a clerk of some kind, Cadmon, who had lost his family in the Norman wars. I felt superior to them both. But Aldwin took no notice of my arguments.

"Everyone has to serve the novitiate," he said. "Becoming a monk asks more of us than other calling. Can you live in charity with your brothers, year upon year? Can you put your life wholly in Christ's hands? It is no light matter. Once the vows are taken there is no going back."

There was nothing for it. I had to give myself up to it all—the ceaseless round of the offices, the rising in the night, the field work that blistered my clerkish hands, the constant company of men I hardly knew. I hated it, yet I stayed. I longed all the time for what I had lost, my wealth and comfort, my importance. Yet in some other half-glimpsed, nearly buried part of me I recognized that Jarrow was where I had to be.

As well as us novices, there were five other men at the monastery at that time. The abbot, of course, and Aelfwy, the monk who had met me. He was a man of such goodness it was impossible not to love him. There were two other monks, Cedd and Albert, who had come to Jarrow from other monasteries, inspired by Aldwin's vision of monastic revival. And there was Reinfrid. Before he opened his mouth, I knew him for a Norman with his black hair and brows. And a black soul too, I thought. He was tall and unsmiling. I hated him at once. I thought he must be some visitor from Durham Castle, an interloper come to inspect the monastery. When I found out that he was in charge of the novices I was aghast. How could I submit myself to such a man? Burning with outrage I rushed straight to Aldwin's cell and burst open the door. It was too important for the normal courtesies. He looked up at me from his table.

"Father, Reinfrid is a Norman! You can't let a Norman be part of the brotherhood! These men are thieves and murderers who have stolen our kingdom! Their souls are stained with mortal sin!"

He waited for several minutes before responding.

"Please learn to curb your anger. And don't enter my cell without knocking and asking permission."

I was speechless. How dare Aldwin speak to me like that? How could he ignore the plain truth? But there was nothing for me to do but back out of the cell.

I watched Aldwin later that day when he was with Reinfrid. He spoke to the Norman with great affection and respect, I saw, whereas he treated me with disdain. He ignored me. I was eaten up with anger and resentment. In desperation I threw myself into work. Work periods at that time were taken up with making another part of the ruins habitable in time for winter. The novices had the task of bringing up reeds from the Don, a stream below the monastery, then binding them up into tight sections for thatching. It was hand-numbing work; the wet reeds soon soaked my habit but tearing them up and trudging up and down the hill gave some vent to my feelings. I spent as little time as possible on the tying and binding. Towards the end of the afternoon I brought up another load of reeds and dumped them on the ground, looking around for rope to bind them. Reinfrid was waiting for me. He picked up one of the bundles I had made with the last load.

"Is not tight. Look."

He shook the bundle hard and some reeds started to slide out.

"You must do again."

I stared at him, at his black-browed Norman face. I had never heard a Norman speak English and it made me even angrier.

"No. I won't. There's nothing wrong with them."

I waited for him to explode. My body tensed, ready to hit him. But his voice didn't change.

"I show you. Look, like this."

He took the bundle, pulled off the loose binding and took up a piece of rope. In spite of the cold, his fingers were deft and careful as he wound it round, knotting and securing each section as he went. When he was done, he held it out to me.

"Nice, no? Try it."

He picked up some loose reeds and gave them to me and took up some for himself. He stood beside me, watching me bind and showing me again how he did it till I had grasped it. My fingers were clumsy and shaking.

"Good."

He turned away and started stacking up the bundles with the same calm carefulness. I stumbled back down the hill, utterly mortified.

I had no sooner recovered from the outrage of having to accept a Norman superior than I set up more turmoil for myself. I found the daily offices tedious. We plodded through the psalms at the pace of the slowest till I was fidgeting with impatience. I missed the chant rising up clear and sweet in the still air. Even more, I missed the sound of my own voice. I decided to speak to the abbot about it. This time I was careful to stand at the door of his cell till I was bidden to enter and to speak respectfully.

"Father, I would like to offer a suggestion regarding the offices."

"Yes?"

"I was Master of Psalmody while in Nidaros. God has blessed me with a good singing voice with which to praise him."

I paused here and sang for him a setting of one of the day's psalms. It was important, I felt, for me to do that. How would he know otherwise the gift that I possessed? He said nothing.

"With your permission, Father, I'd like to offer to lead the brothers in the chanting of the psalms during our offices. My voice is strong enough to support the weaker voices and it would enable us to move our recitations along at a better pace. I am sure it would help the novices, and the other monks too, to find greater joy in our worship."

I felt I had expressed myself modestly, without too much emphasis on my exceptional abilities. I was sure he would be eager to agree. But Aldwin shook his head.

"Your task for the moment is to say the words with faith. To say them with all your heart. Singing or saying, it's not important."

"But Father, to sing the psalms encourages greater feeling. It . . . ."

"Obedience is what is practised in the novitiate. And beyond, of course. If we can't be obedient to our superiors, how can we learn to be obedient to Christ?"

I was, finally, shocked into silence. I lowered my head; he blessed me, and I walked out of his cell in a turmoil of confusion and resentment. I felt as if all the rules had changed. I was always in the wrong. Everything that had won me favour in the past now fell on barren ground. Humility was a hard lesson for me.

As the weeks passed and autumn turned into winter, I started to notice my companions in the novitiate. Morcar was scarcely seventeen. He had been persuaded into the monastery by his father, the Earl, who wanted to show his support for the Church. Morcar often doubted his vocation.

"I'm not like you," he would say. "I don't know all the psalms and the Bible and stuff like you do. And Latin. I can't do it. I don't know if I should be here."

He looked up to me for my learning and experience. It embarrassed me. I could see his modesty was a gift greater than any of mine. I tried to encourage him. I helped him with his Latin and a friendship grew up between us. The other man, Cadmon, was harder. It took me time to understand his silences. One morning at Prime I noticed that he was weeping. It went on all morning, through prayers, through reading, through work. He was still weeping at the noon meal and ate nothing.

"What is it?" I asked him. He tried to check himself, but the sobs grew harder.

"It's her birthday," he said. "My wife's. Last year she was alive. I held her in my arms." Grief choked him. I put my arm round his shoulder and stood with him. How could I not have known? How could I have lived day in day out with this man and not seen his suffering? I was filled with remorse.

I began to understand what Aldwin had said about living in charity with my brothers. We were with each other constantly, praying, eating, working. Only in sleep, in my tiny cell, did I have any privacy. At first it irked me constantly that I was forced to live with men whose company I wouldn't have chosen. But our life bound us together. Through that long winter our life was unrelentingly harsh. All of us were pushed to the limits of our strength. I had to lean on them. Had to accept help.

We had a hall with a hearth where we kept a fire burning through the day. Our daily stew of beans and vegetables was cooked in a heavy pot above it, and bread was baked on the hot stones to the side. Sometimes the people from the villages nearby would bring us a piece of bacon to boil with our stew, or fish from their traps. I thought about food constantly. Fast days passed in dreams of the feasts at Nidaros. We took it in turns to prepare the food, standing close to the fire. I loved to do it, feeling the warmth rise from the pot as I stirred with a long spoon, smelling the fragrance of the stew and remembering the feasts I once enjoyed. We ate in the hall, and it served as our chapter house too. If the cold in our cells was unbearable in the long darkness, we had leave to come to the hall for our times of private study and devotion. Of all those long bleak evenings one stays in my memory. It was in the very depths of winter when it seemed

that the world would never be light again. We were sitting in the hall, all
of us together. The fire gave a leaping light to the room and two candles
stood on the table. Two of the brothers sat close to the candles, reading.
Others sat telling their beads or sitting in contemplation. Outside the
wind howled and buffeted at the roof. A kind of stillness came upon me.
I looked round at the men, my brothers, and found myself filled with love
for them. All of them. Even Reinfrid. I loved them just as they were. Not
the particular love I had for my father, or for a woman, but something
larger and more encompassing.

At last, I thought. At last I feel love. I am changed. But next morning I
had hardly been awake half an hour before I was shouting at Morcar for
spilling cold water down my habit. It was to be a long road.

I thought the Lenten fast might kill me. I had grown thin over the winter,
and even on ordinary days I was still hungry at the end of the meal. During
Lent, days went by without food and during Holy Week we seemed to
stop eating altogether. I was so weak I could hardly walk. The physical
weakness seemed to bring about a kind of lightness in me as if my soul
had been freed from my body, as if I were dead already. All the readings
for the Passion struck me with such force and meaning I was often moved
to tears. We were all slow, spending twice the normal time on every task.
On Holy Saturday, there was a glorious sunrise that turned the water in the
Don to gold and indigo. I stood transfixed, staring at the beauty before me
as if I had entered into Paradise. In some faraway place in myself I could
feel hunger gnawing at my belly, but it no longer seemed to belong to me.

Then Easter Day came, we broke fast in the morning after the dawn
service and later in the day there was a great feast. Morcar's father, the Earl,
sent a lamb for us and his servants roasted it on a spit over a great fire. I can
still remember the taste of that meat—the tender sweetness of the lamb, the
juices dripping from my knife, my mouth full. We drank ale and mead and
soon were drunk with it all. What a joy it was to feel life returning to my body!

What joy, what relief—and yet I felt the loss of spiritual vision I had known. Soon the old grind of our daily life, in all its tedium and discomfort, returned. I chafed with impatience. I wanted to be a saint at once, to be done with the stubbornness of my self.

With the spring a company of masons came, sent by the Earl, to rebuild the west end of the church that had been destroyed by Norman soldiers. The place was filled with their unfamiliar shouts as they started putting up a scaffold of rough-cut tree trunks. I felt again my old fascination with their craft. Whenever I could, I snatched the chance to talk with them and heard of the new tower they were planning at the west door.

"The Romans have done our work for us," the master mason told me. "Look at these stones!"

They were dressed already—weathered for sure, but soon ready to be used again.

"The Romans had a fort near here. When the first monks built this place, they carted the stone here to save themselves the trouble of quarrying. Why not?"

I turned a stone over in my hand and thought of the man who had first cut it. A Roman workman. Even the stone church itself where I stood each day, where Father Bede had stood before me, was four hundred years old. The Roman buildings must have been twice that age.

The Norse had no such history. Nidaros had been founded scarcely fifty years before and everything there, the town, the churches, Olaf's cathedral, was a new beginning. Here at Jarrow, we were blessed to stand within such an ancient tradition. I began to understand Aldwin's vision, his great belief that these places were filled with grace, where we could discover again the first purity of our religion. Centuries separated us from Father Bede and his companions and yet their presence was still close to us. As if they were still here.

I asked if I could work with the masons during work periods, and Aldwin gave me leave. They taught me how to use a chisel to shear away

the stone till it was perfectly formed. I learned to lay a straight row, the
mortar neither too thick or too thin, and each stone exactly square to its
brother. I was sometimes so absorbed that I didn't hear the bell for the
office and had to do penance for my absence. The order and regularity, the
pleasure of watching a line of stones grow straight and true, was pacifying
to me. How much easier it was to shape a stone than my own recalcitrant
nature! Although it was a simple enough building, it was at Jarrow I started
to learn the mason's craft, to see how coarse stone that lies lifeless in the
earth can be transformed into a new form. The great masons understand
the laws that underlie the creation. They know how to shape a building
according to God's own hand. And one day I would know it for myself.

CHAPTER 14

ALL IS TRUE

Jarrow, 1075

It was more than three years since I had set out from Winchcombe with Reinfrid and Aelfwy. Different as we were, our shared gifts had made our new life at Jarrow possible. I had the monastic experience to guide us, Aelfwy had the goodness that inspired us and Reinfrid had the practical skills. He had known how to make the place habitable for us at the beginning, how to start work on the land, how to find food for us. We wouldn't have survived without him. We probably would never have got there. I had come to depend on him more than any of our brothers. And now he was leaving.

De Percy had sent an escort for him, four young men in leather and mail with the Percy colours all over their tunics. All the brothers were waiting by the gate to say their farewells. Reinfrid went over to the horse they'd brought him, letting it nuzzle his hand for a titbit. A memory came to my mind of Reinfrid walking with Freya along some endless road on our journey north, his arm resting on her back, singing a French marching song to keep her moving along and feeding her crusts. I could hardly believe we were saying goodbye. He turned to embrace me.

"Goodbye, Father."

"My dearest brother. May God prosper all you do."

"God bless you, Father. I never forget our time together."

He turned and swung himself up onto the horse. They had brought riding clothes for him and for a moment, sitting tall and straight on his horse, he looked like the warrior knight he had been four years ago. But appearances deceive. I knew he was a changed man.

He had come to my cell a few weeks earlier, soon after the Easter feast. He sat in his usual place on the bench. I noticed there was a special brightness about him. A restlessness. We talked for a while of the novices and the new building work on the church. He paused.

"I have question for you."

"Yes?"

"It is, I want to go now. To Whitby."

"To Whitby?"

"Yes. Tell me, Father. Am I ready?"

With a shock I understood what he was asking me. It was at Whitby, I remembered, that remorse had struck his heart, where he had vowed to give his life to God. I knew that a part of his vow was to restore the ruins of the ancient monastery there, but he hadn't spoken of it since we settled at Jarrow. There was so much to do at Jarrow that I hadn't guessed Whitby was still on his mind. His question took me utterly by surprise. My first impulse was to say no! Not yet! I can't manage without you! But I knew he asked me from his heart, not from his own will. I couldn't withhold the answer.

"Yes," I said. "You're ready."

It was the truth. Reinfrid had taken his vows the year after we arrived at Jarrow and from that time, through Christ's mercy and forgiveness, his guilt had been lifted from him. The dark moods grew fewer. The kindness I had glimpsed on our journey was stronger in him. In spite of his sins he was capable of love.

I had put him in charge of the novices. It was nothing new to Reinfrid to have authority and he took no pride in it, as some men do. He knew the ways of the world and made no judgement about any man's faults or vices, but he was not deceived by them either. He would make a good abbot. He lacked learning, but others could supply that.

It was hard, hard for me to let him go. But he had done all of it, all along, for the sake of his vow. If he felt it was time for him to fulfil it I couldn't hold him back.

"What about the land?" I asked him. "Is Whitby still owned by the Church? How will you manage?"

"God has arranged it. A knight I know from child, we grow up both in Normandy, he comes also to England. The king give him land in the north. He has Whitby."

How did Reinfrid know this? Then I remembered. There had been visitors last week, stopping at Jarrow on their way north from Durham. They had been given refreshment, and Reinfrid had talked with them.

"The men last week—was he one of them?"

"Yes. His name is Percy. Guillaume de Percy. He comes north and he know that I am at Jarrow. So he visit here. When I hear he has Whitby, I think, is God's will. I ask him."

For the sake of his soul, De Percy had agreed to give him the ruined minster at Whitby. And land as well to support the new monastery.

"It's astonishing. It's all been arranged for you."

"Yes." He paused and looked at me in that intense way of his. "I feel now, you know, all is true. All that happen to me. Is God's will."

"Yes. All is true. Praise God."

What else could I say?

Soon after Reinfrid left, two more men came to join us, eager for the monastic life. I put Aelfwy in charge of the novices; he was a seasoned monk now and his gentleness was tempered with more firmness. The new tower was starting to rise over the church. Visitors came to pray with us. Bishop Walcher encouraged us and gifted an estate with all its tithes for our support. I often thought of Reinfrid's words: All is true. I understood what he meant. Like him I had a vision I had given my life to. Almost everyone had thought it a mad folly. Now the truth of it was revealing itself.

And yet, even as Jarrow grew and prospered, I felt a lack. Had Reinfrid's departure made me restless? Yes, we had brought life to this place. We had been guided here by Father Bede himself, and we felt his grace and presence constantly. But I knew there was more. Father Bede's own writings speak of many monasteries and convents, many places blessed with holy saints. I couldn't be content to bring the light of Christ only to one. I had to continue.

Often at that time I contemplated the life of that holy saint, Cuthbert, as set down for us in the writings of Father Bede. I learned that while many honour Lindisfarne as his home, it is only part of the story. His vocation started at Melrose, a monastery at that time newly founded in the light of Christ. It was home to Eata and Boisil, both holy and learned men, and Cuthbert spent many years of his life there. Melrose was the source from which the Saint had drunk. I became more and more certain that Christ meant me to continue his work there. By the time the trees were in leaf and the glorious loveliness of spring was all about us, my resolution was set. I was going to Melrose.

When I told my brothers what I planned, there was a great uproar. But you are the abbot! How can you leave us? Who will give us counsel?

On and on it went, day after day, in all our chapter meetings. I didn't wonder at it. The foundation of the Benedictine Way is stability. They thought I would always remain at Jarrow and they looked to me as their father. I would never have asked this of them had I not been driven by a stronger Will.

"It is the same vision I had from the start," I told them. "If I hadn't believed it then, our monastery here would never have come about. How can I refuse it now?"

Taking the Saint as my example, I wore them down with patience. They would be free to choose their own abbot from among their number, I told them. They no longer had to worry about finding the means to support themselves. God had taken care of it so that they were free to worship him unhindered. Jarrow was under the special grace of Father Bede. He would protect them. The monastery didn't depend on any single person. The more I reasoned with them, the clearer it seemed to me. It was time to go.

I knew I couldn't go alone. The journey north had taught me that. In my heart I wished that Reinfrid had not gone to Whitby. But he had his own vocation, just as I had mine. It wasn't for me to choose anyone. It had to be a calling for any man who would accompany me. I put my request to them and waited.

Late one evening there was a knock at the door of my cell. I said a quick prayer and opened it. I half-expected to find Aelfwy there. But it was Thorgot.

He came into the cell and stood before me. It was almost dark outside, and I had a single candle set on my table. One side of his face was in shadow. One eye sparkled in the reflected light, the other was dark.

"I have come to ask if I may go with you to Melrose."

I looked at the two eyes, one bright, one dark. I asked God to guide me and show me his will.

"May God bless your intention. Tell me why you want to come."

"When first I came to Durham, after I lost my ship, I went to the shrine of St Cuthbert. I first turned to him for help. I want to follow him."

"Yes. It is true, we'll be following in the Saint's footsteps at Melrose." I relented. "Sit down, brother. Let me hear more."

We sat down together, one either side of the table, so I could see his face clearly. I often felt on my guard with Thorgot. He was so persuasive, so intelligent that, as his abbot, I needed to keep a certain distance to be sure I treated him impartially. But he had come now in openness of heart to offer himself, and I owed him more kindness.

"Let me hear more," I prompted him again. "Are you ready for a move, when you've not long been at Jarrow?"

"It's . . . ah . . . "

Thorgot, always ready with his words, was struggling.

"Say what's in your heart. This will be a hard journey, and harder still when we get there. Are you sure?"

"I'm sure. What it is . . . " He took a breath and blew it out fast. "I want to feel faith like you do. Like the Saint did."

He leaned forward towards me across the table, speaking quickly now.

"I say the offices. I fast. I work. I do it all, but it's not there. The light's not there. When I look at you—when I look at our brothers—I can see it's different for them. Their faith is alive. It's real. They find joy in it. Why don't I?"

He was impassioned now. I remembered Aelfwy. He had come on the journey north to try and overcome his weakness. It had nearly driven him from his wits. Was it the same for Thorgot? He wanted the journey to change him. To transform him.

"It's just a journey," I said. "Just another place. If you are ready to endure the hardship of it, you can come, but come without expectation. Let God decide your state."

We talked on. I could see his intention was strong, and I found nothing in my own heart to make me deny him. It was decided.

It was for the best, I thought. Thorgot was so strong and able a man that it was natural for him to take charge of things. Reinfrid had been a match for him, but Aelfwy was novice-master now. There might have been difficulties ahead.

Thorgot and I stepped through the monastery gate on a May morning. A light drizzle was falling, just as it had been three years ago, when we left Winchcombe. And just as then, I felt the tightness in my chest loosen. I was at peace with myself. I was carrying the revelation forward. Of my former companions, only Freya remained. She was docile and patient as ever. She was growing slower, but the journey was far shorter. It would not strain her. She carried all we needed—Mass chalice and patten, vestments, Father Bede's *History*. Thorgot knew the psalms and Gospels as well as I did, as well as hymns and liturgies; we had no need for a library. Thorgot had been anxious to take extra clothing but I quoted Christ's words to him:

"Take nothing for the journey, neither stick nor pack, neither bread nor money; nor are you to have a second coat."

Poor man. He had been used to a life of ease and luxury. In the end, I had pity on him. We would take a change of undergarments. Moreover, since we had a guide to walk with us for the first two days, we took bread so that he would not go hungry. The guide would take us from Jarrow to the crossing over the Tyne and then as far as Corbridge, on the north side of the river. From there, he told us, we had only to follow the ancient route of Dere Street and we would come straight to Melrose.

CHAPTER 15

Melrose

Scotland, 1075

They came to Melrose, which had formerly been a monastery, but was at that time a solitude; and charmed by the seclusion of the place, they began there to serve Christ.

Simeon's "History of the Church of Durham", Chapter LVII

At first, Dere Street took us through wild unpeopled countryside with hardly a hamlet or hut to give us shelter. But by the second day, Thorgot and I were walking among fields and pleasant meadows, prosperous farms where people were happy to give us food, for ourselves and Freya. On the third day, we saw the three peaks of the Eildons ahead. At first, they seemed far away in the distance, then they grew closer by the hour, steep and sudden against the horizon. We had been told to look for them, for they marked the end of our journey. We were to pass close by them till we reached a river called the Tweed, then follow it downstream till we reached the ancient monastery.

But first the street led us directly to a settlement of ruined stone buildings not far from the river. Was this the place? We led Freya closer and wandered here and there between the broken walls.

"It must have been a great monastery. Greater than Jarrow."

"It would have been a fort, Father. Not a monastery. A Roman fort.

141

This is how they laid them out, it was the same at Lincoln. And Chester-le-Street. These would have been stores. Or granaries. And these, look. Barracks for soldiers."

"Not dormitories? Or a refectory perhaps?"

I was struggling to imagine this northern valley filled with Roman soldiers. Surely monks, I thought. But Thorgot shook his head.

"Look at the stonework. Look at the way they turn the corner of the building here, so sharp and square and Roman. Straight lines everywhere."

As I looked around, I began to believe him. There were so many buildings laid out in such a regular way. It would have housed hundreds of monks. Thorgot was right. Father Bede said nothing about such numbers, after all, and we had been told to follow the river. So we left the ruins behind and continued down to the river. We walked alongside it for a couple of miles through rough pasture where sheep were feeding. The banks on the opposite side were thickly wooded with birch and pine and alder and two kites hung above, mewing to each other. I stopped to stare at them, and Freya dropped her head for a quick mouthful of grass. I let her graze. As I stood waiting for her, I saw a tall dyke of earth ahead of us, some four or five feet high. It was overgrown with grass and bushes, but the outline was clear to see. At once I was certain what it was.

"Look, Thorgot! It must be the boundary. For the monastery."

This time he didn't contradict me. The dyke ran in one direction to the banks of the river. We turned in the other direction and followed it along its length, scrambling through brambles and undergrowth till we came to an opening. There was a rough hurdle fence pulled across and a track ran up to it that had signs of recent use. We pulled the hurdles aside, led Freya through and closed them up again. I stood quite still. I was certain now.

"This is the entrance to the monastery," I told Thorgot. "I'm sure of it."

It was this very gate to which Cuthbert must have come, where Boisil welcomed him and foresaw his future. I felt as if we too were standing with Boisil and witnessing the Saint's arrival. I prayed to Christ to bless us in that holy place.

We followed the track through some scrubby woodland before finding ourselves in open meadows. A craggy hill rose steeply up before us; I could see the river flowing on our left side and I realized it must curve around the base of the hill. It would make a kind of half-island of the land, just as at Durham. The monks must have used the dyke to seal off the land side and enclose their sanctuary. I looked around for the monastery buildings. I saw nothing but a few sheep grazing.

"Where can the buildings be?" I asked Thorgot. "Shouldn't they be here, by the gate?"

He was looking round, not attending to me.

"Is that a church? On the rise there?"

We went to look. There was little enough to see, but there were posts set in the ground and some remains of walls made of wattle and daub.

"They were building in wood. Not stone. That's why there's nothing left to see," said Thorgot. "It's all rotted away." He pointed down the slope to the level ground. "Look. Mounds. There are mounds in the grass where their cells were."

He was right. There were a couple of larger mounds in a rectangular form, and many more small circular ones. The monastery was there beneath our feet, and we couldn't see it.

Here was true simplicity. They had taken so little care of their bodily comfort that there was nothing left to be seen of their habitations. I felt a rush of joy to be there. Thorgot stood silent. Perhaps he was disappointed, I thought. He liked buildings. I turned to him, but before I could console him, he said,

"Where are we going to live?"

"We'll make a camp."

He stared at me. I knew he wanted to ask, why did we not bring a tent? I sent him off to look around while I remained in contemplation. He had to learn to trust. Sure enough, he found a shepherd's bothy, not by the monastery but on a low haugh by the river, immediately below the steep crags of the hill opposite. It was snug and newly built. At once he was in better spirits, as if finding it was due to his own merits.

"God has provided for us," I reminded him. He scowled.

We settled into our new home. Thorgot went out each day to beg food for us. I would have been happy never to stir from that blessed place, but Thorgot insisted we should both go out sometimes into the country round about. He had a restless energy.

"Father Bede says it's what the Saint did," he reminded me. "He went out preaching. He did the rounds of the villages. We can't eat people's food and give them nothing in return."

Thorgot was right. The Saint had set great store on supporting himself with his own hands, but with only two of us to dig the land it would be months before we could grow enough to eat. We had to depend on the charity of our neighbours. So once a week we went out to visit the villages nearby. Thorgot would sing a hymn or two and his fine voice soon brought people close, curious to see us. I preached to them and gave them Mass. They were Christians, but it had been many months since they had seen a priest. Soon we were welcomed wherever we went. When we were invited into a house, Thorgot was often called on to sing a ballad or two and soon ale would be flowing. I made no objection. To tell the truth, as the weeks went past, I often forgot I was abbot to his novice. We were companions, just as Aelfwy, Reinfrid and I had been. We said the offices together, worked our plot of land together, slept side by side in the bothy. I found myself depending on him. His easy manners made friends for us among the people. Every day we would find a basket or two set by the gate, with gifts of bread, or some vegetables, or a round of cheese. The food tasted all the sweeter for being freely given. One day two men from a village nearby came and showed Thorgot how to set fish traps in the river. I could hear shouts and laughter. Thorgot came back with his habit half soaked but in high spirits. Later in the summer the same men returned to help him build two withy cells, so that when winter came and the shepherd had need of his bothy, we would not hinder him. How practical he was! I marvelled at him. He could turn his hand to anything. I understood why he had found such favour with the Norse.

I saw too that the grief that had tormented him at Jarrow was easing. His youthful spirits were returning to him. Boisterousness, even. When novices enter a monastery at a young age, they grow accustomed to a quiet deportment. Sometimes this is harder to learn for grown men, and so it was with Thorgot. His monastic robes seemed at odds with him, as if he wore them for a wager and would soon return to the lay clothes he had put off. His sturdy body looked as if it wanted to break out of his habit and go flinging away with arms and legs akimbo. One summer morning before we had broken fast, I heard him singing by the river, a merry song that sent echoes flying round the cliffs. I walked down the track and came up behind him before he noticed me. He spun round, still singing. Then he caught hold of me by the waist and whirled me around in a measure. I had not danced since my childhood and laughter came bubbling up in me. We went spinning down the track beside the river till his song came to an end and we staggered to a halt. At once he flung himself on the ground at my feet.

"I repent! I repent! Give me my penance!"

"Go off with you into that water! An hour or two in there will cool your wanton limbs!"

He looked up at me, eyes still full of laughter. I kept my gaze so severe he was ready to take me at my word. He scrambled up and headed for the river. When he was halfway in, I called him back.

"We'll take breakfast first! What have you got for us?"

We sat together outside the bothy eating bread and curd. He had made a simple bench for us from a fallen tree near the river. The sun warmed us, and the song of the birds was our choir. The bread in our mouths was given in kindness. All God's blessings were upon us. The penance was forgotten.

It was at Melrose that I felt the fulfilment of my revelation. Here, I felt, was the source. Here the word of Christ was first brought to the kingdom. Here it was most pure, least stained by worldly things. The early Fathers had given themselves to God in a life of poverty where they held all in common. Their only purpose was to seek the kingdom of heaven. Just as their intention was unstained so too was the beauty of the place, set apart from worldly cares. The steep cliffs, with their thick forests that rose up on the banks opposite, seemed to enfold the sanctuary and protect it. The air was so tranquil that I felt my spirit fold its wings and come to rest. When I prayed, I felt myself to be in a great company of the saints, with Cuthbert and Boisil at my side. There was such peace there. If we had only been given leave to enjoy it.

From the start of our time at Melrose, Thorgot and I would spend the mornings in prayer and study. A monk is bound to spend time throughout his life in the contemplation of the Word, and learning these skills is one of the main tasks of the novitiate. For many novices it is a long struggle, first to learn Latin, then to grasp the meaning of what they read. But for a few educated men like Thorgot there is a different challenge. He had a fluent grasp of Latin and since boyhood he had studied biblical text and commentary. He often surprised me with the breadth of his knowledge of scripture. But it was like his singing. He could sing a psalm like an angel, so that the listener might be moved to tears, but for Thorgot himself the text was so familiar it no longer touched his heart. He could debate a point of theology as well as any scholar, but it didn't help him find insight.

We began at Melrose with St John's Gospel, called by Jerome "the eagle Gospel", since it touches most nearly the mysteries of God. It was especially beloved by the early saints. Father Bede tells us that when Boisil, Cuthbert's beloved teacher, was dying, he and Cuthbert spent Boisil's last days reading a commentary on it.

I read Bede's remark on this episode to Thorgot: "They were able to finish quickly, because they dealt not with the profound arguments but with the simple things of 'the faith that works by love.'"

"'The faith that works by love'. Can we place that?" I asked Thorgot. Bede was a master of the scriptures; I didn't expect Thorgot to recognize the quotation. He stared at the sky, abstracted. At last he blew out a breath and nodded.

"The apostle James. Letter to the Galatians." He put his head back and quoted: "'For in Christ Jesus there is neither circumcision nor uncircumcision but the faith that works by love.'"

He looked at me with a hint of triumph. He had surprised me again.

"Well remembered indeed! Why should Bede bring it here?"

"Not with profound arguments ... " He pondered it, then looked at me, eyebrow half-raised. "I can guess why you have brought it, Father."

"Yes?"

"Perhaps you think I am too—how to say it? Too fond of the profound arguments. Too much the scholar."

I wanted to smile. He saw through me.

"Well, Bede doesn't dismiss the profound arguments. He was a great scholar himself. But it is like the debate over circumcision in James's day. In the love of Christ, such arguments fall away. It was the same for these saintly men. The simple things of faith were enough for them."

Thorgot ran his fingers through the matted tangle of his hair, as yet untonsured, tugging at it to try and straighten out his thoughts.

"None of it seems simple to me, Father. Sometimes it feels as though my head will burst with all the texts and commentaries."

He gave his hair a final tug and threw his hands down as if to say, I will never get this straight.

"Use Bede's words for private contemplation. Ask to understand them in your heart."

He set his lips tight together, as if to stop himself speaking, frowning with frustration. He wanted to wrestle truth out with his mind. But that is not the way of it.

The long summer days were turning to autumn by the time we came to the end of our study of St John. It was a fine day with a first hint of frost. We read the last chapter, where the risen Christ appears to his disciples on the shores of the Sea of Tiberias. When we finished our reading, it was time for the noon meal. In dry weather, we used a simple hearth outdoors; Thorgot had kept the ashes warm, and now he put a couple of fish on the embers to grill for our meal. I watched him, thinking of Christ and his apostles eating together on the shore of the Sea of Tiberias. I was quite lost in my contemplation and didn't hear the men riding down the grass towards us. When I became aware of their presence, they were dismounting from their horses and walking over. There were four of them. Soldiers of some sort with leather tunics and swords at their sides.

"Good day!" called out Thorgot. One of the men handed his horse's reins to his fellow and walked over.

"By whose authority do you take fish from this river?" the man demanded. He spoke in a rough English I could barely understand.

"Since this is hallowed land, we ask God to feed us," said Thorgot.

The man kicked the fish off the fire with his boot and sent the embers flying.

"This land belongs to Malcolm, King of Scotland. Have you sworn fealty to him?"

I stepped forward to lend Thorgot my support.

"This land was given to God in ancient times. We are servants of Christ and owe fealty to none but him."

"You're thieves and beggars and the King wants you gone from his land."

"We are here with the authority of the Bishop of Durham. He has blessed our mission to this place."

The man glared at me, gave another kick at the fire, then turned away. He got back on his horse and rode off with his fellows.

Our next visitor arrived a week later, a messenger who came cantering down towards us as we were saying Terce. He swung down from his horse and tried to thrust a document into my hands while we were in the very act of saying divine service. I took no notice of him.

"You must take it!" he shouted at me. "It is from the bishop, and I must take back your response today!"

I gave up and took it from him. When I looked it over, I saw that King Malcolm had sent his threats direct to the bishop. Walcher ordered us to return at once to Jarrow. I handed the document back to the messenger.

"Please thank the bishop for his concern. We are here in Christ's service and look for his protection alone."

"The Scots king says he will kill you if you don't swear fealty."

"That's as may be."

At last the man gave up and rode off. We resumed the office. When we were done, Thorgot said:

"What do you mean to do?"

"We are in Christ's hands alone. He will guide us."

Thorgot had a grim look about him that gave me pause. I had no concern for my own safety; the early saints had embraced martyrdom willingly. If that were Christ's will for me, I would not baulk. But I couldn't answer for Thorgot. I waited.

"It's not a religious thing, Father," he said, as if I had not understood. "Not a matter of faith. It's just about jurisdiction. King Malcolm doesn't want a monastery on his territory that owes allegiance elsewhere."

"Why should they think like that? That this place or another is a territory that belongs to this king or that? It was given to God."

"Bishop Walcher has bidden us return. We owe obedience to him."

"I believe that Christ's will is over this place, and that has authority beyond kings and bishops. That's all. But there's no obligation on you. Return if you feel guided to that."

He didn't push the argument any further. He stayed and we continued with our life of devotion as before, but there was fear in the air. If we went out to the villages, no-one came out of their houses. Malcolm's men had warned them off. The baskets of food stopped appearing at the gate. Sometimes Thorgot went out at night to visit the villages secretly and returned with enough bread to last us for a meal or two. We ate much fish from his traps.

Late one afternoon ten or more of Malcolm's soldiers came riding down onto the promontory, across the sanctuary land, filling the quiet air with their curses. We heard them coming. I untethered Freya. She was slow to move; there was no time to wait for her. We ran to the woods behind our cells to hide ourselves in case they meant mischief. As they drew close, I could see they had brought brands of wood as well as swords. One man dismounted and pulled out his tinder to light the wood. When it was flaming, he moved between his fellows to light theirs, till they were all ablaze. Then they rode close to the cells and hurled them in, shouting abuse and blasphemies. The flames soon burst through the roofs. Thorgot tugged at me. We moved deeper back into the woods till we could no longer see them and crouched down in the shelter of the undergrowth. Thorgot was sweating hard, and I could smell his sweat close to me. The leaf mould was damp beneath our feet. A shaft of sunlight fell through the branches. How strange it was to be there in the quiet of the woods while only a hide away flames leapt through the cells where we might have stood. I thought of Freya. For sure, she would have run off, I thought. They would have no interest in a donkey. I fingered the beads in my robe and said the prayers under my breath. After an hour or more Thorgot crept forward to see if they were gone. When he returned, he shook his head.

"They've made camp by the river. They'll sleep here."

That night we lay on the ground beneath the trees, in the thickest part of the wood where the rain hardly touched us. Neither of us slept. At first light we heard the men stirring, talking in their rough voices, the horses whinnying. Soon we felt the ground shake with horses' hooves. They were coming along the track not far from our hiding place. We scarcely breathed. For a time, we could hear them riding around, up and down, across the sanctuary, back down to the river, searching for any sign of us. At last all was quiet. We could hear birds singing in the trees and the scattered sheep bleating to each other. We pushed our way out of the undergrowth and stood giddy in the morning air. I could think of nothing but going out to look for Freya. I stumbled down towards the river.

She had not got far. Her body lay on the ground close to the burnt-out ruins of the cells with a deep gash in her side. I kneeled beside her and laid my hand on her soft coat, that had always been so warm. She was cold now, stiff as stone. Tears fell from my eyes. Is it not always the innocent who suffer? I had brought her to this fate. I wished the spear had pierced my heart, not hers.

Thorgot brought water for me. The cold water in my throat relieved me, but even as I drank, we felt again the movement of hooves on the ground. Thorgot took my arm.

"Quick," he said. "We must hide."

I looked at him, his face urgent. I let him pull me back up towards the wood, but before we reached it the men were there. Two men, leading horses with them.

"It's all right. It's the bishop's men," Thorgot said.

"Are you sure?"

"Look at their colours."

He was right. We turned back and stood before them, twigs and leaves stuck to our clothes, light-headed with lack of sleep and food. The men stared at us, at the burned-out cells and poor Freya's body.

"We've come in good time, Father," said one of the men at last. I had nothing to say. "We are commanded by the bishop to bring you this message."

He pulled a document out of his pack, unrolled it and started to read to us:

> To Aldwin, venerable father and abbot of our monastery at Jarrow,
> I, Walcher, Bishop of Durham do now order and command you in
> Christ's most holy name, on pain of excommunication by all the
> clergy and people of the diocese in the presence of the most holy
> body of St Cuthbert, to withdraw without delay from your residence
> at that former monastery of Melrose, now ruled by Malcolm

> *King of Scots. On receiving this warning of the dreadful threat of*
> *excommunication that awaits your soul, you and your companion*
> *must at once accompany our messenger and return without delay to*
> *our monastery at Jarrow and live henceforth under the protection of*
> *the Saint. And we do solemnly promise and commit to reward your*
> *obedience with the further gift of Monkwearmouth and the ancient*
> *monastery of St Peter, and so in Christ's name we do command you.*
>
> *Given this day of our Lord October seventeenth 1075 at our*
> *episcopal palace of Durham.*

The word "excommunication" fell like a doom in my ears. I staggered and would have fallen but for Thorgot's arm around me. He spoke to the men.

"Thank God you're here. We should leave without delay. Father Aldwin needs your help."

The men came over to me and lifted me up onto the saddle of one of the horses they had brought. I had no strength left to resist.

"Hold the pommel, Father. Look, here. Hold tight."

One of the men took the leading rein, and I felt the horse move forward. I am no rider, but my body soon fell into the rhythm of its gait. I was content to let it move me along. But as we rode through the gate of the monastery, I called out to them to stop. I knew we had to leave, but I wanted a last look.

As I gazed back, I understood that nothing had changed. It was still the same, still a blessed place. The violence we had witnessed had no power to alter it. Nor did our going. Nothing was lost. My heart lightened a little. We had felt the Saint beside us when first we came. I knew his presence was still with us when we left.

CHAPTER 16

JARROW

Jarrow, 1075

There Aldwin conferred the monastic habit upon Thorgot; and as he loved him very dearly as a brother in Christ, he instructed him, by his word and example, how to bear Christ's easy yoke.

Simeon's "History of the Church of Durham", Chapter LVII

During the ride back I was afflicted with a sickness. Whether it was fever or possession, I couldn't tell, but after we got back to Jarrow my sleep was hag-ridden. I woke often, believing that flames were leaping through the windows or that I was choking in dark clouds of smoke. Thorgot slept on the floor of my cell, and minutes after I woke, I would find him at my side, helping me to sit up and giving me water to drink. Just as we had at Melrose, we would say the night office together until the evil spirits took flight. During the day, he was always at my side trying to spoon some broth into my mouth or coaxing me to try a posset he'd made. I took it to please him. I knew he did it out of love for me. Sometimes I could hear him at the door, talking to visitors.

"A little longer," he would say. "Just a day or two more. Oh yes, he's stronger already but he must rest. He sends you his blessing."

It was a relief to feel secure within the peace of my cell. Thorgot understood that my affliction was more than physical weakness. We had spent so many weeks in contemplation, freed from all other burdens. My soul had come to rest in solitude, and now it shrank from all the duties that awaited me as abbot. I thought often of the Saint. The king and all his clergy went to Inner Farne to drag him from his sanctuary. After eight years of solitude, he had to return to the world. Eight years! What torment it must have been to him.

At last one morning I woke refreshed and dreamless. Thorgot brought me porridge to eat, and when I had finished, I asked him what had been happening in the monastery.

"All's well. Two more brothers have joined us. Aelfwy longs to see you. Brother Cedd is eager to give back the abbot's mantle to you."

I nodded. "I'm ready."

He took a long look at me. "Tomorrow," he said. We sat for a while in silence.

"How long have I been here?"

"Eight days. Nine, maybe."

"And you, Thorgot? How is it with you?"

"With me?" More silence, comfortable between us. We'd grown used to waiting for each other's thoughts.

"I've been close to death twice in a year, by water first, and then by fire. I thank God every day I'm still alive."

He paused, looking at me as if he wondered if he should continue.

"But I thought I might lose you, Father. Lose you to this sickness. I blamed myself. I shouldn't have let you stay on at Melrose. We had two warnings. I knew what could happen. I should have brought you away."

He took my hand and squeezed it.

"Faith can go too far, Father."

Gentle though his words were, I felt my innards give way with remorse. I thought, suddenly, of that pelting day on the journey north when I had refused to stop, and of Reinfrid yelling at me, "You are fool!" Thorgot's reproof was far milder but it struck as deep. I wanted to have faith to move mountains, to face any trial, even death. But it wasn't faith. It was my own stubbornness, my own will, my refusal to bow to authority. And it had caused Freya's death. I bowed my head and wept.

Though I would have been pleased enough to return to the monastery as one of the brothers, they pressed me to be their abbot as before. Although I longed for Melrose—indeed, I have never ceased to—I saw that I must accept God's will. I became once more Abbot of Jarrow and bound myself to the loving care of my brothers and the rhythm of the Rule. I missed Thorgot's company constantly; he was a novice still and distanced from me. But November came at last and with it the end of his novitiate. He came to see me, as all novices must, to make his formal request to enter holy orders. I spoke to him as his abbot, in the same way I would have spoken to any novice.

"As God sees the innermost thoughts of your heart, do you believe that he has guided you to serve him and make profession of your vows to him as a monk?"

"I do." Even at this most solemn moment, I caught a glint of laughter in his eye. He still stood respectfully before me, but he spoke directly.

"Father, I will never make a good monk. I will never have your constancy. Your inwardness. I love the world too much. But I swore my oath to God to serve him when he spared me from the sea, and I desire with all my heart to keep my oath."

"My son, all a monk is judged for is his willingness to serve. We are all flawed. If it were not so, how should we have need of God's mercy?"

"Well then. I am ready to swear service."

He made his profession at Christmas and afterwards we celebrated the Christmas feast together. We were nine brothers at that time and two novices. It was a day of special gladness for me. I loved all our brothers, but since Melrose there was a special bond between Thorgot and me. He was my counsellor as well as my brother. I had no doubts of his vocation. God has given men different gifts and if a monastery is to flourish it should make use of all of them. I admitted him into the Order with the certainty that he would become a true servant of Christ.

It was too early for him to hold office within the monastery, but I made a practice of taking him as my companion on the visits to Durham that were required of me. Since our return from Melrose Bishop Walcher seemed to be always sending to speak with me. He was full of schemes, for Monkwearmouth, for increasing our numbers and giving us more land, even for building a monastic cell in Durham itself. His schemes bewildered me. The vision God had granted me was simple and clear: to walk in the footsteps of the saints who had given up everything for the kingdom of heaven. When I was with Walcher, the vision seemed to get lost in deeds and grants and what tithes each hide of land owed us. I knew that the monks needed to eat, but I had rather we simply depended on the charity of those around us, as it had been at Melrose. But Walcher wanted everything set down, everything chartered. Thorgot understood him far better than I.

"You're used to all this," I said to him. "Bishops and noblemen and important people. You know how to deal with them better than I do."

It was true. He knew how to act the courtier, but also, he could go through the deeds and documents with Walcher and see mistakes or clarify wordings. Although he was no longer in thrall to worldly things, he understood them. Besides, I knew how he loved to drink a cup of good wine and eat meat at the bishop's table. I counted it no sin. He had mastered his appetites, and God does not grudge us his bounty.

We learned that much had changed at the Norman court in Durham. King William had deposed the Earl of Northumbria for some treachery. In his place, the king decreed that Walcher should serve as both bishop and earl. I did not trouble myself with the strangeness of such a scheme. I knew already that since Walcher was neither monk nor priest, he was unfit to be a bishop, so it made little difference if he was unfit to be an earl. To house his splendour the earl-bishop was busy with the construction of a new palace next to the castle. He loved to show us the fine hall he was building. It held no interest for me, but Thorgot could spend an hour talking about how the roof trusses would be supported. It gave him a ready subject of conversation with Walcher.

Walcher had sent for two of his kinsmen to help him in his duties. A brutal man named Gilbert had become his sheriff, and a sour-faced cleric, Levin, was made archdeacon and his deputy. Thorgot became silent when we first saw them and slid his head under his hood.

"I could swear I know that Gilbert," he said to me afterwards. "From the time of my escape from Lincoln. I know his face. Please God he doesn't know mine."

There was little fear of it. Gilbert spoke no English, and neither he nor Levin paid us the slightest heed. Englishmen didn't exist for them. Their arrogance made me look with more kindness on Walcher. He, at least, spoke with us as equals. Although he had little English, all three of us had Latin enough to be easy in each other's company. And he was eager to bring monastic life back to full flower in his diocese.

He was, at that time, especially delighted with his new gift to us of Monkwearmouth and the lands that went with it.

"It is a completion of my former gift to you, of Jarrow. They were formerly one, you know. A double monastery. Amazing, isn't it? All those centuries ago. And Monkwearmouth, that was Father Bede's first house!"

He looked at us both in triumph. He knew Bede's *History of the Angles* as well as I did. I reproached myself for judging him. He was, after all, my superior, and we had great cause to be grateful for his generosity. Thorgot was willing to work with him for the sake of the Church. I should do the same. It would, indeed, be a completion to revive the spiritual inheritance of both monasteries.

"Both close to river mouths," remarked Thorgot. "Did you notice that, my lord? St Peter's on the Wear and St Paul's on the Tyne. They must have had plenty of visitors. Or maybe they were travellers?"

"Indeed they were. It's a marvel when you consider how primitive their ships were. They travelled to Frankia, to Rome itself. Brought back treasures. A library, Bede had at Jarrow."

"And you are building a fine library here, my lord," said Thorgot, and soon he and Walcher were deep in talk about his books. Walcher was hungry for such conversation. For all the wealth and power William had heaped on him, he was still a stranger in this wild northern kingdom.

Had he left the comforts of his hall to visit the old monastery of St Peter's? I doubt it. True, Monkwearmouth was closer to Durham than Jarrow, though the two monasteries were scarcely ten miles apart. In Bede's day, the two houses were linked together under one abbot and they became great centres of saintliness and learning. Now it seemed the flourishing of Jarrow was to spread back to its mother house, if God willed. But it would take time. At Jarrow, we had found the church still partly in use, and some of the buildings could be repaired. But the ruin of St Peter's was far gone. Brambles and nettles grew so thickly over the stones that one could scarcely see where the walls had stood. If Walcher had visited, it might have tempered his delight. Thorgot shook his head over it.

"Wait till the spring, Father," he said. "It's too harsh now, in the winter weather. Our hands will freeze to the stones."

I felt relief at his words. Thorgot would take care of the rebuilding. Thorgot would organize whatever needed to be done. I could devote myself to the spiritual life and the pastoral care of our brothers, and I knew that was his intention. I had depended on Reinfrid too, but Thorgot brought something more. He was an Englishman, but because he had known high office he was at ease at court in spite of his antipathy to the Normans. More, I could see there was a friendship growing between him and Walcher. Thorgot was a bridge for us.

PART 3

FIRE IN THE NORTH

1078–1079

CHAPTER 17

HUNRED

Durham, 1078–1079

How strange it is that one's children do not turn out as one expects!

When I first held Mary in my arms, I was overjoyed to have a daughter, a girl who would be close to me, who I could teach all I knew. As soon as she was old enough, I brought out Hunred's old slate and school texts. I taught her to write her name, and she liked that well enough. But she had no patience to learn her letters. She would be fidgeting on the bench before we were well started, tugging at her plaits and squirming away. Her letters were ill-formed, sloppy things, but if I made her rub out and start again, she would lose interest altogether. Soon it became a struggle between us. I would promise her some little treat, a cake or an apple, if she would sit still and do her lessons. She would rush through it for the sake of the treat, but there were still complaints. She looked up at me, round blue eyes and pouting cheeks.

"I don't want to do lessons. None of the other girls have to do lessons."

"You'll be glad you did when you're older. You'll be able to read and learn."

She would pull a face and wriggle away. In the end, I gave up. What was the point of forcing her? No-one else cared. Raedgar would encourage her, but he had no time for teaching her, nor interest either.

She would far rather be with her friends. They did all the things that girls do; plaiting each other's hair with flowers, dressing up as fine ladies in Gudrun's old dresses, winding wool across each other's arms till it was all in a tangle. When she was eight years old, she could sew a straighter seam than me, though she couldn't say the Lord's Prayer to the end. All she thought about was her friends and their games and who was prettiest. Her best friend was Gudrun's daughter Hild. Gudrun had given birth a few months before me, and we were both happy to see our daughters growing together. But the girls were more often at Gudrun's house than mine. Sometimes Gudrun took them both to her father's hall. He had held onto his lands after the Normans and still lived like a lord. Mary loved it. She loved the women in their silks and linen and perfumes, loved the sweetmeats and cakes the grandfather gave her.

At first Hunred liked his little sister well enough and would dance her on his knee, teasing to make her smile. But as he grew older, he took less notice of her—indeed, he turned away from all of us. The laughing boy was gone. I seldom saw him smile when he was at home; always, instead, there was a slight frown between his eyes. Although he was as fair-haired as the rest of us, there was a darkness about him. It was the war years, I thought. The war had changed him. When we came back from Lindisfarne, everything was turned upside down. There had been so much destruction. Our home was always full of strangers who needed a meal or a bed, and when Mary was born, she took up all my attention. Hunred had to fend for himself. I saw him grow sulky and silent, but what could I do?

Then the Normans moved into Durham. It was chaos all over again. Our world was taken from under our feet, the sanctuary ground turned into a building yard full of soldiers and workmen. First the castle rose up like a black shadow in front of us, and then they bound our houses into its yard with their great bailey wall. We became prisoners in our own homes.

Hunred was timid at first, fearful of the soldiers. Then he and his friends started taunting them, goading each other to hurl a stone at a passing sentry or shout an insult from behind a wall. He and two others were caught and whipped. When he came home, he was blubbing like a child. He wept in my arms and let me wash away the blood from his wounds. I covered them in healing herbs and murmured soothing words over him as I'd not done since he was small. But afterwards, he drew away from me as if ashamed. He stopped playing with his friends and buried himself in his schoolwork. It was his way of escaping. He became a scholar and started learning the traditions of the Community. And going to chapter meetings with Raedgar. That was when it all started. One evening he came back with his face alight.

"What did you talk about?" I asked him. Usually he would turn away without responding to my questions. But that evening he was full of it.

"Bishop Walcher told us about his monks. It is a revival of the saints of old. There is a priest called Aldwin, and the bishop plans that one day there will be monks at the shrine."

He turned to Raedgar.

"Did you know about them, Father?"

"Yes."

"Why didn't you tell me?"

"I didn't think you'd be interested."

"But I am, I am! I want to go. I want to know how they live."

"Well—we'll go. It's not far to Jarrow."

The two of them set out together and spent a few days with the monks.

"It's very austere," Raedgar told me afterwards. "Aldwin, the abbot, has a vision of reviving the way of life of the early saints. He and the brothers seem to be ready for any hardship. They live in makeshift huts and eat nothing but beans and barley." He raised an eyebrow. "They're certainly all pretty thin."

We looked at each other. The same thought was in both our minds. Hunred had always loved his comforts, always wanted his bed just so and the softest blankets. He couldn't bear to share an inch of space. And he had an appetite big enough for three. Neither of us could imagine his enthusiasm lasting. But we were wrong.

He was fifteen by then, starting his studies to become a deacon. That was the first step for the inheritors of the Community, as it had been for generations. But after the visit to Jarrow, he started to miss lessons. More and more often, he was at Jarrow. He started criticizing Raedgar.

"The liturgy the Community uses is wrong. You shouldn't be using it."

"It's the liturgy used by the monks of Lindisfarne. You know that. It's part of our tradition."

"Yes, but it was used by monks. That's the point. You're not monks. It should be different."

"What do you have in mind?"

He had no answer for that. He scowled at his father and went out.

He seldom sat with us at the hearth now, however cold the weather. He started going to the church to hold special vigils, all on his own, though they always finished in time for the night meal. He would come in and sit at the table looking as aloof as he could manage before tearing into his bowl of stew and bread, pushing the bowl towards me for more without meeting my eyes. He was growing into a tall man and his body cried out for food. But it didn't stop his complaints.

"Why doesn't the Community observe fast days? They think of nothing but their bellies."

"You know I fast," Raedgar answered him.

"But the others. They don't. They don't care."

"Don't get involved in judging other people. You know what Christ says. Look at the plank in your own eye."

Raedgar was always patient, always reasonable, but the arguments went on. All the anger that had grown in Hunred had found an outlet. Criticizing his father. Criticizing the Community. Perhaps it was something that all young men went through, I thought. But I couldn't remember anything like this. We had always learned respect for everything the Community stood for: the protection of the Saint, the traditions of the Order. Hunred's angry words shocked me.

He was sixteen when he made the decision. We had all been standing together with the rest of the household, for morning prayers. When the prayers were done and the servants were going about their business, Hunred went over to his father.

"I want to speak to you, Father."

Raedgar nodded, then glanced at me to follow him to the office. When I entered behind them, Hunred said:

"I want to speak to you alone, Father."

"If it concerns me, it concerns your mother as well."

"But it doesn't. This has nothing to do with women."

"What do you want to talk to me about?"

"About . . . about the future."

I didn't move. He turned to me.

"Mother, please go."

"What's this?" Raedgar asked him. "Your mother has borne and bred you; she is a daughter of the Community. Can she not speak to you now?"

"It's all part of it," he said. "It's all part of what's wrong. Women. Priests who are married. It's sinful. It's wrong." He was getting agitated now.

"You may hold that view, but while you live under my roof you'll show respect. Invite your mother to join us."

His face turned fiery red. It took him moments to control himself. At last he turned and mumbled something in my direction. We sat down together at the table, both opposite him so he was forced to look at me. For a moment, I saw again the little boy he had been, shouting and banging his spoon on the table. It's just a tantrum, I thought.

"I want to become a monk," he said. His words knocked me sideways; I couldn't take in what he had said. There was a long moment of silence before Raedgar spoke.

"Have you spoken to Abbot Aldwin about this?"

"Yes."

"What has he said to you?"

"He will accept me into the novitiate."

"Does he know who you are?"

"It doesn't matter. Everyone there thinks the same. The servants of God should renounce all worldly things and keep themselves pure for Christ alone."

"But your duty is to serve God here. You are bound to the inheritance of the Saint."

"It's nothing. The Inheritors and all that, it's just stories. What does the Saint care for the sons of men long dead? Yes, they served the Saint then, but the vision has been lost."

"The Community serves the Saint now as it always has."

"Keeps ledgers, you mean. Clings to lands and treasures. Where is the spiritual life? It's dead, dead, dead! Did the Saint live like this? He gave up everything."

His words were like blows, one after the other. Raedgar winced.

"The Community is your family," I said. "Do you want to turn your back on everyone who loves you?"

"I have no family," he said. "That's what Christ says. 'If anyone comes to me and does not hate father and mother, wife and children, brothers and sisters—yes, even their own life—such a person cannot be my disciple.'" He stared at me in triumph.

"It's easy to quote texts. Think about what you're doing."

He shrugged. Raedgar leaned forward.

"Your desire is honourable. Becoming a monk is a formidable undertaking for any man, I'm proud of your courage. But you can't turn your back on your inheritance, and the duty you have to your ancestors and to the Saint. There is no-one else who can step in and take your place, you know. I want you to reflect on this more carefully." He paused. "I will speak to the bishop about the matter."

After all Hunred's wild words, the passion drained out of him. His face set sullen and withdrawn. He got up and left without a word. Raedgar and I sat in the emptiness he left behind. Our son, I thought. Our only son, and we would lose him.

That night, when Raedgar and I lay in bed together, I asked him, "What is this about women? What does Hunred mean, women are part of what's wrong?"

Raedgar was silent. I pushed myself up onto my elbow so I could look at him.

"What is it?" I insisted.

"Well, monks are celibate."

"I know that."

He looked up at me and sighed. He pulled himself up and wrapped the blanket round him. He looked like a kind of monk himself.

"The Pope—the new Pope. Gregory."

"Yes. Pope Gregory."

"He believes that priests should also be celibate. He wants to forbid clerical marriage."

Clerical marriage. That was us. Raedgar was a priest, and I was married to him. The Pope wanted to forbid us!

"He can't," I said. "He'd have to forbid the whole Community. All of us."

"That's right. That's not going to happen. But that's why the bishop is so keen on his monks. He's going to start building a cloister for monks alongside the church. He wants to show the Pope that there is a monastic community at Durham."

"Why didn't you tell me this before?"

Raedgar said nothing.

"Why?"

He put his arm round me and drew me close to him.

"I don't know what it all means, Edith. For the Community. For us. I don't know. And now Hunred has got hold of it. They must be talking about it at Jarrow."

His arm tightened round me. He bent down and kissed my head.

"My dearest love."

Raedgar talked to the bishop. He talked to the other elders. It was agreed that Hunred would go to Jarrow for his novitiate, and then there would be a discussion with chapter. There was no reason why he should not take his place in the Community as a monk. If he would.

So Hunred left us. Though I wept to see him go, I was ashamed to find I felt relief as well. Mary had no such shame.

"Hurrah! That old cross-patch is gone. All he does is argue with Father."

The little girls came to play more often, and our hall was filled with their screams and giggles, their songs and games. It was true. We were all relieved.

CHAPTER 18

THE PERFUME OF ROSES

Durham, 1079

Hunred had hardly been gone a year when there were new troubles. Not for us alone, but for all Northumbria.

At first, when Walcher was appointed earl, the province was more settled. He did his best to make peace with the Northern lords. He set up a council of government, and invited Lord Ligulf, most powerful of the Northern lords, to sit on it. But soon the bishop's kinsmen, Gilbert and Levin, joined the council too. They had different ideas about governing the North. The year after Hunred left everyone could see trouble was coming.

That year, 1079, was one of those summers when warm days follow one on another and it feels as if they will never end, as if life will always be ease and brightness. I wanted it to go on for ever. I shut my ears to the rumours going round the town. When I went to visit Gudrun on those summer days, she was often outside in her garden with her herbs and flowers. She had a lovely garden, divided into four with a hedge all around for shelter and in one quarter of it she grew nothing but roses and gillyflowers. She had sweetbriar, but white and red roses too from Frankia, whose fragrance filled the air. One warm afternoon, when the perfume was at its height, we picked them, placing the petals in our baskets, and took them into the still room. We laid the rose petals on soft goose fat, layer on layer, so that their scent would soak into the fat, and then it would be done again, and again, with more and more petals, till it was saturated with the perfume. Then Gudrun would scrape it up into little jars and seal them with wax. She smelled of roses all winter long.

When we had emptied our baskets, I put my finger in the fat and smeared it on my wrist. I sniffed. It was fragrant already. It made me think of Lindisfarne and the perfume Raedgar had once bought me from a trader.

"How long is it?"

"How long is what?"

"Since Lindisfarne."

"What makes you think of that? It was just before Christmas. It was freezing. That's when my chilblains started."

"You were carrying Hild. Ten years ago."

"The way things are going we'll be back there again. That's what my brother says." She paused. "He says Northumbria is like tinder, waiting for a spark to set it alight. You know the latest thing I heard from him?"

I shook my head. I would sooner not have heard, but Gudrun was loyal to her brother and liked to vent her wrath on his behalf.

"About a man who held land from my father? A freeman, Oswin, his name was. Last month Gilbert's soldiers came riding by his farm. They'd been out hunting and caught nothing, so they went into one of Oswin's fields and started hunting down his sheep. They killed two of them and a lamb. When Oswin heard the commotion in the field he ran out to stop them. When he protested the soldier pulled his sword out and ran it straight through him. They made off with the sheep and left him lying."

"Dear God!"

"So Oswin's son swore he would have justice for his father's death. He took his petition to the bishop's court at Durham, asking wergild for his father and payment for his sheep. When he came into court Levin looked over the petition, tore it into pieces and threw it in the man's face. And Walcher tut tuts, says no no, we must hear the plea, but Levin takes not a scrap of notice of him. He and Gilbert are hand in glove."

I'd heard such stories before. Gilbert's soldiers rode around the countryside acting as they pleased, stealing, raping, even killing without check from their master. If men brought cases to court, Levin laughed in their faces. And Walcher's too. They held the whole province in contempt.

"Northumbria won't stand for it," Gudrun declared, pulling her shoulders back and tossing her head defiantly. For a moment I imagined her brother stood before me. "There'll be an uprising. There will."

The old fear tightened in my belly. I wanted to enjoy the smell of roses and sweet memories of Lindisfarne. But there was no escaping it. Even at home. Raedgar came home day after day with his own complaints. Levin was the villain for the Community. Walcher had appointed him as archdeacon over us. He was supposed to take care of the spiritual needs of the diocese in Walcher's place and to spread the word of Christ through the countryside. But Levin only left Durham to see what lands he might annex, what tithes he might increase. He took charge of the Community's estates and soon all our monies were flowing into his pocket. Raedgar grew hollow-eyed taking his complaints to Walcher but the thefts continued.

Was Gudrun right? Would there be an uprising? Surely, I thought, people had seen that King William would stop at nothing to crush rebellion. Had they forgotten the Harrying and the empty lands? Even suffering injustice was preferable to that.

In the autumn, when those summer days were long forgotten, there was a meeting of the council. Lord Ligulf and his retinue came riding through the gate to the bishop's palace. The bishop came out to greet him, but not Gilbert. Everyone knew that Ligulf and Gilbert were at loggerheads. As sheriff, it was Gilbert's duty to defend the province. But when King Malcolm of Scotland spent the summer rampaging along the border and as far down as Ligulf's estates on the Tyne, Gilbert did nothing. Why would he bother? So long as the Scots kept away from his Durham estates, they could do what they liked. His soldiers had been idle all summer and Ligulf was furious.

Once I had seen Lord Ligulf ride up to the palace I went home. Raedgar was a member of the council, and I would hear any news from him later. But hardly an hour later I heard Gudrun pulling open my door.

"Come quick!" she said. She grabbed my hand and pulled me along towards the castle where a little crowd had gathered.

"Listen!" she said. "You can hear everything!" The casements of the council room stood open and sure enough, the shouting going on inside could be heard halfway across Durham. I heard a Saxon voice first. Ligulf, I thought.

"Malcolm knows he's got nothing to fear from your skulking sheriff, Bishop! He'll be back after Christmas for more. You've a castle full of soldiers doing nothing!"

Walcher started to speak but soon we could hear Levin shouting back at Ligulf.

"Hold your peace, you whining cur! Get to your kennel and learn who's master here!"

"God damn you deep, Levin! May the fires of hell burn you for stealing from the Church! Let Gilbert answer for himself."

It went on with the insults growing fiercer and fouler till I turned away. I wanted to hear no more.

Fear gripped my heart. There would never be peace, I thought. Never. The memory of Lindisfarne came to me again, as sharp as if I stood there still. I thought of the months we had spent there after the flight from Durham; just the three of us, Raedgar, Hunred and me. I wished we had never left.

CHAPTER 19

Bishop Walcher

Jarrow, 1079

I hold 2 October as a special feast-day. My soul's birthday. It is the anniversary of the shipwreck when God saved me from the sea, and each year since I had marked it as a day especially to reflect on God's providence. Five years already! I had been a monk for four of them and now, since last summer, prior of Jarrow-Monkwearmouth monasteries.

I came to England looking for freedom. I found it where I least expected it; through losing everything. I thought it was a calamity. But the months I spent with Aldwin at Melrose showed me something different. He taught me the freedom of living with nothing, with no cares, no possessions. I learned to feel joy in the simplest things. That time was a bond between us, and sometimes I longed to return to Melrose as much as he did. But King Malcolm wasn't waiting to welcome us back, and I had to deal with the world again—the monasteries' estates, the building works and all the rest of it. Still, Melrose had changed me. I no longer felt driven as I once did, with ambition, with desire for power and possession. I had found a different kind of freedom.

So on that bright October day, I gave praise to God for my deliverance and set off to look at the first of the cloister arches that had been completed. I was at Monkwearmouth, where we had finally managed to clear the site and start to build. I prayed that this, our second monastery, might prosper

172

as Jarrow did. But before I could reach the cloister, I was called away to the gatehouse to receive a messenger.

It was Callum, Walcher's manservant, a dapper young man who loved to sport the bishop's colours. Usually he brought a message that I was wanted on such and such a day, and I would travel to Durham at my leisure. But that day brought different news. I was to attend upon the bishop without delay.

"And the abbot?" I asked. "Is he looked for? He is at Jarrow."

"Better you come alone. It will be more delay to fetch the abbot, and Lord Walcher requires you urgently. He has sent a horse for you."

I went to my cell and changed into travelling clothes. Once I was mounted, we set off at a teeth-rattling gallop. I shouted to Callum, 'What's amiss?" But he kept his mouth shut and shook his head. I clutched the pommel and took my mind off my shaken bones by puzzling over what might have caused this urgent summons.

Walcher often sent for us—Aldwin and I, or more often recently, just me. A friendship had grown up between us. He loved to talk to me about the latest books he'd had from Frankia or to hear about King Olaf's palace and his fireplaces. To tell the truth, it pleased me too. My rage with the Normans had cooled; in any case, Walcher was a Frank not a Norman. He came from Liege but had undertaken commissions for King William while the king was still Duke of Normandy. Walcher was ambitious, just as I had been. He wanted high office, whether in the Church or the state. When William offered him the Durham bishopric, he jumped at it. He must have had the means to pay for it too, though if he had known what awaited him, he might have kept his coins in his purse.

He had found, not the gentle water-meadows of Liege, but a wild and windswept northern town, beset by feuding warlords and the hostile Scots, where the Community of the Saint was not a monastic order but a fraternity of landowners.

"My dear fellow," he told me, "I was ready to leave within days. I'd had no idea! Nothing had been explained to me! But what could I do?

How could I tell King William? I would never have received another appointment!"

He loved to tell me of his trials—the barbarous Northern lords and their dreadful table manners, the priests of the Community who could hardly stutter through a sentence in Latin, the Saxon cellarer who brought him wine too sour to swallow. Yet for all that, when the Earl of Northumbria made the mistake of leading a revolt against William and lost his earldom, Walcher stepped up to buy it. He had a vision of himself as a great prince in a new kingdom of the north. But great men need great servants. Walcher sent for his kinsmen, Gilbert and Levin, to serve him, but they wanted to be lords too, not servants. They stirred up new feuds and enmities wherever they went. As the horse's hooves pounded beneath me, I felt certain they were the cause of this sudden summons.

We rode into Durham late in the afternoon. I bade farewell to Callum and went on alone to the bishop's hall, still aching from the ride. I could hear shouting. As I entered, I met Walcher's kinsman, Archdeacon Levin, on his way out. He was a pinch-faced, spiteful man who spent his time filching from the Church's revenues. Walcher was distraught. Tears were running down his face and he tore his bishop's hood from his head, screaming after Levin,

"This is the result of your folly! Of your evil plotting! You have destroyed us all!"

Levin passed me without a word.

"My lord bishop," I said. "What is amiss?"

He threw himself down onto a chair.

"It is the end, Thorgot! It is the end of everything I have tried to do. God knows I have tried to govern justly. All my work is undone! They will rise up against me!"

"My lord, what evil day is this?"

"You have not heard?"

I shook my head. "What, my lord?"

He leaned forward in the chair, holding his head and still racked with sobs. I had never seen him so distressed. I dreaded to hear what might have caused it.

"It is Levin's doing. It is his evil, evil tongue that has caused this. What kin is he of mine? He will destroy us all!"

There was wine on the table. I poured a cup and gave it to him.

"Come, my lord. May God be his judge. Take some wine, lord. Be comforted."

Slowly he became calm enough to tell me the story.

Ligulf, an earl of the Northumbrians, had insulted Levin in council. Levin, priest though he was, could find no forgiveness in his heart. With no word to Walcher he had gone to his sheriff, Gilbert, taunting him for a coward if he would not take revenge on Ligulf. Last night Gilbert had taken his men to Ligulf's hall, and they set it alight. Ligulf, his children and his household were asleep inside. They had all died, save for his wife who was away from home.

"Dear God," I said when he was done. "Dear God." I could find no other words. At once I understood Walcher's grief. So terrible, so barbarous an act, for what? To revenge some petty insult? It was beyond comprehension.

"It was murder, Thorgot. In cold blood."

"A mortal sin. And a folly beyond belief."

"They will never trust me again, these lords. They will rise up against me."

I saw then, beyond the horror of the deed itself, the worse horrors it might bring. Walcher must act, I realized. He must act at once.

"My lord, it is not your doing. Send out messengers, send them at once to every part of the earldom, to declare your abhorrence of this foul act. Tell them that your hand was not on it. Tell them you will dismiss Gilbert."

"Who will heed me, Thorgot?"

"Truly, my lord, I believe they will heed you. They know you as a just man. But you must act swiftly. And you must dismiss Gilbert."

Walcher was silent, rocking himself to and fro in the chair as he thought.

"I believe you are right. Dear God, I will do anything. Do you think it is enough to stay them from revenge?"

"You have been bishop to us for ten years and you are respected here. They will believe you. Gilbert is to blame. And Levin. They must be held to account."

"Help me, Thorgot. Help me write something."

I stayed with him that night and the next. He sent for Raedgar, the dean of the Community, to help us. He too was horrified by the deed and what might come of it. He joined with me to persuade Walcher to rid himself of his evil kinsmen.

Before I returned to Jarrow we had drawn up a declaration. Walcher sent messengers out far and wide. He sent letters to Ligulf's widow offering her money and new lands to make reparation for her losses. For the next few weeks, we held our breath, praying for peace. The Christmas feast came and went. Walcher's messengers went to and fro with the leaders of the Northumbrians and Ligulf's kin to negotiate terms for reconciliation. Walcher continued to swear that he had had no knowledge of Gilbert's plan, and that he was willing to submit to the ecclesiastical judgement of the Pope. But still he would not—dared not—dismiss Gilbert.

The last time I saw him was at the Easter feast. Aldwin and I were invited together. We found Walcher's hall filled with Gilbert's henchmen and Gilbert sprawled across the table, half-wasted even before the feast began. Levin sat on the other side of Walcher, shouting across him to Gilbert. I understood then that Walcher was a weak man. His ambition was his undoing. If he had been satisfied with his bishopric, all might have been well. But he could not manage the earldom. Though Gilbert and Levin had chosen to lie low for a time, they ruled him still.

Aldwin and I found a seat with Dean Raedgar, far down at the bottom of the table. He was happy to see us and greeted Aldwin warmly. There was a sympathy between them. They were both ascetic, other-worldly men who were ill at ease at the banqueting table.

"Nothing has changed, then," I said to Raedgar. He looked at me, torn between his loyalty to the bishop and the truth.

"No," he said. "Not yet." He paused and I saw he had more to tell us. "But there is to be a meeting between Lord Walcher and Ligulf's kin at Gateshead, on the border between the bishopric and the earldom. To negotiate terms." He paused and swallowed. "To make peace."

"What of Gilbert and Levin?"

"They will be part of Lord Walcher's retinue."

"Gilbert and Levin? At Gateshead? Ligulf's kin will never sit down with them!"

Raedgar's face took on a particular look of unease. I was familiar with it in Aldwin too. In his heart he knew what I said to be true, but he felt it wrong to pass judgement. Like Aldwin, he wanted to think the best of men. Even when all the evidence was against them. Aldwin would say that blessed were the peacemakers and I held my tongue. But I couldn't silence the voice within me crying out that this was a trap. I felt an urge to run to Walcher's side and shout in his ear, "Beware! Beware!" But he was like a puppet now, his strings pulled by hands that would soon have silenced me.

The meeting at Gateshead was to be held the day before the ides of May, on the 14th. As the day drew close so my fears grew. I tried to convince Aldwin but he made light of them.

"They are meeting in the church, Thorgot. St Mary's Church. It's hallowed ground and mortal sin to profane it. Ligulf's kinsmen would not have agreed to such a meeting-place if they meant him ill."

His eyes were so clear, so innocent. I couldn't gainsay him. Instead, when I was next at Durham, I looked for Callum, Walcher's man. We knew each other well enough for honesty.

"I fear for your lord at Gateshead," I told him. "Maybe it's folly, but I have a favour to beg of you."

He looked at me, surprised.

"Go with him, even if he doesn't ask for you. When the meeting's done, tell Lord Walcher we have begged him to come and visit us on his return. If he will not come, come yourself and bring us the news of the day."

I saw in his face that he would need a coin or two to undertake my mission. I had resorted to the alms box and come prepared; the deal was struck. At least I would not be kept waiting for days wondering what might have passed between the bishop and his enemies. And at worst, Callum had some warning.

The day dawned fair. The sun rose into a cloudless sky and even the birds singing in the trees seemed to be mocking my fears. But I was restless, gabbling through the morning offices and unable to attend to the simplest task. In the afternoon I went out and walked down to the Don, the little river that flowed past the monastery and out into the Tyne. There was a jetty at the side where supplies for the monastery could be offloaded. When I drew near, I saw Callum tying up his boat to a stanchion. He had come.

He hauled himself up onto the jetty and at once fell forward on his face. He didn't need to speak for me to know his news. His bright tunic was ripped and filthy with dirt and blood. Half the sleeve of his shirt was torn away and as he lay there on the jetty his body shook and trembled. I knelt close, took hold of his shoulders and turned him round till his head and shoulders were resting on my knees.

"You're safe now. You're safe," I told him. Still his body shook. He was too shocked to speak. After a while his eyes opened, staring as if at nothing. Then he saw my face leaning over him and recognized me. Suddenly the words poured out.

"They have killed him! They have killed them all, Master Thorgot! Gilbert, Levin, all their men. They fell on them. I fled into a house and hid myself. There was nothing I could do. No-one could help him. There were so many!"

"They've killed the bishop? Why wasn't he protected?"

"They tricked him. They bid him stay inside the church with only Gilbert and Levin and one or two others. When they had killed the soldiers outside, they set fire to the church; it burned up like a blazing torch, and he was forced to come out."

"What then?"

"He cried out to them for mercy, to spare him, but they ran him through with their swords, stabbing at him till he was slain twenty times over. I ran from my hiding place down to the boat and one came after me with his knife, he tried to drag me down, but I pulled away. I pulled away . . . ."

He started to weep, and I would have wept with him. But my heart was frozen stiff with horror. And with guilt. I had known—and I had done nothing. I had let myself be put off with reasons and excuses and now my friend, my bishop, had met a most horrible death. The shame was mine alone. I would never be able to atone for it. I bowed my head till it rested on his and gave myself up to despair.

At that dark moment, a stillness came upon me. I seemed to be both present on the jetty, with Callum's tears running wet on my knees, and yet removed. I felt as if I were somehow with Walcher, as if his spirit was close. He was asking something of me. A realization came to my mind. We couldn't leave him to rot in a field. Whatever the danger, we had to fetch back his body and give him burial. They couldn't deny us that. It would be my last act of friendship.

My grief and guilt fell away from me. I was conscious only of what I needed to do. I stood up and shouted to two brothers working in the garden. I asked them to look after Callum while I went in search of the abbot. Before I left, Callum caught at my hand.

"They will march on Durham tomorrow. They mean to burn down the castle and drive the Normans out."

I stared at him, trying to grasp what he was saying. I would understand it later. For now, I bent down over him and clasped his hands.

"These men will look after you, Callum. God's blessings on you for what you have done."

✛

Aldwin was shattered by what had happened. He was not a stranger to violence; he had lived through the Conquest as we all had. But it was more frightful than the loss of a friend or the savagery of his murder. The attack profaned God himself. His servant had been slaughtered upon hallowed ground in violation of the deepest oaths. Aldwin could not believe that such a thing was possible. It overwhelmed him. He had only one thought: to summon all the brothers to the church to beg for God's mercy.

"Father," I said, "I have a task to do for Walcher before I join you. I have to bring back his body for burial. I'm going to take a boat for him to Gateshead." I saw he could hardly take in what I was saying but there was no time to debate it. We would have to get there before nightfall.

I sought out three brothers to help me, younger men who were good oarsmen and strong enough to help bear Walcher's body: Hunred, the dean's son, Cadmon, my companion from the novitiate, and Edward, a monk newly come to us from York. We took the lightest boat we could find at the mooring and slipped out into the Don. The day had clouded, and a light drizzle dampened our clothes. I scarcely heeded it. I was still half in that inward state that had overtaken me on the jetty. When the stream joined the Tyne, the current pulled us downstream at first, forcing us to bend down over the oars and stretch in earnest. It took us a couple of hours pulling up the fast water to cover the distance to Gateshead and the effort of it brought me back into myself. As we drew close, I could smell smoke drifting off the land. We pulled over to the shore and tied up on the riverbank below the village. Then we clambered up over the bank. Waiting for us there was a vision of hell.

The villagers had fled; there was not a soul to be seen. The huts still stood but the church was burned almost to the ground, only the corner posts were smouldering still. The ground all about was scorched and black. I saw one, then two bodies lying close to the bank, sprawled out and shocking white in the wet greyness of the afternoon. They had been stripped of anything of value—clothes, weapons, money. Dark wisps of smoke blew here and there in the wind and the rain started to fall more heavily. There was no sound save for a pair of buzzards screeching overhead. Already crows were pecking at other bodies near the church. Lord have mercy, I said to myself, again and again.

I had thought it would be an easy task to find Walcher in his bishop's cope, but I realized they must have stripped his body too in a final act of sacrilege. There were only nameless corpses, the flesh pale but for the blood darkening on their wounds. We started to walk among the dead, searching for Walcher. He had been murdered outside the church, Callum had told me, but how were we to distinguish him? If a body was lying prone, we gently turned it so that we could see the face. Once a man groaned when we turned him. We tried to raise him, but he gasped and fell back, head lolling.

At last one of the brothers called me to a body lying by the well. Why had they dragged him there? Had they meant to throw him in it? The body was so mutilated it was impossible to tell if it were him. There was blood from wounds all over it, and the cheeks and lips were slashed. But I knew his hair, his dark Frankish hair. I knelt down and prised open the eyelids. Brown eyes. Walcher's eyes. They stared back at me lifelessly. Alas for my friend! Alas for the doom that brought him here! I closed his eyes and kissed him.

When we had got the body ashore at Jarrow, we took it first to the infirmary. There was no time to wash it properly. We made him as decent as we could and covered the body with coarse cloth. Then we laid him on a stretcher that was used to bring up sacks of grain, with a sturdy pole at either side. I looked at my companions. Darkness was closing in on us and I could see only the gleam of their eyes.

"Tomorrow the rebels will attack Durham. We need to get the Lord Bishop's body there before dawn. We'll go on foot to Monkwearmouth and carry it between us on the stretcher. Then we'll take it by boat up the Wear to Durham."

I paused. "It'll be a hard journey. None of us will sleep tonight. You've given the bishop faithful service already. There's no shame in letting other brothers take your place." I waited. No-one spoke.

"God bless you all. May he give us strength."

Cadmon spoke up.

"We should send word ahead to Monkwearmouth, so they can ready a boat for us."

"Yes. And let's eat something before we leave."

We set off at last after nightfall. The track between the two monasteries was familiar to us all but we found new stones and ruts to trip over. Every stumble sent the body lurching to the side of the stretcher, once half toppling out. We slowed our pace, and Cadmon, the fittest of us, took one of the front poles and called a marching count for us. We started to move more smoothly, but the weight of the pole pressed painfully into each man's shoulders. We should have brought pads, we muttered to each other. We stopped, laid down the stretcher and swung our arms to loosen the pain. I ripped off the hood of my habit and folded it into a pad. We changed over sides, Cadmon counted us in, and we swung the stretcher back up onto our shoulders. So it went on, hour upon hour. We couldn't walk more than a mile without resting, and as we grew more and more fatigued, we stopped more often. I was conscious of nothing but the pain in my shoulders and the visionless dark of the night. How strange is this, I thought, that I who fled my country to escape the Normans, who swore perpetual hatred of all their kin, should be risking my life to carry home a Norman bishop.

By the time we reached Monkwearmouth, I was in a kind of trance of pain and exhaustion. The relief of laying down the stretcher for the last time was intense. I could scarcely stop myself from lying down beside it, but the brothers were ready for us, putting bowls of hot soup into our hands. I supped it down and felt the warmth through my innards. When I had eaten my fill I knew I could continue. Then Cadmon squatted down beside me.

"There are two fresh men to take the oars, Prior."

"Good. You stay, then. You and Edward. I must go on. Since Hunred is the dean's son, he should come with me."

Cadmon nodded. When all was made ready, Hunred and I got in beside the oarsmen with the body between us. I felt Walcher close to me, as if he were alive and we were taking some excursion on the river. We're going home, I told him. My dear friend. Within five minutes of pushing out into the river fatigue overcame me. I slumped across the bench and slept beside him.

CHAPTER 20

THE SIEGE

Durham, 1079

When the intelligence of the bishop's death reached the brethren of the monastery of Jarrow, they embarked in a little boat and sailed to the spot and having discovered the corpse of the bishop (which they had difficulty in recognizing, in consequence of the abundance of the wounds by which it had been disfigured) they placed it, stripped as it was of every covering, within their vessel, and they carried it back with great grief to their monastery; it was conveyed from there to Durham where it was interred with a funeral less honourable than became a bishop; for immediately after this abominable slaughter, his murderers had come thither and were raging up and down the city, intending to storm the castle and put to death such of the bishop's retainers as still survived.

Simeon's "History of the Church of Durham", Chapter LIX

It was an hour or so after dawn. Raedgar was gone to the church to say Prime. Mary was still abed, and I was knelt at the hearth coaxing the embers back to life. Suddenly, without a knock or greeting, the door was pushed open and a man staggered inside. The dawn light was behind him and for a moment I couldn't tell who it was. Then I realized.

"Hunred!" I got to my feet and ran over to the door.

"Mother," he said, and stumbled into my arms. He was head and shoulders taller than me; I could scarcely bear his weight. His habit was rough against my face and his bony ribs stuck into my breast. I half-carried him over to the table and set him down at the end of the bench. He slumped forward, head in his arms. I stared at him in amazement. My son, I thought. My dearest, dearest son. All the love I had ever felt for him rose up in me, and with it as much bewilderment.

At that moment Mary came into the hall, rubbing the sleep out of her eyes.

"Who is it?"

"It's Hunred."

She ran forward and shook his shoulder. He didn't stir. She stared at me.

"What's the matter with him? Why's he here?"

"I don't know. He just came in." I looked over and saw another man standing at the threshold. Fear tightened me.

"Who are you?" I called out to him. He stepped closer and gave me a little bow.

"My name is Thorgot, Mistress. If I might sit down . . . ."

At that moment the bells started ringing. First the church bells, then the heavy tolling of the single bell at the castle. The air was suddenly shaking with the clamour. Raedgar came breathless into the hall.

"Prior Thorgot!" He clasped the man by the hand. "Hunred is with you?" The man nodded. "They're taking the body to the church."

Was I sleeping still? I was utterly bewildered. Mary started crying and ran over to me. As I held her close to me, I tried to gather my wits. Bells. All the bells. There must be an attack. An attack, and the bishop is from home with half his retinue.

It was only later that I learned he was not.

It was two hours or more before we heard the first shouts of the Northumbrian forces. By then Hunred and Prior Thorgot were so sound asleep that all the armies of King William might have marched through the house and not roused them. But as soon as the shouts started Mary caught my arm, her eyes starting out of her face.

"What will they do? What will they do to us if they get in?"

"Their quarrel's not with us. It's with the Normans."

"How will they know we're not Normans?"

In spite of my fear I laughed at her. "You, a Norman?" I gave her fair pigtails a little tug. "When did we see a Norman like this?"

I made my mind up.

"We'll go to the church. Father's there. Everyone'll be there."

"What about Hunred?"

"Alun and the other servants will stay."

"Will we be safe in the church?"

"Yes. The church is hallowed ground. They won't touch us there."

I knew I lied. Hadn't they burned down the church at Gateshead with the bishop and his men within? Raedgar had tried to reassure me: they were our countrymen. They would respect the shrine. I would have liked to believe him. But I didn't. I trusted no-one. What did it matter what side you were on, whether you were born Saxon or Norman? The church was ruled by Normans, and we were their servants. That was enough. There were treasures to carry off and houses to loot. And women to take. Terror strung me tight.

The attack raged on beyond the walls all morning, but we saw nothing of it. Everyone was in the church; the Community and townspeople too, who had come for sanctuary. We sang psalms and hymns and listened to Raedgar and the other priests praying for deliverance. Usually it was a consolation to me to stand in the church, in the stillness of it, feeling the presence of the Saint close at hand. But that was all lost in the press of people. It was so crowded, so close and stuffy. The fear in the air felt strong enough to touch. I felt as if I was breathing in an infection. Horrible imaginings took hold of me: of the church at Gateshead burning, being swallowed in a sea of red fire. I felt the flames leaping around me, imagined the bishop choking with smoke and fleeing to the waiting swords. I could hardly breathe. What if they set fire to our church, with all of us inside it? What horror there would be of screaming and pushing . . . . "No!" I said aloud. "No! No!" People turned to stare at me. I pulled my shawl further down over my head. I bent down to Mary.

"I'm going back to see to Hunred. You go and stand with Hild and her family."

She brightened up at that and let go of my hand. I waited till she reached them, Gudrun looked over to me and nodded. I pushed my way through the crowd and went out into the daylight. I stood for several minutes, just breathing the freshness of the air, calming myself. I listened. There were cries still from the direction of the castle, but it all seemed quiet at our end of the bailey. I looked around, up and down. There was no-one about. I slipped out onto the path. I made myself walk slowly. I was almost home when a sudden movement caught my eye. Our house was inside the bailey now, but the huge palisade of timber that formed the bailey wall stood only a score of yards from our house. I saw a man had clambered somehow to the top. A helmet half-covered his head, but I could see he was a young man, maybe Hunred's age. He caught sight of me, grinned and flourished his sword. He was just a lad, I realized. No fearsome soldier. He jumped down, and another head appeared above the bailey. They must have made a ladder, I thought.

The next minute there was a sound of hooves on the ground. Two soldiers from the garrison came galloping at full speed alongside the bailey wall. The front one set his horse straight at the young man. It knocked him over and the second one trampled him. The soldiers wheeled their horses round; one jumped off and ran over to where the lad lay writhing on the ground. He drove his sword into him, drawing it out red with blood. Then he was back on his horse and riding off with his companion. The young man lay still, his blood soaking into the earth.

I stood, frozen, in front of it. I couldn't move. But when the lad was dead, I found my wits and ran as fast as I might to the house. I shoved open the door. As soon as I was inside the sobs started; I caught hold of one of the house posts to hold myself upright. I could feel nothing but steel and blood and death.

How long I stood there sobbing I couldn't say. After a time, I knew that someone stood near me. I looked up.

"Mistress Edith."

It was the prior. He was standing in front of me, quite close, and he was holding his hands out towards me. I was too distraught to think if this was seemly. All I knew was that it was comfort. I gave him my hands, and he clasped them in his own. They were strong and warm. He held them tight till I had swallowed the last of my sobs. I looked up at him. I had thought him almost ugly, with his wide nose and pale Norse hair. But when I looked at him then I saw nothing but kindness in his face. He was looking directly at me. I looked back into his eyes and felt some of the tightness leave me.

So it was that I first truly met Thorgot. He sat me down, persuaded me to take some wine and took some himself.

"Don't be afraid," he said. "They won't take the castle. They're just a war-band; they're wild to kill Normans but they haven't the men. If they'd got here at night, without warning, and got through the gates, they might have stood a chance, but even then they wouldn't have got up the motte. Don't worry. There'll be no madmen running amok today."

It was hard to get it out, but I told him what I had seen, the young lad and the soldiers.

"Horrible," he said. "Horrible. May God have mercy on him and rest his soul. These young lads don't realize what they're up against." He looked at me.

"Did he remind you of Hunred?"

It was that, I realized. The tears started to rise again in my eyes. It could have been Hunred.

"He's safe. He's sleeping still. He's shown great strength and courage." I drew a deep breath.

"Are you not wearied still, Prior?"

"Me? Ah, I'm used to running away."

"Running away?"

"Not only once. But I'll tell you about the first time." He leaned forward and started to tell me the story of his escape from Lincoln. He told it in so light and funny a way that I forgot about the attack, forgot my sorrows and wanted only to find out if he would reach the court of Norway. When his tale ended, I saw that Hunred was standing, listening too. What would he think, I wondered, of the prior sitting at table with his mother?

"Were you the king's chaplain, Father?" he asked. Before Thorgot could answer the door was open and Mary ran in.

"It's over!" she shouted. "Gudrun says our prayers have been heard! They couldn't get in! And I didn't have any breakfast, and I'm really, really hungry!"

Then Raedgar was there, and a deacon from the church, and Alun and the servants wanting to know if all was well, and the hall was full of noise and bustle. Raedgar seemed half-dazed. I went to him and took his arm.

"Is it true? Are we safe?" He looked down at me and sighed.

"Yes, for now," he said. "They have withdrawn and thank God that we are spared. But we can't rejoice. They are setting up camp in the town and around. They mean to lay siege."

At once I felt new fears. Did we have enough food? How long could we hold out? I found myself looking at Thorgot. He shook his head.

"I don't think the siege will last long," he said. "A few days. A week maybe. The garrison will find a way to get word to York to send up more troops from there."

Raedgar stared at him as if struggling to understand his words. At last he nodded. "It may be so." He turned away, his shoulders sunk with weariness. "God willing, we will bury the bishop tomorrow."

Bishop Walcher was laid to rest, not in the fine tomb he would have liked but in a simple plot in the cemetery beside the church, with as much ceremony as we could muster. The monks had washed the body and laid him out in his bishop's robes in a rough wooden coffin made by the carpenter from the castle. We couldn't wait for better. His face was covered with a linen cloth to hide his wounds. Once the Mass was over the lid was closed and we followed the coffin out into the cemetery. It was a blustery day with a mad spring wind that whipped up the dirt and small stones from the grave and sent them flying into our faces. Gilbert's deputy and a score of Walcher's Norman retinue came to see the earl-bishop buried, standing aside from us with grim faces. They knew, as we all did, what was likely to follow. Raedgar spoke the prayers in Latin for their sake, though most of them understood it as little as English:

> *"O Lord God most holy, O Lord most mighty, O holy and most*
> *merciful Saviour, deliver us not into the bitter pains of eternal death.*
> *Thou knowest, Lord, the secrets of our hearts; shut not thy*
> *merciful ears to our prayer; but spare us, Lord most holy, thou most*
> *worthy Judge eternal, suffer us not, at our last hour, for any pains*
> *of death, to fall from thee."*

His last hour, I thought. God shield us from such an hour. I prayed God had held him as he fled the flames.

When the prayers were done, we strewed his coffin with rosemary and thyme and flowering currant before the dirt was piled upon him. The wind caught the posies and swept them here and there as if they were loath to lie on him. Prior Thorgot caught hold of one and held it to his heart. I saw there were tears on his cheeks. I felt shame then, that I had none to shed for the bishop, or no more than I would have shed for any man who had met so cruel a death. I had hardly known Walcher. I had seen him in the church on feast days in his robes and mitre, but he did not invite the women of the Community to his palace. Did Raedgar grieve, I wondered, watching him. Yes, but it was more than grief. The shock of Walcher's murder had aged him overnight. He looked old suddenly. His face was grey, and he stumbled over the words as he prayed. Now, with the bishop gone, and Levin the archdeacon too, everything fell on his shoulders. Dear God, I prayed, St Cuthbert, preserve us.

After the funeral, I saw little of Hunred. He and Prior Thorgot, together with the other two monks who had brought the bishop's body, moved into the guesthouse. The Community's liturgy differs from the Benedictine hours, so they kept separate devotions. But at night they came for their meal. We ate only once a day during the siege, to save food. I needed little. It was a greater joy to me to have my son at my table again, to let him have my portion and watch him wolfing it down as he always had. Monastic life hadn't lessened his appetite. He kept silent during the meal, as the other two monks did. Not Prior Thorgot. He talked like any ordinary person at table, complimenting me on the food, asking Raedgar about his day. Mary took a liking to him and brought him her stitching to admire.

"Beautiful!" he said. "What a neat hand you have! And the colours! So beautiful!" She was pink with pleasure. At the end of the meal, when we were trying not to think about how hungry we still were, he would tell a tale of the Norse or sing a ballad to lift our spirits. What a voice he had! We'd never heard such singing in our hall, and while he sang, all thoughts about the siege, about the Normans, all the daily dread went from our minds. He was a welcome guest indeed, and far from what I had expected. There was a fearlessness about him that made light of the dark days.

On the afternoon of the second day I was kneading dough for the evening meal when Hunred came in. My heart lifted. He had come to see me!

"Come and keep me company while I get the kneading done."

He came over and sat on a stool by me while I pushed and pulled at the dough. His tall young body seemed too big for the stool. He fidgeted about, trying to tuck his legs in like a proper monk.

"Tell me how you are. How is it going for you at Jarrow?"

He didn't answer. I looked up at him. There was the old cloud on his forehead, darkening the smooth youthfulness of his skin.

"I wanted to talk to you, Mother."

"Yes."

"About the prior. Prior Thorgot."

"What a good man he is, Hunred. And he thinks very well of you."

"That's not important." He hesitated. "What I wanted to say—you know, our life at the monastery is not like this. We don't talk at table. The prior doesn't talk at table, not usually. We observe the Rule. It's only here, you know, because there are no rules here."

"It sounds very strict."

"It is strict. But Prior Thorgot . . . he is a good prior, but he is, well, more worldly. He became a monk later in his life, he lived at court in Norway before that. You heard all that. He is close to the abbot, it's true, but the abbot is quite different. I wanted you to understand that. The abbot wouldn't speak at table or sit with women. He wouldn't. I know he wouldn't."

"Prior Thorgot wants to put us at our ease. It's good manners, that's all."

Hunred scowled. What a Pharisee he is, I thought. Everything must be done by the rules, by the book. He was blind to Thorgot's virtues.

"The abbot might not like to hear you criticizing your superiors," I added, maliciously.

"I'm not criticizing him. I'm explaining. I want you to understand how our life is."

"I understand. Prior Thorgot says you have great strength and courage."

He reddened and bowed his head.

"I'm very proud of you," I said. It was more than he could bear. He jumped up from his stool and was gone.

Strange to say, in spite of the dread that was constantly with us, the siege was a kind of respite to me. Life became simple. While it lasted, there was no future. All we could do was live from day to day, suspended in time. Hunred was near me, whether he liked it or not.

Little seemed to happen. We waited for new attacks, but they never came. Soldiers on horseback patrolled the bailey wall constantly till I grew used to the sound of hooves pounding past and the men shouting to each other and no longer flinched every time they passed. There was a constant coming and going of men at the castle end of the bailey, changing guard, patrolling, bringing up supplies from the bishop's storehouses. The rebels would have a long wait before they were emptied, I thought. What would they be eating? Everything they could find in the streets and houses of the town, I supposed. Whose food would run out first?

One of those siege mornings I was sat spinning to pass the time while Mary worked at her stitching. I looked up to see Prior Thorgot standing at the door, waiting for permission to enter.

"Look!" said Mary. "It's Prior Thorgot!"

"Come in, Prior," I called out to him.

He came over with a piece of cloth in his hand.

"You'll scold me for this," he said. "When we were carrying the stretcher over to Monkwearmouth the pole cut so sharp into my shoulder that I tore off my hood to make a pad for it to rest on."

He held out the cloth. I saw for the first time that his habit was ripped around the neck.

"You tore it off?" cried Mary.

"I did. And now I have a cold head as a penance."

I went over to him to have a look.

"The cloth is quite frayed," I said. "We may have to take it back, and then it may pull. It won't fit as well."

He shrugged. "If you're willing to do it . . . "

"We'll try. But you'll have to take it off." I looked at Mary. "We can't stitch with you inside!" and Mary broke into giggles.

I looked in the closet and found him a robe of Raedgar's. He went off to change, and when he returned we both laughed. The prior was a stocky, broad-chested man, nothing like tall, lean Raedgar. The robes hung strangely on him, too long and too tight.

"You look funny in father's clothes," said Mary, and Prior Thorgot looked down at himself and gave a great roar of laughter. How merry it was! How long since we had laughed like that. Nor did he leave us to get on with our task. He sat with us while we worked at the habit, Mary on one side of the hood, me on the other. He told us about the monastery and the monks, and how every monk had a different story and what had brought them there, and what jobs Hunred had to do, till it no longer seemed so strange and distant a place.

At last we were done, and he went off to change. When he came back in his habit, with the hood up over his head, Mary and I burst out laughing all over again. We had worked a side each, and I had taken back the cloth on my side further than Mary had done, so the hood was lopsided. It gave him such a raffish air that I couldn't imagine him standing soberly before his novices. I went over and gave the hood a sharp tug.

"Aargh!" he cried out in protest.

"You'll need to pull it like that, whenever you put it up. Otherwise it looks . . . strange."

"Funny!" said Mary. He grinned at us both.

"It'll cure me of vanity. God bless you both for my warm ears!"

Then he was gone, and the hall seemed emptier.

"I like Prior Thorgot," said Mary.

When the news came a few days later that the rebels had struck camp and gone back north, I should have rejoiced with all my heart and given thanks to God, and so I did. But there was fear in my heart as well as thanksgiving. While the siege had lasted, we lived without thought of the future. But once it was over, we had to face what lay in store for us. Of course, we needed a new bishop. But before that the North would have to face King William's vengeance. We knew him to be pitiless and unyielding. After the massacre ten years ago, it had been many months before he unleashed his revenge. Now his power was so much greater, his armies stronger. There was no doubt, no question. There would be war, and soon.

Raedgar and I didn't speak of it. I had known too much of war to heed his reassurances, and I could see for myself what would happen. Just as they had at York, the rebels would disband and slip away into the hills. William's armies were too strong; they wouldn't fight them. Thwarted of their prey, the Normans would lay their lands waste, just as they had done before. It would be the innocent who would suffer. It always was.

The garrison were cautious at first, fearing a ruse on the rebels' part. Patrols were sent out into the town and then further, over the bridge and out into the countryside. After a couple of days, they were content to believe them gone. Townspeople who had taken refuge in the bailey went back to see what destruction had been done to their homes. As soon as the gates were opened, Hunred was eager to be gone, back to his beloved abbot and his rules. But Prior Thorgot was in less of a hurry.

"We have to travel north. The rebels won't be in any hurry. We don't want to run into trouble."

But at last, he judged it time to leave. When he came to say his farewells Mary and I were ready for him.

"We don't want you to remember us for a crooked hood," I told him. "We have gifts for you!"

For once, I had surprised him. He looked at us, his head on one side, unsure. Mary gave him a little keepsake she had stitched for him in different colours.

"Why, Mary! Is it for me?"

"Yes!" she looked up at him, delighted with herself. He bent down and kissed her head.

"What clever fingers you have! I shall keep it always in my habit." He showed her the pocket in the side. Then it was my turn to make my gift.

"It is a little marker to keep place in your books."

I had gone to Raedgar's desk and found a slip of parchment cut from a document. There was just room to copy a verse from the Magnificat on it. It was so long since I had used pen and ink that I feared to blot it, but I made no mistakes. When I was done I traced a little pattern round it in ochre that I found in the back of the cupboard. It was a pretty little thing. What pleasure it had given me to write again!

When Thorgot saw the marker, his expression changed. For a moment he struggled to find words.

"Mistress Edith! You are a scribe!"

"I am the scribe, and Mary is the seamstress. She loves the needle better than the pen, don't you?" I squeezed her hand, but she pulled away from me to stand beside Thorgot.

"Will you come back and see us again, Father Prior?" she said, round-eyed, gazing up at him.

"Well—you've taken me by surprise. Look—I'm empty-handed! I will have to return with gifts for you!"

"We liked all your stories," she said. "And the songs."

"We did," I said. "And your advice and counsel too."

Then Raedgar came to tell him that the boat was ready and the monks were waiting on him. We followed him down to the jetty to bid farewell. Although Hunred shrank away from me in case I should kiss him in front of his fellow brothers, Prior Thorgot looked at me as if he would have been happy to take his place. They unhitched the rope, pushed off from the jetty and took up the oars. I could have wept to see them go. For all Hunred's surliness I knew he loved me, even if he didn't know that himself. And Thorgot's company had been like a spark of light in the darkness that surrounded us.

CHAPTER 21

MAGNIFICAT

Jarrow, 1079

*As soon as the intelligence of this transaction (the murder of Bishop
Walcher and the siege at Durham) was circulated, Odo, bishop of
Bayeux, who was second only to the king, and many of the chief
nobles of the kingdom, came to Durham, with a large body of troops,
and, in revenging the bishop's death, they reduced nearly the whole
land to a wilderness. The miserable inhabitants who, trusting in
their innocence, had remained in their homes, were either beheaded
as criminals, or mutilated by the loss of some of their members. False
accusations were brought against some of them, in order that they
might purchase their safety and their life by money.*
Simeon's "History of the Church of Durham", Chapter LIX

When we returned to Jarrow I felt as if we had been away for months,
though it was scarcely three weeks. Three weeks! It had turned my life
upside down. We found Aldwin and the brothers grieving Walcher's
murder, and so indeed was I, and yet I found myself unaccountably
light-hearted.

It was days before understanding started to come to me. I was working
on the repair of a wall, chipping away at a fresh block of stone that needed
to be fitted in. It started to rain and I pulled up my hood. At once I was

transported back to the dean's house at Durham. I felt again Edith's hand, tugging my crooked hood sideways. I heard her laugh and saw the little girl beside her. I found myself smiling at the memory. My heart lifted and I whistled a little tune under my breath as I worked.

I went inside to wash before the office. As I stood at the washstand and ran the water over my hands, I said to myself, "Edith". What a beautiful name it was! I said it softly again, letting it linger in my mouth. What sweet feelings it evoked in me! As quickly as I felt them, I reproved myself for daydreaming and hurried away into the church. But not the offices, nor the holy Mass itself, could stop the images that kept rising in my mind. I started to recall every meeting I had had with her, over and over, till each scene became jewel-like in my memory.

Then, stronger than such pleasant thoughts and recollections, I found that I wanted urgently to see her again, though I couldn't explain why. I felt she must need me. Even, that I had abandoned her. But why? Dean Raedgar was with her, after all. There was no reason to return to Durham. I had only just got back, and there was no Bishop Walcher to visit now. I was forced, at last, to admit it to myself. I am in love with Edith. Once made, the admission seemed to throw fuel on the fire. I loved her! I wanted more than anything to be with her again, and the longing was worse than bodily pain. I am shamed to confess it, but when I prayed to the Holy Mother of God, it was Edith's image that I saw. Her sweet, pale face, her tender lips, her eyes full of sorrows. I often pictured her as she stood when she was spinning, so straight and slender, her distaff held out before her and the spindle bobbing, the long blue veil of her headdress hanging down her back, so plainly dressed and yet with such grace.

I became absent-minded and found myself forgetting ordinary duties. Aldwin noticed.

"You're not yourself, Thorgot. Do you want to speak of it?"

"No—no. It's . . . I'm unsettled still, from Durham."

He thought I meant all the horrors I had seen, of Walcher's murder, of the siege. I let him think it. It was the first time I had ever concealed something from him. I was filled with guilt at deceiving him—but if he knew, he would forbid me from seeing her. He would keep me from Durham. I couldn't bear it.

I reproached myself, indeed, that Edith filled my thoughts when I should have been mourning my friend. But I knew Walcher would have understood. He was a man of the world. He would have asked me, my dear fellow, are you in love? Who is she? And would have been agog to know every detail and to plague me with taunts and teasing.

I was a man of the world too. Perhaps, I thought, if I had been a monk from my youth I wouldn't be troubled by such torments, or I would have learned to put them from me. But I had lived at court for years and Olaf loved women. There were always beautiful women around him and they didn't disdain me, his favourite, either. I had often been half in love with one pretty face or another and I had known the pleasures of the bedchamber. But I had never felt love like this. It seemed to me a holy love, different to the lusts I had known before. And she was lettered, a cultured woman who read Latin, whose gift to me had been written in her own hand. I kept her bookmark safe inside my habit, and I read it a dozen times a day.

> *"My soul doth magnify the Lord, my heart gives thanks to God my Saviour."*

So does my heart, I thought, but for Edith. Sacrilege was no stranger to me.

I watched Hunred as he stood in church, trying to find her features in him. There was, still, some softness in his cheek, some light in his eye that spoke of her. But he was so full of his youthful self-righteousness that it drove out the semblance and I would drop my gaze, disappointed.

In my calmer moments I knew there was nothing to be done, that I must endure it, that I must allow these feelings, pure and precious though they seemed to me, to burn through me till they were exhausted for want of fuel. I must not see her again. I could not force myself to banish her from my thoughts, but I would not allow myself to make stratagems that might take me back to Durham.

You will wonder at me, that I could have been so taken up with such a passion when we stood in the very shadow of war. How could I have been blind to the horror that was about to be unleashed upon us?

God forbid that you should ever find yourself standing in my shoes at such a time, but if you do you might discover, as I did, that the heart is stronger than the sword. I believe my love for Edith was what sustained me through what was to follow, when the full fury of King William and his myrmidons fell upon us. Aldwin's transcendent faith, his deep love of Christ, was that sustaining light for him. But I, whose soul was still earthbound, needed an earthly image of redemption. Through the murderous destruction of those dark days her image was a star in my heart that could not be put out.

I saw her only once in all that time. Walcher was murdered in May, and by late July the Norman army was in Durham with Bishop Odo at its head. They marched north in search of the rebels, but they had long since disbanded and fled back into the hills north of the Tyne. Odo didn't trouble to cross the Tyne to find them. He would carry out his vengeance on the surrounding countryside from the comfort of his castle at Durham. It was nothing to him whether men were innocent or guilty; they were all Englishmen. He sent out his battalions each day like a pack of wolves to raven through the countryside, to every farm and estate, every village and hamlet. They reached close to Jarrow. Walcher had given half a dozen estates for the monks' support and one of these, Hebburn, was sacked by Odo's men early in August. The soldiers drove off all their sheep and cattle, trampled down the crops, torched the houses and killed an old man too slow to escape. The folk fled to us for shelter, utterly distraught and uncomprehending.

"But we're not rebels! We've done nothing wrong! Why have they done this to us?"

I understood their suffering. I knew what it was to cower in the woods and watch my home burning. The memory of Malcolm's soldiers hunting us down at Melrose was still vivid in my dreams. We had to do anything we could to protect our people. The next day Aldwin and I set out for Durham to plead with Odo, taking the deeds to our holdings with us.

Durham was in a ferment. The town was crowded with people fleeing the savagery beyond. Once inside the bailey gates the uproar was even greater, with battalions of soldiers riding out from the castle, carts rolling in with provisions, servants running to and fro, and the air ringing with shouts and curses. Immediately outside the bishop's palace was a press of people of all kinds, petitioners like us, waiting for their chance.

Aldwin was aghast. "We'll be waiting all day! We'll never get in!"

I grabbed hold of his hand and tugging him behind me I pushed and shoved a way through till we were close to one of the guards. I waved the documents at him.

"We have a special message for the bishop."

Startled, he stared at me. So unexpected was the appearance of a couple of monks bursting out of the crowd that he took us at our word. He led us in and just a few minutes later we found ourselves in Walcher's great hall. At once memories flooded in on me. I took a quick glance upwards. Those roof trusses. There they were, beautifully done in oak, absolutely even and regular. I muttered my congratulations to Walcher's shade before I looked to the end of the hall at the man who had taken his hall. Odo of Bayeux.

Odo was King William's half-brother and they were reputed to be alike in form and temper. He was not a tall man, as I had imagined, but short and stocky, fleshy in the face with a jowly double chin and two small eyes set far apart, shaded with thick brows. Tight brown curls broke out from beneath the embroidered cap he wore, and the same restlessness and impatience seemed ready to break out at any moment from the man himself. He seemed as pugnacious as a village wrestler and looked as ready for a fight.

"What message is this?" he demanded of us. I glanced at Aldwin and saw he was about to tell the bishop that no, it wasn't a message, that was a misunderstanding. Our opportunity would be gone. I had sat through Olaf's audiences in Nidaros scores of times. I knew a successful petitioner had to get the king's attention at once, by whatever means he might. Not to weary him with explanations. I spoke at once.

"Lord Bishop, the righteous anger of the king has fallen upon his enemies. But we beg you to spare those who have rendered him most faithful service. Our monasteries of Jarrow and Monkwearmouth enjoyed Bishop Walcher's special favour. We beseech you to preserve them to offer prayers to God on your behalf."

I wasn't sure if he was listening. I felt his small eyes upon me like a boar peering out of a thicket, deciding if he would charge or no. I fell to my knees in front of him.

"Lord Bishop, we are monks of Jarrow and faithful servants of the reverend Bishop Walcher. I and my companions brought back his body here to Durham after his foul murder. We gave him burial and endured the siege for his sake."

He glared at me. "What do you mean, you brought him back?"

I told him the story of Gateshead and our flight through the night and embellished the tale with as much drama as I could. I felt a little interest flicker in him. When I had finished, I seized my chance to conclude with our petition.

"Lord Bishop, these are the estates granted to our monasteries for the support of the men of God who live in them. As we have shown ourselves to be faithful servants, I beseech you to instruct your men to spare them."

I shuffled forward on my knees and thrust the document into his hands. I took a quick glance at his face. He had taken the document. He was not looking at it, true, but he had not thrown it back at me either.

"You tell a good tale, monk. What's your name?"

"Prior Thorgot, Lord."

"And this man?"

"Abbot Aldwin."

"Where is this monastery of yours?"

"Jarrow, Lord, is close to Tynemouth. And Monkwearmouth is down the river from your castle here at Durham."

He turned to one of his attendants and spoke to him. Then the man came over and took us out. It was over. I'd done what I could.

It was a relief to get away from the castle and the uproar all about us. We trudged away together towards the church to visit the Saint and to beg for the success of our petition. Aldwin shook his head.

"Well, Thorgot," he said. "You certainly have ways of getting heard."

"Didn't it work?" I said. He shook his head again, half-disapproving, half-relieved.

After the clamour of the court it was a kind of miracle to come into the stillness of the church. I knelt before the shrine with Aldwin and stared at the glowing canopy of the coffin. I thought of the siege days when I had come here every day. When I had sat at table with Edith every day. Had watched her at her spinning. Had talked with her, often and again. How I wished for those days again! I had a sudden desire to tell the Saint about her, to tell him the secret that burned my heart. After all, he had been a young man once, back in the Melrose days. I made my intention, prostrated my forehead to the ground and confessed. I love Edith, I told him.

Nothing. No voice, no sudden disturbance in the air. The same calm and stillness. Nothing? I remonstrated. No judgement? Or comfort? Then the response became known to me. I understood it was not to be made clear to me yet. I was to be patient.

I had no idea what it meant. Yet a kind of content came over me. I prostrated myself again, said the prayers of thanksgiving and let myself slip into a dream till Aldwin had finished his prayers. We went outside.

Suddenly, there she was, her head veiled, no doubt because of all the soldiers so close at hand. She was walking along the path to the church, towards us. I felt my heart beating fast in my chest. She looked up, saw us, and at once lifted back the veil to greet us. Ah! How beautiful she was! After all the memories I had cherished, the reality was dazzlingly lovelier. She was smiling and held out her hand to me.

"Why, Prior Thorgot! How happy I am to see you! And your companion?"

"This is Father Aldwin, our abbot."

She gave a little curtsy to him and bowed her head, then looked up again to me.

"Are you visiting us? Raedgar will be so pleased to see you."

Aldwin answered at once,

"We give you thanks, Mistress, but we must return to Monkwearmouth before nightfall."

I wished a thousand curses on his head. Edith must have sensed some disapproval in his tone, for her manner became more formal. She bowed again to him, bid us both God speed and veiled herself again before walking on to the church. I remonstrated with Aldwin.

"Why not stay the night, Father? We ought to speak with the dean. Surely he will be struggling to preserve the Community's lands, just as we are."

"Perhaps you're right. We can call before we leave."

I took him to Raedgar's house but found only his manservant. He was attending on the bishop, he told us. He didn't know how long he would be, and the mistress was gone to church. Aldwin was easily dissuaded.

"We'll go," he told me. "God pity them, but how the dean and the others live with this dreadful clamour of war all about them I do not know."

He wanted only to get back to the peace and seclusion of his cell. He was right, of course. The garrison paid no heed to the sacred precinct next to them and thought nothing of marching soldiers up and down, penning their stolen cattle, drinking and brawling as if the house of God was of no account. Yet I would rather have stayed there than any place on earth. She had smiled to see me! More, she had invited us to stay with her! Had Aldwin some suspicion? He gave no hint.

✤

In the days and weeks that followed our visit to Durham it was quiet at Jarrow. There were no further raids on our lands. We had word from Monkwearmouth that they too were left unscathed. It seemed that Odo had granted the monasteries protection. Both Jarrow and Monkwearmouth became places of sanctuary for survivors of the Normans' war upon the innocent. We often saw men who had been maimed with the loss of an arm, a leg or ear. We cared for them as best we could, but often wounds became infected and fever would carry them off. Beyond such injury the greatest hardship was hunger. The Normans destroyed the crops that would have seen people through the winter, and they stole or killed their beasts. War, famine, death and pestilence stalked our countryside. Sometimes it seemed that apocalypse was upon us.

But by the end of September the last fires were burned out, the last raids ended. Odo took his troops back to York for the winter. People started to return to the ruined countryside though there was nothing left to support them. Rather than starve through the winter many travelled west or north to beg for land, for shelter, to offer themselves as slaves. All around, save for our lands, there was a ravaged stillness. We could do nothing but pray for Christ's mercy on the suffering we had seen.

I drove out all thoughts of Durham and former days from my mind. My duty lay at the monastery and there was to be no flinching from it. But still in my heart I carried a single image of Edith as I had last seen her; Edith as she lifted back her veil and revealed her face to me.

PART 4

THE PRIEST'S WIFE

1081–1082

CHAPTER 22

WILLIAM DE ST CALAIS

Durham, 1081

Six months and ten days having passed after the murder of Bishop Walcher, in the fifteenth year of the reign of William, that king himself elected the abbot of the monastery of Saint Vincent, by name William de Saint Calais; and the rule of the bishopric of the church of Durham was entrusted to him upon the fifth of the ides of November.

Simeon's "History of the Church of Durham", Chapter LX

When he had obtained the episcopal see of Saint Cuthbert by God's favour, William de Saint Calais found that the land which belonged to it was nearly desolated, and he noticed that the locality which the presence of his sacred body made illustrious, was in a condition so neglected as to be by no means consistent with his sanctity. He discovered there neither monks of his own order or any canons regular. He was deeply grieved at this state of things.

Simeon's "History of the Church of Durham", Chapter LXI

To William, most excellent King of the English and Duke of the Normans: William de St Calais, by God's grace bishop of Durham, sends greetings in the Lord.

Inasmuch as it has pleased your most gracious majesty to confer upon me the bishopric belonging to the sacred jurisdiction of that blessed confessor, St Cuthbert, I desire to entreat your further interest and benevolent regard in this northernmost part of your kingdom.

Alas, most gracious king, that I have here discovered not only that the location has been rendered desolate by the late campaign of your brother, the most reverend Bishop Odo, but the holy church and sepulchre of the Saint lacks proper servants to attend upon it.

The estates of the bishopric have been grievously laid waste so that there is no settled income to support the dignity of the office, either of myself as bishop or of those who claim to serve the sacred body of the Saint. That duty is claimed by a hereditary community of priests, who with their families and dependents live within the sacred precinct of the church.

As your highness well knows, that most reverend shepherd of the church, Pope Gregory X has issued his anathema against priests entering upon matrimony, and moreover your servant Lanfranc, Archbishop of Canterbury, has made known his zealous opposition to such abuses.

Since the self-styled priests of Durham have, through marriage, created many ties of kin and friendship with the nobility of the north, they continue to enjoy reverence and respect such that any reformation of their lives may meet with opposition in the locality. I write therefore to seek the support of yourself and your most honoured Queen Matilda to approach Pope Gregory for infallible letters of authority so that it may be seen that, in disbanding the ancient Community of the Saint, I act not from my own will or understanding, but with the authority and blessing of the Pope himself, as well as your most honoured majesty. In their place I will transfer monks of the Benedictine order inhabiting monasteries in the locality to Durham itself.

The monies of the lands of St Cuthbert will then be properly allocated to the support on the one hand of the monastery at Durham and on the other of the bishopric. I also humbly petition your royal majesty for the grant of further lands in more prosperous parts of your kingdom to enable the support and proper dignity of the episcopate.

I give thanks to God for the generosity and benefaction which you have shown to your people and I humbly beseech you to preserve us still in your regard,

William de St Calais, Bishop of Durham

From William, King of England and Duke of Normandy to William de St Calais, Bishop of Durham.

We give thanks to God that you have entered upon the bishopric of Durham. Queen Matilda and I rejoice that with stern justice you seek the reformation of your episcopate and charge you to travel without delay to Pope Gregory's court at Rome to make your petition.

We have sundry further commissions for you to undertake at Rome and desire you to attend upon us at our court in London as soon as may be.

It has pleased us to confer upon the shrine at Durham of the blessed St Cuthbert our estate at Waltham with all its dues and appurtenances in perpetuity. Deeds of gift will be transferred to you in London.

Pray for us and for the state of our kingdom, for we hold you in high esteem and it is our desire, above all things, to love you most sincerely.

William, King of England

CHAPTER 23

Springing The Trap

Durham, 1082

The new bishop was consecrated in York, not Durham. As dean, Raedgar had to attend, though it was January and foul weather. I thought of that other January, of the snowstorm thirteen years ago when de Comines rode his troops into Durham. The Normans cared nothing for weather, nor people, nor for anything but conquest. Now another Norman bishop was to take possession of us whether we liked it or no. Who cared what the Community wished? We were their vassals.

The sky was so black with cloud the day Raedgar returned you might have thought night had fallen early. When I stepped outside to look for him sharp bolts of hail blew into my face and sent me hurrying back inside. I banked up the fire and waited. Alun had gone with him, and it was he who came to the door first.

"The master's worn out. I've got him sitting in the stable, but you'll need to give me a hand to bring him in."

I wrapped a cloak around myself and followed him out. Raedgar was slumped on a bench, his head sunk forward on his chest. When he heard us, he looked up.

"Edith!"

His face was so drawn and grey I was suddenly fearful.

"What's the matter? What is it?"

"I'm tired, that's all. It's my legs."

"He can't walk right, mistress. You take one side; I'll take the other. Now then—up we go!"

We hauled him upright, an arm each under his shoulders, and brought him staggering into the house. We set him on a bench while I took off his wet cloak and tugged off his boots.

"Hold him there. I'll fetch bedding."

We lay him down by the hearth and he was soon asleep. I gave Alun food and blessed him for his good service.

"He was very slow, mistress, yesterday and today. I said to him, let's find lodging and rest up a day, but he was all for getting home. He takes no account of himself—always worrying after his duties. Look where that's got him."

"Why can't he walk?"

Alun shrugged. "He's not used to riding such a distance. His legs'll be too stiff and sore to move."

So it proved. After a couple of days' rest, he could hobble around well enough, though he still looked exhausted.

"You're fifty-three, Raedgar. You're an old man. You must take better care of yourself."

"Fifty-two," he said.

"Well then."

"Thank God for all your care of me, since I am so bad at it." He took me in his arms, and I let my head lie against his shoulder. Once I had felt safe in his embrace. Now I felt that all was changed, that I must protect him. Must try, somehow, to keep him from wearing himself out with all the cares of his office.

"Is the bishop with you?" I asked him. At least, if William de St Calais came, there would be less for Raedgar to do.

"No. He'll come north later. He has business to transact with the king and Bishop Odo. It seems he has served the king before. He was trained at Bayeux where Odo was bishop."

Bishop Odo. I could hardly bear to hear his name. What if our new bishop was made in the same mould?

"What is he like?"

"He is—how can I say it? A piercing man. He has a very piercing way about him, always, whether he is listening or watching. Nothing escapes him. If he thinks you are holding something back, he will press and question till he has found out what he wants."

"Not a comfortable man, then."

"No. Not comfortable. But clever."

When the bishop finally arrived, the Community held a special service of welcome for him. All the families were there, the wives and the children, the deacons, the clerks from the scriptorium, the schoolmaster. Our new bishop was as unlike Walcher as a man could be. He was a monk and wore an abbot's habit in place of the fine robes Walcher used to love. Where Walcher had been corpulent and often flushed with wine, this bishop was a thin man with a lean white face. He had a long jaw and prominent cheekbones. There was a chilliness about him that made the March day seem colder. Even his bright darting eyes were frosty. Raedgar had been right; his gaze was piercing. As he looked us over a little frown formed between his eyebrows.

There was no feasting afterwards. The bishop returned to his palace. Next day Raedgar was summoned to attend on him, and the next, and the next. The bishop, Raedgar said, wished to know every detail of every estate the Community owned, down to the last hide and farthing that it owed. Again and again Raedgar had to tell him, this estate or that was burned last summer and no dues could be collected. At last he told him outright: all the wealth of the Community was gone and there was scarcely enough for us to live on. Bishop Odo spared nothing. He might have added, and your coffers are empty too, but the bishop could see it clearly enough for himself.

When all the accounts had been gone through his next business was with chapter. He had them sit through a long service of psalms and prayers before they began, and then kept them there most of the day, and the next. Raedgar was reluctant to talk about it.

"He wants to know more of the history of the Saint."

"Has he not read Father Bede?"

"Yes, I mean the other history. Our history."

"The Community?"

"Yes."

He would say no more. Next day when they were in chapter again, I took Mary and we went to visit Gudrun.

"What are they talking about?" I asked her. "This is the third day he's been with them."

"Leofric says he is questioning them about the Community. He doesn't understand about the Inheritance and the people of the Saint."

Perhaps it was hard, I thought. Hard for a foreigner to understand our customs and our history. But it made me feel uneasy.

"He should pray to the Saint and ask fewer questions."

"Do you know what I think?" said Gudrun. There was a kind of mischief in her face. I shook my head.

"Did you ever see so cold a man? He hates women, that's what I think. When Leofric presented me to him, he wouldn't take my hand. Wouldn't even look at me. He just turned away."

"He'll have to get used to us."

"I'll never get used to him. I wish he'd go back to his monastery and leave us alone."

I wished so too.

St Calais next wanted to visit the monasteries at Monkwearmouth and Jarrow—and Raedgar must take him.

"Can't someone else take him?"

"I prefer to know what he's thinking. And I'll have a chance to see Hunred."

When he returned, he had news for me of Hunred, of how well he was doing in the novitiate.

"But what did the bishop want of the monks?" I pestered him.

"Oh—I nearly forgot. Prior Thorgot asked to be commended to you. He well remembers the kindness you showed him in the siege."

I felt a rush of pleasure. Prior Thorgot! Did he think of me still? At once I felt reassured. What was there to fear from the monks? Thorgot had always shown friendship to us, to me and Mary as well as Raedgar, and was he not the prior? I had seen for myself what an able man he was. Thorgot would never set himself against us.

The bishop was called to London to attend upon the king for the Easter feast, and that was the last we saw of him for many months. News came that he had been sent as an envoy to the Pope, to Rome itself, with petitions from the king. I tried to imagine our chilly bishop riding through the sweltering fields of Italy, tried to imagine him standing in marble palaces before the Pope. And then I stopped thinking about him altogether.

It was more than a year before St Calais returned. It was April, mild and showery. Out in the countryside the spring sowing was going on. There had been a harvest of sorts the previous autumn, and now people were returning, rebuilding huts, begging a loan to buy a cow. Life seemed in some way to be settling down. The garrison kept to itself, and the rhythm of Community worship had settled into its old pattern. I took spring flowers to the shrine and felt the Saint's pleasure. But I fretted over Raedgar. The last two years had aged him. However hard he tried to drive himself, he couldn't do the work he used to.

"You must ask for help!" I would scold him, and he would smile absent-mindedly to placate me. At least there was more food now, and I could make good stews and broths for him.

When we heard news of the bishop's return, no-one tried to organize a feast or a greeting party to welcome him back. We had all concluded that he was a bishop in name only, whose real job was as councillor and servant to the king. He had no sooner become bishop than he was gone for more than a year. He had shown nothing but disdain for the Community and its traditions. We didn't expect him to stay long.

This time he didn't send for Raedgar but required all the elders to wait on him in chapter. When Raedgar left the house that morning I was thinking about what I should cook for us. The bishop was fond of lengthy services, I recalled. There was no rush. Raedgar wouldn't be back till the evening.

So I was taken by surprise when the door opened only two hours later. I looked up to greet him but when I saw his face the words stopped in my throat. He looked ghastly. I thought a sudden illness must have taken him.

"Edith," he said. "Dear Edith."

"What is it?"

"The bishop has come with letters from the Pope. The news is very grave. I hardly know how I can tell you."

"Sit down, Raedgar. You look sick."

He nodded. We sat down together. I would have taken his hand, but he looked at me so solemnly I kept it in my lap. He spoke in a kind of monotone, forcing the words out of himself.

"The bishop believes that, since St Cuthbert himself was a monk and was, after his death, attended upon by monks, that he should be served in the same way now."

The bishop wanted to bring monks to Durham, I thought. Well, that was not so much of a surprise. Walcher had the same idea. It would be awkward, for sure, housing them and agreeing a common pattern of worship. But why would that need letters from the Pope? Raedgar took a deep breath.

"Since he believes there are not monies enough to support both a monastic community at Durham and the hereditary Community, the bishop has decreed that the hereditary Community must be disbanded. The priests of the Community will only be allowed to stay if they embrace a monastic way of life and join the new order. If they choose to leave, they and their families will be given a priest's living in parishes belonging to St Cuthbert."

At last the news broke upon me. I was filled with fury. I leapt to my feet and shouted at Raedgar,

"He cannot do this. He cannot. There will be an uprising!"

He looked at me with dull eyes.

"There is more."

"Tell me!"

"He wants us to understand that the decree was made not on his wishes alone but in consultation with King William and Lanfranc, the Archbishop of Canterbury. They have approved his plans. He has laid them before the Pope himself. The Pope has issued an anathema against anyone who opposes the bishop's plans. The bishop showed us the document."

In Raedgar's eyes I saw his hopelessness. He had no words to reassure me. No words to comfort me. St Calais had outwitted us in every way. As I stood there, staring at Raedgar, his words sank into me and I understood his despair. We were utterly lost.

Raedgar was right when he called William de St Calais a clever man. How carefully he had set his trap! He meant to seize the land, that the Community had always held for St Cuthbert, in the name of reform. The monks had no families to support and could be relied on to maintain a life of poverty. He could divert the rest of the income into his own coffers. He would get rid of all the women, all the messy lives of their children and servants and families. The church would be cold and silent and orderly. The bishop would be rich. Hunred, I thought: how happy he will be. He'll get rid of us at last.

How could St Calais do it? How could he at a single blow destroy a tradition revered for so many generations? The Community was held in honour and respect throughout the North. I wanted to rail at Raedgar, but he was so haggard that I held my peace.

The elders met day after day. The bishop went to visit Jarrow and Monkwearmouth and was away a week. Telling them the glad news, I thought grimly. By then, Mary had heard about it. She was twelve by then, well able to understand. She would have found out soon enough in any case. But it was hard. She couldn't believe her life was about to fall apart.

"What will happen to us? Will we have to go and live somewhere else?"

"I don't know. Father will decide."

She started to cry. "Hild says we'll be outcasts, and no-one will want to marry us."

"Come here." I took her in my arms and kissed her. "You're as pretty and skilful a girl as any man could wish for, and Hild too. We'll be driving away your suitors from the door wherever we go to live. Stop worrying."

I half believed myself. She was growing up so fast and to my eyes she grew lovelier by the day. Any man would want her. But the hard truth was that it would tarnish our family. When the Community was held in high honour, noble families of the North were proud to marry into it. Look at Gudrun! She was from just such a family. But now? When the Community was no longer in control of St Cuthbert's lands and the shrine, what influence would they have? Who would want the daughter of a village priest?

Mary and I spent our days at Gudrun's house. The girls plaited each other's hair and worried about their marriage prospects. Gudrun and I talked, on and on, twisting and turning inside the trap, trying to find a way out.

"What does your father say? Won't the noble families take up our cause?"

"He thinks no-one has the heart for it now. My father had to pay Odo all his gold to save his land. He says he can do nothing for us." She leaned forward so that no-one should hear.

"Some men say that the Community have betrayed their own people. They think we sided with the Normans to save ourselves from Odo. They won't help us."

One morning we found her getting ready to go out.

"Leofric wants us to look at Easington." I understood. Easington was one of the livings offered to priests of the Community when they left Durham. She looked at me, ill at ease.

"Don't judge me, Edith. All of us are going to have to do it." She paused. "Do you know what? I'll miss it, being close to the shrine and all of that. Of course I will. But we'll be able to live a normal life. I won't have Norman soldiers ogling me every time we leave the house. And Easington is not so far from my father's house."

"I want to go too!" Mary shouted at once. "Can I come with you, Aunt Gudrun?"

Gudrun looked at me and I nodded.

Gudrun has accepted it, I thought. It's over for her. Perhaps it was for other members of the Community too. But how could Raedgar accept it? The tradition, the Saint, the shrine; it was his life.

He spent most of his time in the church now. When he was at home he hardly spoke and wouldn't speak of it with me. He hardly ate. He started to sleep apart, saying he was rising in the night and didn't want to trouble me. Even then I suspected nothing.

CHAPTER 24

Four-and-Twenty Elders

Jarrow, 1082

"You are to be commended, Father Abbot, for rekindling the light of monasticism in this the original land of the saints."

The bishop's Latin was very correct. Very formal. I supposed it to be a Norman inflection.

"It's through God's grace. I am the least of his servants."

He ignored me. Things were to be understood as Bishop St Calais wished them understood. That had been clear as soon as he arrived.

We had received word of his coming the day before and made the guesthouse ready. However, when he arrived with a small retinue of men and pack horses, his servants immediately took over the guesthouse and arranged things to his liking. I made no objection. How could I? He was our bishop.

I had spent time the previous night reading those chapters of Father Bede's *Life of Cuthbert* that deal with the Saint's time as bishop, when he would spend weeks on end travelling to every village and hamlet in his diocese. People would come in great crowds to hear him preach, making themselves huts and shelters of branches so they could be near him. I prayed that the spirit of the Saint might be renewed in our new bishop and resolved I would seek the benefit of his guidance.

"The brothers and I would be greatly honoured if you would preach the word of God to us during your visit, so that we may profit from your wisdom," I said to him before we sat down to eat. He looked at me with his very direct gaze, as if calculating what might have caused me to make such a request.

"I have other business with you on this visit. Although I may give pastoral guidance on future occasions, I will not be speaking to the brethren today."

With that he turned his attention to his meal. He was a precise man who took care to straighten his cup before ale was poured for him. There had been no time to prepare a special feast; we ate our usual stew of beans and whatever herbs and roots Brother Cadmon had managed to find in the garden, with fresh bread. He ate sparingly and pushed the bowl away unfinished. I couldn't tell whether it was not to his taste or if he was rigorous in abstaining from food. He was silent through the meal but watchful, observing the brothers closely. There was something uncomfortable about his straight-backed, unsmiling presence, as if he were in some way judging us. None of the brothers lingered over their food. He rose from the table and turned to me.

"I will attend the next office," he said. "But first I wish to speak to you privately, Father Abbot."

His attendants followed us as we walked to my house. He gestured to his men to wait outside, but as soon as he saw my office he called one of them and spoke to him. The man left, and St Calais remained standing till he returned. He brought cushions, arranged them on my only chair, wrapped a cloak around his master, bowed and left. The bishop settled himself, and I sat on the bench. Then he started to speak.

I spent the next hour in a state of astonishment. I could not believe what he told me: that he planned to take the guardianship of the shrine from the Community. During my years in Northumbria I had learned more about the Community's traditions. I knew how they had preserved the sacred body of the Saint through many dangers, and how they continued to serve him. True, I had met few of the elders save for the dean. But I felt a deep respect for Dean Raedgar. Married though he was, he was a good and holy man and I knew he loved the Saint with all his heart. Just as I had been at Winchcombe, he was worn down with the burdens of his office, but his spirit never wavered. And now it was to be taken from him! I was shocked. Was this really God's will?

The bishop's eyes never left my face as he spoke. He must have seen my dismay, for he brought out from his bag the Papal Bull and handed it to me. I took it with shaking hands. I could scarcely believe what I was touching. It was from the Pope himself, the Holy Father of the Church. His hand had written the words I saw in front of me. He had signed it and his seal hung from it, a great red seal that I had seen only once before, embossed with a winged eagle. I was overwhelmed. I dropped to my knees and kissed the seal. I looked up at the bishop.

"It is truly from the Pope?" I asked him.

"He delivered it into my own hands. You must know, Father Abbot, that His Holiness Pope Gregory has declared his anathema against the marriage of priests. Such an abomination at the very heart of the country's most venerable shrine cannot be permitted to continue. You can see that His Holiness has directed me to undertake this step."

I could. How could I, least of all the servants of Christ, oppose the Pope's will? Yet I felt tears rising within me. I had to drop my head.

When I looked up again, I saw he was holding a book out to me.

"I am told you were inspired to come to this land by Father Bede's *History of the Angles*. Let me lay before you another work by Father Bede."

He put it into my hands. It was a commentary by Father Bede, on the book of the Revelation of St John the Divine. I had never seen it before, nor known of it.

"It is a fine work. Father Bede understands in the vision of St John not only the end of times, but a reflection of the eternal struggle of the Church against the forces of evil in this world. Let me read a section to you which I believe is salient to the realization of your vision."

> *"After these things I looked, and behold, a door was opened in heaven, and immediately I was in the Spirit. And behold, a throne*

set in heaven, and one seated upon the throne, and he who sat
there looked like jasper and sard, and around the throne, a rainbow
that looked like an emerald. And round the throne were twenty-
four seats; and upon them sat twenty-four elders clothed in white
garments and on their heads, crowns of gold."

I had no idea why the bishop might be reading this to me. He continued:
"Father Bede comments on the passage like this:

'The twenty-four elders seated about the throne can be understood as
those who accomplish the perfection of their work, since in the Old
Testament there are twelve Tribes of Israel and in the radiance of the
Gospel of the New Testament there are twelve Apostles of the Lamb.'"

The bishop leaned forward slightly towards me. His pale face flushed a
little and he spoke faster.

"Father Aldwin, God inspired you to renew the holy church in the
place of the saints. Now it has been given to me to complete the task by
cleansing St Cuthbert's shrine of iniquity. The shrine will be once more a
true reflection of the throne of the Lord as revealed to us by St John and
as in his vision it will be served by twenty-four elders. So you must choose
twenty-four of your brothers, of the most worthy and suitable men, who
will be the elders of the monastery."

I was completely bewildered. Was this, indeed, to be the completion
of my vision? I had never dreamed of such a thing. All I had wanted was
to follow Christ in purity of heart, as the early saints had done, letting go
of all possession and earthly attachment. Christ's words: "My kingdom is
not of this world" were my guiding light.

Now, it seemed, St Calais wished to realize Christ's kingdom in this
world. What was this cleansing of the shrine? What business was that of
mine?

I found it hard to listen as he told me his plans; how the Community
would be removed, how the lands of St Cuthbert would be taken from

the Community and divided between the monastery and the bishop. He had much to say about the different estates and their relative value to the bishopric to which I paid scant attention. Even while I was at Winchcombe, I had little interest in such matters. But as I listened to him, a suspicion wormed its way into my thoughts. He is taking their land, my thought remarked. Was that part of his Revelation?

Then he talked about our monasteries at Jarrow and Monkwearmouth, that they appeared to be in conformity with the Rule of Benedict, albeit he had not yet attended the offices, and that this great honour, that of attending upon the shrine of the Saint, would be conferred upon us and upon me as prior. He himself would be both abbot of the monastery and bishop. He paused and I realized he meant me to express my gratitude.

"Lord Bishop, I beg you to give me time to reflect on all that you have told me. I have no words yet for I am still astonished."

His nostrils flared at that, making his lip curl up slightly. I could see he thought me a witless old fool. I spoke again.

"My prior, Master Thorgot, is most able and of sounder understanding than myself. He is presently at Monkwearmouth. I will summon him without delay to make your tidings known to him. Perhaps I may send him on my behalf to attend on you in Durham."

"There's no need. We travelled here from Monkwearmouth, and I have already spoken with him. You and he can judge for yourselves when you wish to make it known to the brothers—perhaps once you have decided upon the most suitable and worthy men. I'll make all other necessary arrangements. Well, Father Abbot, I believe that is the bell for Sext. Shall we attend the office?"

The familiar words of the office settled me. I knew the bishop was observing our practices with occasional grimaces, but I paid no attention. I gave up all my bewilderment to God and begged him to direct me. And as soon as the bishop took his leave, I sent a servant to Monkwearmouth. I needed Thorgot.

While I waited for him, I reflected again upon the vision that had first inspired me. It had come to me of itself. I had never had to think about it or debate its truth. I trusted in it with all my heart and had never doubted it. But St Calais' words filled me with confusion. They found no echo in my heart and yet he, my bishop, had told me that what he meant to do was the completion of my vision. Could it be true?

"What if we refuse?" I asked Thorgot when he arrived.

"He'll send for monks from his abbey in France. From Odo's abbey, God forbid. But truly, we have no choice but to obey him. He has the king's ear. And papal authority."

I couldn't imagine it. I had expected to live out my life at Jarrow.

"It's a new order," Thorgot said. "Our country will never be as it was. All that we were, our traditions, our holy places, it has all been swept away. Do you know what St Calais believes? That all the troubles we have endured, all the trials, are the reflection of the end times. The four horsemen have been loosed upon us—Death, War, Famine and Pestilence—to make way for the coming of the new Jerusalem. And he is going to build that new Jerusalem at Durham."

"At Durham? But Durham is a fortress! Think how it was there when we went to petition Odo. Dear God!"

"The Saint is there, Aldwin."

We were sitting in my office. As usual I sat in my chair, while Thorgot had the bench by the table. Sometimes he brought documents for me to sign and spread them over it, or he had a cup of ale to refresh him after the long walk from Monkwearmouth. Today he leant forward across it to look more directly at me.

"The vision that brought you here, Aldwin. Perhaps you are the real inheritor of the Saint. The spiritual inheritor. Perhaps you are intended to be there."

I was not ready to consider such an idea.

"But what of the Community? Of the dean? He's given his life to the Saint."

"The dean. Yes."

I remembered something the bishop had said.

"St Calais told me—he said that the elders might remain if they renounced their wives. Perhaps—do you think the dean would choose that?"

Thorgot drew back so that I could see his face less clearly. But I saw well enough that he had reddened. Why, I wondered.

"Well, I couldn't say. Though Hunred is on fire with the idea."

I remembered then. Hunred was the dean's son. I hadn't thought of it before. He would have been one of the inheritors of the tradition, but he had renounced it. Indeed, I had had to speak to him about his lack of charity for the Community.

"He wants to go to Durham to speak to his father," Thorgot said.

"Does he know of the bishop's plans already?"

"It's common talk there. The news came from Durham before the bishop, and the whole countryside is talking of it."

"We must pray for guidance." A deep sigh rose up in me. "Ah, if only we had never left Melrose!"

Thorgot laughed.

"When the Normans sign a peace treaty with King Malcolm, I'll build you a hermit's cell at Melrose. St Calais will never find you there."

CHAPTER 25

THE PARTING

Durham, 1082

*As for those individuals who had previously resided in the church
(canons by name but men who in no one respect followed canonical
rule), them the bishop commanded henceforth to lead a monastic
life along with the monks, if they had any wish to continue their
residence within the church. All of them preferred abandoning the
church to retaining it upon such a condition, except one of their
number, the dean, whose son, a monk, with difficulty persuaded
him to follow his own example.*

Simeon's "History of the Church of Durham", Chapter LXII

When Mary returned from her visit to Easington with Gudrun's family,
she was silent. The next day she spent the morning spinning, staring out
of the window. There was none of her usual singing and chatter.

"It was all right," she said, shrugging, when I pressed her. I could see
that it wasn't.

When Raedgar came home at noon he hardly spoke either, refused
food and went into his office. What a sad place our hall was! I would go
to the shrine, I decided. I wrapped a shawl around me and left all the
misery behind.

When I returned, I could hear voices before I reached the door. I recognized one of them. It was Hunred! I hurried inside.

He and Raedgar were standing outside Raedgar's office. They must have just come out. I looked round for Mary and saw her sitting in the shadows. Hunred was shouting at Raedgar.

"You have to, Father! You have to! Do you think you know better than the Pope himself? Have you not seen the anathema the bishop has brought?"

"The bishop does not seek to compel us, Hunred."

"Your own conscience should compel you! God has granted you this time to repent your sin."

Raedgar turned and saw me. He seemed to sag at the knees. He sat down on a bench at the table. Hunred didn't bother to greet me; he was too absorbed in his attack on Raedgar.

"It is an abomination for a priest to marry. It defiles the office."

"It was not always said to be so."

"No, for men wanted to continue in their vile lust and fornication."

I looked at Hunred, at his passionate face, at his limber body beneath the habit. All this ranting and disgust! Where had it come from? For all the pain his words gave me, I could still see my son. It was not so long since he used to run to me for comfort, for hugs and cuddles. He used to hanker after girls like any youth. Then he had taken all his anger to the monastery and made himself a monk. He would never know the sweetness of a woman, so he would have his father suffer as he did, and he would hate women with all the fury of love denied.

"Why did God give Eve to Adam?" I asked him. "Woman is part of man. When did Christ say that men should not marry?"

He turned, irritated to have to turn his attention to me.

"Christ himself was celibate," he said shortly. "Any man who wishes to imitate Christ in his life must live as he did. As the Saint himself did."

"Your father and I took our marriage vows before God. I am sworn to be flesh of his flesh, and he of mine."

"As a priest he had no right to marry. They were false vows."

"You wouldn't be here without them."

"How do you think that is for me? Knowing that I was conceived in mortal sin? That is the burden you have placed on me, that I have to atone for." He paused for breath.

"I will tell you a story, a true story from a monk who came to live with us at Jarrow. A married priest he knew lay with his wife one night and the next day arose from his fornication and went to celebrate the Mass. When he took up the cup to drink, he saw that the wine had turned to blood. Horrified, he dashed it from his mouth. He went to his bishop to beg forgiveness and reform his life."

He stared at us in triumph.

"That is what all priests should do! It is unclean! Do you know what they call the women who tempt such priests into marriage? A priest's whore! Is that the name you would be known by, Mother?"

I wanted to slap him for his cruelty and rudeness. Mary jumped up from the hearth.

"I hate you!" she shouted at him. "You're horrible! You make everybody miserable! It's all your fault, everything that's happening to us. Go away!"

It caught him off guard. His face changed and he flushed.

"You are a foolish child. You understand nothing or you would not speak like that."

"Go away!" she screamed again. He looked across as if expecting me to reprove her, but I said nothing. Raedgar was slumped over the table, his head in his hands. For a moment Hunred looked uncertain. He hesitated, then turned away and was gone.

Mary started crying and ran over to me. I held her tight so she wouldn't see my own tears. Still Raedgar didn't move. Still he said nothing.

I was angry with Raedgar, angry that he should let Hunred speak to me in such a manner, unchecked. But the anger was mixed with a deeper dread. Did it mean he believed Hunred? For the first time, I thought the unthinkable: that Raedgar meant to leave me. It was impossible. I knew it was impossible, we were bound by vow and by law. Yet when I looked at him, at his stricken face, some part of me believed it. At once, I couldn't stand to be near him.

"Come, Mary," I said. We took our shawls and went out into the still-bright afternoon. I felt a sudden impulse to escape. "We'll go down into the town."

We went hand in hand through the gate and out into all the clamour of the street, the noise of workshops, of hawkers shouting their wares and women talking at their doors. The life and business was a relief. We watched a smith hammering out silver till he thought we were customers and tried to sell us a silver necklace. Mary started to laugh. Thank God, I thought. I wished she had not heard what Hunred said. Why had Raedgar not stopped him? We wandered about till twilight came, the townsfolk shuttered up their shops and we had to hurry home through the gate. I squeezed Mary's hand.

"Would you like to go to Gudrun's? She'll have enough food for you."

"Are you going to talk to Father?"

"Yes."

"All right."

When I got home, Raedgar had made up the fire and was sitting by the hearth. As soon as I saw him, I felt a terrible anger rising up in me.

"You have never loved me," I said. "You have been false to me from the day we were married."

"It's not true."

"It is true. You think I am a whore. You think you soil yourself when you lie with me."

He turned his head away from me. It enraged me more. I screamed at him,

"You have betrayed me from the start. Your vows were nothing but perjury. God will punish you for your falsehood!"

Suddenly he got up. He came over and took hold of me.

"You are wrong, Edith." He held me till I was silent. "I adore you. Since we first married, you have been everything to me. I love you with all my heart. I always will."

At once I was undone. All my fear and rage came sobbing out as he held me.

"What are we to do, Raedgar? What is to become of us?"

He said nothing, and in his silence I found his answer. I knew he would leave me. It made no difference that he loved me. He was the dean. He had given his life to the service of the Saint and it was impossible for him to change. But I could not face that knowledge then. I stayed in his arms till all my tears were done. He wiped the tears from my cheeks and kissed me.

We sat together then in such peace and amity with each other that I wished it would never end. Although it was weeks before the separation came, when I look back, I remember that evening as the last we spent together. The last evening we were truly man and wife. I persuaded him to take some soup and scolded him for neglecting himself. We talked of old times, of the years when we were first married, before the Normans came. We could never have guessed then what was to befall us. When Mary came back from Gudrun, she found us still sitting together on the bench, his hand in mine. She came over and squeezed herself in between us, and Raedgar kissed her head.

The next morning he was up and gone to the church before Mary and I were awake. It was then that the realization came upon me. Raedgar was leaving me. I would be alone, for always, for ever. A great wave of grief rushed in upon me and drowned me in salt tears. I couldn't stop crying. Mary came and found me.

"What's the matter, Mother?"

"Father is going to join the monks."

At once she started crying too. I couldn't comfort her. Her loss was different, but as great as mine. When Alun came in with wood, he found us weeping still and nearly dropped his logs.

"Why mistress, what is it? God forbid, is someone dead?"

Yes! I thought. Yes, he is dead, he is dead to us. But to Alun I only shook my head.

Over the next few days, Raedgar and I were like strangers to each other. We hardly spoke. He slept on his own and spent most of the day in church, or with the bishop, or wherever it was he went. I didn't ask. Then one evening I saw he wanted to talk to me.

"Edith. We must talk. About where you and Mary are to live."

His words were like a knife in my heart. I couldn't bear to think about it.

"I have spoken with the other elders to see if . . . if . . . ah . . . "

"If there are others like me."

"Like you. But—no, there are not. The other elders have decided to go with their families and take up the priestly livings which have been offered to them."

It was only us. Only me. All the rest were leaving. All the other women would still be married, would still have their families, their homes. I pulled my shawl around me. I was shivering as if it were midwinter. The anguish was unbearable, for both of us, but he couldn't touch me now. He couldn't hold me or comfort me. Already we were separated. When he spoke again the words were choking him.

"Where do you want to live?"

It was too much. I broke down into tears and covered my face with my hands.

"Later," I sobbed at him. "I'll tell you later."

Then I ran out of the door and went straight to the church. I was weeping still and had no care for who saw me or what they thought. There was no-one inside. I went and knelt by the Saint's shrine, as I had done since I was a child. I had always lived within a few minutes of this church, of this shrine. I asked the Saint, how could I leave? Was it not as terrible for me as for Raedgar? Why did I count for less? I flung all my furious questions at him, wept all my tears. As I wept, Father Bede's stories of the Saint came into my mind, of how, when he was a hermit on the island, he would sit in his cell with the window open, listening to all the sorrows of his visitors and giving them his counsel. I am sitting by your window, Father, I said to him. Counsel me.

It was then I thought, I will go to Lindisfarne. I will still be close to you there. Even though your mortal remains are here, your spirit is over the place. It will be a solace to me. I prostrated my head to the floor and then kissed the coffin. The Community owned land on the island. Something could be arranged for me. I had decided.

Not for Mary, though. She looked at me in horror when I told her.

"Lindisfarne? It's a four-day ride away! It's almost Scotland! I'll never see anybody, ever again! I can't, Mother. I can't."

I went to see Gudrun. What a true friend she was! Raedgar's decision had horrified her, but she never criticized him, never railed against him as some of the others did. Her house was our second home during that time. We could always go there, always feel the familiar warmth of her hall, always be welcomed and comforted. When I told her about Lindisfarne and about Mary, she went quiet. I knew she was pondering.

"Would you not come and live with us?" she said. "You and Mary both? We could make an extra room for you."

Dear Gudrun! How generous she was! Perhaps I should have accepted her offer there and then. But I was still too used to being mistress of my own home. I didn't want to be a dependent in another woman's household.

"What about Mary, though?" she asked, when I made my refusal. "Mary could come and live with us. Hild would love it. And she'd be better placed."

I knew what Gudrun was saying. Mary would have a chance of finding a husband. Who would marry the daughter of a priest's discarded wife? Had Raedgar considered that? Did he realize he was destroying his daughter's life as well as his wife's?

"Yes. How kind you are, Gudrun. I'll ask her."

As I spoke, I felt another knife enter my heart. I would lose Mary as well. I would be utterly alone.

✤

I told Raedgar my decision. I thought he might be surprised, or he might remember the days we had spent there together. Maybe we would talk of them. He might try and persuade me to live closer to him. I even dreamed he might tell me to stay in the town so he could visit me. I imagined myself in a little house down in the town where he could come and take his meals with me. Where he could come and sleep with me on Mondays when the Mass was done. But of course it was all folly. He said only: "I will speak to the bishop. I'll arrange it." He didn't even ask about Mary.

The days went past in a daze. I wept so constantly that I marvelled I should have any tears left. Such grief and anger and fear assailed me that my mind was in turmoil. I could understand nothing clearly. It was to be, but it was not yet. Raedgar still walked through the door each evening, still took food from me without a word. In the close outside, there was turmoil too, with everyone starting to pack up, to complain about their livings, to rail against the bishop. I felt I was going mad.

One morning I woke up with a feeling of doom in my heart. I got up. The door to his work room was open, and I went inside. The pallet he had been sleeping on was untouched. He had gone. I knew it. He had slipped away without a word. I knelt down on the pallet and pulled the blanket tightly to me. It still smelled of him. I buried my face in it and howled.

On the day of my departure, there was not the slightest glimmer of sunlight through the clouds. The sky was a deep, dull grey, an unrelenting gloom. It was the absolute reflection of my heart and I wished for nothing different. Outside my house stood a horse and cart, piled up with all I would take with me. There was a chest with my clothes in it, another with blankets and a couple of hangings, my distaff and spindle and needles. I took my cooking pots and bowls and all my household gear. But for furniture I took only a chair and a bed. What good was such a large table for me? Who would sit now on my benches? There was one more box. I took all the books that Raedgar had left behind, his inks, his parchment, everything.

Had he meant me to take them? I didn't care. They were the only things that set a small spark of joy alight in my heart. I would have them.

Alun would go with me on the journey. He was almost as grieved as I. He had served Raedgar since he was a boy, and me too since I married him. He was family. Raedgar had cast him off, and he couldn't forgive him. He even asked if he could serve me on Lindisfarne. But what need would I have for him? I would have no servants. I would take care of myself.

It was still very early in the morning. I had been to every household in the close and said my farewells the night before, so that I could leave quietly. I had no wish for the townsfolk to witness my shame. There was only Mary now, clinging to me as if she could never bear to let me go.

"We'll come and see you! Gudrun has promised! It won't be long. I love you! I love you!"

At last, we made our final kisses, and Alun lifted me up onto the horse. He gave a tug at the cart-horse's bridle and our little procession moved away towards the gate. I thought of Lot's wife. I wouldn't look back. After so many tears there could be little salt left in me, but still, I wouldn't risk it. Forwards, now, I told myself, but I felt only dullness.

As we crossed the bridge over the Wear and set out on the track, I saw a rider coming towards us. As he drew closer, I saw it was a monk. For a moment, joy surged within me. It was Raedgar! He had come after all! He had changed his mind! But within minutes I knew it was not him. It was a stockier, shorter man, who looked at ease on his horse, with none of Raedgar's stiffness and pain. It was Prior Thorgot. I hardly knew whether I was pleased or sorry to see him.

"Raedgar has asked me to ride with you to Lindisfarne. To show you the house. I have deeds and a letter for the priest."

So Raedgar had thought of me. He had tried in some way to take care of me. And Prior Thorgot was a good man, I remembered. A kind man. I did my best to find a smile to greet him.

So it was that Thorgot bore us company to Lindisfarne. Both Alun and I found we were glad of it. He and Alun took turns to ride and to lead the cart-horse, and I could hear Thorgot talking to Alun, whiling away the journey with stories and songs. He saw my distress and took care not to trouble me, but his presence was a mercy on that journey. It would have been a long, gloomy march with just Alun and me. It eased the shame too. To have a monk ride with us announced to the world that I was an honourable woman. That the Church did not, after all, despise me.

We crossed the sands to Lindisfarne on a clear day, the skies wide above us and the sea no more than a white edge of surf far in the distance. Curlews rose up into the air in front of us, their calls ringing in the stillness. The emptiness of it was a solace. We crossed like pilgrims without a word spoken between us, the cart lurching through the mud and Alun tugging at the horse to keep him moving. Then we were onto the solid ground of the Island. I felt that I had left the world behind for good.

The village priest came to see us as Alun started hauling down my boxes from the cart. Thorgot greeted him at once, and soon they were talking like old friends. I stopped by the cart and listened.

"Mistress Edith is a deaconess," I heard him say. "She is a scholar, a very learned woman. She has a great love for St Cuthbert, so she has chosen Lindisfarne as her retreat. I believe her presence here will be a light to his memory."

All at once I found myself wanting to laugh. He was making my introductions for me, so that I would be treated with respect. None of it was untrue, but he made it sound so plausible. There was a kind of boldness and dash about the way Thorgot spoke that made him hard to resist. I could see the priest had fallen under his spell. Soon Thorgot was being taken off to see the church and to be told about all the repairs it needed. I went into the little cottage that was to be mine, and found Alun crouched over the hearth blowing sparks onto the bundle of twigs he'd brought for the purpose. Soon he had flames leaping up and logs piled on. The first fire of my new life. I sat on my chair beside it and Alun dragged over a chest, and we sat like old companions staring into the fire till Thorgot returned. "The tide's coming in!" he cried out, and all at once they were in a bustle to get the horses ready and be off, and all of us glad that there were no lingering farewells. Then they were gone. I was alone.

PART 5

A Woman Clothed In The Sun

1083–1092

CHAPTER 26

The Inheritors

Durham, 1083

"The inheritor of the Saint." In the days before we left Jarrow, I often thought of Thorgot's words. But was I in service now to the Saint or to St Calais? The move to Durham was not what I would have chosen. I was growing old, and I wanted more than ever to free myself of the world. I thought of Cuthbert on his island, in a cell built with his own hands, tending his plot of land. I wanted to live as he did, free of possession, depending only on God.

But Cuthbert had returned to the world, I reminded myself. Even in old age, he renounced his hermit's life to serve his people. I had to do the same. St Calais was taken up with his mystical visions, with Revelation and his four-and-twenty elders, but he took no interest in the brothers as men. Although he styled himself abbot of the monastery, he seldom attended the offices or gave the brothers spiritual counsel. He was more often at the king's court than in Durham. As prior now, it fell to me to oversee the new Order. At least, as Thorgot had reminded me, the Saint was there. I wouldn't carry the burden alone.

As abbot, St Calais laid down the rules for the new monastery. I had to carry them out and they were a vexation to me. He set up many different offices: sacristan, precentor, infirmerer, kitchener, cellarer, chamberlain. I felt as if I had returned to Winchcombe. All that these titles do is sow division. It makes men vie for position and become puffed up with pride in them. At Jarrow we'd lived and worked together with no man set over another.

The brothers slept in dormitories now, but St Calais insisted that as prior I should have a house. I was lodged in one that had belonged to the Community. It was far too big for me. The walls seemed still to speak of the family who had been forced to leave it, and I felt like an intruder.

"Why don't you come and live here? Take part of the house?" I said to Thorgot when he came to visit me one day.

"The bishop wouldn't hear of it. He wants you to have your full dignity as prior."

"Dignity!"

"Better if I'm over there, Father." He took my arm. "Have you been out in your garden?"

I shook my head.

"It's a fine day. Let's go and have a look."

He took me outside. The herb bed was running wild and the roses were a tangle of thorns.

"I feel like a thief, Thorgot. I've stolen another man's property."

"It won't be for ever. The new buildings—there'll be a prior's house there. I'll talk to St Calais about it."

"You are always talking to St Calais."

"I know. It's not what I'd choose."

He led me to a bench at the side of the garden. I sat beside him and felt the sun on my face. I remembered how we used to sit on the log by the river at Melrose, just Thorgot and myself. Tears rose in my eyes; foolish old man's tears. Thorgot went on talking.

"But it's better that we work with St Calais. For the sake of the Saint. What if there were four-and-twenty Norman monks here with not the slightest notion of him? Your presence here with the brothers, your vision—that's what'll preserve the tradition. That's what's important."

"I've grown too used to having things my own way. And to having you by my side."

"I'm still here." He leaned over towards me till I was half crushed. "Still leaning on you."

I had to push him off and then we were laughing. Thorgot's good nature could restore my spirits like no-one else. He was wasted on St Calais, who had no spirits to restore. But the bishop understood well enough how able Thorgot was. He was put in charge of the building work to extend the new monastery and the scriptorium. That was only the start, Thorgot told me. The bishop was planning a new cathedral in the image of the New Jerusalem.

How could they think of such things? The countryside was still recovering from famine after Odo's devastation. Where was the money to come from? What was wrong with the fine old church we had? But I kept these thoughts from Thorgot. I knew he loved to build, to lose himself in the mason's art, to dream of spires and domes. There are many ways to praise God and that was Thorgot's.

A few months after we arrived in Durham, St Calais was called away on the king's business. I was happy enough for him to be gone, but I soon discovered it meant I saw even less of Thorgot. Although St Calais had given him no title, Thorgot seemed to have become the bishop's deputy. He received visitors and attended meetings on the bishop's behalf; he organized the bishop's court; he even took charge of the estate office. It would have ground down another man entirely. But Thorgot still had that brightness about him that all the weighty duties of his life never seemed able to extinguish. He'd known what it was to lose everything. Although it seemed in a rush to return, the world sat lightly on him.

St Calais was busy with the king's Domesday census, Thorgot had explained to me. It must have been the bishop's idea. It seemed so like him: to count up every hide of land, every goose, every hut, every labourer and write it all down in a great book, as if the country could be added up in a ledger and possessed by an earthly king.

There were others who felt as I did about the bishop—my oldest friends, Aelfwy, Cadmon. But gossiping and backbiting are forbidden to us. We never spoke of it. Instead, the shrine became my refuge, where I took my grievances and confessed my resentments. It was a relief to enter the quiet space, to feel that intersection of the heavenly world with our mortal cares. I always had a sense of being received, of a spaciousness that encompassed me. At first, I wanted the Saint to share my anger, wanted him to put right my wrongs. Or, when I was mortified by my own ill-will I expected to feel his stern judgement. But I felt neither. As the psalmist says, the rain falls on the just and the unjust alike. I found the mercy of the Saint's presence to be like the rain. It was beyond right and wrong. Beyond deserving. I had to learn to quieten my grievances in order to find it.

Another man was often at the shrine, hood pulled low over his forehead to hide his weeping. My brother Raedgar smelled of sorrow. He was dean no longer, though his tears were not for that. Raedgar knew more about the inheritance of the Saint than any man living, yet the bishop had stripped him of his title. I knew it didn't trouble Raedgar; indeed, he was relieved to have all duties taken from him. He had deeper griefs.

Although he was unrelenting in his spiritual duties, as his confessor I knew he was tormented. Sometimes he would come to my house early in the morning, distracted with grief. It was pitiful to see him.

"I have been awake all night, Father. My heart hurts me till I think it will break. I feel Edith's pain as though it were my own. I am the cause of it. I can't bear that she should suffer so."

"Think of her eternal soul and yours."

"Better I were damned than this. Give me leave to go to Lindisfarne."

"I can't, Raedgar. Be calm. However sore the pain you must endure on this earth you have freed her from judgement in the hereafter. Trust that she will be comforted."

"I can't, Father! I must go to her!"

The best comfort I could give him was to let him voice his grief, to empty himself of his torment till he could return to reason. I couldn't dispute the judgement of the Pope himself, yet it seemed a cruel thing to make a man betray his wife.

His son, Hunred, was no comfort to him. He was blind to his father's goodness. Gaining the bishop's favour was Hunred's only thought; he had the book of Revelation by heart and loved to talk of plagues and rivers of blood. I prayed he might one day come to know the love of Christ.

I grew close to Raedgar. I would often go with him to the shrine and afterwards we would talk about the customs of the old Community. A notion came to me that this might be the purpose of his presence among us.

"I want you to talk to the brothers," I said to him one evening after we had left the shrine. "I want you to tell us all that you know, the history of the shrine, how the Saint came to be at Durham, the customs of former times. All the stories."

He looked at me. He was so modest a man he doubted his own worthiness.

"You are the inheritor," I said to him. "All the others have gone. The traditions are known to you alone. Surely the Saint would wish it."

St Calais was still busy with his Domesday Book, so there was no-one to gainsay me. I announced to the monks that once a week, in chapter, we would learn the traditions of the Saint from our brother Raedgar.

So it started. At that time, before the chapter house was built, we used the hall of the prior's house for meetings. When we gathered there, with a fire in the hearth, it felt like a feast of former times, when a scop would come to tell tales to the company. Raedgar knew the stories better than any scop and soon we were all immersed in them.

He began each recitation in the same way:

> "We give praise to God who has poured out the light of His Word
> upon Northumbria and for the life of his holy saint Cuthbert. From
> the year in which Aidan ascended the Bishop's seat on Lindisfarne
> to our present time is 450 years and from the death of Father
> Cuthbert on Inner Farne 398 years. We remember our forefathers,

> the Haliwerfolc, who preserved the holy relics of the Saint from
> destruction. As the fourteenth generation of the servants of the
> Saint we swear to defend him with the fortitude of those who have
> gone before us."

We heard of the monks' flight from Lindisfarne as the Danes laid waste
to Northumbria. We heard all the adventures of their seven-year diaspora
and the seven faithful bearers. Even Hunred took an interest in what his
father had to say then, since seven is the number of Revelation. We heard
how the Saint appeared to the Danish king in a vision, bidding him to
protect the people of the Saint and give them land. We learned of the new
shrine at Chester-le-Street and the translation into English of the Gospels.
We heard the miraculous stopping of the coffin on its journey as the Saint
made his wish known to move to Durham. We rejoiced that all the people
of Northumbria came together to clear the land and make a new resting
place for the Saint and his community.

As we heard Raedgar's words, week by week, I felt a new understanding
growing amongst us. Coming to Durham was more than just a change
of place. It was a change of purpose. Our duty now was to preserve the
traditions of the shrine for all who were to come. Not I alone, but all of
us had become the new inheritors of the Saint.

Raedgar stood tall and gaunt before us, recounting the tales like a
messenger from the other world. There was scarcely any flesh left on his
face, only white skin stretched over bones, the eyes sunk dark in their
sockets. I feared he wouldn't be with us for long. I ordered Simeon the
precentor to write down all that he told us, to write Raedgar's stories of
the Saints from the earliest days, so that nothing should be forgotten.

Did it give some satisfaction to Raedgar, to hand the traditions on? At
the least, while he spoke it gave him respite from his thoughts. But I could
see that no sooner had he finished speaking to us, his spirit turned back
to his wife and he longed again to be restored to her.

On Good Friday, three years after we were brought into Durham, Raedgar suffered a seizure that left him paralysed in part of his body. His left leg and arm hung heavy, and his face on the same side sagged so that he couldn't speak clearly. I gave orders for him to be brought to the house and I sent for Hunred.

"Your father is close to death. You're relieved of all your duties for this time. I want you to be able to care for him."

Hunred wouldn't meet my eyes.

"Shouldn't he be in the infirmary, Father? Where they have the skills to care for him?"

"He's dying, Hunred. Your presence will be a comfort to him."

Hunred liked to think of himself as a scholar. He spent most of the day in the scriptorium and I could see he hated to be away from it. But I insisted.

"I'll be here too. I'll help you. You must keep close to him so you can hear if he wants to speak. Give him water as often as he wants, and these herbs to ease his pain."

Hunred was a poor nurse. He was awkward with his father and more broth slopped down Raedgar's habit than went in his mouth. I didn't relent. I showed him how to tend to Raedgar.

"Put your hand on his forehead, look, like this. Does it feel hot to you, or cold?"

He mumbled some response.

"Does he need a cooling cloth, or does he need to be well covered and warmed? Think of his comfort as if it were your own."

I couldn't tell if Raedgar heard us or not, or if he knew that Hunred attended on him. At night I stayed with him for the offices instead of joining the brothers. Sometimes I saw his lips moving with mine. One night after Matins I saw he was awake. He lay, his eyes wide open, looking directly at me. I leaned over, trying to understand what he was saying. Lindisfarne? I asked him. He nodded. I knew what he wanted. I clasped his hands. "Yes," I said.

CHAPTER 27

WIDOWED BUT STILL WED

Lindisfarne, 1085

It was more than two years after I went to live on Lindisfarne that the masons arrived. By then I no longer suffered the sharp, bitter anguish that had sent me howling and heartsore to the island's distant shores. My grief had become a duller pain, so constant I was hardened to it. I no longer climbed the ridge overlooking the sea and ached to throw myself into the waves below. I worked constantly to still my thoughts. I dragged kelp up from the shore for my garden, I grew roots and onions enough to feed myself, I got wool from the farm and spent half the day spinning or weaving, filling the hours till another joyless day should be done. Sometimes I clambered over the rocks to the tiny island where the Saint first made his retreats. I sat there while the tide rose and fell, watching the water moving till I was numbed in mind and body. I knew the Saint's presence but felt distant from him. I was distant from everyone. The rumour had spread around the island that I was a religious, that I was in retreat, and no-one bothered me.

So when the masons arrived, I took little notice at first. There were just two of them, Yann-Luc and his labourer, Herve. St Calais had sent them to repair St Peter's church, I heard, and St Calais' name was enough to make me hate them for their master. They built themselves a couple of simple huts to live in and set up their workshop alongside. The island whinstone was too hard for them to work, so carters brought over blocks of pink sandstone from further north. As the wall of the tower started to rise, though, I found pleasure watching them at their work. I marvelled at the smooth blocks the mason fashioned out of the rough stone. One day Yann-Luc straightened up from his work.

"Good day, mistress."

I was surprised to hear him speak English. "Good day," I replied. Although I had walked past him day after day, he had always been bent over the stone and I had hardly seen his face. He had an open sunburnt face, black hair and a short-trimmed beard that made it hard to tell his age. Not old, perhaps, but no youth either. He was broad-shouldered and hardy with peat-brown eyes. I could think of nothing else to say to him, so I went on my way. But after that, I greeted him whenever I passed. One day I saw he had started working on a carving for the head of a pillar. It was entrancing. Suddenly the stone had blossomed out into curving leaves.

"Oh, how beautiful!" I said. "What will it be?"

"They are leaves of—acanthus." He pronounced it "acantus".

"Where are you from?" I asked him.

"From France."

"From Normandy?"

"No. Not Norman." He spat on the ground. "I am from Bretagne."

He set his tools down and leaned back on a stone. I could see he was ready for a talk. I might have walked on, but I didn't. I stopped and listened.

Yann-Luc could work for hours on end with nothing before him but a piece of stone and the chips and dust flying up from his chisel, on and on. But I was to learn that when he stopped, he liked to talk. He talked to me then of his travels, of the places where he had worked, of the great churches and castles he had seen. He would talk for an hour or more, but I was not bored. He had a lively way of telling his tales, and I found myself able to imagine him carving his stone in all those faraway places.

After that first conversation, I would often stop for a while. If he put down his tools, I knew it was an invitation. If he called out a greeting but went on working, I would know he was not to be disturbed, that he was in the midst of his creation, and I walked on.

Sometimes he told me stories from his country, and I grew familiar with the strange names and places of Bretagne. Or he told me of marvels and miracles that had happened in the different churches where he worked. One day he told me about his wife.

"You wonder, why do I travel alone? Why is no wife with Yann-Luc?" He looked at me rhetorically. "She will not come. She will not travel. I say to her, masons have to travel. How else we work? Walls do not walk towards us. But she would not follow me."

"I've lost my husband too," I told him. "He has left me." Yann-Luc stared at me in astonishment.

"He leave you? He leave his wife?"

"He is a priest. The Pope has forbidden the marriage of priests, so he cast me off."

His eyebrows rose almost to his hair. Then he nodded. "I have heard this, this business of priests." He was silent for a moment.

"We are both widowed but still wed," he said.

After that he started to come to my house after his work was finished, and I would cook a meal for him. I washed his clothes. One day he came carrying a bundle of oiled cloth. I unwrapped it. It was a flat square of stone, carved with a rose and a little bee flying above it. For the first time in so many months I felt a thrill of pleasure rise in me. How wonderful that he could make so sweet a thing, that he could bring such beauty out of blank stone. I set it on my shelf, and every day I looked at it I loved it.

One night after he had eaten, he did not leave the house. He sat by the hearth till it was long dark outside. Then he took me in his arms. I knew that he would do it, and I felt no shame, no shock. Why shouldn't we? Had we not both been abandoned?

We lay together that night and most nights after, though he would be gone before dawn. Herve could see what was happening, but he scarcely had a word of English. There was no fear of gossip from him.

Raedgar had been a creature of fire and air, halfway between a man and an angel. Yann-Luc was different. He was made of earth. When he held me in his arms, I felt nothing but his body against mine, solid and strong. It brought me back to myself. He knew that I belonged to another man, and he asked nothing of me, nor I of him.

I started to feel life returning to me. I had an appetite for my breakfast, and I smiled at the blackbird feeding its nestlings in the garden. But I no longer went to sit on the Saint's tiny island, nor did I set a candle on his shrine altar. When I went to the church, I covered my head and stood at the back.

One afternoon in June when I was in the garden digging ground elder out from between my rows of beans, I heard a voice call my name. I knew it at once and felt a leap of joy.

"Mary!"

There she was, standing at the door, looking as lovely as a rose. She wore a dusty old travelling gown, but there was no hiding her lissom body. She was sixteen and a woman. She had sent news a few weeks before that she was to marry a young cousin of Gudrun's in the autumn, so at first I thought she had come to talk to me of bridal chests and linen and lovers' secrets. But her face was grave. At once I felt misgivings. Why had she come all the way to Lindisfarne? What was amiss?

I put my fears aside to greet her and hugged her close.

"Have you come alone?"

"One of Gudrun's men came with me. I wanted to come as soon as I could."

I knew then she had bad news. I stood back, braced for what it would be. She looked at me directly.

"It's Father."

Then she faltered and dropped her gaze.

"He's dead."

There was a long silence, her words hanging like a knell between us. I was frozen still. Then she stammered onwards.

"It was a seizure. He couldn't move, it was only a few days before . . . "

"Did Hunred send word to you?"

"No. I heard it from Gudrun. Leofric and the other priests were told."

"Did you go to the funeral?"

"It was too late."

Then all my rage burst from me. I fell onto the bench and beat on the table with my fists.

"How could they do that? How could they bury him without telling us? May they rot in hell." Tears rushed from my eyes. "He need not have died, Mary. I could have cared for him! I could have nursed him if they had sent for me! He would be alive still."

"Mother." She sat beside me and held my shoulders. "Don't torment yourself. Father will have been all right. He was such a good man. That's what everyone says. He'll be at peace."

She was right. Who could doubt his salvation? He would be with the Saint at last. But that didn't comfort me. Whatever the pain of our separation, there had still been a thread of hope that tied me to him. With his death it was cut for ever. It was unbearable to me that I hadn't seen him before the end. Unbearable that I hadn't been able to care for him or say farewell. What cruelty was it of the monks not to have sent for me? Not even Hunred, my own son, had thought of me.

Mary stayed with me for a few days, and we grieved together. We told each other tales of Raedgar from when she was still a child, and I let myself be comforted by her. I heard about Kenelm who she would marry, and all her stories of life in Gudrun's hall. But once she was gone my grief was consumed by an anger that burned in me every moment of the day. I cursed the monks of Durham. I begged God to swallow them up. I renounced all morality, all obedience to their laws and their commandments. They were as vile to me as dust beneath my feet.

✝

Yann-Luc pitied me. He still came to me for his meal in the evening, but he didn't trouble me with his usual jokes and talk. He left when he was done. Sometimes he brought me little gifts—a bunch of pink thrift from the shore or a couple of gull's eggs. One evening he came in with his hands cupped together, holding something. He opened two fingers for me to look. Inside I could see two bright eyes staring up at me.

"Is baby. Levre. A dog catches his mother."

It was a little leveret, so small it fitted easily in his hand, covered already with spiky black-brown fur. I found a basket for it and lined it with grass and set it in the quiet darkness of my storeroom. When Yann-Luc was gone, I took milk and sat with it, coaxing it to lick from my finger. At last I felt the tiny rasping of its tongue. For the next few weeks, I thought of nothing but the care of my leveret. He learned to take his milk from a little leather dropper that Yann-Luc made for me. He started to grow, to get bolder. When I set his basket in my room he would jump out and lope around the room, sniffing at my wool. Already his back legs were growing strong and sometimes he would dash so suddenly from one end of the room to the other that I would laugh out loud. One evening when Yann-Luc was eating supper the leveret took a sudden mad hurtle round the room, leaping into the air and cannoning into my legs.

"Is time he go out," said Yann-Luc.

"No. I'll keep him as a pet."

Yann-Luc shook his head. "How he can run inside? Better he is free."

So one evening at dusk I put him in his basket and covered him. Yann-Luc and I went together to a field outside the village. I set the basket down and took off the cloth. At once he was alert, his long ears set forward, sniffing the air, his eyes darting to and fro. Then he hopped out and at first loped around beside us, biting off the tips of the grass and chewing. Then suddenly he leapt into the air like a dancer and was racing away across the field faster than I could have imagined. Not a backward look. He was gone. I felt a tear rise to my eye. Yann-Luc took my hand.

"Time to let go."

CHAPTER 28

THE CONFESSOR

Durham, 1086

After Raedgar's passing, I felt myself drawing closer to the other world. He was often in my thoughts, and I prayed that his tormented soul had found peace in Christ. I blamed myself that I had not sent for his wife sooner. It was his last wish, but the next morning I could see his death was close. I sent Hunred for holy oil for the last rites. When his son was gone, Raedgar opened his eyes again and tried to speak. I knew what he was asking.

"She's coming," I told him. "She'll be here very soon. Don't fear."

God will forgive a falsehood told for love. He fell back and his breath grew fainter. Hunred returned with the oils. I anointed Raedgar and together Hunred and I said the prayers for the dying. He was gone before we finished. I pray he died at peace.

I knew it would not be long before I lay, like him, taking my last breath of life. All the activity of the world started to seem meaningless to me. I spent more and more time withdrawn in contemplation.

One day Thorgot burst in upon me, full of high spirits and news. He took hold of my hands, pulled me up from my bench and hugged me. I laughed in spite of myself.

"Come, Father—are you moping still? The sun's shining outside, and all the birds are singing. Let's take a stroll."

I couldn't resist him. He bundled me up in a cloak, took me on his arm and out we went. In his company the air was all the sweeter.

"Let's go and take a look at the river and I'll tell you my news."

"Slower," I said. "Have mercy on an old man." He squeezed my arm tightly to him and pretended to break into a run till I was tripping and stumbling and out of breath.

"Thorgot!" I cried out at him, and he slowed down at last, grinning at me.

"It's just to remind you," he said. "Do you remember how we fled from Malcolm's men, when we were at Melrose?"

"Yes. Of course I do."

"Well—where do you think I'm to go? To visit King Malcolm and his queen!"

"You're teasing me."

"No—it's true. King Malcolm has married Princess Margaret, the Aetheling's sister. By all accounts she is a very pious lady and finds the Church in Scotland primitive. She wants to build a monastery at Dunfermline near the royal court and has asked St Calais for his help."

"And St Calais is sending you."

"Yes! I received the message this morning. I must go in his place. Of course, St Calais knows nothing of our adventures. And I'll take care not to remind King Malcolm."

"Well, my son. Have a care. There are temptations at the courts of kings."

"It's true. You must pray for me."

I couldn't imagine why such a visit would fill him with high spirits. It would have been a hard penance for me. But Thorgot still had a taste for adventure. How could I begrudge it him?

He was gone all summer, and I missed him sorely. Sometimes I woke feeling so weak I feared I wouldn't last till he returned. I begged God to preserve me till I could make my farewell.

✟

When he returned, I knew at once something had changed. Gone were all the high spirits, the jokes, the teasing. He greeted me as lovingly as ever, but I knew his attention was elsewhere. As the days went by my anxiety grew. I couldn't tell how he was in his work, but when I saw him, he could hardly concentrate on what I was saying long enough to respond to me. There were dark shadows under his eyes. I knew he wasn't sleeping but it was more than that. We had been companions twelve years or more and I could sense a deep disturbance in him. Once or twice I asked, "How are you, my son?", but he would shrug and turn away with some offhand remark, that he was weary still. At last, when he came to see me one evening, I stood up and walked over to the door. I closed it and bolted it behind him.

"You don't leave till you have told me what's burdening your soul."

He sank down on the bench without a word.

CHAPTER 29

A VISIT TO LINDISFARNE

Lindisfarne, 1086

And there appeared a great wonder in heaven; a woman clothed with the sun, and the moon under her feet, and upon her head a crown of twelve stars.

Book of Revelation, Chapter 12, verse 1

After we left Dunfermline and had taken ship across the Firth, I told my men we would visit Lindisfarne on our way south. I wished to pay my respects on the island where the Saint had been both prior and bishop, and I would take the opportunity to see how the building work on St Peter's Church was going.

I didn't mention my other business. Ever since Raedgar's death I'd promised myself I would visit Edith to offer my condolences, to make sure she wanted for nothing, but there had never been time. She had been a widow for months now, but St Calais always had another task for me. Now that the journey from Scotland had brought me close to Lindisfarne, I felt I had been presented with the opportunity.

When we reached the island, the tide had not yet gone out. We had to wait an hour or two, so I left my men to their ale and walked apart. Now that we were close, I wondered at myself, that I should still be running after my memories of Edith. It was years since I'd seen her, years since her grief-stricken flight to Lindisfarne. If she had needed anything, she could have sent word. Was it curiosity on my part, to see what had become of her?

At last the tide fell. We rode the horses down onto the wet sands, and they plunged and stumbled across to the island. There is something unearthly about those marshes; the vast emptiness of sand and the pale clouded sky above, and the marram grass where flocks of birds rise suddenly with their haunting cries. As we rode across, I felt the ties that bound me to the ordinary world slipping away. However hard I tried to hold them back, thoughts of Edith crowded in on me.

We put up at the little guesthouse. I left my men to make arrangements; I found myself on edge with impatience. I couldn't wait to be outside Edith's cottage. But when I got there and knocked at the door all was silent. At once I was in turmoil. What if she were from home? What if she had gone to visit her daughter? But after a few minutes the door opened and there she was.

"Edith!"

She was astonished. "Why, Prior Thorgot! Good day!"

We stood on the doorstep staring at each other. Then she gathered up her gown to make way for me and stood aside.

"Will you come in?"

I followed her inside. When she had closed the door, I took her hands in mine.

"Dear Edith. Forgive me for surprising you. I should have sent a man on to warn you."

"But you are here yourself now."

"Yes. I am here."

I looked around. It was a simple hall room, no different from a thousand other cottages, but everything about it was fascinating to me. The casement stood half open so I could see clearly enough. The embers of the fire glowed under a pot that stood over the hearth. A chair was alongside with a bright embroidered cushion and her distaff at the side.

Two long pitchers stood against the wall, and there were shelves with her bowls and dishes. In one corner was a table with books and parchment.

"You are reading still?"

"Yes. I was very pleased to have the books you sent."

"You must tell me what you like to read, and I'll send more."

She smiled and said nothing, gesturing to me to take the chair by the hearth, while she pulled up a stool.

"Will you take some ale?" she said. "It's honey ale. It has honey in it from the island's flowers."

As I drank the ale, I felt like the wanderer in the folktale, who drinks a draught of Faery Land and forgets his home and his people and where he has come from. I felt all my tasks and projects falling away from me. I knew only the cup in my hand, the flame leaping from the fire and Edith sitting with me. I looked at her, looked more deeply, saw how she had changed. There was a hardness about her like a piece of wood that has weathered through storms and freezing winters till only what is lasting survives. She was still beautiful, but there were lines on her face I didn't remember. Her eyes seemed to have grown larger, her face thinner, and her gaze had a new directness. I couldn't stop myself gazing at her. I started talking, talking about anything, to stop myself dissolving completely.

"We are returning from Scotland," I said. "I was sent to the court at Dunfermline. The new queen, Margaret, wants to build a monastery there."

"To Dunfermline? To the court? Why, Thorgot! You've become an adventurer! What's the queen like? Is she beautiful?"

"She is sister to the Aetheling and spent her youth in Frankia. She finds the Scots a rough bunch. And King Malcolm . . . well . . . ." I did a little impersonation of Malcolm for her, of Malcolm with his growling gravelly voice talking to his young Frankish wife. Edith laughed aloud. It was enough to encourage me. I told her how life went on in Malcolm's hall, how Margaret led the king a merry dance with all her fasting and praying, and about the strange food I had eaten, the great whales I had seen in the

Firth, till we were both easy with each other again, like the days of the siege when I had stayed in Raedgar's hall. At last I got up.

"I should go and see to my men, and I must pay a visit to the priest. May I come and bid you goodnight when I am done?"

She smiled at me and nodded.

I walked back to the guesthouse with a light step. There, I told myself. What was there to worry about? Edith and I are old friends, that's all. I'll call again to bid her goodnight and we'll be away in the morning.

I found my men had already been given a meal and were busy with a game of dice and cups of ale. "Here's food for you, Prior!" called out one of them, pushing a bowl towards me. I shook my head. I had no appetite for food. I told the men I might stay late at the priest's house and that they shouldn't wait for me. They hardly heard me.

When I arrived at the priest's house, I found him eating too, but he laid it aside long enough to take me to the church. In the first days of the Lindisfarne monastery, there had been two churches, St Mary's for the laity and St Peter's for the monks. St Mary's was still in use, but St Peter's had suffered at the hands of the Danes and was half-ruined. Since St Calais planned to have a new monastic cell on the island, he wanted St Peter's rebuilt for his monks. Two masons' huts stood outside it and under a canopy was their workbench with several blocks of stone. I love to see stone worked and took a closer look. Four of the blocks were being dressed ready for the building. The fifth was a section of an arch, and the mason was carving it. I could see it was part of a Tree of Life, showing a tree branch and a bird's head peeping out between leaves.

"He's a good mason," I remarked to the priest. "This is a fine piece of work."

"Yes. His name is Yann-Luc. He learned his trade in Frankia. The other man, Herve, is his labourer."

Another time I would have wanted to meet the man, to hear more of what he was doing. But already I was impatient, and I could see the priest was eager to return to his pottage. He finished showing me around, I promised to call on him in the morning and we parted.

When I returned to Edith's cottage, a new idea had started bubbling up inside me. Instead of simply bidding her goodnight I thought I would talk to her of it. As soon as she opened the door I started.

"Edith. I won't trouble you for long, but I have an idea I want to put to you."

She looked at me, with that new direct look I had noticed before, that made my heart beat faster. It felt as if she were looking into my soul and I was not sure what she saw there. She stood aside again to let me in. When we were seated, now with the casement closed and candles burning on the table, I suddenly doubted what I was going to say. Was it presumptuous of me? Would I offend her? But I couldn't stop now.

"You've been here a long time, Edith. Years. Life must be hard for you here on the island. Hard for you to be alone." I took a breath. "You are a widow now. There's no need for you to stay here. You could come back to Durham. I could arrange it for you. A house in the lower town, perhaps."

She was silent for a moment before replying.

"You are kind to think of it, Thorgot. But the island is a consolation to me. I don't wish to be elsewhere. Mary comes to see me. And sometimes Yann-Luc bears me company."

"Yann-Luc? The mason?"

"Yes, the French mason. He works on the church. His wife wouldn't follow him to England. We both know abandonment."

"He stays with you?"

She looked at me with her fearless eyes.

"Yes."

At that moment everything I had thought, had believed about Edith was shattered into a thousand pieces. I had believed her to be pure, to be holy, to be beyond desire. In my mind, I had made her into an angel of light. Suddenly my ideal love was ripped to shreds and I saw not only the truth of her, but of myself. I wanted her, and I wanted her for myself alone. I was overwhelmed with rage. How dared this Frenchman have her! How dared he touch her! I wanted to put my hands round his neck and throttle him. I put my head in my hands to hide my face. I heard her voice continue speaking.

"I am a widow, Thorgot. Before that, so they say, I was a whore. I count for nothing. I am nobody. All the oaths and commandments of the Church, what are they to me? Men set them aside as they will. The Pope himself made Raedgar break his vows. I keep my own laws now."

She was like an angel still, but an angel at the gate of Eden with a flaming sword in her hand, driving me out. I couldn't bear it.

"I am the only sinner here, Edith. I want you. I have always wanted you. You are the only woman I have truly loved."

She stood then and moved away into the darkness so I couldn't see her face. There was a long silence. I could hear the distant roar of the sea. The candlelight cast great shadows on the wall. I felt a kind of relief. I had told the truth. What penance I would have to do for it I couldn't say, but it was out.

When she turned round, I saw she had loosened her girdle so that her gown hung loose. She undid the clasp at her shoulders and let it drop to the floor. Then she undid her head covering and shook out her hair. She stood in her shift with her bright hair around her shoulders and waited for me.

I lay with her that night till dawn. Did I hesitate? Did I remind myself of my monastic vows? No. When I took her body in my arms, her slender warm body, I felt only that I would explode with joy. Everything about her, from the lovely roundness of her breasts and her long soft hair to her ready mouth filled me with ecstasy. The old Thorgot was lost, was gone, was drowned in Edith, and there was nothing left in me but her, nothing but love. She was right. What were oaths, what were vows to this? They were nothing but dry leaves burned up in the fire.

When the first light showed through the cracks in the casement, I took her in my arms.

"I will never leave you," I told her. "My old life is done, is gone forever. I'll stay with you here."

She wriggled away from me, propping herself up on her elbow.

"Stay here? You'd go mad in a week. What are you going to do, mend wattle fences and follow the plough? You're the bishop's deputy, Thorgot. They all depend on you. You are confessor to the Queen of Scotland!"

"Don't you want me here? Don't you love me?"

"I loved once. Not again."

I caught hold of her and buried my head between her breasts. I couldn't bear it. She let me lie there, stroking my head.

"You must go, Thorgot. Before the village starts moving. And then go, go with your men and don't look back."

She kissed me and then was gone from my grasp. She came back with my clothes and tugged at my arm.

"Up, up, come on, up now!" I had to obey her. She thrust the tunic over my head, and then the habit, and tugged and pulled at me till somehow I was dressed and the cord pulled around my waist and I was a monk again.

"Another kiss!" I begged, and she kissed me till I was mad for her all over again, but she opened the door and pushed me out into the dawn. I turned back, but the door closed behind me.

I stumbled away, down the village lane. I knew I couldn't face the guesthouse. I went down to the harbour, over the pebbled shore to the water and waded in. It was icy. I bent down, splashed my face and ducked my head under till I was gasping for air. When my legs were half-frozen, I came out and headed up onto the ridge that stands above the harbour and let the dawn wind scour me. I stayed there till sunrise.

When I went into the guesthouse, the men were quiet and respectful. I could see they thought, he has fasted and prayed all night. They put breakfast before me and suddenly I was ravenous, trying not to tear and gobble at the bread and cheese. As soon as I was done, I nodded to them.

"We'll leave right away. We've got a long journey ahead," and as I said it, I felt like weeping. How could they know how long the journey was that lay ahead of me?

We rode down across the sandy turf of the island back to the shore and urged our horses out across the sands. I felt myself sway from side to side as my horse picked his way through the sinking mud. The sun was well risen, and I felt its warmth on my shoulders. Don't look back, she had told me, but I couldn't stop myself. I twisted round in the saddle, and there she was, standing on the shore. She was too distant for me to see her face, but I knew it was her. She cared enough for me to see me gone. The sun was behind her so that the light made a glowing aureole about her. A verse from Revelation came to my mind, of the great wonder that John sees: a woman clothed with the sun, the moon at her feet and twelve stars about her head. Surely it was she.

When I got back to Durham, I couldn't hide the turmoil in my soul from Aldwin. He knew me too well. Once he bolted the door behind me, I knew I would have to confess. Should I tell him the whole story? How could I? He was my father and my dearest friend, but he was an innocent. He had been a monk all his life. He didn't hate women as St Calais did, but he had never known one. He was an old man close to death and I feared to shock him. I said,

"Father, before I made my profession, I told you I would never make a good monk."

He said nothing. I knew he would keep silent for as long as it took me to tell him. There was nothing for it but to continue.

"What I have to tell you will grieve you. I have broken my vow. I have lain with a woman."

It was shock enough. His face was filled with horror.

"No. No, Thorgot. Surely not."

"Yes."

He clasped his hands before him, and tears sprang from his eyes. How could I cause him such grief? I wished I had kept it to myself, but he knew me too well. He had seen my distraction. I put my arms round him and we stood together, both weeping. At last he wiped his face with his cuff and stood away from me. He tried to speak with his usual firmness, but his voice shook.

"You have committed a mortal sin, and you have broken the sacred vow of your profession. You must repent now before Almighty God and beg that he restore you to his love and favour. Do you repent of your sin?"

I wanted to shout aloud, No! No! I will never repent of it! I want only to return to her! But for Aldwin's sake, I knelt down before him and mumbled out, "I repent."

He heaped on me every penance he could think of. I hardly paid attention. I felt as if I had betrayed her.

Aldwin's penances didn't touch me. I poured out streams of prayers and fasted for days till physical weakness distracted me from the torment in my heart. I did it for Aldwin's sake, so that he wouldn't be worrying about me when his time came. But my suffering was the same. I have never known such pain as my longing for Edith. When I woke up each morning, my first thought was, Edith! And then, immediately after, I may not have her! And tears would rush to my eyes.

Deeper even than the pain, though, was the insurgency in my being. I could not repent of what I had done. How could such joy be evil? I thought, again and again, of Edith's words: "I make my own laws now." How could I live as a monk without hypocrisy when I refused to believe my love a sin?

As the weeks went by, I hid my anguish deep within myself and bound it about with chains of iron. One day, I knew, I would have to confront it. For now, it lay within me, beyond even Aldwin's gaze.

Such was my state for many long months.

CHAPTER 30

THE FRENCHWOMAN

Jumieges, 1087

When Thorgot came to my door that summer evening, I was still full of hatred for the monks of Durham. If it had been any other of the brothers, or my son, I would have closed it in his face. But Thorgot? Alone of all the monks he had shown me kindness. I let him in.

For all that, when I let him lie with me there was revenge in my heart. See! I wanted to say to all the holy brethren. See! You are sinners too. Your hearts are filled with the same lust you punish others for.

Afterwards I was ashamed. Thorgot was a true man. There was no pretence or hypocrisy about him. He loved me, and when I lay with him that night, the anger drained from my heart. In its place something woke in me I had not thought to feel again. I refused to heed it. I couldn't endure the suffering of another forbidden love. But Thorgot had been ready to give up everything for my sake, and he deserved better of me. One day, I thought, I will make amends.

I told Yann-Luc nothing. He thought the priest had come to hear my confession and left me alone. At first, in the weeks after Thorgot's visit I thought, I will not lie with Yann-Luc again. But I did. It was as if I had become his wife, whether I would or not, and even though he was still wed. I let him back into my bed and soon we were as before. If thoughts of Thorgot tormented me, what of that? I held Yann-Luc closer.

As the autumn days grew shorter, the masons' work on the church was close to ending. Yann-Luc wanted to be done before the first frosts came and made it impossible to work the mortar. He and Herve worked without a break during daylight hours, and we ate the evening meal by candlelight.

"What will happen?" I asked him. "When you are finished? What then?"

He cut himself off a piece of bread, dipped it in the soup, and chewed while he thought about it.

"First I finish here. It will be a few more weeks yet. Then I go to Durham."

"Why?"

"Get money from St Calais. See where he want me next. Maybe back to France."

"I'll come with you. Not to Durham. To France."

He frowned and picked up another bit of bread.

"No nice hall like this, Edith. No hearth and chair. A mason's hut."

"I don't mind."

"Perhaps you think, this is not so good. I will go and live with my friends."

"No. I won't."

"Are you sure?"

"I'll stay with you, Yann-Luc."

He pulled me over to him and kissed my mouth. As he held me, I thought, how will I tell Mary? She would be horrified to think of her mother living in a mason's hut. When she came to visit Lindisfarne, Yann-Luc kept out the way. I would have to think of some story. Perhaps I would tell her I was going on a pilgrimage, all the way to Rome, to have absolution from my sins as a priest's wife. I would be gone a long time.

I pushed Yann-Luc off me.

"Your mouth tastes of soup," I told him.

In the spring, Yann-Luc returned from Durham in good humour. He had silver in his pockets, and he and Herve had passed the winter nights with their friends in the alehouses. He was full of news.

"Your priest friend, Thorgot, the man who come here, yes?"

"Yes?"

"He does the bishop's work now. St Calais is at court. Who cares? Master Thorgot, the men like him better."

A pang struck my heart. "He's a good man."

"Yes, he's good. He say, you and Herve must go to Normandy. You do work at Jumieges for Duke Robert."

He looked at me and tossed a coin into the air.

"You come still?"

All through his absence I had resolved to deny him. In the long dreary days of winter, I swore to myself, I will turn away from my sin. I will repent and live decently as a widow. But now, with him standing before me and images of Normandy filling my head, the answer was out of my mouth before I could stop it.

"Yes. I'm coming."

To stop myself thinking I threw myself into a fever of preparation and packing, trying to imagine what I might need in Normandy.

"What's all this?" Yann-Luc said, when he saw the chests and boxes I had prepared for the journey. "We take ship. One small chest, or they not take us."

"But I need it all!"

"One cooking pot. Spoon, knife, cup, bowl. Change of clothes. Distaff and spindle." He checked them off on his fingers.

"I have to take all the cooking gear."

"I have my tools too. Look, my box."

It was so small. I had never thought about how little Yann-Luc had with him. "I am nothing," I had said to Thorgot, and believed it, but now

I saw how much I still had. Must I leave everything behind? I thought. Suddenly I felt sympathy with Yann-Luc's wife. I pictured her in her hall with her carved chairs, her silver candlesticks, and her good clothes. I knew why she hadn't followed him.

I unpacked the chests and boxes. We had to wait for weeks till a trader came into the harbour who would take us to Normandy, and I spent the time storing everything away as carefully as I could so it would wait for my return. It might be a small house, but it was mine and it had become my home. What folly had possessed me, to follow this man across the sea?

But when we were at last on board with our boxes crammed in beside us, feeling for the first time the rock and heave of the ship as she took the swell, my fears left me. We were out on the blue sea with the wind billowing in the sail above us; the ship was leaping over the waves like a living thing, and my heart sang in my breast. I was free. The salt spray on my lips was the taste of a new life.

Jumieges, where Yann-Luc was to work, lay on the banks of a great river called the Seine. Like Durham, it was built on a part-island formed by a loop in the river. On the far bank, the land was thickly forested and sloped upwards from the river, just as at Durham. But on the town side the land was flat so that you could walk directly to the water's edge. I had never seen anywhere so beautiful. Spring came earlier here, and already when we arrived the countryside was filled with apple blossom. The meadows were full of daisies and the cows that grazed in them were sleek with heavy udders. Our cattle at home would have been still scrawny from the winter. Goslings tumbled after the geese that the village girls herded down to the river and swallows swooped low over the water.

The abbey was a marvel. I had thought our church at Durham the equal of any, but Jumieges taught me differently. I had never seen so magnificent a building. When I stood at the entrance, the two great towers on either side seemed to reach upwards endlessly, one row of colonnades after another.

I felt tiny before them. How could they have built so high? How could every arch of the windows be so perfectly rounded, so exactly measured from its neighbours? It was built of pure white stone that dazzled in the sun. Inside the walls were covered in bright paintings and light streamed in from the high clerestory windows. On a fine day, the whole lofty space seemed to be alive with colour and light. At the far end of the nave was a breathtaking arch that rose from the floor to the roof of the building. It filled my heart with wonder. The church was dedicated to the Blessed Virgin, and it had a purity that seemed her gift alone.

"The bishop," Yann-Luc told me, "he want to build like this at Durham. Greater, even."

"It would be fine for the Saint to have such a shrine."

He laughed, put his arm around me and squeezed me close.

"I build it for you!"

He was happy at Jumieges. The abbey church itself was almost complete and had been consecrated already, but there was still work in the close, on the chapter house and cloisters. We would be there till the end of the year, Yann-Luc reckoned. There were two other masons, as well as carpenters and workmen, and Yann-Luc liked nothing better than an evening drinking wine with them and telling tales of the places they had worked. There were women too, wives or just women. No-one cared. It was a wandering community, always on the move to wherever there was work, and the townsfolk left us alone. I was one of them now. I went with the other women to buy food with Yann-Luc's coin, and then we sat together, grinding grain and singing, telling tales as we cooked and baked on the fire we used together. I started to learn French, and though Yann-Luc still spoke to me in English, I spoke more French than English. Once I would sooner have spat than speak the Normans' tongue, but now I was glad of it. The new language made me another person. Aydit, they called me. Aydit. I forgot about Edith, forgot about the woman who had been the dean's wife, forgot about her modesty and good behaviour and learning. I went with the other women to swim in pools in the river on hot summer days and thought nothing of stripping off every stitch of clothing. It was so hot! I had never known the sun could burn so fiercely. My woollen clothes were unbearable. I made Yann-Luc buy me a length of linen, so I could make myself a light shift. I learned to sleep in the heat of the day and then stay up half the night drinking and talking in the firelight, men and women together. The Normans made a drink with apples, cidre, and it made me drunk as ale never had. Such food there was too! I ate plums and peaches, grapes and luscious figs, rich cheeses, and butter as yellow as the sun. There were fish for the taking in the river, wildfowl, rabbits. It was a summer of marvels. I felt as if I had stumbled into the Garden of Eden.

"Why?" I asked Yann-Luc. "Why did Duke William and his knights leave Normandy? Why did they want England? Why rain and wind and rough weather when they already had this?"

It baffled me. They had seized our lands, our people, possessed us, murdered us—for what? They had all this. All this richness of their own. Yann-Luc shrugged.

"Always knights want more," he said. "Always to own more land, more rents, more men. Then they can pay us to build a castle for them. Or a church. Then they think, God will not punish them for their thieving ways."

He laughed. Yann-Luc was like that. He didn't trouble himself with the world, nor the world with him. He did his work and what he touched turned to beauty. As long as he had silver in his purse, a pitcher of wine in the evening and a woman in his bed, he cared for nothing.

CHAPTER 31

BEYOND THE GRAVE

Durham, 1087–1091

The winter after my visit to Scotland seemed endlessly dreary. The Rule rubbed on my restless spirit like a sore. How could I counsel others in such a state? And there was more than ever for me to do. Aldwin was sick, and I had to take over his duties. The care of the monastery and the brothers was on my shoulders, and all the while my heart was heavy with loss. Not only Edith. It seemed I would lose Aldwin too.

All through that winter he suffered a low fever that kept him constantly abed. Through the blustery days of March his life hung by a thread, but when April came with softer days, I hoped spring might heal him. When I went to see him, I set the door open to let the sunshine in.

"Listen to that, Father." He looked up at me from his bed, confused.

"The birds. Listen to them! They know its spring!"

A thrush was singing in the garden, such a sweet song it made him smile. He shifted in his bed, and I saw he was trying to sit up. I put my arm round his shoulders to lift him and tucked a couple of pillows behind him. He was so thin I feared to crush him. The effort left him breathless for a while, but he took my hand in his. I saw he was trying to speak, and I leaned close to hear him.

"Sing. Sing for me."

I understood. I thought of those days long ago, when I'd first arrived at

Jarrow and in my arrogance had begged him to let me teach the brothers psalmody. His reproof still stung my memory: "Your task is to say the words with faith. To say them with all your heart."

I would do it for him now. I would sing the psalms with all my heart. We sat together that bright April morning, his hand in mine and the words of the psalms in the air between us.

> *"Surely His salvation is nigh to them that fear Him*
> *That glory may dwell in our land*
> *Mercy and Truth are met together;*
> *Righteousness and Peace have kissed each other*
> *Truth shall spring out of the earth*
> *And Righteousness shall look down from heaven."*

How tranquil he seemed, lying there in the spring sunshine. How peaceful it was between us. I must have been singing for an hour or more when I felt his hand grow stiff in mine. I glanced down at him. His forehead was smooth, his face clear as a young man again. I saw that all his cares had been lifted from him.

It was then I heard him first. There was no sound, his lips were still and yet it was his voice. I heard it distinctly at first, and then it trailed away. "Take me back . . . ," he said.

Back? Back where? Where did he want me to take him? Melrose, I thought. He wants to be buried at Melrose. I placed his hands together on his chest and said the prayers for the dead, but I still heard the echo of his voice.

The brothers wanted him to be buried at Durham, of course, next to the church, where they could visit him and honour his grave. It would be impossible for me to bury him at Melrose, even though I was in favour at the Scottish court. Besides, I doubted myself. Had I really heard him? I was sure I had imagined it.

But as the coffin was lowered into the earth, I was aware of his presence again.

"You'll be all right here," I said. "You're close to the Saint."

One of the brothers standing next to me stared, and I realized I'd spoken aloud. Hurriedly I pulled the hood over my head.

That was how it started. Aldwin and I had talked almost every day of the last twelve years. He'd been my abbot and my confessor all that time. We'd built Jarrow and Monkwearmouth together. When we moved to Durham, there were more demands on me from the bishop, but our companionship never faltered. It seemed we were talking still.

After his death I was appointed archdeacon, second in authority to the bishop. It wasn't so great a change. I'd been carrying out Aldwin's duties since he became sick. But now, when there was some difficulty in the monastery, I found myself discussing it with Aldwin as if he were still alive. I even caught myself muttering at table a couple of times and saw Aelfwy gazing at me with concern. It was just an old habit, I told myself. But the strangeness of it was, I didn't feel the conversations were one-sided. Aldwin was there. I was conscious of his presence distinctly and of his responses. At last I said to him,

"Father, you must be at peace. You have desired so long to be with Christ. Don't trouble yourself with our doings."

He could be so stubborn sometimes, just as when he was alive. I knew he did not intend to leave me.

"Stop worrying about me. I have done penance for my sins."

But he wanted me to have another confessor. In my office, it was the bishop's duty, but he was seldom in Durham. King William had died not long after Aldwin and St Calais had got involved in schemes to depose his heir, William Rufus, in favour of his brother, Robert of Normandy. I knew what Aldwin felt about that. It was not a bishop's place to interfere in affairs of state.

"The Saint did," I reminded him. "It was the Saint who brought Oswy's bastard son to power."

He ignored me. I returned to the matter of my confessor.

"I often have to travel now. I go to synods and other gatherings to represent the bishop. Perhaps a godly priest from the bishop's court in York would hear me."

Silence. I wanted to laugh. I wanted to hug him as I used to in the old days.

"I miss you, Father!" I cried out aloud.

After a few months I made an agreement with him. While St Calais was away, I would stand at his graveside once a week. If he was present, I would confess. Otherwise he was to leave me alone. And I him. No muttering at the table or talking aloud in my cell.

So I started my weekly vigils. Perhaps since I'd known him so long my mind could make up what he said. Yet the things I heard him say often surprised me. And I still had the sense of his presence, though not always. There were weeks when I felt that the graveyard was empty, when I was conscious of nothing but the rain falling on my face and the rooks cawing from the woods by the river. He still didn't like to hear of St Calais and his Revelation. I talked of it just the same. It was often on my mind.

St Calais believed that all the destruction that had been visited on Durham was God's punishment for the sinful decadence of the Community serving the Saint. Aldwin hated that argument. It was the greed and cruelty of the Normans, he said, and there was nothing special about Durham. They had wreaked destruction wherever they went. I thought of Lincoln and knew he was right. Why did I listen to St Calais? Had I not suffered enough at the hands of the Normans?

Yet the next part of the bishop's vision, the church of the New Jerusalem he meant to build, still captivated me. How different Aldwin and I were! Nothing had delighted Aldwin more than the empty post-rings of the cells at Melrose. The more simple, the more saintly. But I remembered the loveliness of the Byzantine dome in Nidaros and how sound echoed around it. I still felt the excitement of laying out the new cathedral with Olaf. Somehow in such buildings the rough matter of the world is transformed by the mason's art into something new and glorious. It woke praise in me like nothing else. Or like one thing else. The love that still burned me, day after day. I never spoke of that to Aldwin. It lay bound in my heart with iron chains.

For once, St Calais had misjudged. The rebellion against William Rufus failed. St Calais refused to stand trial for his part in it, saying he would answer to the Pope alone. William Rufus cared nothing for that. He banished him to Normandy and confiscated all his lands. By the first anniversary of Aldwin's death, 11 April, St Calais was gone, and I found myself bishop in all but name.

It was a fearful time for the brothers, with no-one to defend us from a vengeful king who might have a mind to take our land too. I needed all my strength to keep them from faltering. When we sat together in chapter, monks argued that we should leave, should return to Jarrow or Monkwearmouth. I knew Aldwin agreed with them, but I would have none of it.

"We have undertaken to become the guardians of the Saint," I reminded them—and him. "We must hold fast. Pray to the Saint for his protection."

We had newly started on building our refectory at that time, and I insisted that the work should continue. We went on building and praying and living the Rule. After a while things settled down and there was no more talk of Jarrow. The king didn't trouble us; indeed, by the end of the year I had messages from the court summoning me to a synod in London.

By the second anniversary, I had different news for Aldwin. "I've been to London," I told him. "To court. I have sat at table with lords and bishops."

There was absolute silence from Aldwin, but I was full of it and would not be quieted. What a time of wonders it had been! Durham was a village compared to London. The Thames was alive with ships, and I had felt my old trading days stirring in me. The sight of a Norse trader brought tears to my eyes. "I'll never be reformed," I said to Aldwin. I knew he agreed.

Yet it had been like visiting a foreign court. I heard not a word of English spoken, and the king's halls were full of Norman lords in their finery. I had learned enough French to speak with them, but I could see that they disdained me. Not so the king. Why, I could not tell, but he rose to greet me and paid me every courtesy. He gave me audience three days together with his priests beside him, and by the end of it he had signed a new charter for the monastery that confirmed all our rights and privileges.

"Look! Look at it!" I cried out to Aldwin. "You needn't worry. It hasn't gone to my head. I know it is the Saint's doing, not mine. I know the king did it for the sake of the Saint."

"You are the servant of the servants of St Cuthbert," said Aldwin. "Nothing more."

By the time Aldwin's third anniversary came around, St Calais was back in favour. He had negotiated a peace between the two brothers, William Rufus and Robert of Normandy, and there were celebrations on both sides of the Channel. I received letters from St Calais in London. All the lands of the bishopric had been restored to him, I learned, and new gifts made by the king, that would need to be surveyed and administered without delay. William Rufus had discovered, like his father before him, that he couldn't do without St Calais. Loaded carts started to arrive at the bishop's palace, with fine vestments and ornaments for the church, some in pure gold. There were books for the scriptorium, sacred vessels for the altar. At last, four years after he'd left, the bishop himself returned to Durham.

Around that time the graveyard fell silent for good, though I still returned there. Aldwin had never liked St Calais.

Indeed, it was impossible to truly like William de St Calais, let alone love him. After a four-year absence, we greeted each other as formally as strangers, though he commended my work in managing the diocese. He was such a cold man that any expression of feeling would have seemed close to blasphemy. He was formidable in his understanding and relentless in his governance. But I had learned to see that another kind of passion burned in him; a transcendent vision that was his private religion. It was surprising that so worldly a man should be also a mystic. He knew the text of Revelation by heart, and most of Bede's commentary on it. He wanted to realize the New Jerusalem on this earth; to take the coarse substance of the world and transmute it, just as the alchemists sought to turn base metal into gold. The book of Revelation was his Philosopher's Stone, where he found the wisdom that would transform things material into their spiritual reality. His mind was full of sacred numbers, of horned beasts and angels, of apocalypse and salvation. He had spent his time in Normandy visiting the great churches that were being built at Lisieux and Jumieges, and he wanted to outdo them all.

How unlike Aldwin he was. Aldwin had turned his back on the world. As far as he could, he renounced it altogether. The less he had the more his heart found peace. St Calais was his opposite; he lived in the world and was skilled in all its ways. But he wanted to transcend it in a different way. He wanted to bring about the kingdom of heaven upon earth, to transform the physical world into a higher spiritual state.

And me? God forgive me, but I love the world. I love it in all its ways and forms, from the smell of varnish on a ship to the sound of a canticle rising to heaven. Nor had I renounced my passion for Edith. I still worshipped the memory of her body, the softness of her hair on my shoulder and her fearless gaze, though time had softened the anguish of separation. I am neither ascetic nor mystic. Nevertheless in St Calais' cathedral I was to discover a vision that would, for me, unite both heaven and earth.

As much as he ever showed passion, St Calais was on fire with his new cathedral. He summoned me to the palace for my instructions. We stood in his chambers, the table covered in plans. He had another man with him, a man with wide shoulders who looked as if he could pick up St Calais in one hand. Although he seemed no older than me his hair was completely white. It gave him an impressive air of dignity.

"This is Master Kennet, Archdeacon. He will direct the masons." An English master, I thought. I was glad of it.

St Calais turned to the master. "And this, Master Kennet, is Archdeacon Turgot." Like all the Normans, St Calais was defeated by the th of my name. I had become Turgot, as the master had become Kennet. I would tell Master Kenneth my real name later. "He will oversee the works on my behalf and deal with procurement."

We bowed, both making our first judgements of each other. For years to come, we would be seeing each other day after day. All that was to follow would fall on our shoulders.

The bishop pulled one of the plans towards him. On it, Master Kenneth had drawn a series of overlapping squares, laid across each other in a beautiful geometric design. *Ad quadratum*, I thought. It was the basis of the geometry the master masons used. Within it I could see sketched out the choir, the nave and the crossing tower at the centre where all the squares met.

"The cathedral will be built according to St John's vision of the New Jerusalem," St Calais said. He recited the passage from Revelation that was to become so familiar to us:

> *"And I saw a new heaven and a new earth ... and the holy city, New Jerusalem, coming down from God out of heaven ... and the wall of the city had twelve foundations ... and the City lieth four square, and the length is as large as the breadth, and he measured the city with a reed, twelve thousand furlongs: the length, the breadth, and the height of it are equal."*

In case I had not understood, he stabbed at the diagram with his finger. "The New Jerusalem is perfectly equal on all its sides and so that must be the basis of the building."

I looked more closely. The first two squares were set beside each other, with two further squares overlaying them at forty-five degrees, forming two eight-pointed stars. A fifth, slightly larger square was overlaid at the centre, at the same forty-five-degree angle, forming a central sixth square at the centre where they all overlapped.

"It is a dodecaid," said St Calais triumphantly. "A twelve-pointed star."

As he spoke a realization exploded in my head like a sudden shower of meteorites flinging light across the heavens.

"A woman clothed with the sun," I said. "And the moon under her feet and on her head a crown of twelve stars."

"Exactly," said St Calais. "As Father Bede says, she is the Church, girded with the light of Christ, treading upon temporal glory. The twelve stars represent the twelve apostles."

I paid him no heed. Edith, I thought. Treading upon temporal glory. She is the Church, she is the stones and the spaces, she is the pillars and the dome. She is the light. At once the chains around my heart broke open, the iron links shattered, and joy burst out of me. I would build this church for Edith. I threw my head back and laughed aloud.

St Calais and the mason stared at me.

"I laugh for joy, Lord Bishop. At the vision of this great cathedral."

"It is well that it rejoices you, Archdeacon. It will take you many years of toil to accomplish."

CHAPTER 32

THE RETURN

Durham, 1092

I was to be five years a Frenchwoman. After the first year, we moved from Jumieges to Caen, and there seemed to be enough work there at St Etienne's Cathedral to keep Yann-Luc busy for ever. I had no thought of returning to England. I had forgotten who I was. I refused to think about the past. I lived from day to day.

But my past life, that destiny that bound me to the Saint, was not done with me yet. In the world beyond the masons' camp St Calais was pardoned and Durham was restored to him. His first act was to recall every mason he could to start work on his new cathedral. Yann-Luc made no complaint. He wanted to be part of it. He set about packing up without delay. But I was filled with sudden fears. Would the Saint turn me away? Would he judge me for my sin? True, I was a widow now. But I was not a wife. Yann-Luc could not wed me. Would I be twice damned? As the priest's whore, and the mason's?

I had other worries too. What if I saw people who knew me? What if I saw Hunred? How could I atone to Mary for abandoning her? I had told her I was going to make a pilgrimage, but that was years ago. She must think me dead by now.

Yann-Luc, Herve and I left Caen in the pleasant warmth of early autumn and sailed on calm seas to London. But then we had to stay a

week or more in a filthy inn till a ship could be found to take us north with
Yann-Luc grumbling all the time at the cost of it. By the time we found a
ship, the weather had changed, with a blustery west wind bringing squalls
of heavy rain, driving the ship out from the land. We were days at sea, and
each day I was sicker than the last. When they set us down on the shore
in pelting rain, I felt as if my punishment had begun. All the strength and
health I had from Normandy had been beaten out of me. I could scarcely
move, and it was a day's walk to Durham.

"I can't. I have to rest first."

He sighed. Yann-Luc hated to part with his silver.

"You'll have to carry me otherwise."

He found a house that would give us lodgings and paid for a hot meal
for us all and a bed to sleep on. I slept all night and half the morning too,
before Yann-Luc shook me awake, impatient to be on the road. So we set
out for Durham.

Although I had some notion that there would be new buildings for the
monks, I still thought of Durham as I had known it. I expected everything
still to be as it was when I'd left, to walk through the gates across the close
to the cathedral. I could never have imagined what I was to find.

We made our way up through the town, pushing along the crowded
dirty streets. It was much as it had ever been, though I could see it was
growing larger, with new houses stretching further away to the north. But
when we walked through the bailey gate into the church close, it was as
if I had stepped into another world. Everything was strange to me. I had
been away for many years, I told myself. Had I forgotten my home, the
place where I was born?

The first shock was the castle. I seemed to have driven it from my
memory. Now it towered higher than ever, the old wooden fortress
rebuilt in stone and with more tall stone buildings beside it. That I could
understand, could explain to myself. I had forgotten. I could not explain
what I seemed to see beyond the castle. If ever I had been away from
Durham in the past, when I returned it was the sight of the two towers
of the church that made me know I was home; the west tower at the

entrance and the great crossing tower at the centre. To me they were as unchangeable as the rock on which they stood; they were part of what Durham was. They were eternal. But they had gone. Was I looking in the wrong direction? Had I forgotten so much? I twisted around, trying to get my bearings. No. They were not there. In front of where the towers had stood, there was a pale ungainly web of wood scaffolding and the outline of a new wall.

In a panic now, I looked for my house. It was nowhere to be seen. Where it had stood was a stack of stone and a covered workshop. Not only my house, but all of them, save only one, were gone. There was no trace of where they might have been, for the whole extent of the sanctuary ground was divided up with tracks and makeshift huts and piles of wood and stone. There were carts loaded with timber being led across to the new half-finished wall that stood in front of where the church had been. Men were busy cutting stone, sawing wood, mixing mortar. Women stood talking outside huts. What had been my home had become a building yard. Insight suddenly struck me. This is the truth, I saw. This is how the world is. Nothing lasts. Nothing is permanent. Everything we try to hold on to, that we believe to be real, is swept away from us. I understand, I cried out to the Saint. I understand.

In a daze, I followed Yann-Luc and Herve to the last house left standing, where the master mason now lived. As soon as he opened the door and I heard the heavy wood scrape on the threshold, I realized it was Gudrun's house. I peered in, half expecting to see her standing there. But all her chairs and cushions and wall hangings were gone. It was bare but for a rough table and benches, yet a scent of roses seemed to linger in the air. Gudrun! What a kind friend she had been to me. Memories of my former life flooded through my mind, one after another.

I thought of that January day long ago when we had drawn down the honey ale, when she and Hunred and I had gone to watch the Norman soldiers riding through the snow. Then the terrors of that night came back to me; Hunred and I huddled together in the hayloft, the flames leaping up from the bishop's palace set ablaze in the darkness. Did he ever think of that now, I wondered, as he came and went in his new monastery? That night was where it all began. What I saw all about me now was the fruit of it. The thoughts made me giddy.

"Come," said Yann-Luc. "I show you where we are to stay."

I caught hold of his arm like one drowning. There was nothing strange about the place in his eyes. It was a building yard like any other. He was in a bad temper because the day was cold and wet, we'd been travelling for days, and he'd had to spend money. When we reached the hut we had been given, the bad temper became fury.

"These huts, they expect we live in them? They are better for pigs."

It was true. The hut we'd been given was hardly big enough for both of us to sleep in, let alone make a hearth and fire. Yann-Luc was off again to Master Kenneth with Herve trailing behind him.

At last they came back, carrying pitchers and an armful of bread, and took me away to a hut close to the mason's house. It would do, I thought when I saw it. It was secluded and spacious enough, with a hearth ready to use. Herve would have the other hut, poor thing, but we all sat down together to eat. My first evening back in Durham, I thought, and I am sitting on straw in a workman's hut, with nothing but bread and sour ale for supper. By then I was too tired to care.

As soon as I woke the next morning, I took my shawl and slipped out of the hut before Yann-Luc was stirring. If the church had been pulled down, where was the Saint? I made my way along the cart tracks towards where the church had been. I peeped over the wall now in front of it. I saw it had not been destroyed entirely. The east end, where the Saint's shrine had always been, seemed to be a chapel now, with its own entrance. My spirits lifted. The Saint was still here. They must have spared that part of the old church to house the shrine till the new building was ready. Something, then, had stayed the same. But it was difficult to reach it, since the foundations for the new cathedral seemed to stretch almost the whole extent of the ground. I had to skirt right around the far end of the foundations. When I reached the other side, I saw more buildings there as well. I realized it was the new monastery; I could see a dormitory, refectory, a chapter house. But I could get to the shrine without passing them. I pulled my shawl over my head and made my way to the new entrance. Before I could open the door, I heard a man call out to me.

"Stop!" he said. "Come away from there."

I turned round and saw a monk coming towards me. For a moment I thought, it is Hunred, and everything froze within me. But it was not. It was a smaller, older man.

"You mustn't go in there."

"Are the brothers at prayer?"

"No, but it is forbidden for women to enter the shrine."

"Forbidden? By whose order?"

"It is well known that it displeases the Saint to have women in the church. Did you not know this?"

"I have visited the Saint in this church since I was a child. It has never displeased him before."

"It was part of the error of former times. It must be a long time since you have visited. The Saint has made his displeasure known."

He saw my disbelief and came closer to me, poking his finger at me.

"I'll tell you a story. When a certain noble lady came to visit the shrine, she refused to believe it was so, and sent her maidservant secretly into the church. The woman was struck down with terrible pains in her limbs. She died only two days later. Take care that you don't suffer her fate."

I stared at the monk. I had a desire to laugh—at the folly of his words, at his red-faced earnestness that made his Adam's apple jig up and down. It was pointless to argue. I turned and walked away. My heart was thumping hard in my chest.

I thought of Gudrun's words, when St Calais first came to Durham. "He hates women!" Now, it seemed, the Saint must hate women too, at St Calais' behest. I felt sick. I thought of all the feast days of my life, when the women of the Community had spent the day decorating the shrine, of all the vigils I had kept at the Saint's side through all my life, of the flight to Lindisfarne, when all of us, men, women and children, travelled with the Saint and cared for him. We were his and he was ours. No-one was turned away. I was utterly certain of it.

But what was I going to do? How was I going to visit the Saint? I needed to talk to Yann-Luc.

That evening we made a plan. I would have to wait, for he was busy setting up his workshop in the masons' lodge. And there was plenty for me to do too, once I had coaxed some more silver from his purse, making the bare hut into a home for us. I bought cloth to make a mattress and blankets, and a new pot for the hearth. I talked to the other women, finding out how things went on the yard. Have you visited the shrine? I asked them, and all of them gave me the same answer: the Saint will not have women near him. Hunred, I thought. He had been brought up in the Community. He and I had stood by the shrine countless times together. He must know it was a lie. But then, I thought, he would like it. He would like to keep women away. He would argue, like the monk I had talked to, that allowing women to visit the Saint was part of the error of former times. Hunred. I drove him out of my mind. He had been my beloved son, but he was no part of me now.

CHAPTER 33

THE WOMAN TAKEN
IN ADULTERY

Durham, 1092

*Jesus said unto them, "He that is without sin among you, let him
cast the first stone at her." And again he stooped down, and wrote
on the ground.*

*And they which heard it, being convicted by their own conscience,
left one after another and Jesus was left alone, and the woman
standing in the midst. When Jesus had lifted up himself, and saw
none but the woman, he said unto her,*

*"Woman, where are those thine accusers? Hath no man
condemned thee?"*

*She said, "No man, Lord." And Jesus said unto her, "Neither do
I condemn thee: go, and sin no more."*

St John's Gospel, Chapter 8, verses 2–11

One evening Yann-Luc came home with a pile of clothing in his arms. He
held them out to me.

"Boy's clothes. Same height as you, same thin. Try them."

I took them—tunic, jerkin, hose. They were well worn. I took off my
gown and shift and pulled on the hose. They were stiff with sweat and

dirt and I had to force myself to pull them up. Then the tunic. I turned to show Yann-Luc.

"No. Take it off. First, give me girdle."

He took hold of the girdle and started to strap it round my breasts, flattening them against my chest.

"Ow! Not so tight."

"They show too much. How is 'at?"

I squashed my breasts under it till he was satisfied and knotted the girdle at the back.

"Must be tight or it slip. Try now."

I put the tunic on again, and the jerkin.

"Yes! Good. Nice boy! Now—the hair."

He had brought a hood that half covered my face, but still he shook his head.

"We have to cut hair. You want to?"

"How much?"

"Like a boy. To your shoulders."

"Yes. Do it."

He gathered up all my hair in his hands, sighing and shaking his head.

"It'll grow again," I said.

Picking up his shears, he cut away at it till he held the long bunch of my hair loose in his hands. It was strange to feel my head light, the hair brushing at my shoulders. I pulled the hood down over my head.

Yann-Luc stared at me for a while. "It's good. You are boy." Then he took me in his arms, biting my short hair between his teeth.

I waited till the next afternoon, for the period between the offices when I knew the monks would be working. I peered out of the hut to make sure no-one saw me—but what if they did? They would think Yann-Luc had brought home an apprentice. I set off through the yard. No-one gave me a second look. I tried to stride along like a lad on an errand, round the edge of the new foundations and up the other side towards the shrine. There were workmen around but not a monk to be seen. I strode up to the door, my heart beating. I opened it, and I was in. I had a quick look round. It was empty.

They had built a new wall at the west end to make a chapel of it, but it was still the old building. It had the same silence and tranquillity, and the Saint's shrine stood where it always had. I went over to it, kissed the coffin and knelt close beside it to pray. It was very quiet. My fear lessened. I was here, at last. I felt again the wings of angels stir the air. As I prayed my father's words came back to my mind as they always had.

"Don't trouble the Saint with your petty worries," he had said. "Just listen. Wait and listen."

It's not a petty worry, I told him. I am an adulteress. But when I knelt before the shrine my guilt for the sins I had committed, the fear that the Saint would turn me away, seemed to fade. Time passed, the silence deepened, and I felt the mercy of the Saint's presence I had always known. As I knelt there, the words of Christ to the woman taken in adultery came into my mind unbidden, as if they were the Saint's words to me: "Neither do I condemn thee. Go and sin no more." My heart opened. I went deeper into contemplation, for how long I couldn't say. I was hardly aware when a man entered the church and came over to the shrine. He didn't disturb me and for a time we knelt together in silence. Then, I couldn't say how, I realized that I knew him, although I hadn't looked up. I knew the man. It was Thorgot.

I felt no surprise or alarm. I lifted my head and glanced at him. I saw he had changed. The old passion had turned into something steadier and more definite. There was a new strength about him. Then he looked up and met my eyes. I could tell my disguise did not conceal me from him; he knew at once that it was me. There was a flicker of shock for an instant, but he gave no other sign. He held my gaze in his till all constraint was gone between us. I felt joy such as I have never felt in this life, a joy that seemed to embrace the Saint, Thorgot and myself within it. All my sins and failures dropped away from me till there was only love. I know that Thorgot felt it too. The air was filled with light.

I couldn't say how long we stayed there before I dropped my gaze. When I looked up, he was gone.

I was glad to take off the boy's clothes. I bundled them up and gave them back to Yann-Luc.

"Not go again?" he asked.

"No."

During the next few days, I spent time making enquiries among the other women in the camp. I knew there were often women looking for support, who had been widowed or who had lost their home for one reason or another. When I had found what I was looking for I spoke to Yann-Luc. It was just another evening; he was weary from hours of work, and I ladled out a good stew into his bowl and set a jar of ale beside him. I ate with him, as I had a thousand times. When we were done, I spoke.

"I have had word from Mary, my daughter. She is sick with a new babe. I must go to her."

Yann-Luc's eyes snapped open at that.

"How you have had word? Where is this daughter?"

"It's not so far. It is a day's walk."

"I need you too. Who cook my food? Mend my tunic?"

"Don't worry. I have arranged it. There's a woman I have talked to, you know, whose husband fell in the quarry? Sarah, her name is. You'll like her. She's young. A good cook."

Yann-Luc looked at me, half-trusting, half-suspicious.

"How long you go for?"

"I don't know. But if you want me you can come and get me. The name of the village is . . . "

I explained to him where the village was, what road to take, the name of Mary's family.

"You'll know where I am. I won't be anywhere else."

Perhaps he guessed then that I was giving him a choice, or perhaps he didn't. There was no need to upset him.

The next morning Sarah came early to the hut. He seemed pleased enough with her and let her take a look round. When she had gone, we embraced, kissed farewell, and then he was ready to be off to the lodge. I watched him walk off across the yard, tool bag over his shoulder, whistling a Breton song just as he did every day. Then I turned back into the hut, made up a pack with food for the journey and bound on my boots. I stepped out into the morning, passed across the close, through the bailey gate and out into the din and clamour of the streets. By the time the sun was up Durham was far behind me.

Afterword

The Chronicler: Simeon of Durham

The contemporary sources for the remarkable stories of Thorgot and Aldwin are two twelfth-century histories written by Simeon of Durham. Simeon was an Anglo-Saxon monk who entered the monastery at Jarrow soon after its foundation. He was one of the brothers who moved to Durham in 1083 and took holy orders shortly afterwards.

Between 1104 and 1107, Simeon wrote the *Historia Ecclesiae Dunelmensis* (History of the Church at Durham). It tells the story of the Community of St Cuthbert from the first days of Christianity in Northumberland right up to the death of William de St Calais in 1096. Simeon's task was to demonstrate the continuity of Durham's history through the centuries—and to justify the expulsion of the hereditary Community in 1083.

Simeon was one of Aldwin's monks, so he is a trustworthy narrator for Aldwin's story. He also served under Thorgot, whose story is mainly told in a later work of Simeon's, *Historia regum Anglorum et Dacorum* (A History of the Kings of England), composed around 1129.

✝HORGO✝

When the same Aldwin died, by order of bishop William, Turgot succeeded him in the priory of the church of Durham, which he ably administered for twenty years all but twelve days. For in the eighth year of the episcopate of Ranulph, who succeeded William, at the request of Alexander king of Scots, he was elevated by Henry, king of the English, to the episcopate of the church of Saint Andrew in Scotland, which is the see of the primate of the whole nation of the Scots.

After an episcopate of eight years, two months and ten days, he obtained of God the gift which he had earnestly sought, that he might breathe he last breath near the sacred body of Saint Cuthbert. He was buried in the chapter house, where his body lies between that of bishop Walcher on the south and bishop William on the north.

Simeon's "History of the Kings of England"

With William de St Calais frequently absent at court, Thorgot continued to run the bishopric of Durham. Through his relationship with Queen Margaret, he established good relationships with the Scottish court, and on 11 August 1093, King Malcolm, together with Bishop de St Calais and Prior Thorgot, laid the foundation stone of the new cathedral at Durham.

William de St Calais died on 1 January 1096. The king, William Rufus, left the see empty for three years, so he could claim its revenues. Eventually it was bought by Ranulf Flambard, the king's unscrupulous treasurer, whose only interest in Durham was in its revenues. His nickname, Flambard, means fiery or flamboyant, and his arrogance and greed made him many enemies. Immediately after the sudden death of William Rufus, Flambard was arrested and imprisoned, and subsequently fled to Normandy.

Once again, Thorgot was left in charge of the diocese from 1096 to 1107. During that time, he carried out all the duties of a bishop, including preaching, visitations, patronage, and consecration of new churches and investing priests. He was also in charge of the construction and fitting out of the new cathedral. Working with an unknown master mason, Thorgot was responsible for the construction of the most innovative and beautiful Romanesque building in the country. During his period of supervision, the choir, transepts and eastern apse were completed, and the crossing and the nave commenced. Thorgot was also responsible for the construction of the claustral buildings for the monks.

On 4 September 1104, the Saint's coffin was translated from the old church to the new. Beforehand, the monks decided to open the coffin and report on its contents. Thorgot, with nine of his brothers, was present. They found two coffins, one within another, with a Gospel of St John laid within. When the lid was lifted the witnesses smelled

> *an odour of the greatest fragrancy; and behold, they found the venerable body of the blessed Father, lying on its right side in a perfect state, and from the flexibility of its joints representing a person asleep rather than dead.*
>
> **Simeon's "History of the Kings of England"**

It was opened twice more for doubters, including a visiting French abbot. The incorrupt nature of Cuthbert's body was established beyond doubt and with it his saintly authority. The final translation was an intensely emotional event with huge crowds in attendance.

Ranulf Flambard was briefly present for the translation before returning to Normandy. He was eventually pardoned and returned to England in 1107. But he remained out of favour at court and had to reside in Durham. His relationship with his deputy, Prior Thorgot, quickly started to go downhill.

It was fraught from the beginning. As soon as he arrived, Flambard attempted to take over the revenues belonging to the monastery. However, he found in Thorgot a formidable prior willing to resist him and a monastic community used to independence. Clashes also took place over the building work at the cathedral. Flambard wanted to take direction of the work in order to make a name for himself, but Thorgot was effectively in charge of all aspects of the construction. When an opportunity arose to get rid of Thorgot, Flambard jumped at it.

Queen Margaret's son Andrew, now King of Scotland, invited Thorgot to become Bishop of St Andrews and Primate of Scotland. Flambard accepted at once on Thorgot's behalf and pushed forward his consecration with unseemly haste. Thorgot finally left Durham in 1109.

He was fifty-nine. He had to leave behind the cathedral that had become his life's work and the saint to whom he was devoted. He was going to a country where the Church had little in common with his Benedictine heritage and no tradition of building. It was dominated by a sect called the Culdees whose doctrines were not recognized by the Pope. The authority of Canterbury over the Scottish Church was bitterly disputed by King Andrew, who also supported the Culdees. For Thorgot, it was like finding himself back in Nidaros thirty-five years earlier, back at the beginning of a Church, but he no longer had the energy of his youth. After five years of factionalism and conflict his health broke down and he asked leave to visit St Cuthbert's shrine for healing.

He called first at Monkwearmouth, where he had received holy orders, then continued on to Durham. He spent two months close to the shrine, suffering attacks of fever. He died in Durham on 31 August 1115. He is buried at Durham, between Bishop Walcher and Bishop William de St Calais.

EDITH

Edith was one of the many thousands of nameless women who suffered rejection, penury and abuse during the clerical reforms of the eleventh and twelfth centuries. Clerical celibacy was strongly promoted by Pope Gregory and supported by the Norman Church.

In 1108, the Synod of London under Anselm, Archbishop of Canterbury, decreed clerical celibacy as English Church law:

> *It was enacted that priests, deacons and sub-deacons should live chastely, and should not have in their houses any women except those allied to them by near relationship, according to what the holy Nicene council has decreed. Those priests, deacons or sub-deacons who after the prohibition of the synod of London have retained their wives, or married others, if they wish any more to celebrate Mass, shall put them away from them entirely, that neither shall they enter the women's houses, nor the women theirs; and neither shall they knowingly meet in any house, nor shall any women of this sort reside in the territory of the church; and if for any proper reason it be necessary to confer with them, they shall meet out of doors in the presence of two lawful witnesses.*

As descendants of Eve, women were held responsible for luring priests into the sin of fornication, thanks to their sexually insatiable and irrational natures. Hence in the case of clerical marriage women were held blameworthy rather than men and deserving of both temporal and eternal punishment. Simeon of Durham quotes the following episode that occurs in the Dream of Boso, a knight who has a near-death vision of the afterlife:

> *Casting my eyes over the field once more, I saw it covered, for some miles, with a large body of women; and while I was in astonishment at their number, my guide informed me they were the wives of priests. He spoke thus: "these wretched women, and those persons also who were consecrated for sacrificing to God, but who, unworthy, have become enchained to the pleasures of the flesh, are awaiting the eternal sentence of condemnation, and the severe punishment in the fires of hell."*

Simeon's "History of the Church of Durham", Chapter LXVII

At Durham, it is particularly sad that the bishop and monks recruited St Cuthbert as their misogynistic champion, creating a whole new body of legends purporting to show his antipathy towards women. None of them existed before the eleventh and twelfth centuries. One need only to return to the contemporary account of the Saint in the Venerable Bede's *Life of Cuthbert* to understand what a falsification the new legends represent. Throughout Bede's *Life*, we see Cuthbert in warm relationships with women, from his much-loved foster mother Kenswith, to Princess Aelflaed, subsequently Abbess of Whitby, with whom he had a close relationship as mentor and counsellor. He is recorded as having healed several women as well as staying at convents on pastoral journeys. As far as we know he was celibate throughout his life, but it did not prevent him having loving relationships with women.

Edith is referred to by Simeon only once, as the dean's wife. Her story here is fictional; it is up to the reader to decide how the rest of her story might have turned out.

Bibliography

Primary sources

The Venerable Bede, *Ecclesiastical History of the English People*, ed. Farmer (Penguin Classics, 1990).

The Venerable Bede, *Life of Cuthbert* in *The Age of Bede*, ed. Farmer (Penguin Classics, 1998).

The Venerable Bede, *Commentary on Revelation*, tr. Wallis (Liverpool University Press, 2013).

Simeon of Durham, *A History of the Church of Durham*, tr. Stephenson (Llanerch Press, 1988).

Simeon of Durham. *A History of the Kings of England*, tr. Stephenson (Kindle edition, 2016).

Ecclesiastical History of Orderic Vitalis, tr. Chibnall (Oxford Medieval Texts, 1983).

Reference

Kapelle, *The Norman Conquest of the North* (Croom Helm, 1979).

Aird, *Saint Cuthbert and the Normans* (Boydell and Brewer, 1998).

Rollason et al., *Anglo-Norman Durham* (Boydell and Brewer, 1998).

Golding, *Conquest and Colonisation* (Palgrave MacMillan, 2013).

Green, *Building Saint Cuthbert's Shrine*, ed. Hopkins (Sacristy Press, 2013).

Field, *Durham Cathedral* (Third Millennium, 2006).

Turner et al., *Wearmouth and Jarrow* (University of Hertfordshire for English Heritage, 2013).

Lacey and Danziger, *The Year 1000* (Little, Brown, 1999).

Timeline

St Cuthbert and his cult

687	Death of Cuthbert, 20 March
710—20	Lindisfarne Gospels written and illuminated
721	Life of Cuthbert written by the Venerable Bede

The Vikings and the Danish Invasion

793	First raid on Lindisfarne
866	Danish Invasion of Northumbria
875	Lindisfarne abandoned
875—81	The flight of St Cuthbert's Community
882	Establishment of the shrine at Chester-le-Street

Durham

995	Community moves to Durham

The Conquest

1066	Battle of Hastings. William of Normandy crowned King of England
1068	Construction of Lincoln Castle and imprisonment of hostages
	Thorgot escapes to Norway
1069	Massacre at Durham of Robert de Comines and his army
1069—70	The Harrying of the North
	Community flees to Lindisfarne
1071	Walcher appointed Bishop of Durham

1072	Building of Durham Castle
1073	Aldwin travels to Northumbria, establishment of monastery at Jarrow
1074	Thorgot leaves Norway and returns to England
1075	Thorgot and Aldwin go to Melrose
1080	Walcher murdered. Siege of Durham
	Odo sacks Northumbria
1081	William de St Calais appointed Bishop of Durham
1083	The Community ousted from Durham. Aldwin and his monks take their place
1086	Raedgar dies
1087	Aldwin dies. Thorgot becomes Prior
	King William dies, William Rufus becomes king
1088	St Calais exiled. Thorgot in charge of the diocese
1091	St Calais pardoned and returns to Durham
1092	Saxon church demolished
1093	Foundation stone of the cathedral laid and building work started
1096	Death of William de St Calais
1104	Simeon starts composing the *History of the Church at Durham*

Acknowledgements

A New Heaven and A New Earth is my third novel tracing the history of the iconic saint of the North and his Community. My grateful thanks to all the team at Sacristy Press for their support and encouragement for the project: Richard Hilton, Erik Sharman, and my editor Natalie Watson.

Warm thanks to family and friends for their interest and support, in particular to Piers Claxton for some great discussions and his insistence on details I was hoping to ignore, and to Patricia Coleman for her willingness to be a first reader and her insights from lockdown.

Finally, all my thanks and love to Michael Tiernan, editor-in-chief and first reader in the ongoing process of writing the novel. His unfailing support made it all possible.

CPSIA information can be obtained
at www.ICGtesting.com
Printed in the USA
LVHW041520210920
666682LV00003B/692